I0668599

Wanted

DEMON FAMILIAR

BELLORA QUINN &
SADIE ROSE BERMINHAM

Demon Familiar
ISBN # 978-1-78686-362-1
©Copyright Bellora Quinn and Sadie Rose Bermingham 2018
Cover Art by Cherith Vaughan ©Copyright June 2018
Interior text design by Claire Siemaszkiewicz
Pride Publishing

This is a work of fiction. All characters, places and events are from the author's imagination and should not be confused with fact. Any resemblance to persons, living or dead, events or places is purely coincidental.

All rights reserved. No part of this publication may be reproduced in any material form, whether by printing, photocopying, scanning or otherwise without the written permission of the publisher, Pride Publishing.

Applications should be addressed in the first instance, in writing, to Pride Publishing. Unauthorised or restricted acts in relation to this publication may result in civil proceedings and/or criminal prosecution.

The author and illustrator have asserted their respective rights under the Copyright Designs and Patents Acts 1988 (as amended) to be identified as the author of this book and illustrator of the artwork.

Published in 2018 by Pride Publishing, United Kingdom.

No part of this book may be reproduced, scanned, or distributed in any printed or electronic form without permission. Please do not participate in or encourage piracy of copyrighted materials in violation of the authors' rights. Purchase only authorised copies.

Pride Publishing is an imprint of Totally Entwined Group Limited.

If you purchased this book without a cover you should be aware that this book is stolen property. It was reported as "unsold and destroyed" to the publisher and neither the author nor the publisher has received any payment for this "stripped book".

DEMON
FAMILIAR

Dedication

Dear Reader,

This book is set in the invented city of Or d'Roit. The city is loosely based on an alternate reality version of Detroit, Michigan. Its grim industrial foundation mingled with flashes of art deco grandeur, the glittering majesty of a river clogged with ships and pollution, and the slow, crumbling decline of once stately houses all add to the landscape of our fictional city. More importantly, it is the spirit of the people living in the midst of ruin, but still fighting, still surviving, and determined to grow new roots in the fertile ashes of what others have abandoned, that inspired us. This book is dedicated to the indomitable spirit of Detroit and the people who live there.

Love, Bellora and Sadie

Chapter One

Neil set the bushel of summer squash into the panel van with the rest of the produce ready to go to market tomorrow morning and jumped down. Mr. Yaetz patted him on the back. "That's the last one. Good job, Neil. You best head home now. Don't want to get caught outside the wards after nightfall, 'specially not in that fancy car."

Neil stifled a wince and forced himself not to look around to see who might have overheard the mention of his 'fancy car'. Mr. Yaetz didn't mean anything by it, but the car was a sore point with his co-workers at the small greenhouse and urban farm lot. None of them had their own vehicle, much less a sleek convertible sports car. Explaining that it was his mother's, not his, hadn't stopped the digs about his 'slumming with the common folk' or brought him any closer to the camaraderie the rest of them shared.

"Thanks, Mr. Yaetz. I'll see you tomorrow," Neil told him and turned toward the front lot. He glanced at the horizon automatically, judging how much time he had.

About forty-five minutes, maybe an hour. More than enough for the short drive home. He wasn't likely to come across any shadow beasts here on the outskirts of the city but a pack hunting farther afield was always a possibility. Of course, if he did run across shadow beasts, they would have to catch him first and the Maserati was both fast and agile.

Neil slid behind the wheel and the powerful engine purred to life. With the sun slowly sinking behind him, he swung the car out onto the road and headed for home.

As expected, Neil pulled into the driveway with plenty of daylight left and no encounters with any creatures that came out after dark. Climbing the front steps, his thoughts preoccupied with a shower and dinner, he almost missed the broken seal on his front door. He stopped cold. The warding glyph, usually a subtle shimmering gold, was inert, dull gray and cracked with lines of black. A sick knot cramped in his belly and Neil pressed his thumb down on the latch and pushed the door open but hesitated on the threshold.

"Mom?"

He listened. No answer.

Neil stepped into the foyer and slowly moved into the hall. A picture had been knocked off the wall and the broken glass from the frame glittered in the fading sunlight streaming in behind him.

"Mom?" he called again, louder.

Something crashed in the kitchen, the metallic clatter of pans hitting the tile floor. Neil ran in that direction.

His mother screamed, "Neil, get out! Get out!"

Heart hammering, he skidded into the kitchen. A black-clad, hooded man held on to his struggling mother. Another man stood next to them with a curved knife in his hand – his eyes were flat black and icy cold as they slid over him. Neil rushed them, yelling, "Get away from her!" The man with the knife lifted his free arm and flung the outstretched fingers of his empty hand at him. Neil hit the stop spell so hard it jarred him from teeth to toes, knocking him on his ass.

"Neil!" his mother shrieked.

He lifted his head in time to see the man who had floored him lift the knife and draw it down the side of her throat and across her shoulder in two professional, vicious slashes. The other man let her go as her eyes went wide and her hands flew up to clutch at the wounds. The blood didn't spray everywhere like it did in the movies. It welled up in a gush of red that soaked the front of her shirt as she choked and gasped then fell down on her knees.

"Mom! No!" Neil scrambled to his feet. The two men moved toward him in unison as his mother crumpled, face down on the floor. Her body sounded like a wet rag hitting the tiles and a shocking pool of red spread under her.

"Take him," the one holding the bloody knife said. His voice was low, emotionless and without accent, like an automaton in one of the old films they occasionally streamed when the comms satellite was functioning.

On autopilot, Neil grabbed the pendant that hung on the chain around his neck and ripped it off, throwing it on the floor. The man reached to stop him, but it was too late. The glass pendant shattered and a wall of noxious smoke rose between him and the killers. It wouldn't hold them long, a minute if he was lucky. Probably less. He turned and ran back down the hall, fleeing the house.

He stumbled down the steps and fumbled the keys from his pocket, hitting the lock button. He yanked the door open and was shaking so badly he dropped the keys on the floor.

"Fuck! Fuck!" He reached down and his fingers just touched the ring as the killers came running out of the front door. Neil grabbed the keyring and jammed the right key in the ignition. For one horrible second, he was sure it wouldn't start even though he'd just driven the car home. The engine turned over as smooth as a kitten's purr and he slammed the shifter in reverse just as the man with the blade grabbed the driver's door handle. Neil put his foot down on the pedal. The tires squealed and the car shot backward down the driveway and into the street.

Blood pounded in his ears, almost drowning out the engine sounds as he threw the car into drive and floored the gas, clutching the steering wheel hard enough to turn his knuckles white. He looked in the rear-view mirror as he sped away. They would come after him. He turned at the next intersection. Then turned again. And again. He tried to focus on what to do next but all he could see was the shock and anguish on his mother's face before she fell, and that bright pool of red spreading out under her. He looked in the mirror again but saw no sign of the men that had killed her. That didn't mean anything. They could come, he knew it. He was heading out of the city following pure instinct, but now he slowed the car for just a moment. At the next turn, he doubled back the way he'd come.

Out of the city might seem safer, but it wasn't. He had little money and the car would take him only so far. He needed resources.

He forced his fingers to relax on the steering wheel but his hands still shook. When he took a breath, it was shaky too. The red had been so stark against her blonde hair. Her eyes…had they been blank before she fell or after she hit the floor? No. No he couldn't think of that now. He raised and hand and swiped at his wet cheeks.

Bone Men. Their name whispered across Neil's mind in his father's voice, from one of his many lessons. Assassins. Twisted by the sorcery that enhanced them, marked by the lives they took. Had she been their target? Was her death retribution for something his father had done? Or…or were they there for him?

His mind raced as fast as his pulse and the car he was driving. He took another deep breath and eased his foot back off the pedal a few degrees. He needed a clear head. He needed a plan. But first he needed somewhere to hide. Instinct told him to find someone he trusted, but his training overrode that idea. He could hear his father's voice in his ear again. *Trust no one, Nielob. If they come for you, go to ground. Speak to no one you know. Hide and wait. I will find you.*

Not if he could help it. If he had his way, he'd lose both the Bone Men and his father, for good. The car would get him a good distance but he couldn't keep it. It was traceable. He'd drive into the city, find someone he could sell the car to for scrap and use the money to get a ticket to as far away as it would take him.

He couldn't take the car directly to a salvage yard without a title, too risky. He needed a fence. Months ago, while he'd been watering seedlings at work, he'd overheard Carl bragging about how his uncle was going to get a real car, one with a combustion engine. No one had believed him and Carl had gotten mad. Insisted his uncle knew a guy that dealt in contraband autos in the city. Hammersfell Road, next to the old Ackard Motors factory. There was a warehouse where they had raves. The fence organized them. Neil had no way of knowing if the bragging was just lies, but he had filed the information away anyway. His chin gave an odd quiver and the tightness in his throat squeezed hard enough to choke him. No. He couldn't give in to tears now. He couldn't afford to let out the sobs that threatened him. A safe place first. The grief tasted of bitter acid and wanted to strangle him, but he swallowed it down and kept going.

Chapter Two

Mal's morning routine rarely varied. As the first light spilled through the cracks in the warped shutters and poked at his thinly veiled eyes, he shifted out of the realm of uncomfortable dreams and rolled off the thin mattress on its base of wooden pallets. The old injury to his lower back and right leg still twisted his muscles tight until he'd been mobile for a few minutes and he grimaced as he ran cold water from the rusty faucet into his cupped hands and used it to splash his face and rinse out his mouth. Spitting into the chipped basin, he watched the dregs go swirling down the dark maw of the drain then ran wet hands through his unruly hair and pulled on his faded jeans and desert boots. Wriggling his arms into the close-fitting leather jacket that kept the worst of the early-morning chill off, he headed down the creaking staircase into the workshop below.

Merc already had the stove fired up and Mal's nostrils twitched at the smell of strong, fresh coffee perking in the pot over the welcome heat. Mal stretched out his fingers to the warmth and flexed his shoulders, wincing at the crack as his back protested this exercise. His wings fluttered deep beneath the subcutaneous layer of meat that trapped them, a discomfort he had grown used to over the years that never failed to make him shiver. His partner poured two mugs of the steaming brew and Mal wrapped his hands around the vessel he passed over, inhaling the delicious, bitter steam.

"The nightmares were a bitch last night, huh?" Merc grunted as he swigged the coffee black, immune to the incendiary heat.

Mal took a sip and winced then added a couple of drops of caramel to his.

"A bitch and all her hell-spawn," he agreed. "And the wings are restless, on top. Did I keep you awake?"

Merc shook his hoary head and rubbed at his wire-wool beard with one callused finger. "I slept 'til first light, got the heat going then went for a walk before the dog boys were stirring."

"Get far?" Mal asked him. He had long since given up trying to discourage the old man from walking out alone. Downtown was dangerous at all hours but Mercurio Geiger was a grown-up — the fellow looked as old as Malachai's father but Mal knew he could probably add another fifty years at least on top of that. Merc was capable of making his own choices.

"'Bout a mile up Shaftesbury then back along Crown and down through the Pieces," Merc told him. "There's an old Buick Wildcat been dumped up there, 1967, practically intact. 'Cept for the wheels."

That figured, Mal snorted silently. The wheels were always the first to go.

"Thought I'd head back up there with the truck and arc welder and see if we can't get us some salvage."

"There won't be anything left by the time you go back, Merc," he predicted. "Just a pile of rust."

"Still, if there is, we get first shout." The old gremlin chuckled without humor.

"You're an eternal optimist. Want a hand?" Mal took a longer gulp of the steaming brew. The caramel lent a whisper of sweetness to the powerful caffeine hit and he rolled it around in his mouth for a moment before letting it burn down his throat.

"You got that order for Del Vargas to finish," Merc reminded him. "Don't want that piece of shit banging down my doors at all hours if you ain't done on time."

"It'll be done. He'll get his juice," Mal said with a shrug. He drained the coffee mug down to the dregs then tipped those in the sluice. "If you're going to go and get that Buick, you'd better get a wriggle on, Mercurio. The dog boys are going to be sniffing around once the ground warms up and Castille runs the area 'round Sixth and Crown. If he catches you nicking his salvage, you're dead meat, old chap."

"Thanks for the warning," Merc said with a flash of sarcasm. "Get that fuel oil flowing, I'll be back before the sun's over the top of the M'riott Tower."

Merc had been gone about an hour and Malachai was settling down at the still with a pile of rocks for company and another mug of coffee slowly going cold beside him when he heard the vehicle pull up outside. His first thought was Vargas, turned up early for his consignment, but the engine noise was minimal, not the rattle and clatter of Del Vargas' old van. His curiosity piqued, he pushed himself to his feet again, wandering through to the shop front, flexing his shoulders to ease the twitching under the skin. Wiping the dusty window with one hand, he squinted out. He had to be dreaming, or the petrol fumes had caused him to hallucinate. The car that was still thrumming softly by the curb was a Maserati GranCabrio, in 'arrest me now, officer' carmine metallic, with a folding titanium roof that was tucked back into the trunk. Not the sort of motor anyone drove around Downtown if they weren't packing serious weaponry or under protection from the Sorcery Guilds. Mal moved silently to the door and opened it a crack.

A lanky figure in muted, gray-camo cargo pants and a sleeveless vest hopped out without opening the driver's door and came loping over, tugging at the dark blue goatee that clung to his chin. Mal relaxed at the sight of him and let the door open wider. No sorcerer, this one.

"Where did you hotwire that, Dooley?" he wanted to know. "And why is it parked outside my shop, like a red flag to every cop in the district?"

"Chill, Valentine." Rex Dooley smirked at him. "Come for a ride and I'll make you a proposition. The car's legit, right. Just looking to offload it for a friend of a friend."

"And I'm the Queen of the fucking Fairies, Dooley. I wasn't born yesterday." Mal folded his arms and drew himself up to his full height, which meant that Rex had to look up at him just a bit. "Where did it come from and why is it here?"

"Malachai, everyone knows that you and Merc can make it disappear. You're the motor magicians, right?" he crooned. "You're not telling me that you can't make decent money off of this baby? 'Course you can."

"Only if we melt the damned thing down," Mal grumbled. "I'd be willing to bet that every damned part is wizard-marked and if it's stolen…"

"It's not," Dooley argued at once. "Mal, it's legit. I told you a f —"

"Friend of a friend, yes. I heard you." Malachai sighed. "How much?"

"You'll have to talk to the owner about that. I'm just the broker, man." Dooley beamed at him. "So…wanna come and say hello? The keys could be yours by midday."

"And a crack team of sorcerers from the Guild over on Crown could have incinerated my workshop by nightfall," Mal said with some skepticism.

"He's a poor little rich boy, down on his luck. He turned up at Corvo's out of the blue at sundown last night and he's been hanging tight ever since. The boss doesn't have time to deal with it, he's arranging some drug-fueled shindig for his eldest's twenty-first tonight, so he sent me along to show you the goods. Maybe you guys would have something in common," Dooley hedged. "Just come and talk to the brat. He needs a hand up and the car's his only asset."

Mal sighed again but the fuel consignment was over three-quarters complete. He'd still have time to finish if they were quick. If Rex was right and the deal could be done by noon.

"Okay. You have one hour to get me back here, Dooley. If you don't, I will sell you for parts, do you understand?"

"You are scary when you get all British on me," Dooley said with an irreverent grin and returned to the still-purring Maserati, hopping in over the door again.

Mal sighed and grabbed his keys and rucksack, locked up and followed him to the car.

Chapter Three

Neil had spent a sleepless night on a cold floor in a filthy old warehouse, but at least he'd been behind wards and survived the night. The muscles along his shoulders ached and every time he closed his eyes, he saw the cold edge of a curved knife slice into his mother's throat.

He'd found Rex Dooley right where Carl had claimed he would be, then had promptly seen his hopes of a fast sale and an even faster ticket out of the city shot down. Rex didn't have the kind of cash on hand to give him even a quarter of what the car was worth. At least, that was what he'd said. Neil suspected that what he really didn't have was the skill it would take to remove all the magical tracking from the car that would allow him to safely take it off Neil's hands. Instead, Neil had let himself be convinced to stay and wait for another buyer, one Dooley assured him wouldn't be able to resist his car.

This was probably a bad idea. He would probably get ripped off. He would *undoubtedly* get ripped off but if he expected it, maybe it wouldn't feel so bad. He jumped when Rex clapped him on the shoulder.

"Still here?"

No answer seemed expected of him and Neil gave none. Dooley jerked a thumb toward the guy standing next to him. "This is Malachai. The tinker I tol' you about. He's interested in the car."

Malachai was tall, even given the way he slouched. He had long hair in a dark-ish shade of red, kind of shaggy where it had escaped the tail that cascaded down his back. His eyes were clear and a piercing pale gray, almost silvery, and he was giving him a narrow look that said Malachai put up with zero bullshit from anyone.

Neil said, "Hi."

The tinker stared at him without speaking for so long that Neil got nervous then wondered if the guy even spoke English. What sort of name was Malachai, anyway?

"Where did you get it?"

His speech was very clipped and precise. Even in just those few words, Neil could hear the hint of some kind of accent. Something he wasn't used to hearing.

"Get what?" Neil asked. One of the man's eyebrows lifted and he almost smacked his forehead with his palm. "Oh! The car. It's mine."

"Yeah, right!" Malachai laughed but Neil got the feeling it wasn't because he thought Neil was funny. There was no humor in that laugh at all. "Do you have papers for it? Because I'm not looking to get myself roasted by the guilds for handling stolen goods, okay?

Let's start again, shall we? Where did the car come from?"

"I, um, I don't have the papers..." Neil said. "Unless they're with the log book in the dash."

Malachai snorted. "For fuck's sake, waste of time..."

"No...wait. I don't have them, but it's not stolen. It was my mom's car."

"This just gets better and better," Malachai declared, shoving his hands into the pockets of his battered leather coat. "It isn't yours. You don't have documentation. You don't even look old enough to legally drive. I'm out of here. There is a bad-tempered Panamanian fae up on Delancey waiting on me for a consignment of fuel oil. And it's gonna take me thirty minutes to get back to work. Thanks for nothing, Dooley!" This last remark was aimed at the scrawny, rat-faced man standing by Neil's right side.

Dooley shrugged and spread his hands and the tinker turned on his heel and strode away. Neil followed after him, nearly breaking into a run to keep up with that long-legged, angry stride.

"Wait...hang on. It is mine, now. I just... Would you listen a minute...please?"

He didn't even slow down and Neil followed him out into the yard and across to the parking garage ramp. "I need the money. I'll give it to you for half what it's worth. I thought you could just part it out."

"Do I look stupid?" Malachai turned back to face him so smartly that Neil almost ran into him. "Listen to me. I was not shipped in from the Green Isle yesterday, boy. If you're so desperate to get rid of a motor like that, it's either hot, or you are. Either way, I don't want any part of it."

"Fine. But, you know someone that will? Take it? It's the only thing I have and I need the cash."

Briefly, the tinker seemed to consider. His pale, silvery gaze roamed over Neil slowly, assessing him.

"What do you need the money for?" he asked at last. "Drugs? Blackmail?"

Neil debated lying. He hesitated, licked his lips, but it wasn't like he was going to tell him *where* he was going. "I need a train ticket."

One of the fellow's fine, bronze eyebrows rose again. In the daylight, his long hair was the color of dry rust, streaked intermittently with paler threads. His skeptical expression did not wane.

"Why can't you drive wherever it is you're going?"

Damn. He should have guessed that question was coming. He never got away with lying, even when he was telling the truth. He was trying to figure out a good answer, without telling him that he couldn't keep the car because it was trackable, when the door they had exited through swung open. Neil glanced over his shoulder and his heart just about stopped in his chest as he recognized the skeletal shape of one of the Bone Men who had murdered his mother. He was looking down the alley toward the street, but all he would have to do was turn his head to spot them.

"Forget it," Neil whispered, already moving, suppressing the urge to break into a run, which would only draw the assassin's attention. It was just a few more strides to the ramp. Other people were milling around. If he could get back to the car, he could get away again.

His heart was trying to hammer its way out of his ribcage as he reached the shadowy interior of the garage. He was about to break into a run when

Malachai asked, "Who's after you?" He hadn't even realized the tinker had followed.

"No one..." Neil murmured then stopped dead as he spotted the shadow of a man cast on the concrete floor by his car. He ducked left behind a pillar, keeping away from the vehicle, and Malachai mirrored him.

Shit, shit, shit!

"No one, huh?" Malachai lowered his voice but he gave a thoughtful nod. "That one feels like trouble with bells and whistles on. This way."

He turned back into a patch of deeper shadows and Neil followed because he couldn't think what else to do.

Malachai crouched beside a station wagon and jimmied the driver's door open with something he slid out of his inside jacket pocket. He nudged Neil and moved to his feet, pulling him along as the station wagon alarm blared.

They darted between parked cars, keeping low, out of sight, Neil's heart pumping harder at the clatter of booted feet on the concrete floor. The sounds echoed off the ceiling and his companion zigzagged back and forth between parked cars, ducking into the shadows whenever he could. Neil stuck to him because right now he was the lesser of two evils.

Beside a black Chevrolet Impala, Malachai dropped to one knee and forced the driver's door again. The alarm sang out, a shrill scream that fought with the blare of the station wagon across the garage.

"What are you doing?" Neil whispered through clenched teeth.

Malachai put a finger to his lips and scuttled between cars, keeping low as the men following them hastened over to the shrieking vehicles. Once the route toward the scarlet Maserati was clear, he made a beeline for it and hopped over the driver's door, turning the key that Rex had left in it.

Neil froze for a moment, staring at him as the engine revved. Silver eyes met his own.

"Get in," Malachai said. "Or stay and ask what they want. Not my problem, kid."

A line of flames sprung up on the opposite side of the garage. Not regular flame. These were blue-black and moved as if they had thought and purpose. Shadow fire. Demon magic. Neil took one look and jumped into the car.

"Go! Go!" he yelled as the black flames suddenly raced across the ground like they were following a trail of fuel. Malachai cursed under his breath and yanked the Maserati into reverse as the men in the garage began shouting. He hit the accelerator and the tires shrieked on the pavement.

"Shadow fire… Fuck, kid, who did you piss off? That kind of magic doesn't come cheap!"

"I didn't piss anyone off," Neil said. His hands shook as he grabbed for the seat belt and pulled it across his body.

"So these demonic gentlemen are just casual acquaintances? Charming. I'd hate to meet anyone you'd actually crossed." He spun the wheel and the sports car slid into a graceful curve, turned ninety degrees and came to an abrupt halt. Malachai began flicking switches on the dash but his silver eyes gleamed like mercury as they stayed fixed on the flames.

Neil had his eyes peeled so wide they were in danger of falling out. His pulse was racing as the flames got closer and the stealthy figures ran toward them.

"You need to turn around. Turn around!" Neil yelled at last.

Malachai ignored the order, hit another switch, and the whirr of the internal motors came to life as the roof unfolded from the trunk, rose up and finally clicked shut over their heads.

"Oh my god...we're gonna die." Neil grabbed the door handle, about to jump out and take his chances when Malachai jammed the car into drive. The tires screamed again as he floored the pedal and the powerful engine shot them forward, straight for the line of fire.

Neil had a couple of gut-liquidizing moments to process that he'd just been abducted by a madman.

"You're going the wrong way! You're going the wrong way!" Neil's voice went from a normal shout to a near scream as the flames spread side to side in front of them.

Malachai closed his eyes. With one hand on the wheel, he reached for something in the open neckline of his shirt, closing his fingers around it, whispering words that spilled like oil into Neil's ears but made no sense. His skin felt tight for a heartbeat and he braced himself.

They hit the flames and all around them the fire turned to water, spilling over the roof and windows of the flying Maserati, sluicing up from under the wide-wall tires and arcing out behind them in wings of glistening silver droplets that hung in the air for a few seconds like a magical veil.

Malachai opened his eyes and they were the color of water. The color of the silvery stone on its chain, hanging around his neck. He swung the car into the sharp bend at the foot of the exit ramp and floored the gas again, throwing them back into their leather seats as they roared out of the subterranean garage and emerged, blinking, into the sunlight.

Neil looked in the mirror, watching behind them, then around, then back to the mirror. He did this for a couple of minutes, front, sides, back, front again. He expected Malachai to start questioning him, but the man kept silent, eyes forward on the road ahead.

When the acid in his stomach had churned to the point he couldn't stand it anymore, Neil asked, "Where are we going?"

"Away from your friends with the nasty incineration habit," Malachai said. His gaze also flicked from road to mirror and back again as he eased off the gas. His sun-bronzed fingers held the wheel steady, though. He drove like the car was an extension of his body. "This is a nice motor. Is it seriously yours to sell?"

"Yeah," Neil answered, the words tightening his throat. "It was my mom's car, I told you. And she's...not... Well—it's mine now. I guess." Neil didn't actually know that but who else was the car going to go to? Since the adrenaline rush was ebbing, he had time to wonder just how the Bone Men had found him. It had to be the car. He'd been worried it was trackable, but it must have taken some serious pull to find it so fast. "Listen, I have to get rid of this car."

Malachai's gaze flitted to the mirrors again then back to the road ahead. He said, "If I didn't live Downtown, I'd say deal and drop you on the next corner. A beast like this is gonna draw attention, mind you. I can hide it for a day or two but long-term... No dice. I can get rid of it, though. Heartbreaking as that would be."

"Please, I have to get rid of it. Now," Neil said and cringed inwardly at how desperate that sounded.

Malachai took his eyes off the road for a second to look at him. "What's the hurry?"

"It's got a tracer on it."

"Wouldn't it be easier to find the tracer and get rid of it?" the other man asked.

"If I knew how, don't you think I would have done it?"

That got him a sharp look but he was tired and had been riding a crest of fear and stress for hours. He didn't have much left in the way of tact.

"There's magic worked into the tracer. I don't understand how it works or what it might do if it was taken off," he said, trying for a calmer tone. That much was true at least. A physical tracking device would probably be simple enough to remove but since the boundaries between the human world and the demon planes had blurred, demonic magic was more in vogue. That had been good from his family's perspective, at least financially. At least until now.

Malachai gave him a sidelong look. Nothing more. An assessing look, like he was reevaluating Neil, deciding whether or not to just stop and kick him out of the car anyway.

"How do you know that?"

How he knew that would require more of an explanation than he wanted to give. He didn't want to get into a discussion with a stranger about how his dad wanted to keep tabs on his mom — and him — so he lied. "Mom paid a sorcerer to have it put on, in case it was stolen."

He saw a swift frown crease Malachai's forehead, between his eyebrows — there then gone.

"Every nerve in my body is telling me you're bad news, kid," the man said at last. Rex had called him a tinker but Neil was pretty sure that no tinker on the earth talked like Malachai. He had a smooth, cultured voice. English, maybe? Irish? It made Neil's skin prickle all over.

He had no idea how to reply to that unspoken question. If he switched places with Malachai, he'd probably think the same. Logic said he shouldn't trust anyone but currently it was looking like he didn't have much choice.

"Those men...you were right. They are looking for me. I'm not sure why. Not exactly. Something to do with...with my family. I know you've got no reason, but I need your help. I can't keep the car, they'll use it to find me again."

Malachai drew a long breath then eased it out in a steady sigh. "In that case, it looks like we're going to have to take a detour."

The tinker drove them off the Court Circular and west, into a part of town that Neil was aware of in the same way he was aware of Hel, the demon plane. In the few short decades since the three planes had become accessible to one another, and the lives of humans, demonkind and fae had been thrown together, the fortunes of areas like this had fallen into a sharp decline. This might as well be Hel, at least from the stories his father had told him of what it was like there. He'd never had cause to be in either place and had no particular desire to be here now, but the choice was out of his hands. The Maserati pulled up outside a unit on a single block, with boarded-up windows, emblazoned with the graffiti of many ages and a heavy iron grille over the central recessed doorway. He could tell the beat-up sign on the front of the building had once read *AUTO PARTS*. The shadows of the missing letter A and

TS were still outlined on the wall. Some enterprising soul had added a bit of red spray paint to what remained of the sign so that it appeared to read *UTOPIA*. Neil figured he'd never seen a less likely Utopia in his life.

He held his tongue as Malachai took them around to the back of the block where there was a yard with a heavy, rusted-metal sliding gate. The unlikely tinker hopped out of the car, leaving the engine running, and unfastened the three large metal padlocks that kept the gate moored. He put his shoulder to the edge of the gate and rolled it back then returned to the car and drove them inside. Once in the yard, the corners of which were piled high with scrap metal, he jumped out again, shutting the gate behind him and padlocking it from the inside for good measure.

There was a roller door into the back of the building and he unlocked this, pushing it up to head height to reveal a darkened garage bay, probably three cars wide, the same depth and the height of a medium-sized box van. Within it were two vehicles in advanced states of deconstruction.

Once they were parked inside, his companion finally cut the engine and climbed out to pull the shutter down behind them. He returned to the car, running dusty fingers through his disheveled, flame-red hair.

"We'll be safe here for a while," he said. "It doesn't look like much, but it's secure and there are wards on the bay that'll scramble the signal from that damned tracker until we can offload the car."

Neil closed the car door and looked around, trying to spot the wards, but whoever had laid them must have been good. He couldn't detect any telltale shimmer or wavering over the bays. Either that or there actually wasn't anything there and Malachai hadn't a clue what he was talking about.

"Are you sure the wards will work?" he asked, trailing after him.

"They usually do," he said brusquely. "Merc deals with the wards. He's the best at such matters. I simply transmute things."

"Who?"

"Mercurio. My—"

He was cut off by an angry voice. "Where the fuck have you been? And where the fuck did the car come from? Who the fuck is he?" The man doing the asking stabbed a stubby, oil-encrusted finger in Neil's face. He was shorter and way older than either of them, but stocky in a way that suggested there was still muscle under his bulk.

Malachai brushed his accusing finger aside easily and patted the burly, bald-headed fellow attached to it on one shoulder in an amiable fashion.

"Hello, Merc. Neil, this is Mercurio Geiger, mechanic extraordinaire and the warding wizard of this operation. Merc, this is Neil...don't know his second name. The Maserati comes with him. I liberated them both from a very boring warehouse, which was considerably enlivened by some filthy, demonic blackguards trying to kill us. Why are you so antsy, anyway?"

Merc didn't answer the question. Instead he hooked his thumbs in his suspenders, actual suspenders, and eyed the car with what Neil could only describe as a greedy expression. "That's some tincan. Has to be hot enough to burn the place down around us. What are you thinking, Mal, bringing it here?"

He still sounded gruff but not as antagonistic as he had a moment ago. Neil didn't think he could get his frozen tongue to make words just yet so he kept silent.

"Neil needs us to make it disappear. I told him you were the very best at that. He also needs to make some money out of the deal so that he can disappear too. You can relax when that's happened, can't you, Merc?" The younger man was smiling, just for a moment, as he pushed one hand through his tangled red hair. "Did you get what you went out for?"

Mercurio glowered at Neil a moment longer then scratched his nose and turned back to Mal. "Got some parts. Most of it had gone, you were right." He stared at the Maserati again. "Be a shame to dismantle that beauty. But you'd be converting rocks all night every night if we was to try and run it. Speaking of rocks...Del Vargas was round here looking for his fuel. I told him you were out. He was not a happy chappy, Mal."

"It's mostly done. I'll run it over there later." Mal patted Neil on the back. "You two play nicely while I finish it off then we can decide what to do with the pretty car. Sound good?"

That sounded horrible actually, but Neil didn't dare say so. Instead he mumbled, "Is there a bathroom I can use?"

Merc squinted at him again but pointed toward a door. "Through there. Third door on the left."

Neil murmured his thanks and hurried off the way he'd been told.

Mal let the kid get out of earshot then returned to the garage where he walked around the car, admiring it and trailing his fingers across its still gleaming flanks. Merc cleared his throat.

"No, you can't fucking keep it. It's gotta be hot. Where did the kid steal it?"

"He *says* it was his mother's." Mal raised one copper-colored eyebrow.

"Right. And she's gonna be overjoyed if we cut it into tiny bits and sell them to the highest bidders." Merc grunted. "What is his mother? The Witch Queen of fucking Angmar?"

"She isn't our problem. No one knows the car is here, apart from you, me and him. It's a pity, but we have to get rid of it." He sighed and looked up at Mercurio. "I'll leave that in your hands, old friend. I have some gas to wring out of a handful of rocks."

"Smug limey bastard," Merc snorted, but there was a half-smile on his face as he said it.

"When you figure out how to do my job, be sure to come and tell me." Mal wagged one long finger in his face then returned to his still to finish off the fuel consignment for Del. They had dodged a bullet there — the shop was still standing, but Vargas would not wait forever.

He had some time to think while he was refining the bluestones, carefully distilling them down into the purest liquid form, breathing shallowly so as not to make himself dizzy from the vapors coming off the fresh gasoline. Neil could be a problem for them. The kid had to be hiding something, though he was barely out of school, to Mal's reckoning. It would be down to Neil at the end of the day to square things with his mother about the missing car. Mal refused to feel guilty on that count.

It was a lovely car, though. Such a shame.

His hands trembled at the thought of the drive back here, which had stirred up memories he'd buried deep. They belonged to a different life, one he had come here to forget. Mal forced himself to focus on Neil again, pushing the past aside.

The lad was trying to be tough but was so obviously scared out of his mind. Malachai had been a new boy at enough boarding schools to recognize that brittle, defensive stare when he saw it. Hell, he'd probably worn that look himself a few times. He wouldn't be the first kid to run away with a fancy car and not look back. As he was finishing off the transmutation, he looked up to find that the boy was back, watching him warily from the edge of the room, close to the door where there was a draft of clearer air.

"You've not seen an alchemist at work before then?" he ventured, capping off the jars once the last of the fuel oil had trickled down into them.

Neil shook his head and Mal got his first real look at him in good light. He was as young and green as a spring blade, but he could just make out the hint of stubble on his chin and an angular cast to his cheekbones and jaw that had him thinking that maybe he'd reached his majority at least. He had a mop of dark hair that came down to just below his ears, but it had a singular sameness to it that told Mal the color probably came out of a bottle, or maybe a bit of glamouring. Yeah, a bit of glamouring might also explain the vivid blue hue of his eyes, too, and why he was feeling drawn to the pretty softness about him when that usually wasn't what he went for at all.

"Is that real gasoline?" the youngster asked.

"I wouldn't be in business long if it were fake, would I?"

The kid didn't drop his eyes but Mal saw the stain of color flush his neck. "I guess not."

What a study of contradictions. He stole a car, either from his family or not, was running from a pack of sorcerous killers and hadn't batted an eye at shadow magic, yet he about pissed himself when Merc was mildly grumpy and blushed at the mildest of teasing. Mal wouldn't lay a bet on him lasting a week on his own. Not that it was his problem.

"All right, kid, here's the plan. Merc's gonna work on deactivating the tracer. Once that's done, we'll chop the car up and part it out. It's not worth as much as parts but that's the only way."

"Okay."

No argument. No questions. No haggling. This was not good. And not his problem.

Neil shifted from foot to foot and Mal transferred his gaze back to the fuel jars and started packing them.

"Um...so, what will you give me for it?"

"Nothing. Yet. Once Merc gets the tracker off, I'll throw out some lures on the parts, see who nibbles, and I'll have a better idea what I can give you for it."

"Okay. How long will that take?"

"A week, maybe two."

"A week! But—"

"A week, at least."

Neil went silent and Mal waited. Asking him straight out, why the hurry, wouldn't get him anywhere, he already knew. He could practically smell the distrust coming off Neil—if that was even his name. Patience would be a better tool. Fortunately he didn't need much of it.

"Is there anywhere around here I can get a room for a week and pay later?"

Mal snorted. "Not a chance."

Neil crossed his arms. "Okay then, I need to stay in the car. I don't have anywhere else to go."

"How about just going home?"

Neil brought a hand up and wiped it over his face. Maybe there wasn't any glamour on him after all, or surely it'd be concealing the shadows under his eyes.

"I can't. Not if I want to stay alive."

That was interesting. Was it the kid's family that was the problem? Or something threatening the family as a whole? Mal pushed himself to his feet and came back toward the door where the air was better. He still gave the kid some room.

"Let's backtrack here a bit. You knew who those guys were, back at the garage, didn't you? Or at least, you knew what they were."

He could practically see the wheels turning in the kid's head, working out if he should trust him and how much — whether he should lie, or tell the truth, and what to reveal. The hesitation was only a moment but it was enough. He watched the flicker of his eyes, away and back, the nervous licking of his lips, then the resigned slump of his shoulders before he nodded slowly.

"Bone Men. Sent by a sorcerer after my dad, probably. I don't know if their orders were to kill his family, or if they wanted to try and use me as bait, or if it's just because of what I saw that they are trying to find me. Whatever they want with him, I'll probably end up dead if they find me."

Mal knew from the way the kid's face closed up that his eyes must have widened at this revelation. The Bone Men were not sent to Neil's house on any petty debt-collection mission. If he was right about them and —

given some of the magical firepower at their disposal, shadow flame was no hedge witch trick, it took blood and demon fire to raise a true shadow flame — he most probably was, these guys had a serious grudge to settle.

"Who the hell is your dad, kid?"

"No one you're likely to know," Neil answered quietly but firmly. Probably hoping he wouldn't press the issue. Mal wasn't in the mood to let him play coy. Not when there was an expensive piece of evidence with a tracking device on it sitting in his garage and a kid who said magical assassins might be trying to kill him.

"Tell me anyway."

Neil sighed. "His name is Vukasin Markovic."

"What is that, something Balkan?"

"Serbian." Neil nodded.

Mal gave him a narrow look. "He's in the military?"

Neil snorted. "Mafija."

"That makes me feel so much better!" Mal told him with a cynical sneer. "Please tell me we're not about to be shut down by them."

"I don't want my dad to find me anymore than those guys back at the garage. But can you at least see why I just want to get the money and clear out of here?"

"It's just you and him, I take it?" Mal found a crate and began to pack the bottles of gasoline into it for the sake of not looking like he was actively hassling Neil for clues. He kind of understood that sort of relationship. He and the old man were hardly on speaking terms these days, after all.

Neil was silent so long Mal threw a glance back at him. The pain in those pretty blue eyes was so deep he could have gone swimming in them, then he blinked and it was gone.

"It doesn't matter. I can't go anywhere that either my dad might find me or the assassins looking for him might find me. I am pretty much fucked. I've got one thing. That fucking car. It's got to be my ticket out of here."

Mal mellowed because he understood that look too well. He had fled across oceans to escape his family ties but still feared every day that it wouldn't be far enough.

"Where will you go?" he asked, leaning on the edge of the crate for a moment.

Another one of those long, thoughtful pauses followed before Neil answered. "I don't know."

Mal pressed a grin on his face. "Where would you like to go?"

"I don't... Look, I didn't really plan this out. I sorta just...had to go."

"So where will you stay until we can scrap the car for you?" Mal pushed him. "Do you have anywhere you can hang out. Friends? Girlfriend?"

And there was that pretty blush again. "I-I don't... No, no. I don't think you're hearing me. There isn't anywhere I can go. Nowhere that I've been before anyway. And anywhere else is going to require money." He pulled out his wallet from his back pocket and opened it up, extracting a few low-denomination bills. "This isn't enough to get a bowl of noodles, much less somewhere to stay."

Mal huffed as he ferried the last of the gas bottles into crates. He found lids for them and tapped them into place with a handful of panel pins.

"Come and give me a hand with these," he suggested. "I need to get them over to Del's place before it starts getting dark. You don't want to be out in that neighborhood when night falls. But it will be fine for an hour or so."

Mercurio fired a curious look at them both as he and Neil lugged the three crates out to the street between them and wedged them into place in the back of Mal's ancient pickup.

"Got myself an assistant," Mal told him. "What? What's that look for? You wanted the gas delivered. We're doing it!"

"Just watch yourself out there, Malachai Valentine," Merc said in a gruff tone. His gaze flitted to Neil briefly and there was no warmth there. Mal wondered if the old boy had been eavesdropping on their chat.

"Don't call me Valentine," he drawled and hopped up into the truck, gunning the engines. "Come on, kid. Let's hit the trail."

Neil scrambled up into the seat and fumbled with the seat belt. Mal pulled the old beast smoothly out onto the street.

"Um…this, uh, doesn't seem to work," Neil said.

"Nope."

"Oh. Okay."

Neil didn't fidget but the tension around him was palpable. Mal wondered what he was going to have to do to get the kid to relax, because if he was going to be hanging around for a few days, that was a must, or Merc might do something rash.

"You like music?" Mal asked.

Neil nodded and Mal turned the knob on the ancient radio, flicking through some of the stations until he found something not too offensive. He left the volume low but surprisingly Neil didn't try to fill the space between them with empty chatter. That was a plus anyway.

It was about ten or fifteen minutes before Neil finally asked, "If you're an alchemist, how come you're making bootleg gas instead of working in some lab?"

Mal muttered something under his breath but when he looked sidelong to discover Neil still looking at him with a question on his face, he repeated himself. "I don't have a work permit. Actually I don't have a visa, either. And if you tell anyone that, I may have to kill you myself."

Neil frowned. "Why would I tell anyone?"

He looked and sounded so serious Mal had to chuckle. "It's an expression. Just keep your mouth shut, right?"

"Okay."

Another few minutes went by before Neil asked, "Do you make anything other than fuel?"

Mal felt a smile ghost across his lips. "I make whiskey. Quite good whiskey, on the whole. I need water to do it, though, and the supply to the store isn't reliable. Should have collected the stuff I turned the shadow-fire into, shouldn't I? Do you suppose magically twice-transformed substance would lend itself well to alcohol?"

Neil turned his head and blinked at him. "I don't think I'd want to find out. If it tasted anything like shadow fire feels..." He shuddered.

"True. It would be something of an acquired taste." Mal nodded. His fingers tapped against the wheel in time with a song on the radio channel. "A special vintage for the discerning sorcerer in your life. Where have you felt shadow-flame before today? Not the sort of thing they teach in senior high, I'd have thought."

"An accident. A neighbor was experimenting and lost control."

This time the answer came without any hesitation. Flat. Rehearsed. Why would he lie, though? Mal glanced at Neil. He was looking out of the passenger window, still and calm, but he'd gone pale as milk.

"If rogue sorcerers are the kind of neighbors you get in upmarket districts, I'll stick with Downtown, thanks," Mal told him, deliberately not pushing for more.

Chapter Four

From the moment he had come home from work to find assassins in his home, Neil had been riding an adrenaline high that felt like it would never end. As they finally rolled to a stop in front of a crumbling old Victorian home on a street that was all but dead, Neil stifled a yawn.

"Am I keeping you up?" Mal asked him with a half-grin that told him it wasn't a question that demanded answers. "C'mon, give me a hand. This won't take long."

As they got busy dropping the tailgate and hiking the three heavy crates of gasoline out of the back of the ancient pickup, Neil got the chance to take a better look at the alchemist without necessarily seeming like he was staring. He had to watch what Malachai was doing, after all, didn't he?

If his face had not been so gaunt—his cheek and jawbones etched in sharp relief under the tan skin—he might have described Mal as pretty. There was a roughness to him that precluded that. His face was unshaven, sporting a fiery, two-day fuzz and his mouth was wide, thin lipped. He took two or three strides to start moving properly when they got to work, hauling each crate up the pathway to the side door of the house, as if his muscles were cramped from the brief halt.

As they reached a wooden door, its glass paneling now boarded over crudely with whatever had come to hand, Neil's attention diverted to the house. This was a part of town he'd never been to and he was beginning to see why. As they'd first driven down Delancey, he had not really been looking at the buildings but he'd been kind of aware that these were large, spaced-out properties — more affluent looking than the ones in Mal's neighborhood. This house had seen better days, though. The yard was overgrown and full of rubbish — oil cans and empty crates, car parts and an old, rusting refrigerator that looked like it belonged in one of the 1950s movies his mother loved to watch.

His thoughts derailed, thinking of her, and he pushed his attention right back to the house, blinking away angry tears. He could not afford to get emotional.

The house stood over four stories, including a basement that was half-visible through the weeds and junk, and attic rooms with broken windows, ragged curtains flapping through the fractured glass. There was a bay section at the front that took up almost half of the facade, with huge, curved windows rising up to the roof level, and a dome on the top whose remaining tiles blended smoothly with the angular slope of the main roof. A broad chimney stack ran up the other side of the house, topped with six elegant terracotta pots, shaped like tall, orangey crowns of differing heights.

Neil imagined sitting on the deep sill in one of those bay windows, a fire crackling in the hearth behind him as he watched the world go by out on this street. Then he looked around and registered for the first time just how quiet it was here. They had not seen another soul since they'd pulled up. No vehicles passed them on the potholed road. The house facing this one had lost half its roof, joists pushing through the shattered slate into the sunset skies like yellowing bones, reaching out of the grave. The lower floor windows were covered in metal grilles and decorated with stark graffiti.

"Where have you brought me?" he muttered under his breath.

"It looks worse than it is," Mal said with a half-shrug. "Hardly anyone lives out here these days. Once the Adjuntament gets their collective heads around the fact that all these bricks are sitting here, they'll come and demolish it, turn it into a labor park or something."

Neil had no idea what a labor park was, but he had a hard time imagining anyone wanting to build any type of park here. Old maples and oaks lined the street but where they should have made it leafy and green, they seemed to cast only brooding shadows and the overgrown lots might have been small meadows with wildflowers but instead they looked like they hid secrets. The whole street was wrong, broken, and Neil shivered in the lengthening shadows.

They hauled the crates up a cracked two-track concrete drive to the side of the house and Mal lifted his hand to knock on the door. It opened before his knuckles touched it.

"You're late!" A squat figure in a long gray duster coat and battered denim jeans glared out at them.

For a moment, Neil stared then looked away because he had always been taught that it was rude. The speaker had a round, pale, silver-whiskered face, like a large meerkat. Dark eyes bored into Mal and the occupant of the mysterious house snapped, "Vargas is pissed. What did you bring that here for?"

Neil looked over his shoulder then back at the creature as he realized it was talking about him.

"He's my assistant," Mal answered, apparently unconcerned with the fellow's rudeness. "The delay was unavoidable, but the fuel is here. Does Del want it or not?"

Neil stole a glance at Mal from the corner of his eye. He didn't sound irked. In fact, he looked calm and sounded rather bored, but there was just something about him that made Neil think it was no idle threat. That'd if he got any hassle at all, he'd haul those crates right back to his truck and not bat an eye over it.

The...man? — Neil still wasn't sure if it was a man — wrinkled his nose and Neil noticed a few longer, thicker hairs stuck out a bit under it, like feelers or animal whiskers. Was he in some kind of half-form? Part human, part...what, exactly? His father occasionally talked about 'half-breeds', usually with his lip curled, much like the one he was receiving now. If it wasn't a half-shifted form, maybe it was a glamour. Why he would want to look like that Neil couldn't guess. If it was a glamour, though, that meant fae magic.

"Beggars can't be choosers, I guess. Bring those crates inside."

Neil bent to grab one and the...the otter man — that was what he looked like — stopped him with an upheld hand. "Not you. You wait here. I don't want you tracking the taint on you inside."

Neil stopped in his tracks. He wished he could feel insulted. If he were insulted, maybe he could deny it, maybe he wouldn't be standing here like a mute simpleton or feel the shame heating up his cheeks. He wondered briefly how the fellow knew what he was, when he could count on one hand the number of times someone had reacted like this to him. It was just his luck that it happened here, when he didn't want to be noticed.

"Don't be a pillock, Crow. We just want to get the gas inside and get our money, then we'll be out of here. He's a kid." Mal definitely sounded irritable now.

"Even you're not so blind, Lord Valentine," the little fellow sneered at him. "Don't you feel the black magic cracking off of him?"

"I'll crack something off you, if you don't stop pratting about and let us in," Mal warned him, drawing himself up to his full, impressive height and folding his arms so that he could glare down at Crow. "Does Del want this shit, or doesn't he? Because you guys can eat dead grass and shiver in the dark tonight for all I care! We are going to be out of here well before the sun goes down, whether you let me in or not."

The crate Neil had picked up was heavy and his arms were starting to shake, the tremor making the glass jars clink together faintly, before Crow relented at last and stepped back to let them pass.

Neil followed Mal into the dim recesses of the entryway. The linoleum tiles underfoot were probably as old as his grandfather, and worn so thin there wasn't any discernible pattern on them, but in spite of this, the place was spotlessly clean inside. Mal turned to his right. The hallway beyond led to a staircase down into the cellar, lit only from the watery afternoon light that made it through the surviving windows and the cracks in the ones that had been boarded over.

The fine hairs on the back of Neil's neck rose. The only reason he kept moving down was because Mal was ahead of him and if he didn't follow, he'd be left alone with Crow behind him. He set the crate down next to where Mal placed his, under the stairs.

As he straightened and turned around, he saw the fellow called Crow make a hasty warding gesture, a fleeting motion of his pasty fingers. Mal must have seen it too because he murmured, "Enough of that! We're all on the same side, Three Crow Tree."

The weight of those dark, hateful eyes bore into Neil and while he couldn't exactly dredge up an insult, the acid churning in his gut and the chafe of chaining the urge to lash out were as familiar as old friends.

"It's not my fault," he ground out, aware of how childish that sounded.

"Well, it speaks at least. Should I be surprised the first thing it says is a lie?"

Neil scowled. "I don't owe you any explanation."

"Maybe not," a silky voice from behind them said. "But I would certainly like to know why the darkness of sorcery is suddenly in my home."

All eyes shifted to the figure in the doorway at the top of the stairs. The voice that addressed them was most assuredly masculine in pitch and timbre, but the figure that met their eyes was draped in some kind of neck-to-ankle gown that fell in folds of sateen material to almost pool on the ground. Long silvery hair was piled up on the speaker's head, trickling down to his shoulders in places and large sunray-disc earrings hung, sparkling from his earlobes.

"Delilah," Mal said, the first to break the uneasy silence. He had pressed a smile onto his face and came forward to meet their host as he descended to the basement one graceful step at a time. "This is Neil. He's helping me out. We brought you some gasoline, isn't that kind of us? But the sun is beginning to go down and it's time we were out of here."

He had been advancing toward the stairs as he spoke and Del Vargas descended slowly to meet him so that they faced off at the very bottom step. Vargas was tall, because with the benefit of that final stair riser, the fellow towered over Malachai by a good seven inches. Vargas put out one hand, resting it on Mal's chest, stopping his advance. His fingernails were long and painted purple. In the light from the top of the stairwell, Neil could see that streaks in his hair were a similar shade of rich, royal purple too. His features might have been described as beautiful, sharp and sculpted, like the statue of some ancient goddess, but there was a hardness to that face which made Neil uneasy.

"Malachai Valentine," Vargas purred and Neil could hear the hint of an accent in his voice, too — something more Latin than Malachai's odd, lilting brogue. "So long since you have graced us with your delightful presence. Is this creature the reason why?"

Kohl-rimmed eyes darted in Neil's direction and the hints of softness vanished as Vargas glared at him.

If he'd felt the weight of Crow's disapproval, Delilah's glare was like being punched in the gut. Or maybe the forehead, because he had an almost uncontrollable urge to rub there, to cover that vulnerable spot from his prying. Any streak of defiance had been pummeled out of him long ago but he found it in him to lift his chin and glare back.

"If I felt danger on him, I wouldn't have him in the store, Delilah," Mal said in a softer tone. "Mercurio wouldn't let him through the gates if he was serious trouble."

Vargas was still staring at Neil when he whispered, "Don't you feel it? Like ants under your skin?"

Mal managed a small, humorless smile. "I feel it, Del."

"How can you stand it?"

"Perhaps I'm more used to it. You forget, I'm from the Old Country. We're all made of magic," he said and the smile was in his voice this time.

"If you're going to keep him around, a cleansing is in order," Crow said.

All the anger and shame Neil had been feeling drained out of him to be replaced by something much colder and slimier. He swallowed hard and the sole of his sneaker scuffed lightly on the floor. How stupid was he for coming down here? He didn't know Malachai. There was no reason he should trust him or think he'd protect him from whatever brand of torture Crow thought would scour off the indelible marks on his soul.

His brain took about half a minute to process Mal's response. The flame-haired alchemist chuckled softly. "I think he's quite clean enough for us, Crow. Though a bath might be in order once we're done humping these boxes around for you."

"Lord Valentine, proximity to new magic is making you careless, I think," Vargas said, tapping one immaculate fingernail against his chest. "Be careful, Malachai. Your ancestors cannot protect you here."

"I'm always careful, Delilah." Mal smiled at Vargas and closed his hand gently around the one holding him back, moving it aside. "You have some money for me, I believe. My side of the bargain is fulfilled. Once you've paid me, you will thank us both for upholding the compact, I will take my assistant out of your house and we will not trouble you again."

Neil saw the tight scowl on Vargas' face. The fellow wanted very much to argue but Malachai was looking him directly in the eyes and his smile was gone. The expression on his face was stern and unbending, the countenance of a man unused to being denied. Mal folded his arms across his chest again, not blinking as he faced him down.

Finally, Vargas snapped his fingers, making both Neil and the chap named Crow jump.

"Fetch Malachai his due, Crow," Vargas said in a cold voice. "He and his playmate are leaving."

"Spite doesn't suit you, Delilah Vargas. Didn't your mama ever tell you, if the wind changes, your face will stick that way?" Mal said, turning away and winking at Neil like nothing more than a game had just taken place. "Come on, kid. We'll have to get a wriggle on if we're going to be back at the shop by nightfall."

Neil had no idea what had just passed between them, or what it meant, but he didn't need to be told twice. He skirted Vargas, giving him as wide a berth as possible, around Mal and up the stairs. He didn't break into a run, but it was a near thing and he was more than happy to step back outside into the rapidly disappearing afternoon light while Mal concluded his business.

He was outside for only a few moments before Mal joined him. His mouth was set in such a grim line Neil was convinced he was about to tell him to get lost.

"Get in the truck," Mal said, without looking at him.

He wasn't sure he should, but the alternative was less appealing, so Neil did as he was told. Mal got behind the wheel and started the engine, dropping the old beast in gear and pulling away.

"Don't pay any attention to him, he's just jealous."

"Jealous of what?" Neil asked.

"Everyone. He used to be a favorite in the unseighlie court down in Panama City, but a few indiscreet affairs made him some powerful enemies. He and his half-brother had to relocate and they ended up here. His brother, Felipe, is younger and more tolerant, but exile has made Del bitter. Now he collects refugees from the human and fae communities and hoards them there, plotting revenges he's never going to carry out and living off grid in case people like your friends the Bone Men catch up with him," Mal said. "The ones that can still use their gifts, he farms out to make money for essentials like food and fuel for that wreck they hide in. The ungifted humans, he trains as scouts and thieves and pickpockets, they handle the iron for him. Del is one screwed-up son of a bitch. I'm sorry you had to listen to all that shit from him."

"Delilah's fae?" Neil asked. He'd heard there were fae living in the city, but he'd never met one before.

"Yes. He has old magic but the kind of spells he can cast will only defend him. He talks big but he can't attack us, not unless we strike first."

"I'm sorry if I caused you any trouble. I didn't think that...most people can't tell...about the sorcery."

"You'd be surprised." Mal's chuckle sounded almost sad, Neil thought. "There are a lot of the old kin here. For some reason we seem to be drawn to this shithole city. The difference between myself and someone like Vargas, and especially that cursed slimerag, Crow, is that I don't tar all magic users with the same brush. I've seen too much bad in supposedly good people and maybe a bit of good in too many allegedly irredeemable villains."

"It sounds like Delilah and Crow are made for each other," Neil muttered.

"More than you could know." Mal smirked at him sidelong. "Vargas was something of a hex-breaker, before he was cast out, but he's too fond of human moonshine to be good at anything much these days. Still, Crow sticks with him in the hope that one day Del will figure out how to lift the curse that he's under. What?" he asked when Neil looked a question at him. "You don't think anything natural looks like that, do you? Crow crossed the wrong hex master and that was his payback. Little wonder he's such a grouch."

"Your friends are the sweetest people," Neil huffed.

"Friends? Hah! Del needs me to keep that ratpile of his running, that's all. I don't know of another reputable alchemist in this part of town. Not one that he can afford, in any case." Malachai winked at him again. "Now, are you going to tell me your side of the story?"

He shifted the topic so deftly Neil was pretty sure there was more that he was trying to avoid discussing. A lie automatically started to form on his tongue but he stopped before he spit it out. He had hidden who and what he was for so long it was second nature, but did it really matter? He'd already told Mal more than he'd planned on saying. What would it hurt if he told him about his father? Not everything of course, but some. "Do you remember how I said I knew how shadow fire felt because of a neighbor? Well, that wasn't really true. My dad was trying to teach me how to use it."

Malachai's arched an eyebrow, but he kept driving and his attention returned to the road. He waited a beat for a bigger reaction, for a lip curled in disgust at least. Shadow fire was banned and only the blackest sorcerers dared use it, much less teach it to a child.

"So the Weird Sisters were right, there is a bit of black magic in you?" He whistled through his teeth, softly. "Your father is a sorcerer."

Neil stared down at his hands. "I'm not...not like him. At all. I don't want to be a sorcerer. I can't help it if some of my relatives are."

Mal mellowed again. "None of us can help who our parents are," he agreed, tapping the wheel as he took a turn toward the heart of the city. The setting sun was painting the world in a rich palette of reds and golds and the urban heartlands almost looked glorious, the old skyscrapers casting long fingers of shadow as the pickup wound between them. "Did you want to learn? About the shadow fire, I mean?"

Neil closed his eyes for a second and tried hard not to remember how the shadows had come so eagerly to his fingertips, how it had felt like pouring dirty oil down his throat until he'd vomited and lost control of it. But trying not to think of it only brought to mind the image of his mother's terrified face and how dark her blood had been.

"No. I didn't want to learn any of it."

Mal nodded for a few seconds. "Understandable."

Neil turned to stare at him. Of all the things he'd steeled himself to hear, that wasn't one.

"How? How could you understand it?"

"What? You think that I grew up on an island with more sheep than people and all I ever had to worry myself with was changing rocks into fuel oil?" Malachai laughed and it was a rich, rippling sound, like a harp. A sound that made Neil believe there was old magic and old music in his veins. He talked like no one Neil had ever heard, his words sculpted and soft, sometimes like stone, sometimes like velvet. "Trust me, Neil, there are also things I have seen that I would rather have not. We cannot always choose our pasts, but the future is in our hands alone. If you have no desire to embrace the darkness, I am not unhappy with your choice."

Mal was quiet for a while as they rumbled along the rough-hewn roads into the older parts of the city. Downtown might have been subject to neglect, but once it had been glorious, and tonight with the last gold of the day touching the ancient buildings that still stood here, it felt like a place out of myths. Neil could believe that magic had always lived here, growing stronger as the city fell into decline.

"Where do you want to go?" Malachai asked him, at last.

Neil sighed, but he did it quietly enough that he didn't think Mal heard him. "Where I want to go doesn't exist. I just want to be somewhere that no one who knows who I am can find me. I want to go somewhere that I'm not going to run into anyone that calls me tainted and makes warding signs at me. If I thought for a minute that torturing the evil out of me would actually work, I would have let them do it."

Mal looked his way briefly and the smile on his face seemed genuine.

"Maybe you struck lucky. I'm sure Merc might disagree on the torturing front but his bark is generally worse than his bite. He's a grouchy old bugger but he wouldn't harm anyone. He didn't kill me, anyway." He was quiet for a moment, watching the road ahead again, but at last he said, "It wouldn't work, by the way. And evil is as evil does. I don't think you're evil, for what it's worth."

"You're in a tiny minority," Neil said. Then, took a breath and added, "But thanks."

Mal didn't respond because he was watching the road and his smile had waned. For an instant his pale eyes flickered like nacre again as the last rays of sunlight dipped out of sight and the shadows between buildings lengthened and merged. Neil was reminded of his companion's urgency back at the house on Delancey.

"The sun is down…" Neil breathed the words as they reached an avenue he recognized and the darkness grew to an impossible pitch. It was too quick. Too intense.

Malachai muttered something that he did not understand, guttural-sounding words, in an alien language. He pushed the full beam headlamps on and even those powerful rays were slowly swallowed by the blackness that wrapped around them. It gave them just enough light to make out the front of the parts shop, its crooked, weather-beaten sign proclaiming UTOPIA, before it too was shrouded in darkness.

Mal's gaze was like ice, fixed on the road. He kept on murmuring the words that became a restless mantra. "Tabhair dom na Gréine."

Over and over, the same words. As the pickup cornered, practically on two wheels, into the alleyway between the store and the next block, they lost the last of the daylight and were plunged into an unnatural darkness. By the faint threads of illumination from the truck's headlamps, Neil made out the iron barrier of the gate up ahead. Then his heart almost stopped in his chest.

Standing between them and the gate was a figure even darker than the street, shrouded from head to foot in tattered shadows. It held out a black hand and that seemed to suck the last of the light out of the pickup.

Mal swore and hit the horn, one long blast and two short ones.

"Shadow beast." Neil gasped. He'd never actually seen one before but he instinctively knew what he was looking at.

"Yes," Mal said through gritted teeth. "Durka. Lighteaters. They take the light and transform it into power."

He banged out the same tattoo on the horn again. One long tone and two short sharp ones. Before the last of the echoes died, a cascade of light spilled down from overhead and cast the cab of the pickup into silver-edged shadows. The Durka threw up its hands, covering its face, struggling to devour the intense shafts of illumination as one after another the floodlights on their high poles around the edge of the yard came on. Soon it was brighter than day in the narrow back alley behind the store. Blinded by the lights, the shrouded figure stumbled and fled for the darker side streets beyond the yard, vanishing into the shadows. With a bang and a creak of metal the gate slid open and Mal drove the pickup through and into the garage bay. Neil turned to watch as Mercurio towed the gate shut again, bolting and chaining it securely. Beside him, Mal killed the engine. "That was close!"

"If yer done being a moron, there's grub in the kitchen," Merc said as he walked by the driver's side window.

Neil's stomach gave a lurch. When was the last time he'd eaten? He thought he remembered grabbing some kind of cereal bar before he'd left for work yesterday.

"Hungry?" Mal asked.

Neil nodded. "Starving."

"Good." Mal swung out of the pickup and led the way up into the store.

The kitchen was in the back and something smelled good as they walked through the door and shut it behind them. Mal dropped the envelope Del had given him onto the table and ran water into the ceramic basin, splashing his face and running wet hands through his hair.

Merc ladled something that steamed and smelled of meat and onions into three bowls on the scrubbed wooden table in the middle of the room. He pulled up a stool to join the two ancient-looking wooden chairs already at each end and broke a long loaf into three roughly equal pieces.

"For what we are about to receive, et cetera," Mal said gruffly, coming to sit on one of the chairs. "Is that the last of the crocodile?"

"For now," Mercurio acknowledged. "What you doing luring Durka down the back of my shop?"

"I hoped they'd have a bit of sirloin on them." Mal grinned at him. "Oh, lighten up, Merc. We got paid."

Merc grunted and spooned some soup into his mouth. Mal dug in as well and Neil lifted his own spoon. He was a bit more careful with the hot liquid and blew on it first. For all that he was hungry, he was still leery. He didn't know if Mal was kidding about the crocodile thing, but he couldn't readily identify the meat and all he could smell were the onions. The broth itself was kind of strange, but rich, and didn't taste terrible. He took a bigger bite then ate some of the bread and after that hunger won out and he hit the bottom of the bowl and the end of the bread before he looked up again.

Merc grunted. "More?"

"Sure, please…"

He grunted again and put another ladle full of the meaty soup into Neil's empty bowl.

"I don't think I've ever seen anyone have seconds of Merc's croc stew," Malachai said. "You must be starved."

"At least someone around here has some manners." Merc sniffed.

"Something like that." Mal looked pleased with himself. He used the last hunk of his bread to wipe around the bottom of the bowl in front of him then popped it in his mouth, chewing happily.

"So…Durka?" Merc prompted.

"We were running a bit late," Mal said with his mouth full. He chewed some more and swallowed, and Merc put a bottle of budget-price lager in front of him and popped the cap. The older man opened a second and swigged some of it down.

Mal took a quick slurp, pulled a face, but swallowed.

"Is that it?" Merc persisted. "You had me put the floods on because you were running a bit late?"

"You wanted the money, right? Because we could have just let him suck us dry and take the lot." Mal looked injured.

"It was my fault," Neil said.

Both Malachai and Merc stared at him in surprise.

He cleared his throat. "They uh, didn't really like that he brought me with him on the delivery and gave him a hard time about it. That's why it took longer."

Merc swallowed another long chug from his bottle. He set it down on the table and muttered, "Figures."

"Mercurio, be nice," Mal said.

"Valentine, you took him into a magical war zone and expected Del Vargas to just roll over and let him walk inside. You're not an innocent. What the fuck were you thinking?" Merc growled. "He's been fighting the Bone Men since I was a boy. I'm amazed he didn't take your head off your shoulders and introduce it to your arse."

"Del likes me," Mal said with a shrug. "Crow wasn't too happy, though."

"Three Crow Tree has a stick up his arse as long as my arm." Merc laughed bitterly. "He could spell you from here to Ground Zero, mind, so watch your back." He turned and looked at Neil more shrewdly. "Since they didn't kill you, either Malachai was the soul of diplomacy or they decided you weren't the biggest threat to their security. And since I know that Mal is as subtle as a brick in the face, I'm going to let you stay. But if we have a sniff of trouble around this block tonight, you're out on your arse and we'll keep the car as collateral. Understood?"

Malachai might or might not understand anything about diplomacy, but as much as Neil disliked what he was, he wasn't the son of a sorcerer for nothing. He knew when to keep his mouth shut and bide his time.

If any trouble did come sniffing around, they were keeping his car over his dead body.

"Sure," Neil said. "There won't be any trouble, though."

"Good. Let's keep it that way." Merc sniffed and finished his broth and his beer. "Where's the brat sleeping? He ain't having my bed."

"He can stay in mine," Mal said in an amiable tone but his expression clearly showed that he'd not given this much thought.

"Figures!" Merc huffed again and this time Malachai shot him a narrow-eyed look.

"I'll sleep in the shop."

"You don't have to do that. I can sleep out there," Neil said.

"And rob us blind while we sleep?" Merc snorted. "That's not happening. You'll sleep in his room."

"It'll be fine," Mal said, pushing himself to his feet. "I'll show you where everything is. You must be exhausted."

Neil rose and said, "Thanks for the food."

Merc grunted and Neil turned to follow Malachai down the hall and up a flight of stairs that doubled back on itself. Mal showed him to a small room with a narrow bed.

"It isn't much, I'm afraid, but it's reasonably comfortable," he said. "And clean. You can take a shower down the hall, first door on the right. The water should be warm enough by now, we have solar panels on the roof. It can just be a bit lively in the mornings, so be warned."

"Um, thanks." The food in his belly was warm and heavy and the bed looked inviting enough. Still, he felt weird taking Malachai's bed from him and as the man turned to leave, he suddenly didn't want to be all alone with his thoughts. "Uh, what did Mercurio mean when he said 'figures'?"

Mal rose from the trunk he'd pulled from under the bed, where he had been gathering a change of clothing. He straightened, hugging the items to his chest and watching Neil with a strange, almost wistful expression.

"Ignore him. He thinks he's being clever. In truth he's merely being salacious."

Neil frowned. What did that mean?

Before he had a chance to ask, Malachai slipped out of the door with a murmured, "G'night."

Neil thought about taking a shower but the effort was too much and he lay down on the bed, fully clothed, instead. He figured he would just close his eyes for a few minutes until he could convince himself to go wash up but once closed, they stayed that way until morning.

Chapter Five

Mal slept fitfully that night. He had grabbed a couple of blankets from the airing cupboard on the main landing and they were enough to keep him warm and provide some respite from the chill of the shop space at the front of their building, but he could not stop thinking about the events of the previous day. Scenes kept replaying themselves in his head. The Bone Men in the parking garage, the way Crow and Vargas had looked at Neil over at the house on Delancey and the Durka in the alleyway, the way it had seemed to be waiting for them patiently. He shivered, though it was not a cold night.

He had seen Durka before, in the old country. Usually they appeared when there was a death in the family. Sometimes they were seen as heralds of a death foretold. He had never seen one come so close to the shop before. Utopia was warded against magical beings. A magic user could come inside if he left his casting habits at the door. Durka were channels for magic, though. It was part of their being. He had never seen the face of a Durka and he didn't want to.

The boy upstairs was a different matter entirely. He was definitely human but with a frisson of something other. Whatever was in his physical makeup, it hadn't completely triggered the wards, but Mal felt them quivering and he was sure that Merc did too. It was Merc's job to keep them maintained and if the boy wandered before dawn, Mercurio would know of it. Mal thought he would too. He knew every loose board and each different floor surface in this building and how it sounded to tread upon them. If the lad shifted, he would hear it.

Eventually he slept. His gift took a lot out of him and he had worked it hard yesterday. His dreams were difficult, though. When he woke, they were mostly scattered moments in his mind but he remembered the old man, and the whip, a screech of locked brakes and the crunch of crumpled metal, throwing him into darkness, the folding and sealing of his wings and the pain that had screamed through his imprisoned body for months afterward.

At first light he forced himself up off the floor and spent a few minutes slowly and painfully working the kinks out of his muscles and waiting for his scarred back to stop its restless shivering. Then he made his way up the stairs, leaning heavily on the crooked wooden rail. Neil was still sound asleep when he poked his head around the door to check. Mercurio was snoring down the other end of the hallway and Mal braved the shower.

The water wasn't stone cold but sharp enough that he flinched as he eased his dusty body under it and reached for the soap. He was still half-hard. These days those first minutes of wakefulness, when his body was coming to life, were the only times he got an erection. Like everything else, its timing sucked. Malachai was not a natural morning person.

He leaned against the tiles, under the thin fall of cool water, and lathered his right hand nevertheless, sliding it down his belly 'til it met his cock and stroking it, slow at first, but soon gathering pace as it responded. He closed his eyes.

Normally it was Emeline he saw when he wanked. He wasn't sure why. The bitch had poured cold water on his lust for her by abandoning him when someone with a fatter wallet came along, but her pert tits and silken skin were a better fantasy than most. It felt mechanical, today, a routine rather than a real passion. This morning, he saw a different face as he fisted away.

Neil had beautiful eyes. He'd been struck by them the first time he saw the lad. That black hair was too severe for his face. He guessed it was normally something fairer — blond or a mousey brown — but a lot of the kids still went for that half-starved emo look. Mal wasn't sure why.

He was still pretty and for some unhinged reason, Mal found himself dwelling on that as he pumped himself harder. He had a soft-looking mouth and that unnatural hair was probably soft as silk too. Mal cursed Mercurio, silently, for even getting him thinking on it. He'd made the mistake once of admitting to the old boy, when they were drunk, that he'd enjoyed his first proper release in the mouth of another lad at his school. Merc had never let it drop, even if he'd barely looked at another man in that way since.

Idiot!

Mal rolled the pad of his thumb back and forth over the head of his cock as he inched up and his breathing grew more ragged, less controlled. He slowed his strokes and as he idly wondered how Neil's soft mouth might feel around his cock, he burst like a dancing fountain, coming in thick, hot spurts until his balls were empty and his body was shaking.

Rapidly then, he soaped away the sweat and grime of the previous day, and the traces of his release. Limping out of the shower, he snared a long strip of towel and began to slowly rub his body down, avoiding views of the scarring on his back and shoulders in the sliver of mirror still clinging to the wall beside him. It took him time to get dry and to awkwardly massage rose oil into the pale welts that he could reach. When the dry itch of the scars between his shoulder blades became unbearable, he gave in and got Merc to oil his back for him. He'd told the man that he'd gotten them in a car accident but he could see from the look on Mercurio's face, each time, that the old bastard didn't believe him. Today he could let them be.

He was just about to put the cap back on the oil when the door opened and Neil stumbled in, yawning and knuckling sleep from his eyes. He was still dressed in the clothes he'd been wearing the day before, and his hair looked as sleep mussed as the rest of him. Neil stopped dead when he spotted him standing there and the unguarded moment of surprise on his face couldn't be described any other way than 'cute'.

"Oh shit, I'm sorry... I didn't realize you were in here!" he said, quickly backing up.

Mal fought the urge to grin. That wouldn't help. Neil didn't quite blush but there was a hint of color to his cheeks. Malachai didn't miss the way those big blue eyes moved over his body before he backed toward the door.

Hmm…maybe Neil wasn't as green as he thought.

"It's okay. I'm done here, you can stay," he offered, wrapping the towel around his middle. To spare further blushes.

Okay, so he wasn't above making sure the towel was tucked low on his hips and taking his time tightening the cap on the bottle and placing it just so on the shelf while watching Neil from the corner of his eye. He stood perfectly still, like he wasn't sure if he should stay or bolt, but it gave Mal enough time to see Neil's eyes stray back down to his arse and watch the way his throat moved as he swallowed. He turned around to pick up his clothes and slid out of the door.

Mal got dressed while he thought about those not-so-sly looks of Neil's, also that while he'd not run like a rabbit, he'd also not said another word. He was a quiet one. Other than when he'd been answering direct questions, the only times he'd spoken up were to apologize for something. He wondered if that was a habit, or just that he was scared out of his mind from having sorcerers trying to kill him. If that were true.

By the time he got back down to the kitchen, he was dressed in jeans and a fitted tee, with a shirt slung about his shoulders. Merc must have woken and come down while he was showering because he'd found a news sheet somewhere since the previous evening and a handful of eggs, too, which he had begun frying off in the skillet. He'd also got the coffee on and Mal poured himself a mug with a grateful sigh.

"Did you sleep okay?" Merc asked in a gruff tone, without looking around.

"So-so," Mal admitted.

"At least you didn't get your throat cut," Merc grumbled, turning to push the newspaper across to him. "Take a look at that once you've had your breakfast. Our house guest is a wanted man."

Mal blinked at him and picked up the folded sheet, unfurling it single handed as he continued to sip his coffee.

The caffeine was waking his brain up slowly but the headline screaming across the front page woke him a damned sight faster.

Necromancer's Wife Slain in Her Home! Police Seek Missing Son.

Below was a blurry photo of a much younger-looking Neil, wide eyed with soft, pale curls, but undeniably the same boy who had just been scanning his arse in the bathroom. He felt some of the coffee bubble up in his throat and put the mug down with a bang.

"Fuck!"

"Good job you didn't," Merc observed. "There's a reward."

"What?" Mal stared at him for a full ten seconds.

"For handing in the killer. A reward. Cash, it says. *Mucho mas mazoola!*"

He scanned the article again. "It doesn't say he killed her."

"It doesn't say he didn't, either," Merc reminded him darkly. "What it does say is 'Money for information leading to the retrieval of…'"

His eyes shifted up and to the doorway behind Mal and he turned in his seat as Neil stepped into the room, his hair still wet from the shower. He smelled good, Mal thought and immediately pushed that thought away. The kid was the son of a death mage and a possible killer. What was he doing, still thinking with his dick?

He could only guess at how long Neil had been standing there, but it had apparently been long enough. His already pale face was positively ashen and the shadows under his eyes had deepened to nearly a blue shade despite a night's sleep. His eyes were fixed on the paper in front of Mal and those soft-looking lips trembled, just the once, before he pressed them together.

"I didn't kill my mother," he said, perfectly calm. "The Bone Men killed her before I ran."

Merc made a rude noise through his nostrils. "Sure, he'll tell us that now, when his neck's in the noose."

"It's true!" Neil glared at him. Mal could see that his hands shook just a shade and his face turned paler.

He held up a hand before they could begin shouting at each other.

"You're not gonna defend him in the face of this?" Merc pointed at the news sheet.

"If he's telling us the truth, he saw Bone Men murder his mother. Mercurio, cut him some slack here."

"If he isn't, we're sheltering a fugitive and a sorcerous murderer," Merc snarled.

"Why don't you tell us what happened, from the start," Malachai said, ignoring Merc.

Neil stood where he was, just a step inside the kitchen. He didn't fidget or talk with his hands. The stillness was quite eerie, almost military, but Mal recognized how he was braced. Hoping not to draw attention, waiting for a strike, poised to flee.

"I came home from work—" Neil started.

"Where did you work?" Merc put emphasis on the word *work*, like he didn't believe Neil knew what it meant.

"At the Yaetz greenhouses — "

"Doing what?" Merc interrupted again. Mal shot him an annoyed look for trying to trip the boy up but Neil didn't miss a beat.

"I watered plants, checked temperatures and fans, got shipments ready, loaded trucks…"

Merc snorted. "I doubt it. You're no bigger'n a stick and yer hands are soft as butter. Never worked a day."

Neil glared at him. "I don't know if you've ever heard of gloves, but they exist. And you don't have to be huge to lug some bags of dirt around. There are these things called trolleys…"

"Ignore him, Neil. Go on. What happened?" Mal pressed him.

Neil took a breath. "I came home and I saw the ward was broken." He paused, swallowed and continued. "I pushed the door open and called out for my mom, but she didn't answer, so I went in. There was broken glass in the hallway, I heard a crash in the kitchen and ran that way, and…and…" He took another breath and although his voice didn't waver, he'd gone so white Mal was worried he was going to faint.

"I heard Mom yell my name, tell me to run. There were two Bone Men, one held her arms, the other had a knife. I tried to get to her. I tried…but he stopped me. The other one cut her…before I could get back up. There w-was a lot of blood and she…w-went down…and I knew she was dead. I used a charm…" He reached up absently and Mal didn't think he even knew he was moving. Slender fingers touched just below his throat, where a pendant might sit if he were wearing a chain. "It blocked them long enough for me to run out of the house."

"You stopped trained killers with a three-dollar charm?" Merc sneered, shaking his head. "Tell me another. I like my fairy tales, kid."

Neil didn't respond. He'd gone from milk pale to slightly green.

Mal held his hand up for quiet again. "Where did you get the charm from, Neil?"

"My mom made me wear it. Just in case. We had a plan. Like you do fire and shooter drills in school, you know? Only this was in case anyone ever came after us." He looked at Merc. "And it didn't stop them, not really. Only held for a few seconds, but it was long enough."

"You can stop with the soulful looks, kid. I'm not buying any of this and I don't swing that way anyway," Merc said.

Neil's brow furrowed. "I don't understand what you're talking about. Everything I told you is the truth."

Merc opened his mouth to say something more but Mal cut him off. "I believe you." He watched Neil's face, his body language. His shoulders lowered a fraction and the tightness around his mouth eased. Relief showed in his face, but he was still wary. Mal didn't blame him. "Sit. Have something to eat."

Neil came toward them like a watchful alley cat, scooting closer to him and staying out of Merc's reach. His partner scraped the chair back and stood.

"A word, Valentine." Mercurio jabbed his thumb over his shoulder toward the corridor leading out back.

Mal took his time, making sure that Neil had coffee and food on his plate before he followed Merc back down the hallway and stone steps to the workshop. In his experience a man was less likely to run when he was hungry.

His partner was pacing back and forth irately and Mal leaned in the doorway, watching with his thumbs tucked into his jean pockets until Merc realized he was there. It did not do to provoke the man and Malachai was happy to wait for him to unburden himself of his grievance.

Merc did so by stopping his pacing abruptly and pointing a finger at him. "You are thinking with your dick."

Instead of denying it, Mal said, "And you are thinking from your wallet."

That took some of the huff out of him but Merc still looked far from pleased. "He smelled like trouble the second you drove him and that fancy piece of metal into the garage. Do you even have a clue what he is? He's not human, not fully. Do you know what's in his blood?"

"What difference does it make? He's human, Merc. And if what he says is true, he's been through a hell of a lot in the last couple of days."

"Malachai…"

Mal held up a hand. "He was being chased. That much I know is true because I saw them at Corvo's with my own eyes. They were willing to risk using shadow fire in public, in full daylight, to get to him. That makes me inclined to believe the rest of his story is true."

Merc still had a stubborn set to his jaw and Malachai sighed. "For fuck's sake, Merc, look at him. Does he look like a cold-blooded killer to you? Does he feel as if he could slit his own mother's throat?"

The older man bit his tongue and Mal took that for assent. Mercurio Geiger didn't do apologies and he was getting used to that. The old bastard had taken some adapting to when he first landed in Or d'Roit and Malachai had stopped short of killing him in his sleep himself, more than once. He would not have blamed Neil for considering it.

"He's barely more than a kid. And he's alone, with no real idea of what he's running from, except that he watched it kill his mother. What would you have done, Merc?"

"What I would'a done don't matter. It's what we're gonna do that matters. That kid's worth a small fortune. You think nobody's gonna come looking for him?"

"We'll keep it low key for a while until we figure out—"

"Shit." Merc cut him off, his body giving a jerk. "I think your chicken just flew the coop. Just felt a ward on the front door snap."

Mal stared at him for a full second. He'd figured they were safe leaving Neil in the kitchen, since he'd only come and gone via the workshop before. Clearly Neil liked to think outside the box.

"Fuck!"

He was on the stairs before his head had processed what to do next, running for the front of the building. Mercurio kept pace with him as far as the kitchen, where Mal heard him swearing as he discovered their cash box was empty of everything but small change.

"Merc…go back to the garage. Take the pickup round to the street. He isn't going to get far on foot," he yelled as he reached the front of the shop and found the door still swinging open. On the street there was no sign of

Neil. Under his breath he muttered, "Gods damn it! You little bastard! Which way did you fucking go?"

If he went west, he'd be running down to the docks and no good could come of him or their takings there. But maybe he hoped for a fast boat out of Shitsville.

Mal locked the shop and set off that way. As Merc came out of the alley in the truck, Mal sent him in the opposite direction. It didn't hurt to cover every possible escape route.

Well, if Merc caught him first, it might hurt Neil a bit.

Merc shook his head, though. "Get in the fucking truck, Valentine. This is your fault. I'm not having you go soft on the thieving brat. We're running a business here, unless you forgot."

Mal considered arguing but the longer they stood here, the further Neil would get. He popped the door open and climbed in. Merc had the gas floored before he shut it behind him.

"It would be quicker if I drove," he said.

"Shut the fuck up." Merc growled and drove several blocks before he added, "What's your instinct then, Lord Smartass? Where's the brat going?"

"He wants to get the hell out of Dodge," Mal said, his tone cooler than he felt. "I'd head for the docks. Try and pay passage on a ship."

"He'll be robbed and raped before they put him overboard then. Which is good but it ain't gonna get us our money back," Merc grumbled.

"You really are an intolerant old goat, aren't you?" Mal leaned his elbow on the sill as the pickup bounced and jolted over every pothole Downtown.

"I take my business interests seriously. Unlike you, your fucking lordship. You might be able to run back to Daddy if things go tits up—"

"I can't do that and you know it," Mal countered softly, but Merc ignored him.

"...but I gotta sit this out. If I don't wanna grow old and feeble on the fucking streets of this hellhole, I gotta make money while I can. And that brat is not gonna bilk me out of every last penny."

"We'll find him, Mercurio," Mal assured. "Damn it, he can't have gone this route. We'd have caught him already. Try Fifth and Lensfield. Then head down to the wharf. If we go that way, the road will be quicker. We might get there before him."

Quicker still if you'd let me drive, he thought but knew better than to say it.

Chapter Six

Neil slunk through the shadows, which there were plenty of, even in the bright light of morning. It was an odd thing he'd done for as long as he could remember. As much as he was afraid of the darkness, seeking out those pathways through the light came to him as naturally as breathing and felt like running along old, familiar roads.

He pulled up the hood of the sweatshirt he'd taken off a hook by the door in the kitchen and tried to convince himself not to feel guilty about that or the money in his pocket. He was sure that Malachai would get triple the amount he'd taken from the cash box after he chopped up the car and sold it off. And really, he was doing the man a favor by leaving like this. He'd already caused him trouble with his clients and his partner and the longer he stayed, the more trouble was likely to come. He'd been nice to him and Neil didn't want to repay that kindness by bringing problems down around his ears. Besides that, he didn't trust

Mercurio not to sell him out, no matter what Malachai said.

No, it was better they part company before he was any more tempted to find out exactly what Malachai's lips would feel like on his or how his tongue would taste. He stuffed his hands in the pockets of the hoodie and tried not to think about the long, lean body he'd gotten a good eyeful of when he'd walked in on Mal in the bathroom.

He must have looked a complete idiot, frozen there, gawking at him but at least Malachai had been kind enough not to tease him about it, or the hard-on he'd desperately tried to will down while he'd waited to piss. And oh man, thinking about all that sleek, naked skin was not helping him focus on where the hell he was going. It had taken an act of sheer willpower not to drop to his knees in that bathroom and beg to suck him off. Well, willpower and the thought that he'd probably get his ass kicked out on the street if he did.

But what if he *had* done it and Mal hadn't kicked him out? What if he'd tugged his towel off and instead of asking what he thought he was doing, Mal had smiled that sly smile of his and pushed his fingers into his hair? Neil swallowed the saliva that flooded his mouth at the thought. *Focus.* He needed to focus. He'd told Malachai he'd needed a train ticket so he headed the opposite direction of the depot. His plan was to find a place he could chill and hide for a day, wait to make sure that if Malachai did go to the railroad, that he wasn't there.

As he cut down a side street between two tall buildings, his nose caught the sharp tang of moving water and the garbage-y rotten smell of wet earth. He must be close to the river. He stopped for a second and looked around. He was in a pocket of the city that was still alive, still active. People and vehicles moved on the streets. Businesses were actually open and running. He could probably disappear among them for a day or even two and work his way back toward the city center and the trains.

Or...or maybe he could leave another way sooner. Boats took passengers as well as cargo. He wasn't sure if it would cost more to leave that way, but it couldn't hurt to find out. He lifted his head and sniffed, following his nose toward the green smell of water and the sound of gulls.

When he reached the wharf, it took him some time to orientate. The shadows were fewer and farther between here and he slunk from one to another, looking up in wonderment at the tall, iron-flanked vessels moored along the embankment. He had never traveled by ship before and had no idea how anyone went about it but there were guys coming and going from all the boats so he supposed it was just a question of stopping one of them long enough to ask.

As he was debating this, a guy in denim dungarees and a gray shirt, sleeves rolled back to bare brawny forearms, came barreling down the nearest gangplank and almost ran into him.

"Oi, watch out!" he snapped.

"Sorry." Neil recoiled a step and bumped right into someone else, who gave him a none too gentle shove back toward the man who had told him to watch out.

"Git outta the way!"

"Sorry!" Neil said again, attempting to squeeze through another clutch of workers going the opposite direction.

"What the fuck you doing down here, sonny?" one man asked. His accent reminded Neil acutely of Mal, though he did not speak nearly so gentle a tone as his handsome, flame-haired rescuer.

"I um, I was just going to see if…if I could get passage on a boat."

"Oh, you was, was you?" The man looked him up and down with more consideration and Neil felt the fine hairs on the back of his neck rise.

"That'll cost you. It ain't cheap."

"It's not? I mean…how much?"

"Depends." The man pursed his lips. "Course you could maybe work out a trade. Work your way to where you're headed."

"I could?" If he could work for passage, that would be awesome. He'd be able to get off the boat far away and still have enough money to get settled in a new city.

The man grinned at him. "Sure. You'd make a fine cabin boy. Just talk to the cap'n."

Neil had no clue what a cabin boy might be expected to do but he asked where he might find the captain anyway and was waved up the gangplank and directed to the bridge. The fellows he found up there were as rough as the men down on the wharf and the man who identified himself as the captain, was about six foot three, with a raft of intriguing tattoos running from his neck right down his chest in the open collar of his shirt and both his arms. Neil tried not to stare at them but his eye was drawn to a young, naked boy angel on his left upper arm. The angel was in chains, his wings crooked and broken, but he had the most beautiful, sorrowful face.

"So," the captain interrupted his admiration gruffly, "exactly what sort of skills do you think you can bring to this vessel, lad?"

Neil tried to recall some long-ago pirate movies he'd watched as a kid to think up what sort of chores might be required on a boat but all he could come up with was something about swabbing decks. "I'm a quick learner, and I'm stronger than I look. If you need cabins cleaned, or cooking done, I can cook a bit, and um, swab decks?"

The captain cracked a grin then laughed and Neil wasn't sure if that was a good sign or bad. Probably bad.

"I'm not sure what you need done. There was a man down on the dock that said I could maybe work for my passage as a cabin boy, so whatever they do, I guess."

The captain laughed at that and his crewmen joined in. One of them, a striking, dark-skinned fellow — whose silver eyes made him think, with a pang of regret, about Malachai — said, "You heard the boy. He's a fast learner. That's the kind of attitude we need. Are you versatile, young man? Can you apply yourself to any position?"

Neil blinked. The way he said it made it sound like a joke but Neil didn't get what was funny. "I can do more than one thing at a time, if that's what you mean."

"That's worth knowing. You'll almost certainly be doing more than one thing at a time, sweet stuff."

The other crew members chortled at the captain's comment so he added, "Unless you're working directly under me. I don't share."

"Whatever position you need me in most is fine," Neil said, wondering what it was he didn't share. He figured, if he was just working for the captain, that would probably mean less work, not that he was afraid of hard work.

The men all laughed uproariously at that and the captain patted him on the shoulder and said, "You're going to be a good fit with this crew, I can feel it. I hope you've got plenty of stamina and you don't mind spending a lot of time on your hands and knees, lad. It can be a satisfying position, for the right candidate."

The men were howling with laughter now and slapping their thighs, pounding one another on the back.

A trickle of cold crept down Neil's back and he finally got the joke. He cursed himself silently for his stupidity and wished very much that a hole would open up below him that he could sink into and disappear, flaming cheeks and all.

"I-I um, think I've made a mistake."

"Oh, don't be like that, kid. The lads can be a bit rowdy but they're a good-hearted bunch. The best crew a bloke could wish for." The captain rested both hands on Neil's shoulders as he turned toward the door. He felt a bit sick. The captain was leering down at him. "Why don't you stay and have a tot of rum, get to know us before we make out...to sea, I mean." He winked at Neil.

Another of the crewmen moved in behind him and he suddenly felt a warm hand on his backside, squeezing firmly there.

Neil reached down and grabbed his wrist. "No, really. I made a mistake. I'll just go."

The guy behind him shook his hand off and the captain moved his hands from his shoulders down to his arms. "I think you'll stay."

"But I'm not— I'm not a..."

"What? Not into men? Don't worry your pretty head none. One hole is as good as another once there's nothing but wind and waves around you."

The cold feeling in the pit of his stomach blossomed and grew. He tried to pull free of the captain's grip but his hands tightened around his arms and the man drew him up close, planting a hard kiss on his lips. Neil tried to twist away. "Let me go."

The crewmen who had groped his ass pressed in closer and kissed his neck while he reached around to stroke Neil's crotch through his jeans. His voice was like swirling smoke as he whispered, "You don't wanna go, hot stuff. Stay and have some fun with us. Let us get your engines running. We understand how to entertain naughty little lads like you."

The captain was still holding Neil tightly by the wrists as his crewman unbuttoned Neil's pants and yanked them down roughly. He pulled Neil's underwear down too and whistled appreciatively.

"That is a nice, round ass. Just the kind I like."

His heart did a double beat against his ribs and his breath whistled harshly in his throat but Neil forced the panic down. He could not afford to wallow in his own stupidity and embarrassment. Not if he was going to get himself out of here in one piece. He stopped fighting to pull away and drew in a breath, consciously relaxing the muscles in his arms and torso as he exhaled. He blinked once and made his eyes wider, staring directly into the captain's eyes.

He'd discovered a few years ago, right about the time his voice had settled into a deeper register, that if he relaxed and looked at someone with just the right amount of finesse, he could sometimes get them to do what he wanted. At first he'd thought it was just something kind of weird that he could do, and it wasn't until he'd learned why he could do it that it sickened him. He hated it, but he wasn't above using it if it meant he could get out of this situation.

"You want me for yourself," Neil murmured to the captain.

He held his breath as confusion clouded the man's hard brown eyes. He held his stare, feeling the subtle hints of resistance, and knew the moment the compulsion took.

"Mr. Brogan, I am captain of this ship. If someone is to take that peachy ass first, it is my due as your captain. Take the brat to my cabin and strip him," he ordered.

"Aye, sir," Brogan said, his tone sullen.

Neil steeled himself to be pushed and dragged down to the lower decks but Brogan simply put him over one shoulder and carried him below like a sack of coal.

A door banged open and Brogan set him down hard on his feet. Before Neil could even take a step back, his hands were on him, pulling his sweatshirt off and throwing it aside. He reached for him again and Neil made his move. He threw himself against Brogan, wrapping his arms around his neck and kissing him to get his attention. It certainly worked and when Neil broke the kiss, Brogan was already falling into his eyes. "It's not fair, what the captain wants," Neil murmured to him, his lips so close to his they nearly brushed together. "You need to go drink, work out the frustration…leave the door open."

It was risky giving him so much at once. Simple was definitely better when he was trying to lust someone into obeying him. He was desperate, though.

Brogan took some work. He looked confused for a moment then tried to kiss Neil on the mouth again, nudging him toward the bed with his knees.

"We can do this. We can be done before he comes down," he whined. "I know you want it."

Neil changed tactics. He rubbed up against him so he'd stop trying to push him backward. "Oh yes…yes, I want you…but I need a drink. Go get me a drink first. Leave the door open," he said again.

This time it worked. Brogan was already erect in his tight pants and that was some hard-on he was struggling with, but he stumbled to the door like a man sleepwalking and out into the hall, obediently leaving the door ajar behind him.

Neil grabbed the sweatshirt, pulled up his pants and ran for the door. He looked both ways. The hallway was empty but there was only the one set of stairs going up. The other way led to darkness and uncertainty. There was a window in the cabin behind him but it was so tiny he doubted even he'd be able to squeeze through it, and he'd rather avoid jumping in the river if he could help it.

The suggestions he'd given the captain and Brogan wouldn't hold long. He had only moments to decide what to do and he chose running over hiding. He barreled up the stairs as fast as he could and it was only surprise and luck that the crew milling at the top didn't immediately grab him. He could see that he'd never make the gangway, so he took off to the side of the boat as fast as his legs would take him, leaped up on a pile of crates and jumped over the rail.

As he was falling, he thought he should have jumped in the river after all. He was probably less likely to break his leg. Or his neck. It was a long way down to the dock. A lot longer than it had seemed on the way up. Fortunately he hadn't lied when he'd told Merc and the captain both that he was stronger than he looked. Well, tougher anyway. He landed hard, pinwheeling his arms as he took two steps forward and fell on his hands and knees. Gasping, he groaned at the stabbing pain that shot up his legs and he squeezed his eyes shut. His ankles and knees stung like hives of angry wasps were attacking him. He swallowed down the pain and got up, slower than he wanted to. He had no idea if they would chase him now that he was off the boat, but he wasn't going to hang around to find out.

The dock was still crowded with workers, some of whom had stopped to stare after watching his drop. He darted into the throng, hoping the surprise of seeing someone jump off a boat would be enough to keep anyone from grabbing him. It was a sound thought and probably he would have got clean away if he hadn't still been a bit disorientated and run smack into someone.

He bounced off a hard chest and would have stumbled back if the man hadn't grabbed his arms. He wasn't sure if he just meant to steady him but he'd been grabbed enough today and he threw his weight back, trying to pull away. "Let go!"

He lifted his head and got a surprise of his own when he saw a familiar halo of dark red hair and stern silver-gray eyes. It was Malachai. For a split second Neil's knees turned to jelly and he wanted to fall into his arms with a sigh of relief. Then he remembered he'd stolen from him. A yell from behind drew his attention and Neil glanced over his shoulder to see the captain and some of his crew coming down the gangplank. He stopped trying to pull away and pushed forward instead.

"We have to go!" he murmured urgently.

Mal looked up at the mob hurrying down the gangplank and his eyes narrowed for a moment.

"This is getting to be something of a habit. Did you steal from them too?" he demanded, keeping a tight hold on Neil's arms. His touch was firm but not rough, just enough to stop him running away again.

"No!" Neil couldn't believe he was quibbling at a time like this. "Look, I'm sorry. Can we please just get out of here?"

As the captain's feet hit the concrete of the moll, Neil struggled again but Mal held his ground. His pale eyes were fixed on the ship's crew, still half-closed. Neil heard their footsteps slowing and the cold, sick sense of panic gripped his gut once more.

"Captain Kenneally," Mal said and his tone was cordial but not warm. "What an unexpected pleasure."

"Please don't give me back to him." Neil's words were hardly more than a strangled whisper but he put every ounce of the siphoned lust remaining in him into that plea.

"Shhh now," Mal told him, lips barely moving. He did not look down, but his fingers squeezed then slackened on Neil's wrists. "Don't run."

He let go of one of Neil's hands, turning him to face the men from the ship as he did so. The captain had a wary look on his face. Brogan was flustered and sweating but he'd lost his erection at least.

"Malachai Valentine, as I live and breathe," Captain Kenneally said. "What brings you down to the quayside? Do you know this scamp?"

"Business, as usual," Mal replied, his tone giving nothing away. "And I might ask the same of you. He's not exactly your type, Kenneally. Bit old for you, I'd have said."

Kenneally didn't seem insulted by what Malachai was insinuating, which Neil supposed was good, but he didn't look in any way deterred, either. "When such pretty fruit drops right into your lap, why complain if it's a touch ripe? He's just signed onto the crew and had a bout of cold feet. I'll have him back, if you please, with my thanks for your help catching the bugger."

Mal gave him a sideways glance and Neil cringed at that look that asked without words how dumb could he be.

"Did you sign any crew papers?" Mal asked.

Neil shook his head.

Kenneally turned a baleful glare on him and it was only Malachai's hand on his arm that kept him from bolting again.

"You came on board my ship, asked me to take you on for cabin boy and all but crawled into my lap to seal the deal."

"I didn't realize what that meant," Neil said, his stomach fluttering uneasily at the way Kenneally put it.

"Misleading job description, you can't blame the lad for that," Mal said, his tone still mild and his manner laid-back.

"Tell you what. Let us take him back on board. We'll all sample the goods, then he's free to go," Kenneally said with a hungry smirk. "I'll even let you have first dibs, Master Malachai. Can't say fairer than that."

Neil was not about to get back on the ship, not even for a chance to play out his early-morning fantasy with Malachai. The more people around and the more stress he was under the less likely he was to be able to influence anyone, but he couldn't just meekly go along and hope for the best. They weren't likely to give him another chance to get away. Which one, though?

Captain Kenneally had been like trying to move a rock earlier. Malachai was closest but the thought of using him that way made the acid churn in his stomach. Brogan had been pretty malleable but he was the farthest away. He had to try.

Catching Brogan's eyes was easy. He softened the tension around his mouth, stared into his eyes hard and licked his lips for good measure. "You'd rather fight him for me, wouldn't you?" he said, his voice pitched low, just a purr of sound.

Brogan's body tensed up and his brow scrunched. He balled up a fist and turned to his captain but Kenneally shoved him out of the way. "You skinny fuck! I'll fucking flay you alive, witch!" he roared, swinging a meaty fist at the side of Neil's head.

Malachai moved so fast that one moment he was by Neil's side and the next the pressure on his wrist was gone and Mal was behind Kenneally, holding him back. Brogan charged the two of them, driving his shoulder into Kenneally's midsection, which caused him to double over and almost throw Mal off. Neil didn't wait to see what happened next. He turned and ran, weaving his way into the crowd as more angry shouts rose up behind them.

A hand reached out to grab him as he raced by and he was swung off his feet and hauled around to face a livid Mercurio.

"You thieving little shit!" the salvage merchant raged at him.

Neil groaned. He had absolutely no luck today. Before he had a chance to explain anything, a howl of rage and pain cut across the general chaos. Neil craned his neck to make sure it wasn't Malachai but he didn't catch sight of his red hair anywhere. The howl came from Captain Kenneally, who was clutching bloody hands to his face. Brogan was laid out on the dock, unmoving.

Finally he saw Malachai. His expression was dark as a storm cloud and he plowed through the milling throng directly toward them. Neil got that weird sensation in his belly again, a kind of swooping feeling that made his knees weaken, but it wasn't exactly fear. Then he saw one of the crew running up behind Mal and the glint of sun on a blade. He stopped trying to pull free of Merc and lurched toward Mal instead.

"Behind you!" he yelled.

When the red-haired man did not even look over his shoulder, Neil thought his heart would stop. There was black anger in his glare and Neil struggled to reach him again. When Merc pulled him into the equivalent of a bearhug, he wanted to scream at the man not to be so blind.

Mal raised his left hand and without breaking stride or even blinking, he grabbed a loop of rope from a roadside chandlery stall and cast it back over his head.

Neil heard screaming but he was transfixed, unable to take his eyes off Malachai. He reached him and Merc before Neil was able to focus on what had happened behind Mal.

The pirate was writhing around on the quayside trying to stab a ten-foot anaconda that had coiled around him and was slowly crushing the life out of his body.

Neil closed his mouth and gulped as he and Mal came face to face and he stared up into his angry scowl. "I'm sorry…"

Malachai grabbed his chin and Neil flinched.

"Stop saying that." He gave his cheek a tap that wasn't quite a slap but was more than just a pat. Neil ignored the sting and bit his lip to keep from saying he was sorry again. "Put him in the truck, Merc," Malachai said.

Merc half-carried, half-dragged him toward the street where the truck was parked. Neil had dug in his heels but he wasn't really putting up any kind of fight. Mal hadn't said another word and he still looked pissed. When they got to the truck, Merc opened the driver's door and pushed Neil up and over while Mal got in on the other side and they slammed the doors closed at nearly the same time.

Neil sat squished between them, trying to make himself as small as possible. Merc started the truck.

"Where's my money, kid?" he demanded.

Neil reached into his back pocket and pulled out the envelope of cash, handing it over. Merc looked at him in disgust. "You put it in your back pocket? Gods a'mighty. Probably the only reason you weren't robbed was no one else is that stupid."

"I only took what I thought you'd get for the car."

Merc glared at him, getting so close Neil thought he might bite him. He cringed back but that only pressed him up against Malachai's hard, unyielding body. "Don't you ever rob from me again."

"You were going to turn me in for money!" Neil protested.

"I might still do!"

"Mercurio, shush," Mal said. "You got your money back."

"And whose fault is it that we had to go hunting after it?" Merc snarled.

"He's a child, Merc. Let it go." Malachai was quiet again, calm as a gentle sea.

"I'm not a child," Neil muttered. "I'm twenty...next month."

That got him a snort from Merc and he put the truck in gear and pulled into traffic. After a few minutes of silence, Neil figured their argument had stalled and asked Malachai, "Where did the snake come from?"

"Just thank your stars it did," Mal told him with a rueful shake of his head. "Unless you'd rather go back and play with the pirates?"

"I didn't know they were pirates," Neil said, feeling defensive again. "Someone told me I could probably work for passage. I didn't know how...what they meant." His cheeks were getting hot again as he thought of their laughter and how all the things they'd said suddenly made sense. He must have looked like such an idiot.

"You struck lucky when you stole from us, in that case. How did you survive the jump? Most men trying a stunt like that would have broken their legs at least."

"I'll break his fucking legs," Merc grumbled, guiding the pickup through the quayside crowds.

Neil sighed and leaned his head back, closing his eyes for a second. Actually his ankles and knees — and even his hips — still hurt some. Sore. Like he'd been running all day. Or maybe doing something else.

"Lucky, I guess. Like you said," Neil answered.

"Goddess touched," Mal exhaled. "Neil, I am an alchemist but my kin were a shade more than human. I am able to alter forms. The snake was not real, it was a magical transformation. The man who wanted to kill me simply believed it was real. Let's start again. How did you survive that jump with your bones intact?"

Funny how when Merc barked at him Neil could more or less brush it off, or at least stand up to him, but when Malachai lost patience and pierced him with those silver-gray eyes, it was like he reached deep inside him and plucked a string that made him quiver from head to toe.

"I-I don't —"

"Neil. Tell. Me."

Each word dropped on him like a stone and he scrunched down in his seat. He tried to look away and found he couldn't. His tongue was stuck to the roof of his mouth and a small whimper of sound gurgled in his throat.

"If he pisses himself, you're cleaning it up!" Merc grumbled.

Malachai didn't even blink and Neil made another sound, trying to get words out.

"Tell me what you are, exactly," Malachai insisted.

The only thing that made it past Neil's lips was the one word he didn't want to say. "Demon."

Malachai didn't recoil. Didn't flinch away or curl his lip in disgust. In fact he didn't seem much bothered or surprised at all. "What type?"'

Neil still couldn't look away from him, though his cheeks were positively on fire. "An incubus."

"Aww, fuck it!" Merc growled. "Just what we need. That explains a lot!"

"Hush, Mercurio." Mal's voice was not loud but there was command in his quiet tone and Neil found himself wondering who really held the reins in their business relationship. "That's why they attacked me. You inflamed them. I did wonder how they grew balls so large since our last encounter." Mal smiled. "No matter. They will rue it the next time we meet."

"I only meant for them to attack each other," Neil said in a small voice. Malachai didn't seem to take umbrage. In fact, furnished with an answer to what exactly he was, he relaxed into his seat.

Neil took a shaky breath. He waited, but they didn't pull over and tell him to get out. Other than Merc's grumble, there was no reaction at all. Neil stole a glance at Mal. He looked perfectly at ease, amused even. Bizarre. He had never met anyone that didn't even flinch when they discovered what he was. Not that many knew, but the few who had found out had been universally horrified or appalled.

Malachai's non-reaction got him wondering.

"So...umm...you said that you weren't entirely human." Neil started, anxious. If Malachai was a higher-ranking demon, or had more blood in him than Neil's grandfather had passed down to him, this could end badly for him. Demon kind — and he could not think the words without hearing the sneering way a teacher of his had said them once in a class on interdimensional beings — were notoriously territorial and hierarchical.

If Malachai *was* demon bred, Neil had gotten no sense of it off him. Mal had made his skin tingle all right, but not that way. Which would mean he was either very low level or very powerful. If he were a demon at all.

Mal smiled, an expression that softened the angular lines of his face. His pale gray eyes had a glitter of mischief, almost.

"My mother is human, from an old family of powerful alchemists," he said in reverent tones. "My father is fae, from the seighlie court."

"Understatement of the year," Merc muttered.

"You're fae…" Neil couldn't keep the surprise out of his voice. There weren't a lot of fae living in the country, as far as he knew. "I thought they hated cities and metal?"

Merc snorted. "I thought incubi seduced young virgins and sucked out their souls."

"Some of them do, I guess." Neil shifted on the seat. His grandfather probably had. The thought of siphoning off someone's soul like that made him feel sick and dirty. "I wouldn't."

"Said the fox to the chicken," Merc muttered.

Neil ignored him and after another long, silent pause, he asked Malachai, "Are you here on your own? I thought fae liked to live together? Like, they needed to be part of a court?"

"Like to? Some do. Need to? No, it isn't entirely necessary." Mal heaved a sigh. "My paternal kin are leprechauns. The lure of gold is stronger in them than the pull of clan loyalty, to be frank, but my mother was human. I take more after her side of the family, truth be told."

"Huh." Neil rolled that around with vaguely remembered rumors about there being colonies of fae out west, ancestors of settlers that had gone in search of mines.

"And if you're lucky enough to find their pot o' gold, some might even grant you three wishes," Mercurio muttered. Neil didn't know him well enough to guess if the sneering tone was sarcasm or if he was just making fun of him. He snuck a glance at Mal from the corner of his eye but his face was impassive.

They pulled into the garage bay and got out of the truck. Neil had taken two steps when Mercurio whirled around, grabbed him by the front of the shirt and slammed him against the hood. "We have rules. No lying. No stealing. No magickin' each other. And if you make a mess, you damn well better clean it up." He hauled Neil back upright and practically threw him at Mal, who caught him by the arm before he fell on his face. "Clean up your mess, yer lordship."

And with that, he stormed off, muttering to himself under his breath.

Chapter Seven

Mal heaved a deep sigh as Mercurio went stomping off into the store without a backward glance. His partner was a diamond and Mal trusted no man here more to watch his back, but he did not mince his words. Merc had been with the US Marine Corps for many years, keeping his fae heritage hidden. Traditionally gremlins were supposed to jinx anything mechanical but Merc was the opposite. He'd fixed tanks and helicopters in parts of the world that most ordinary folk couldn't even spell, let alone find on a map. Give him a broken machine and he would nurse it back to health no matter how long the job might take. The gremlins were the only full-blood fae who could work magic with iron and that was their strength.

Merc had no patience with people, though. Their chatter incensed him. Most of their habits were alien to him. Mercurio Geiger was a private soul at heart.

Alchemists weren't exactly ten a penny out here, but it was Mal's stint in Iraq and Afghanistan with the

Parachute Regiment that had won the older man over, he was sure. Most folk were more impressed by his tales of driving Lamborghinis for the Coulson Team out in Monza and Mal was not averse to talking about that part of his life. It was a world away from the bombs and guns in the desert but he'd come closer to death at the wheel of a Lambo than he ever had in uniform.

Merc didn't care for any of that. He had satisfied himself that Mal knew his way around a petrol engine then left him pretty much to his own devices.

Neil was a different kettle of fish.

The boy was an incubus, for crying out loud! And an active one, if the events down on the quay were to be taken seriously. He should probably stop thinking of Neil as a 'boy', in any case.

Neil trailed him quietly back to the kitchen and Mal was aware of him like a prickle of heat down his back every step of the way. They sat down at the table, Neil still watching him with wary eyes. When Mal poured them both a glass of fruit juice and pushed one across the table to him, Neil asked, "Why does he call you 'your lordship'? Is he just making fun of you?"

"Not entirely," Mal replied. He had no particular desire to explain that mess in detail. "It's not relevant to my life here. Since we've got the business of what you are and what I am out of the way, would you care to change any of your story about why the Bone Men were so keen to get ahold of you?"

Mal watched how he shifted his shoulders, how he went very still. He was learning to read Neil already. The way he moved, like a cringe that was interrupted, some might have taken that for evasiveness. Mal was pretty certain what he was seeing was fear. Specifically the kind of fear that came with years of learning to hide it.

"I don't know why."

"But you have an idea. You were prepared. You were wearing a charm to help you escape, you knew who they were and knew you had to run from them if you wanted to live. Someone taught you that. Readied you for the possibility. You said they were probably after your father. Why?"

Neil sagged and he stared down at the table then shrugged. "He's not just a sorcerer. He's Black Mafija." Neil dragged his eyes off the spot in front of him and met his eyes. "He's killed people. A lot of people. He has a lot of enemies. I really don't understand why they came after Mom and me but my guess is someone found out what he is, or the family of someone he killed wanted revenge. If they were hired to kill me they could have done it at least twice already, so I'm thinking they want me alive."

It was not a bad assumption and one Mal had been thinking himself. It also put a couple of large holes in his theory that this was all about the father. If Neil's father had carried out a hit and a grieving widow wanted revenge for it, both Neil and his mother would be dead. Same if it was just some self-righteous nutjobs that wanted to purge a sorcerer and his family from their neighborhood. Those were not the type of people to do things in half-measures — but if it wasn't about his father…

"You put the stir on anyone's libido lately? Like you did those pirates?"

There was that pretty pink flush again. An incubus that blushed. How did that even happen?

"No. I only did that because I had to. It was the only way I could think to get off that boat, once I figured...figured out I made a mistake. I don't ever do that to people...usually."

"How do you feed then?"

"I don't. Not like that. I'm far enough down the bloodline that I don't have to feed off people."

"But you could?"

"I've no idea. I never tried. And I don't want to."

Malachai drummed his fingers on the table. "So you have the Bone Men, the police and possibly your father, all looking for you. And your plan is to buy a train ticket with some pocket change and hope none of them thinks to look for you two towns over."

He could see defiance, the denial then the last thread of hope all crumble from Neil's expression in the few seconds it took him to process that his plan really wasn't much of a plan at all.

"What else am I supposed to do? Just lay down and let them come find me?" Neil said at last.

"You really have no one else to turn to?" Mal was surprised, even in view of his assessment of Neil's character. "No one who will shelter you if the worst happens?"

Neil shrugged. "I wouldn't be running if there was. What my father does... He's never told me all the details but it's always been enough to protect us before."

"So something changed." Mal nodded.

"I don't know. Maybe. Even if I did, I don't think it would matter. I never wanted any part of what my father does. It's not stopped him from trying to get me to carry on the family legacy but I never will. I don't care what he does, I never will. And now my mom's gone and that's all his fault too, I've got no reason to stay here."

"Do you think he will search for you?" Mal propped his chin on his palm and his elbow on the table. Neil's anger was kept well under wraps but he could feel it simmering under the surface of his apparent composure as he spoke of his mother.

Chronologically he wasn't that much older than Neil, but watching him struggle, watching him try to hide his expressions, gauge how much he could tell him, how deep he could trust, it was like looking into a mirror that showed his own past.

"If he's alive, and he knows I'm alive, he'll hunt for me," Neil said quietly.

Interesting choice of words.

"Wouldn't it be easier to go to him? If he's that well connected, surely he could protect you."

"From the Bone Men, maybe. From the police, definitely. But the price is too high." Neil's lips thinned as he pressed them together, as if tasting something sour and unpleasant. "Every time he uses his sorcery, it eats more of him. Unless he binds a familiar to him, to take the strain for him, he doesn't have much longer. I'll turn myself over to the police and let them hang me before I let that happen."

"No one is going to hang you, Neil. You didn't kill her." Mal reached across to squeeze his hand. "Merc has a mouth on him, but he won't hurt you. He won't betray you. Just…don't lie to us. No one here will ask you to spend yourself against your will. We work together. We stand together. And if we fall, then we fall together."

Neil gave him another of those silent, soulful stares, but this time there was more confusion in it than anything else.

"Why would you help me? You can make more money than you'd get for the car if you turned me over."

"Don't tell me that. I might change my mind." Mal laughed. It was a challenge, truth be told.

Gold was in his blood. And money could be gold but he could not think about that yet. His own sire would have sold Neil to the highest bidder and not turned a hair.

Malachai Valentine was not his father, though. Another thing he and Neil had in common. He was starting to feel, maybe, it wasn't just chance that had put Neil in his path. Best not start thinking like that. Connections with random waifs and strays were not what he needed.

Mal pushed himself to his feet and emptied the glass of apple juice in front of him.

"If those Bone Men bastards are going to come after you, I guess we need to get things moving," he said. "How are you with motor mechanics?"

"How am I what?"

Mal stifled a sigh. "Do you know anything about how an engine works?"

"Sort of," Neil answered. "There's fuel, spark, pistons, rods, other stuff probably that moves around to make it go."

"Ever taken a car to pieces?" he asked, suspecting that the answer would be no. "It's not so hard once you get started. But if there's a tracking charm on it, you need to have the feelers out for it, otherwise it'll go off like a burglar alarm when you try to mess with it."

Neil stared at him. "You want me to take apart a car? You don't want it to run again, right?"

"It doesn't even have to be recognizable," Mal said. He was trying to keep his lips from twitching at the totally incredulous look he was getting. To Neil's credit he didn't say he couldn't do it and he got up and followed him out to the garage.

Somewhere in the back corner, Mal heard Merc tinkering with something but he didn't call him over. It was probably for the best to keep him and Neil working separately for the time being. He went to one of the long metal tool boxes and opened it, taking out a set of wrenches and sockets.

"We'll start on this," he told Neil, handing him the tools and leading him over to an old buggy with the interior missing and half the engine disassembled. "The rest of the engine block needs to come out."

Neil stood, wide-eyed, holding the wrenches as Mal pushed the cherry picker over. "You put the chains around it, unbolt everything then haul it out. Easy."

Neil's look was frankly doubtful but he still didn't complain or say he couldn't do it. He watched everything Mal did like a hawk, standing stone still and clutching the tools. At last he took a couple of steps and peered into the well of the engine compartment.

"How do you hook the chains up to it?" he asked.

Mal smiled and showed him the hooks. "Just have to slide under and hook them together around the fattest part.

"I can do that," Neil said.

Mal heard a faint snort from somewhere in the dark recesses but if Neil heard, he didn't say anything. He set the tools down and got down on the floor, looking underneath.

"Hold on a sec," Mal told him and slid a hydraulic jack out from its spot by the wall and under the axle. "Make sure it's on the frame, would you." He already knew he'd placed it right where it should be but Neil double-checked then looked up and him and nodded. Mal jacked the car up and Neil slid under. Mal fed the chains down from the top. They rattled and Neil moved them around and tried to hook them together. He heard some faint muttered cursing, some more chain rattling, then Neil slid back out.

"Okay. It's secure."

"Good. Can you take the wrench and...do you see that bolt down there over the axle?"

"I see it." Neil's slender hand snaked up to take the wrench.

"Can you get it loose?" Mal leaned on the edge of the chassis, peering down into the engine well.

Despite having just watched Neil jump from a height that would almost certainly have broken bones on a regular human, he was still having trouble seeing past the slender build and smaller stature to the hidden strength below Neil's surface. He watched him place the socket on the bolt, the tension in his wrist and forearm straining for a moment, then it broke free and he cranked it back again to loosen it further.

"There's about six on that side and six more on the other," Mal explained and let him work on those while he started on the side mounts. The steady ratchet sound of the wrench and clank of metal on metal assured him Neil wasn't having any trouble finding the bolts. Mal glanced down occasionally to make sure he wasn't about to step on his feet but Neil seemed to instinctively shimmy over, or stay still, while he was moving around the car.

In about twenty minutes or so, he scooted out from under the engine and handed Mal a small pile of rusted bolts. He hadn't even broken any off.

"Good. Come look over here, I'll show you how to disconnect the transmission lines."

There were smudges of oil on Neil's face and he had to sit down hard on the urge to wet his thumb and wipe them away, the way his mother used to wipe his and Mortie's faces when they were small. Neil must have seen him looking because he asked, "What?"

Then rubbed at his nose with his sleeve.

"You missed a bit." Mal circled his cheek with one finger but didn't touch.

"Kiss him, already!" Merc grumbled from under the Maserati, where he was feeling for the tracer charm.

"Fuck off!" Mal laughed but it felt strained and he knew Merc would hear the difference in his voice.

Damnit!

Neil had just started to look a bit more relaxed but at Merc's teasing the guarded expression snapped back in place. Mal sighed and bent over to start on the transmission lines. He'd half-expected Neil to retreat but he only stood for a moment before leaning over to see what he was doing. Only, he couldn't see much. There was zero room to maneuver and Mal was having a hard time getting to the nuts he was trying to reach.

"I can get it for you," Neil said.

Mal pulled his arm out and gestured for Neil to come take his place. His reach wasn't as long, but his arm was thinner and he had no problem getting it down between the engine block and the wall of the chassis. He had to practically lay across the motor to do it, but he didn't seem to mind. He made short work of the connections and it was just a matter of a few more bolts and some shifting and cursing on both their parts but in almost no time, they had the engine hanging free.

"Well done." Mal gave Neil a friendly clap on the shoulder. He wasn't patronizing him, either. He'd planned an afternoon to pull that bitch out and he could hardly believe they'd managed it in about an hour. The flash of a smile crossed Neil's face and lingered on his lips and made him realize it was the first he'd seen on him.

"You're a natural at this," he said because he wanted to keep that smile there. It warmed his heart to see Neil happy. "D'you want to tackle the wheels too? Should be a piece of cake after that."

"Sure. But if we take the wheels off, how are you going to get it out of here?"

"Merc will get his torch out and cut the frame into pieces. Then it goes for scrap."

"Can I cut it up?"

"You ever used an oxy-acetylene torch, kid?" Merc's asked from under the Maserati. A moment later he slid out, eyeballing Neil.

Mal recognized the signs of mellowing in his partner and suppressed another smile. Mercurio had been just as cynical of his abilities to begin with. More so, in fact.

"No, but you can show me how, right?"

Mercurio wiped his hands on a dirty rag, still looking Neil up and down as if measuring whether he had enough balls to handle the torch or not. Without answering specifically, he went to the rig and picked up a welding mask and handed it to Neil along with a long pair of heavy leather gloves.

"Put these on."

Neil examined the mask, how it balanced on a hinge before he put it on and propped it up so he could see, then pulled the gloves on while Merc got the hose for the torch unwound and turned the valves on the tanks.

"Awright," Merc said, handing Neil the torch. "You see the blue valve, that's the oxygen. Turn that all the way up. The red one's the acetylene, turn that just a bit...right, okay, now take this here and spark it..."

Neil followed Merc's instruction and produced a smoky red-orange flame.

"Awright, bring up the acetylene slowly, not too much...just until the flame turns blue."

Neil twisted the knob and there was that satisfied grin again as the flame steadied and burned a blue-white color.

"Okay, you see this lever here, keep your thumb off that until you're ready to cut."

"How do I know when I'm ready to cut?"

"Good question. Put your top down and bring the torch over here."

Neil flipped the welding mask down and followed Merc, who instructed him, "Put the flame on the steel, just on the edge there."

Neil put the torch to the frame and sparks sprayed. The boy held steady, though.

"Okay, when it starts to turn molten, makes a little puddle like, you push the lever down and move it to make the cut, that's right, nice and slow, keep it steady. You gotta get a feel for it."

It wasn't as perfectly neat as Merc's cuts but Neil kept it going nice and smooth until he was through the beam, then let off on the lever and flipped his mask back to inspect the clean cut straight through the metal.

"Cool."

"Not bad, kid," Merc said grudgingly.

Was Mal imagining the half-smile on his face? He thought not. "See, he's going to settle in just fine," he said.

Merc fired an unreadable look at him but all he said was, "Have another go, kid. Cut across from here to here." He pointed to spots on the chassis. "Make a grid pattern, smaller sections are easier to shift out."

Mal got to work taking tires off and a few other incidentals while Merc hovered behind Neil like a mother hen. He needn't have worried. Neil seemed to already be developing a feel for the torch and started moving through the car like he was cutting up cake. For someone Mal doubted had ever even given more than a passing glance under the hood, or knew which end of a wrench to hold, he was getting into the work, unafraid of the sparks flying or the slag dripping. When a section came away, he moved it, crouched and got right back to cutting.

Mal was somewhat amazed that by lunchtime the entire thing lay in pieces. He'd expected to finish up on it tomorrow.

Neil looked at all the metal stacked around him, torch in one hand and the mask flipped up, a contented grin on his lips.

"Got anything else you want cut up?" he asked Merc, who laughed. Actually laughed. Out loud.

"That's it for today," Merc said, shutting down the tanks and taking the torch to put away. "Good work. Only thing left is to put the hunks of metal in the trailer."

Neil took the welding mask off and hung it on the peg, and Mal noticed he canted it at exactly the angle Merc always hung it. That was some attention to detail. He wondered if it was on purpose or if he did it naturally. Neil picked up a chunk of metal and started carrying it toward the back bay door, where the skip sat outside. He opened his mouth to tell him he didn't need to do that right away, they could get to it later, but Merc made a motion with his hand.

When Neil was outside, the old tinker murmured, "Let him keep busy. Better if he wears himself out with work than looking for trouble." He added the last gruffly.

Mal was still watching the doorway through which Neil had exited with the scrap.

"Maybe you're right," he mused. "I think trouble is looking for him, though. He seems to me like he's just trying to keep his head down."

Mercurio graced him with a look that clearly said he'd lost his mind. "Were you or were you not on the docks this morning when he near 'bout caused a small riot? He's got demon blood. Finding trouble is in his genetic makeup."

"He can't help that, Merc. It doesn't make him inherently evil." Mal turned to face his friend at last. "My ancestry didn't make me a bad person, did it? Just give him a chance. Once we've sorted out the car, we can give him his share and he'll be on his way."

Merc snorted and shook his head. "If you believe that, you really are crazy."

He didn't look angry when he said it. His expression had shifted from a pissed-off scowl back to its normal mild grimace, meaning he was more concerned than riled.

Chapter Eight

Neil was glad when Malachai started helping Mercurio work on his car and left him to haul out all the scrap metal himself. Not that he hadn't liked working with him, getting the buggy chopped up. Just the opposite — it felt natural to work side by side with him, fun even. But Mal was distracting when he was so close, even if he wasn't doing anything more than turning a wrench. Thinking about anything was nearly impossible when he found his eyes straying to Mal's arms, his hands, the way he moved, the way he pressed his lips together when he had to put extra muscle into breaking a bolt free.

He needed a clear head to think and hauling each piece of the cut-up buggy out to the trailer seemed a good time to do that. Malachai was right. The money he got from the car wasn't going to take him far or last long. There had to be a better way to disappear, but exactly how he was going to do that wasn't clear at all.

The afternoon sun beat down in the dusty yard as Neil hauled pieces of metal across it and went back for more. It was heavy, dirty, hot work but it also felt good in a way. Cleansing somehow, even if he was covered in sweat, grease and a fine film of dirt from all the dust that rose and stuck to him.

By the time he'd carried the last piece out and stacked it precariously on top of the rest, the sun was on its way toward the horizon and his arms, legs and back ached. He was still no closer to an answer to his problems but he was so tired he didn't have the energy to worry. Mal and Merc had disappeared inside the shop some time ago. Neil peeled off the gloves he'd been wearing and laid them near the welding stuff before heading inside himself.

The smell of something savory on the stove made his stomach tighten and rumble but he headed up to the bathroom instead of the kitchen. He didn't mind getting dirty but there was no reason to stay filthy when he didn't have to.

The water was nice and hot and Neil scrubbed himself down in the shower with the cake of hard soap that was nothing like the soft, scented bars his mother had always splurged on. He scrubbed his hair and rinsed, then made another pass with the soap before he finally shut off the tap. A steamy cloud followed him out of the shower stall. He dried off, raked a brush through his hair, then wrinkled his nose at his clothes. They were pretty nasty.

Instead of putting them back on, he wrapped a towel around his waist and picked them up off the floor. He could hear Mal and Merc talking in the kitchen and headed in that direction. They both looked up when he entered.

"Do you have a tub I can wash these in?" he asked.

Mercurio laughed uproariously. "Boy, you're as skinny as a starved dog. What you gonna wear while they wash an' dry?"

Mal's expression remained sober, though. His pale gaze slid up Neil's body from his toes to the roots of his hair, making him shiver, though he wasn't cold. At last he held out one hand. "Give them here. I'll put them in the machine. Do you have anything else to wear?"

Neil shook his head and adjusted the towel around his hips.

"I'll see if I have anything of mine you can fit." Malachai sighed.

Merc chuckled. "You think Mal's skinny now, kid, you should'a seen him when he first got here. He's Mr. Universe compared with that sack of bones."

"Hush, Merc," Malachai breathed, gliding from the kitchen with Neil's things.

Neil followed him with his eyes but made his feet stay put. The starved remark didn't bother him. He wasn't buff and probably never would be, and he was fine with that. Being as normal and plain looking as possible was the goal. It was why he dyed his hair dark too.

Malachai certainly wasn't plain looking. Neil wouldn't mind filling his eyes all day on him. He kept the spill of his thick, red and gold-streaked hair tied back, and the rough, unkempt tail fell nearly to the middle of his back. Neil still wanted to run his fingers through it, to find out how that felt. His skin was a soft golden brown, not quite as ruddy as Mercurio's weather-beaten features, and Neil knew that color was the same all over. He wondered how that could be. The city was no place for bare sun worship. He pushed his mind away from the vision of Malachai nude and wet from the shower. Dangerous thought. Mal was the only person in the whole damn world, at this moment, that was willing to help. He didn't need to screw that up.

Mal came back and Neil shifted his feet and looked away quickly. He'd just stood there the whole time, staring after the way he'd gone. They must think he was an idiot.

Mal made a 'follow me' gesture and led Neil back upstairs to the bedroom he'd slept in last night. After a bit of rummaging in a long, low trunk under the bed, he handed him some T-shirts and a pair of jeans.

"Thanks." Neil set the clothes on the bed and, before Mal could leave, an imp in him made him drop the towel. Stupid. Really stupid but he didn't care how vain it was, he wanted Mal to look at him for just a second like *that*. Like those pirates had. To his embarrassment, Mal barely spared him a glance. Neil grabbed the jeans and pulled them on.

They were way too long but didn't hang off his hips too badly and the T-shirt was long enough to cover the ill-fit. He turned up the cuffs so that he wouldn't trip on them. Finished dressing, he dawdled with hanging the towel up and told himself he wasn't disappointed Mal hadn't stuck around to ogle him, or maybe even kiss him.

The smell of food lured him back down to the kitchen.

Mercurio had a griddle pan on the range and bacon and sausages sizzling away while Malachai was chopping onions and mushrooms on the scarred wooden worktop next to him. Merc wolf-whistled him when Neil came in but Mal just carried on dicing away with that gentle, dreamy smile that Neil wished he would wear when he looked at him.

"Hungry?" he asked, scooping up the pieces on the edge of his broad-bladed utility knife and dumping them into the pan. Neil nodded then sat in the chair Mal pointed him to.

He watched the two of them work, Mal giving the vegetables an occasional stir while Merc cracked eggs into a bowl and whipped them up with a fork. His stomach started making embarrassing growls and he tightened his muscles in an effort to shut it up.

By the time the omelets were done and they filled his plate, Neil practically fell on the food like he hadn't eaten in a week. He ate every speck that was put in front of him and only just managed not to lick the plate clean.

"I guess he earned that," Merc said grudgingly.

"He certainly did," Mal agreed, nibbling on the end of a sausage he had left until last, in a way that made Neil's insides clench for entirely different reasons.

Before he had a chance to contemplate that, a loud knock from somewhere at the front of the building made him jump.

Mercurio scraped his chair back. "I'll see who it is."

"That doesn't get you out of your turn to do the dishes," Malachai called after him.

He winked at Neil and carried on eating, which he did in the same methodical way that he did everything bar driving. He ate like each mouthful posed a potential hazard and needed to be properly assimilated into his lean body. Neil wondered if that was why he didn't put weight on. He didn't have long to ponder that thought because the sound of other voices soon drifted down the hallway to his ears.

He thought he recognized the nasal drawl just before Merc appeared back in the kitchen with Vargas and a rather quiet and sullen Crow at his heels.

Mal put his fork down at once. "I wasn't expecting dinner guests, I'd have laid out an extra space," he said, and his tone was so icily polite Neil was pretty sure that was sarcasm.

If Vargas picked up on the tone, he didn't give any indication. His smile settled on him and Neil's skin crawled. There was something about him that was just disturbing and he couldn't even say it was because he knew the man didn't like him.

"I see your young protege is still around," Vargas said.

"Nothing wrong with your eyes, then." Mal rose from the table and moved between Vargas and Neil, doing so in a way that seemed very calm and relaxed though his tone was still cool. "What can we do for you? Was the fuel order not sufficient?"

"No, we have enough fuel. There's something else you have that I'm interested in," Vargas said. "I'm hoping we can come to an agreement."

"And it couldn't wait until office hours?" Mal's tone was casual but his back was stiff and straight, definitely not as relaxed as he wanted to appear. A small scowl crossed Mercurio's features as he circled them both.

"What is the expression? If you snooze, you lose. I don't like to miss out on an opportunity, you know that, Malachai. Now, you currently have possession of one fledgling sorcerer. I'm sure you have no practical use for him but you found him first, so I'm willing to go halves."

Mal made a soft, strangled sound but he didn't step out of the way. "I'm not entirely sure I comprehend what you mean," he said.

The fake smile on Vargas' face turned brittle. "I think you know exactly what I mean. That" — he pointed over Malachai's shoulder at Neil — "is a wanted criminal and worth quite a hefty purse. When were you planning on turning him in?"

Mal tilted his head and surveyed Neil as if he'd only just noticed him sitting there. His expression was calm, composed, but his eyes were like moonlight on still water. He came back to face Vargas and replied, "He's a person, not a thing, Delilah. Not a commodity to be traded and shipped off like cattle."

"Do you think I am a fool, Valentine? The boy is a sorcerer and he is wanted for murder." Vargas laughed huskily. "Do you really think I believe that one of your bloodline would not recognize the worth of such a haul?"

"I am not my father, Delmont Vargas. Neil is not for sale. Nor is he a proven killer, that much is speculation. He is going nowhere. Not with you." There was a chill in Malachai's voice, a rim of frost Neil hadn't heard from him before, and he shivered. The name he spoke to Vargas dropped like a stone between them, making Vargas bristle with barely suppressed fury. In some murky corner of Neil's brain, he thought he remembered something about the fae and true names. Whatever it was, it had power. Neil could feel the way it raised the fine hairs on his arms and the back of his neck.

As much as Neil was loath to draw any attention to himself, the skin-crawling feeling made it impossible to sit and he carefully pushed back his chair.

"Stay where you are," Mal said without looking at him.

"Very wise, Lord Valentine. You will appreciate the wisdom—" Vargas didn't finish the sentence because Mal stepped forward and unfolded, jabbing him in the chest with a long forefinger.

"Shut up! Get out of my home, now!"

Vargas clucked his tongue. Just the one small sound but Neil swore there was power behind it. The start of a spell? It froze his blood and he glanced toward the opening behind him that led to the stairs.

"Such ingratitude," Vargas said in a low, menacing voice. "Such greed…or is it greed? Don't tell me a bit of boy flesh has turned your head, Valentine? Thinking with your dick instead of your wallet? My, how you have changed."

"Don't tar me with your filthy brush, Vargas. I'm serious. Leave him be. You really don't want to push this." Mal stood his ground. Merc had moved in to flank him and Neil saw that Crow was hovering close by Vargas too, his small black eyes darting from one to the other of them.

There was a long, pregnant pause, then everything happened at once. The temperature in the room plunged, like they were suddenly inside a chest freezer, and the air pressure changed, making Neil's ears pop. Malachai lifted his hand as if he would shove Vargas but Vargas mirrored him at the same time and flung an open hand at Mal.

A dark shape coiled around Mal's neck, like a shadowy rope. Mercurio gave an enraged bellow and charged but Crow grappled with him and they both went down.

"Neil! Run!" Malachai called out, his hands flying to his throat. Neil thought he saw a shimmer of energy run from them through the coil of magical smoke and it splintered like glass, falling to the ground at his feet.

Mercurio was wrestling with Crow and had landed a couple of punches, making the nasty little man squeak like a cornered rat.

Neil knew he was outclassed in every possible way for this fight and he whipped around and sprinted for the stairs at the back of the building. He made it up three before a shape at the top caught his attention and he lifted his head to see another man waiting there. He had a long blade in one hand and a sneer on his face as he made his way down the steps. Neil backed up and sidled along the kitchen wall.

There was a roar of sound and the table they had eaten at flew up into the air and splintered into a million shards. Mal raised his arm to shield his head from the falling debris and Vargas pulled something from inside his robe. He blew on it and the room went dark. Neil couldn't make out what happened but Mal gasped audibly. The light flickered again and Mal fell to his knees. Another flick of Vargas' wrist and Mercurio shouted in pain. Then Vargas settled his eyes on him and his teeth were very white and large in the darkened room.

"Grab him!" he ordered the man with the blade.

He was backed into a corner quite literally and even if he had a clear shot to get away, he couldn't just leave Merc and Malachai like that. He knew better than to try seduction. It worked only if there was already an interest and, even then, only if Neil could focus on the person. Too much was happening for that at the moment. He did have one more ace up his sleeve, and that talent was even less under his control, but it was all he had.

He closed his eyes and whispered a word. The power welled up inside, violent and hungry as ever. His throat tightened like invisible hands were choking him and he opened his eyes and spoke the phrase to release the shadow fire.

He didn't have nearly the same amount of power as the assassins in the garage who had attacked them this way, but even so the smoky black flames leaped around him eagerly, an oily blue at their center that danced wickedly and raced along the floor toward Vargas.

The man shouted an ugly word, his lip curled in outrage, or maybe disgust. He brought his arm up defensively much as Mal had done and the flames jerked and leaped onto Crow, who howled and writhed in their midst.

Vargas turned to Crow and Neil darted forward to Mal, who was curled on the floor. "Malachai...Mal..." Neil grabbed him but he didn't have a clue how to counter whatever had been done to him.

Vargas was quickly pouring some kind of energy into the dark flames that threatened to devour Crow's remaining sanity. Before he was done, the man with the knife snaked an arm around Neil's chest and hauled him up so high that his feet did not touch the floor. Vargas pulled Crow to his feet at the same time and gestured toward the front of the building where they had initially entered.

As they headed for the door, Mercurio hurled himself at them in a last-ditch attempt to stop them. Vargas put himself between the enraged mechanic and the man carrying Neil. Crow cut around behind Merc and grabbed the iron pan from the counter, bringing it down on Mercurio's head in a final act of revenge for the magical and non-magical strikes he had received.

Neil twisted around in his captor's arms, trying to catch a last glimpse of Malachai, but the red-haired man was still on the ground as he was hauled out of the store and into a waiting van.

Doors slammed and Vargas shouted, "Drive!"

The panic surging between his ears was not helping him think. All he could see in his mind's eye was Mal curled into a ball on the floor and Merc going down in a heap. They needed help. And where was Vargas taking him? Directly to the police? Neil was dead if he did. They wouldn't believe he didn't kill his mother, and even if they did, their witches would smell the demon blood in him.

"I didn't do it! Please, don't take me to the cops."

"That's what they all say, demon. I watched you unleash the shadow fire. You're a dangerous criminal and if Valentine can't see that, he's a fool." Vargas hissed his disgust, narrowing his eyes at Neil. "You're worth more to me dead than to him alive."

From the creases in his face, Neil guessed that he was hurting. Whatever he or Mal had thrown at him, something had done him damage.

Good! Neil thought with a small, vindictive smile.

Think, Neil. Think! "You're turning me in for a reward that isn't even a tiny bit of what I'm worth."

"I'm not interested in your lies."

"You don't even realize what I am. How would you know?"

"I've seen what you are, demon spawn," Vargas spat. "You're a filthy kinslayer and you are going to dance in a bespelled noose."

Neil's stomach fluttered at the venomous words and he quailed at the vivid image they brought to mind. He caught his breath and forced himself to speak calmly. "I know what you do. Malachai told me. How you...help people who can do things." Neil nearly choked on the word 'help' but there was nothing to gain from being antagonistic. He swallowed hard at what he was about to do but couldn't see any other way of getting out of being taken in to the police, and that was almost certainly a death sentence.

"I can do things," Neil finished in nearly a whisper.

"I know what you can do, brat," Vargas said, his tone cold, though he was looking Neil over with a speculative gaze. They clung to the insides of the van while it bounced and swayed over the rutted roads. "That's why there's a price on your head that would buy my place twice over."

"I can make you more than that reward. A lot more."

Crow uttered a high-pitched cackle and sneered, "We'd be selling your arse until you were a hundred years old to make that much gold, demon."

Vargas just glared at the Crow, and his giggles quickly stifled.

"How?" the dark fae asked him.

Neil wondered if the meal he ate was going to stay down for a moment then took a breath and said, "I can make someone empty their pockets and give it to me..."

Crow snorted but Vargas looked at him intently. "I'll only ask once more. How?"

Neil licked his lips. "I'm an incubus." There. He'd said it out loud, twice in one day.

Those intense eyes blinked just once. "I see."

Vargas did not elaborate but Crow was suddenly staring at him like he was poison and Neil felt uneasy under that beady glare. Once more he swallowed rising bile.

"Show me," Vargas ordered him.

"Show you?"

"He's lying," Crow muttered.

"I'm not. I just... It's... I need to, uh..."

Crow laughed. "What? You need flowers and wine first?"

"No. I need a...victim."

"He needs a donor," Vargas sneered. "Well, I'm sure we can find you a willing...victim. You're easy on the eye, at least."

"He is that!" The man who had grabbed Neil and bundled him into the van had not spoken until this point but his master's humor seemed to have unglued his tongue.

"Good," Vargas declared, nodding once. "I'm glad you see things that way, Trellick. It will make things much simpler. Demon, you have your tribute. Show me what you can do."

Neil squirmed. He wanted to protest that he couldn't just do it here, while they were watching, but he had a feeling that if he balked, they would take him directly to the jail to collect their reward.

He turned to look at the man that had carried him away from Malachai at knifepoint. He waited until he started to smirk, to get that look that both dismissed him and spoke of longing at the same time. Then he softened his gaze, let his eyes unfocus, easing one shoulder back in an inviting pose. So subtle, he hardly moved, but the man Vargas called Trellick leaned toward him, his expression going slack, lips parting as he sucked in a breath.

Neil brought a hand up to rest on his chest as he moved in closer for a kiss. "Not yet," he said, soft, gentle as a caress. "I need something first."

"What?" Trellick asked.

"Give me your knife."

Trellick hesitated. "No, no, I can't give you that."

Neil took a deep breath so that his chest rose and he brought his lips closer, close enough he could feel his breath. "I need your knife... You want me, don't you? Just give it to me and I'm yours..."

Trellick dropped his hand to the sheath on his belt and flicked the knife out. For just a second, Neil's heart leaped into his throat, but at last Trellick offered it to him by the hilt.

Vargas clapped his hands together once, loudly. "And that...that is how a man finds himself in an alley drained of his life with a knife between his ribs."

Trellick blinked slow and stupid at him then stared at the knife in Neil's hands as if wondering how it had gotten there. Vargas leaned over Neil's shoulder and retrieved it before he could do any lasting damage.

"Nice work," he commented. "So, if he mounts you, how strong a compulsion could you put on him then?"

"I...I don't understand," Neil said, although he did know. Still, they wouldn't expect a demonstration like that right here in front of them, would they? His stomach churned at the thought.

"Is the power you exert stronger if your tribute makes more of an effort?" Vargas asked.

"If he bends you over and bangs you hard, could you make him pick the knife up and slit his own throat with it?" Crow laughed, a grating, high-pitched sound that hurt his ears.

Trellick looked wary.

"No," Neil answered. It was a lie, sort of. He wasn't really sure if he could make the compulsion stronger, or longer lasting, if he had sex with a victim. He'd never tried. In theory, the more lust he could make someone feel, the more likely they were to do what he told them. He wasn't about to admit to that if he didn't have to. "I don't have to go that far, they'll follow simple commands, as long as I...um, have their lust. I can make them give me something or go somewhere else."

"Tell you something they wouldn't ordinarily tell?" Vargas asked.

"Yes."

"Interesting." Vargas drummed his fingers on one knee then tapped on the Perspex panel separating them from the driver's position up front. "Change of plan," he called. "Take us back to Delancey."

Chapter Nine

Neil couldn't say his second visit to Del Vargas' house was any more pleasant than the first. At least they hadn't put him down in the cellar. Instead he was in a windowless room hardly larger than a closet. There wasn't space enough for a bed or anything so grand, but there was a thin pad on the floor and that was about it. The only light came from the crack under the door. He could hear Vargas and Crow talking but they were far enough out of his range that he could only make out maybe one or two words in a dozen.

They were busy making plans for him, that much he'd figured out. How best to use his dubious 'talent'. Would it have been better to just let them take him to the police? He might have been able to clear his name, convince them he wasn't a murderer. He didn't have much faith in that panning out. The 'police' were nothing more than paid thugs with a rough and swift sense of justice. And if the reward for him was that big, someone was bankrolling them. Neil would lay money on it being the same people who had killed his mother and come after him.

Instead of a swift hanging, he might instead be tragically killed in jail, his body destroyed. At least that's what the papers would say. He could just be paranoid...but he didn't think so. His current bout of worry came to an abrupt end when the door opened. He squinted in the light, dim as it was. Crow and a woman stood in the entrance.

"Stand up," Crow barked.

Neil got warily to his feet and the woman came closer, looking him up and down. "Hmm." She took one of his arms and held it to one side, turned her head this way and that as she sized him up. "I think Charlie's about the same size. I'll find him something."

More borrowed clothes, Neil guessed. He didn't really want to give up the ones Malachai had given him, even if they were too big.

"In the meantime, I need to do something about that hair."

"What's wrong with my hair?" Neil had visions of being shaved bald. He didn't relish the idea, but it might change how he looked enough that he wouldn't be so easily recognizable. He should have thought of that already and done it himself. Maybe he wouldn't be here if he had.

"That color is all wrong for you. Makes you look older and even more drawn-out than you are. I'm Amy, by the way." She stuck her hand out and Neil automatically shook it. "Come on, let's get to work."

Neil followed her out, squeezing as close as he could to the doorjamb so that he didn't touch Crow at all on the way through the door.

Amy took him to the kitchen and pointed to a chair. "Sit. Let's have a look."

Neil sat and Amy picked up a silver comb. It was more than a little surreal to have her drag it through his hair, pulling out small snarls.

"Tch." She clucked her tongue but it was just an ordinary sound, not filled with power like it had been when Vargas had done it back at Utopia. "Blond under all this dye, yeah?"

Neil grunted a vaguely affirmative sound. When he was little, his hair had been nearly white gold. Fortunately it had darkened a bit as he got older, to a deeper blond. Even so he'd been teased mercilessly by kids at school about being 'goldilocks' until he'd started dying it.

Amy pinched a curl of his hair between her fingers and rubbed the strands together, murmuring words to a spell that Neil heard and forgot just as quickly.

"There we go, that's much better," she chirped and ran her hands through his hair. Tiny dried flecks of black sifted down around him like ash.

Another man came in, carrying a bundle of clothes in his arms. No, not a man, he had to be even younger than Neil was.

"Crow said you needed some clothes for going out," the boy said to Amy then cast a glance at Neil. "These must be for you."

He handed him the bundle and Neil said, "Thanks." Then he examined what he'd been given. These were clothes for 'going out'? There was a long-sleeved shirt but it was made out of some kind of netting, so sheer it hardly seemed right to call it a shirt. The trousers were at least opaque but felt like slinky pajamas. Neil scowled at the clothes but the boy, presumably Charlie, was ushering him into a bathroom just off the kitchen. "Go try 'em on."

Thankfully they let him go into the bathroom by himself. There was no lock on the door that he could see, so he set the clothes down on the sink and went straight to the curtain on the wall. He pulled it aside, only to find a sheet of plywood nailed over the window.

"Damnit!" he muttered. He turned back toward the bundle of clothes and stopped as he got a look at himself in the mirror. It had been at least five years since he'd seen himself without any form of dye in his hair. All the dark brown had been stripped out and what was left was a sandy blond with hints of copper and gold. He smoothed a dismayed hand over the light-colored curls.

"Shit!" The blond brought out all the fine-boned angles in his cheeks and jaw and warmed the pallor of his skin to something creamier.

He was going to have to cut it all off if he couldn't get his hands on some dye. A sharp rap on the door made him jump. "Do you have them on yet?"

"No," Neil answered. "Give me a minute." He entertained the thought of trying to pry the board off the window for a second or two but they would probably hear it and stop him before he got anywhere with it. Sighing, he shed his clothes and put on the ones they'd given him. It felt like he was wearing nothing. Actually, he'd probably feel less exposed if he was wearing nothing.

Another knock made him jump again. "Come out and let us see."

Amy this time. He wondered if they'd just come in and drag him out if he didn't answer. *Probably.* He picked up his other clothes and clutched them defensively before he opened the door and stepped out into the kitchen.

"Well, don't you clean up nice," Amy said. Charlie just glared. Neil couldn't figure out what he could have done to piss him off so he didn't say anything. "Here, hand those over." Amy held out her hand for Neil's clothes and he very reluctantly let her have them.

Vargas walked in. Amy and Charlie both backed up some but he ignored them and looked Neil over. "Oh, I think that will do. Come, Neil."

He bristled at being summoned like a dog to heel but he didn't have much choice.

"I'm taking you to a party," Vargas announced. "Once there I'll let you know who your mark is. The man is a slaver and he's been undercutting my business interests. This will be your first test. I want you to find out where he's been picking up his new flesh and where he's housing them."

Neil nodded and without warning Vargas grabbed him and slammed him with one arm against the wall. He got very close and Neil held his breath.

"If you try to leave, if you try to double cross me, I will hunt you down and that is the end of our deal. When I find you, and I will, the least of your worries will be the police. Do you understand?"

Neil nodded again, slowly, not taking his eyes off Vargas.

"Good. And just for a bit of insurance..." Vargas snapped a piece of metal around his neck.

Neil grabbed at it but it clicked loudly and a buzz like angry bees stung at his fingers and throat. "That will let me find you, no matter where you go. Don't waste your time trying to remove it, if you value your skin."

Vargas stepped back and Neil sagged against the wall, trying to catch his breath. A collar. Not just a collar. He forced himself to acknowledge the words swimming in the stunned murky depths of his head. A slave collar. This couldn't be happening. It couldn't be real.

"Get a move on," Vargas barked.

Numbly Neil followed Vargas out to the van they had come here in. In the gray twilight, he was able to pay it more heed and realized it was more of an armored car. It had a side door that slid open to admit them and thunked shut again behind them, sealing him inside with Vargas — and Crow, who seemed to go everywhere with his boss. The whiskery otter-like man stared at Neil with the same level of loathing that Charlie had and he huddled, against the wall of the truck with his arms wrapped around himself, beginning to wish that they'd just taken him to the cops and made an end of it.

Neil watched out of the front window, trying to memorize the turns, but they didn't seem to be going in any logical pattern. The driver took them two streets, turned, drove another street, turned back the way they'd come, kept going four blocks and turned again in a crazy zigzag.

It took almost an hour to arrive at their destination and by then Neil was thoroughly lost. He probably couldn't have found his way back to Mal and Merc's shop, even with a map. His mind's eye brought up the image of Mal curled on the floor again. Was he okay? If Neil actually did find his way back, Mal would probably slam the door in his face. He'd brought the man nothing but trouble after trouble.

The van pulled up outside a long, low building. Neil could hear the music playing even from the street, as the door slid open and Vargas pushed him out ahead of them. The place did not look like a house. It was more like an empty store, some kind of warehouse, with long, full-length windows that were all boarded up. Light pulsed around the entranceways, glimmering like a dark rainbow, every color, putting feelers out into the night, one by one.

There was a tall creature manning the main entrance and creature was the only way that Neil could think of it because the security on this party was not human. He was taller even than Vargas and skeletal thin, clad in a long black coat done up with leather straps and buckles. Dark gray, metallic-looking skin covered his elongated skull and shiny black eyes swiveled about, high in the dome of his head, to look Neil up and down before flicking to Vargas.

"What do you want, Cluricaun?" he said in a voice that was like metal fingernails, drawn across a sheet of glass.

"We have an invitation." Vargas drew himself up to his full height to glare back at the creature then held out his hand. His nails were painted scarlet metallic and there were ruby streaks in the tumble of his royal purple hair tonight. "Delilah Vargas, plus one."

The skeletal doorman produced an object that Neil initially thought was a gun. His gut clenched but the creature merely passed it over Vargas' hand and it beeped in an innocuous fashion.

"There are three of you," it said tersely.

"Crow will wait here with you," Vargas declared. "Wait here, Crow."

His henchman looked like he wanted to object but Vargas and the doorman were both glaring at him and he kept silent. That was a good thing, at least.

Then Vargas pushed him forward again and Neil entered a dimly lit hallway, where the rainbow lights flickered like ghostly fingers, luring him in. The music grew louder as he made his way down the passage and stepped out into a bowl-shaped auditorium with steeply terraced sides. Down on the floor of the bowl, figures were moving in time to the pulse of the music which was almost unbearably loud here. Strings clashed and whined and drums pulsed a steady rhythm, and all around him people moved and swayed and ground against one another to the music.

As his eyes adjusted to the darkness, he saw that a number of the people here wore metal collars like his own. Some were dancing with uncollared guests. And some of those guests were human-looking, but quite a few were not.

Neil saw skeletal creatures like the doorman but garbed in bright, metallic colors, like Vargas. He saw a huge, burly being covered from head to toe in dark red fur, who was pawing two collared girls in a booth on one of the terraces. A lean fellow, dressed in a silver catsuit that appeared to be made entirely from foil, stopped and looked him up and down. His admirer almost seemed human but his chin and ears were long and pointed—oh, and his skin was a pasty grayish color.

"My...aren't you pretty."

Was that supposed to be a compliment? He never could tell. He hated when people called him pretty. The music was so loud and the colored lights so disorientating he didn't know how to respond and looked to Vargas for a clue.

Vargas nodded once and flicked his fingers in a gesture Neil took to mean this was his mark.

The elegant, cat-suited stranger took his hand — his fingers were cold — and led him down the terraced steps to the dancefloor below. Neil looked around, trying to take everything in, but there were so many people he felt overcrowded and his senses were reeling from the loud music and the weird, almost strobe-like colored lights.

The tall, pointy-eared stranger began to dance with him and his cool hands moved over his body, caressing him through the shimmery shirt and lightweight pants.

"You are so soft," his companion cooed. "Quite delicious. Do you like the music? You move very nicely."

No, he didn't. He had about enough rhythm to sway along with the music. Anything more energetic and he looked about as coordinated as a drunken donkey. He smiled up at the man — at least he assumed he was a man, given that he had no breasts and was so tall — but everything else about him was vaguely feminine. This was just about the worst scenario he could have come up with. His concentration was blown, there were people pressed all around them, and it was so dark he wasn't sure if he could capture his eyes.

Maybe he could use that, though.

"It's a little loud." He shouted to be heard. If he was going to get any information from him, he was going to have to get him somewhere more private.

"We can go to another part of the house if you prefer?" His dance partner stroked those cool fingers down Neil's cheek, smiling hopefully. "I would enjoy that. A more quiet room, yes? We can talk and...do other things."

Neil nodded his agreement and felt the weight of the collar with the movement. How had things gone so wrong so fast? More importantly, would he ever be able to get himself out of this, or was he doomed to be Vargas' pet? Pet was a better word than what he felt like as he followed the man away from all the dancing, swirling, laughing bodies.

The hallway was only marginally quieter than the auditorium had been but once they were around a bend and through a doorway into another room, it quietened to bearable levels.

The silvery man pulled him close the moment Neil was through the door and for a second he stiffened, but made himself relax.

"What's your name?"

The fellow smiled. "You may call me Madran. And what should I call you, pretty one?"

Anything but that.

"I'm Neil," he said. "What is this place?"

Madran gestured to a low sofa, upholstered in soft cream leather and sat down there. When Neil warily perched on the edge of the cushions beside him he murmured, "This is La Sala, a pleasure house. It is a very exclusive place. I have not seen you here before and I come here frequently. How do you come to belong to Delilah?"

"I um, needed a place to stay," he improvised. Actually, it was true enough. The music and the lights and the half-naked people groping one another suddenly made sense. So did the disorientation and the way his skin felt like he would give off static if he was touched. A 'pleasure house'. It was the last place in the world Neil wanted to be. All the lust and desperation out there made his teeth itch.

"That is Delilah's way," Madran said and Neil detected a hint of derision in his tone. He touched the collar at Neil's throat with one finger, briefly. "This, however, is not. Is he afraid you'll run away? Or afraid someone will steal you?"

Neil dragged his eyes up. "Maybe both," he said, trying to get Madran under his gaze, but he kept looking at his lips, his neck, his shoulders. Neil could practically map himself just by watching Madran's eyes on him. "How do you know Delilah?"

Madran uttered a musical laugh. For a second his eyes shimmered like silver and it reminded Neil, with a sharp pang, of Malachai. Malachai...who he had left sprawled on the floor, not sure if he was dead or alive.

"Delilah Vargas is fae, as am I. He has brought many of his waifs here in the past. I sense that you are different. I feel something in you that vibrates in my bones, Neil. What are you?"

"Nothing special," Neil answered.

Focus, Neil! He needed to focus! He was part incubus, seduction should come naturally, but it never had for him. Getting people to do what he wanted while they were looking deep into his eyes, that was something he'd discovered by accident and wasn't difficult. But stirring lust, nudging someone from mild interest to passion, that was a more nebulous concept. Flirting felt awkward. He remembered something Malachai had said about Vargas and his mind cleared.

"Does that make you jealous? That Del has so many...'waifs'?" Neil wasn't even sure what that was supposed to mean but he couldn't think of a better word.

Madran laughed. An odd sound, like clucking hens.

"Jealous. Oh no. All those ungrateful mouths to feed. Better Delilah than me. I much prefer to get them into my bed."

Neil forced a smile. "But you get your penny for a pound of flesh, don't you? You look like someone that knows how to cut a deal." He risked leaning in closer and ran a finger over the back of Madran's hand where it rested on his knee.

Those silvery eyes lowered to his fingers for a moment then rose to meet his gaze. "Are you offering a deal? I thought you were sent here to fuck?"

Neil felt the tiny hairs on the back of his neck rise and badly wanted to swallow but knew it would give away his nerves.

"I can't offer a deal. I belong to Delilah, remember?" The words tasted bitter and Neil wondered how he even managed to say them without gagging. *Okay. Time for another tactic.* He licked his lips. "But you can have me for tonight." Or for as long as it took him to get him to spit out what he needed to discover.

"Aren't you just the sweetest thing." Madran purred and brought his hand up to comb his fingers through Neil's hair. Cupping the back of his head, Madran pulled him in for a kiss.

As kisses went, it wasn't the worst Neil had endured. He could feel the edges of Madran's lust tickling at his skin, just a trickle of energy. Not anywhere near enough for him to try a command yet.

Madran swept his tongue over his lips and Neil opened his mouth a tiny bit. Madran was not subtle in the way he stabbed his tongue inside and pulled back on his hair. There, that was better. The energy had started to rise. Then Madran pushed a hand between his legs and Neil gulped in a breath. He wasn't the least bit aroused and he hoped Madran wasn't going to care too much.

"You're exotic, sweet thing," Madran whispered, nuzzling his neck. "Where in the world did he get you from?"

"Just…around. I'm more interested in where I'll end up." Neil purposefully sagged a bit, pressing against Madran. "There's a rumor in the house that a lot of Delilah's charges have gone missing." He put a whisper of his power into the statement. Not asking the question just yet but softening him up.

Madran slid an arm around his shoulders, pulling him in close. He stroked his fingers through Neil's curls, tugging his head back, kissing his throat.

"Delilah wants to take more care of his pets, in that case," he whispered, his words blowing softly over wet skin, making Neil shiver.

His hands were roaming again, one sliding under the edge of Neil's shirt and over his stomach. There still wasn't a big surge of lust coming from Madran, but there might be enough desire there. Maybe.

"You can tell me what's happened to them, can't you?" Neil said, feeding more power into the words and looking Madran in the eyes. Sometimes if the question was coaxing rather than demanding it worked better. He had a feeling subtle would be the right track to take here.

Silver eyes narrowed shrewdly in response. Madran trailed the tip of his tongue over Neil's lower lip.

"I might be able to. If someone were to make it worth my while," he said at last.

Damn it. How far was he going to have to let this go? He took a small breath and tamped down on his frustration. That wouldn't help. Cupping Madran's face in his hands, he kissed him, parting his lips to coax his tongue out and tentatively stroking it with his own. Madran slid his hand higher under his shirt and pinched his nipple. Hard. Neil gasped and Madran pushed him back on the couch, coming up over him to kiss him again. Neil shoved his fingers into Madran's hair and tightened his grip just as Madran had done to him.

There. Right there was a spike of lust. Madran lifted up a bit, his breath coming faster, and Neil kept his hands in his hair, forcing him to look into his eyes.

"Tell me what's happened to them."

"My master," Madran gasped, his hips moving in a lazy circle against Neil's thigh. "He is building a Court here in Or d'Roit. He desires only the most gifted of our children."

Did Vargas realize who Madran's master was? Probably...maybe. If he didn't get the exact name, would it be good enough?

"Who is your master?" Neil kept his tone light, conversational, but he didn't let Madran look away.

"You truly do not know?" Madran sought another kiss and Neil let him have it because that rough contact provoked another stab of lust that had Madran practically drowning in his power. Madran ground his hips against him and the thin pants he was wearing let Neil feel everything. The hardness of his cock in the hollow of his hip made his stomach roll and he had to stomp on the urge to be sick.

"His name. Tell me his name," Neil gasped when he had his lips free once more. He reeled Madran's lust in and poured it back out as power in those words.

The voice that answered him seemed to come from all directions at once and Neil's heart jumped against his ribs violently. He felt Madran start too, pulling away from him quickly.

"My name is Felipe Drasnil and who, pray tell, are you?"

Madran let him go and practically oozed off the sofa to bend his head to the ground at the feet of a short fellow. Long, oiled curls of pewter-colored hair tumbled down over the shoulders of his very sharp, metallic blue suit. His eyes were the same metal blue and they pinned Neil to the seat, ignoring his fawning molester completely.

"I'm Neil," he answered simply, keeping a wary eye on him. "I should probably go." He rose, inching toward the door.

"Sit!" Drasnil pointed one finger at him and he felt invisible weights drag him down again. "You are not one of us. What are you, Neil? Why are you here?"

Neil's mouth went dry as he frantically weighed his options. Vargas was far from his friend and he faced a very uncertain future with the fae, but this man terrified him with a look and a sharp word. The thought of throwing himself on his mercy, hoping that he might free him from Vargas, seemed like a very long shot. Especially considering, if what Vargas had said was true, that this man was already in the habit of collecting slaves that were never seen again.

That was all very rational, but another part of Neil said he'd rather stay with Vargas because if Malachai did come looking for him, he would start at the run-down house on Delancey.

"I was brought here by my master. He bid me to go with Madran. That's all," Neil said.

"And your master is…?" Drasnil raised one pewter eyebrow.

From his polished boots, Madran piped, "Delilah, Master Drasnil."

Those petrol-blue eyes returned to Neil. Drasnil's suspicion was written plain in the tightness of his lips and the lowering of those perfect eyebrows.

"Delilah did not bring you here just so that my men might sow their seed in you, Neil. What does the sly creature want?"

"Maybe you should ask him yourself," Neil said.

For a moment Drasnil stared at him with no expression and the very blankness made Neil regret his words. He glanced at the door and wondered if he could make it if the man attacked him, whether anyone would hear if he yelled.

"You are feisty," Drasnil said at last, slowly, as if measuring his words and measuring Neil at the same time. "Not as meek as some of the children he fosters."

"You mean the ones you're kidnapping and enslaving?" His temper felt like static running along his skin, but still, he could hardly believe that had just popped out of his mouth. What was wrong with him? It was supposed to be simple. Get a name, give it to Vargas, leave. Not provoke the guy that Vargas was looking for.

"That's what he believes, is it? Interesting." Drasnil shook his head, spilling the silvery curls over his forehead and face. "Precious! His pets simply knew a good thing when they saw it. I am not a kidnapper, Neil. Go back and tell him that, if you wish." Drasnil paused for a second. "Or stay and test out the truth of my words."

"Why should I trust you any more than him?" Neil asked.

"A good question." Drasnil shrugged. "Why would you trust anyone? I suppose only your heart can answer that question."

"Or you could, if you'll deliver a message for me."

Drasnil lifted a brow and Neil went on quickly, "Do you know Malachai and Mercurio? They own Utopia salvage? If you could get a message to them that I'm still with Vargas, then I might trust you."

Those blue eyes widened. "You are a dark horse, aren't you? I might ask of you also, what is your connection to Lord Valentine? But if that is what it takes to earn your trust, I shall send word to them on your behalf." A thin smile tugged at his lips. "And how shall I return his reply to you?"

Neil shrugged. "I don't need a reply. If you tell them, I'll find out." At least he hoped he would. If Mal knew Vargas hadn't turned him into the police, he'd come and tell Vargas to let him go. Maybe. And if he was just glad to be shot of him, he'd know that too, when Mal didn't come. He told himself not to get his hopes up but it was hard not to.

He also didn't miss that this was the second time someone had called Mal 'Lord Valentine'. Vargas too had used the honorific. Mal had brushed him off, but maybe there was more to it.

"Why do you call him Lord Valentine? Are you being sarcastic?"

Drasnil raised one silvery eyebrow. "You truly have no idea who he is?"

"Master, the boy is not Court-born. He is not seighlie," Madran pointed out. The skinny fae was still kneeling by Drasnil's feet and the smaller fellow stroked his hair, as if he were a lapdog.

"Of course," Drasnil murmured absently. "How would you? Foolish!" He tapped his teeth with a long silver fingernail. "How much do you know of the fae, Neil?"

"That they aren't really all three inches tall," Neil answered.

Drasnil uttered a quick, low bark of laughter. Was Neil imagining it or did he see mischief in the man's eyes?

"No. You are correct. I am small by the standards of my kind but even I am taller than that. Fortunately, height is not a determining factor in the selection of those who would rule us." He tugged on one coil of hair. "Our kind, it is said, came first upon this world in Ireland, the Green Isle, some call it. We quickly spread across the globe. Those who remained in the old country are among the oldest of our ruling clans. Their bloodlines go back over thousands of years. The Valentine clan of Kinvarra are one such line. Young Lord Valentine is the heir to that powerful barony. His father is the 40th Baron Kinvarra, the richest and most powerful of the leprechauns on this earth."

Neil stared at him. Waited for him to laugh. Crack a smile. Giggle. Something. Maybe he didn't know what he was talking about. Maybe he was just crazy. He didn't seem like either, but he couldn't be right. Malachai brewed up illegal gasoline to sell on the black market and chopped up cars and other garbage for scrap metal. Why in the world would he do that if he was the heir to some rich, powerful family? And leprechauns were green, weren't they?

"You don't believe me?" Drasnil inquired when Neil waited too long to reply.

"I find it hard to, yes," Neil admitted.

Drasnil smiled at him. "It does seem fanciful, so I won't take insult. This time."

"You'll give Mal my message, though?"

Drasnil gave him a good, long look before nodding. "I will. If for no other reason than to spite Delilah. Whom I believe you should be getting back to."

Neil knew when he was dismissed and he stood.

"Perhaps I should escort him, Master," Madran offered, looking at Neil and all but licking his chops.

"I can find my own way back," Neil said quickly.

* * * *

Vargas was waiting in a booth by the edge of the main auditorium and he narrowed his eyes when he spotted Neil coming toward him.

"Well? You were a time. What did you find out, boy?" he snapped.

"Can we go outside first?"

Vargas scowled at him, maybe not accustomed to having his demands countermanded, maybe just because he didn't like him. Neil couldn't decide. He conceded at last, curiosity winning out.

When they were back out on the street and heading for the van—ignored by the buglike doorman, once his venue was free of them—and with Crow trailing them like a sulky child, Vargas repeated his question.

"What did you discover?"

"Felipe Drasnil. He said to tell you he wasn't kidnapping anyone. They just recognize a better deal when they see one...or something like that."

Vargas stopped so fast that he almost broke a heel. His kohl-rimmed eyes were wide as he turned to face Neil, pulling him around with both hands on his shoulders.

"You worked your lust on Drasnil?" His tone veered between horror and admiration.

"No," Neil said, pulling back. Vargas tightened his grip and didn't let go so he went on. "I didn't have to. Madran told me it was his master that your…people were going to. I was working on getting more info from him when Drasnil interrupted. I got the impression he thinks you're dumb for believing they were all kidnapped," he couldn't resist adding.

Vargas pushed him away with a snort of disgust. "Well, he would say something like that, of course. What was he even doing in a place like this? His minions I can believe, but my baby brother?"

He made a sound somewhere between a spit and a sneeze and cursed in a tongue that was alien to Neil's ears. Crow snickered but shut his mouth when his master turned that glare on him. That made Neil feel better about the situation.

His brother? Drasnil could have told him that. He wondered if the little fae really would find Mal and tell him where he was…and if Malachai would even care. Maybe it had been stupid to ask him to relay a message. Too late.

"Can we go? I got you what you wanted," Neil asked.

Vargas directed a dark look his way, but he didn't contest Neil's claim. All he said was, "Get in the van."

* * * *

When they returned to the house Neil asked Vargas to remove the collar but he only scowled and walked away. He was not returned to the closet, at least. He was shown to a room upstairs that had four narrow beds shoved against the walls. Charlie was there, along with another guy.

"Can I have my clothes back?" Neil asked.

Charlie pointed to the jeans and T-shirt that were on one of the beds and some of the tension eased in Neil's shoulders. It was a small thing, but having his own clothes, even if they were Malachai's cast-offs, made him feel better. Maybe even because they were Malachai's cast-offs. He picked up the clothes and headed to the bathroom across the hall.

The water was cold but looked fairly clean. He couldn't say the same for the tub. Still, he stood under the water and used the small sliver of soap to scrub himself head to toe, twice. There weren't any towels so Neil pushed the water from his skin as best he could. His hands scraping down his chest and belly reminded him of how Madran's hands had been all over him and he shuddered before pulling on his clothes. He didn't want to touch the clothes Charlie had given him but he supposed if he left them in the bathroom, he would get mad.

He needn't have worried. When he tried to hand them back, Charlie waved him off. "Keep 'em. You'll need 'em again soon enough."

That sunk his already low mood.

The lad on the other bed was watching them both in silence. His reddish-blond hair and pale blue eyes reminded Neil, with another pang, of Malachai. Was he even alive? Would Drasnil pass on the message? Would it matter?

"What can you do?" the red-haired boy asked him, breaking into his thoughts. "I'm Eithne, by the way."

He pronounced his name very precisely. It sounded like Edney, to Neil's ears.

Why was everyone here obsessed with what he could or couldn't do?

He shrugged. "Nothing much."

"Neil here does fuck magic," Charlie said.

Neil gaped at him and Charlie gave him a sly look.

"Where did you hear that?" Neil demanded.

"Madame Del said you fuck the truth out from between their ears." Charlie snickered. It was not a pleasant sound. "Crow reckons anything that rides you is fucked in more ways than one."

Neil didn't know if he was disgusted or just angry. "Whatever!" he muttered and turned toward the bed his clothes had been sitting on.

Charlie stood up quick and got in his way. "You better lose that attitude." He pushed his finger against Neil's chest and Neil took a step back. "You think you can come in here and make eyes at Del and put your cute little arse around but let me tell you, pretty looks don't mean shit here. Everyone pulls their weight."

It had been a very, very long few days, full of anguish and fear and uncertainty, and the frayed ends of Neil nerves snapped. He knocked Charlie's hand away, put both his hands on the other boy's chest and shoved him back hard. He avoided fights whenever he could, but that didn't mean he hadn't had to defend himself many times. Mostly he'd ignored taunts and walked away when kids at school had tripped him or pushed him around, but he hadn't always been able to walk away, and those times had taught him the only way his classmates could get the best of him was if they ganged up. He wasn't afraid of Charlie.

Charlie swung and Neil ducked but the fist still caught him on the side of the head. He charged, putting his shoulder down and rammed it just under Charlie's ribs. It would have been more effective if he'd had more room to build up steam but it still took him back a few steps and slammed him up against a wall. Charlie brought a knee up and got his thigh and jabbed him a few times in the side with his fist while Neil got in a few punches to his midsection.

Someone grabbed his hair and he resisted until his head was tugged back. Eithne got between them and pushed them apart.

"Stop it! Both of you." His voice was husky and he didn't land the weight of Charlie's punches. "What's wrong with you two? Fuck!"

Neil backed away from them both, balanced lightly on the balls of his feet, ready if they came at him together.

Eithne only stood between them, arms outspread to keep them from fighting, and Charlie stayed where he was, propped against the wall, holding a hand to his side. Finally he took a step and spat on the floor at their feet. Eithne made a sound of disgust. Neil tensed but Charlie stomped out of the room and Neil heard his footfalls pounding all the way down the stairs.

He slumped down on the bed and put a hand to his own tender ribs with a groan.

"Why did you have to go and push him like that?" Eithne demanded.

"Because if I didn't, he was never going to stop trying to see how far he could push me," Neil said quietly.

"He's just a child. He doesn't get any of this." Eithne sighed. "He wants to be someone's favorite. You pushed his nose out of joint, that's all. Be the bigger guy here."

"I pushed... Are you serious? He got in my face first. Look, I just want to be left alone." To that end, Neil lay back on the bed and turned to face away from Eithne.

"You're stronger than he is, Neil," Eithne said quietly. "You just don't realize that yet."

Neil sighed. "Yes, I do. And now he knows it too. So maybe next time he'll think twice before he—" His words cut off like someone had thrown a switch. A jolt went through him so painful it made his back bow and his teeth clench. It lasted maybe half a minute and left him panting and shaking. He groaned as Eithne asked him what was wrong.

"He'll be fine, Eithne." Delilah's silky voice reached Neil's ringing ears from the door.

Neil lifted his trembling fingers to the collar at his throat. It took effort—he was weak as a kitten.

"There is no fighting allowed under this roof," Vargas said. "Consider this your first warning."

Neil tried to say something, but only a small huff of sound came out.

"Don't make me punish you for real," Vargas warned.

He stalked out, in a swirl of purple silk and Neil stared after him, his stomach churning with acid. His eyes burned but he stubbornly gritted his teeth and rolled over, facing toward the wall, determined to ignore everyone.

The mattress subsided behind him and moments later he felt cool fingers stroke through his hair, then brush over his neck, sliding between collar and skin. The sensation welling out from that touch was oddly soothing.

"Don't fight him, Neil. You won't win," Eithne said in a soft voice.

Neil closed his eyes tight and swallowed around a painful lump. His mother had said almost exactly those same words to him, more than once. Along with "Just do what you father says, Neil." And "Don't make him angry, Neil." And "Just try to please him, that's all he wants from you, Neil."

He could feel the hot sting behind his closed eyelids but he wouldn't let any tears fall. Not here. Not now. Tears were a weakness he couldn't afford to let anyone see.

"Leave me alone. Please. Just leave me alone." His voice was so tight and hoarse it came out raspy.

Eithne's gentle hand made one final pass over his whole body then the mattress shifted again and that calming presence was gone.

"Try to rest," Eithne said. And amazingly, he did. The blackness of exhaustion swallowed him and he slept.

Chapter Ten

Neil slept longer than he thought possible, given the circumstances. As he lay with his eyes open, staring up at the ceiling, he took stock. He was wanted by the police, hunted by assassins and probably his father, his mother was dead, Malachai was injured or dead, he'd lost his only asset, and he'd been blackmailed into slavery to a psychotic fairy who had no compunction about whoring him out for his benefit.

Fear, together with the need to get away as fast and as far as he could, had been driving him for days. Since any sort of immediate escape looked impossible, the weight of grief was pulling him down into despair. A lump the size of a whole walnut felt like it was lodged in his throat but he kept swallowing it down, refusing to cry. His footing here was still too uncertain to allow himself the luxury to grieve.

"Time to get up, lazy bones," Amy said.

Neil turned his head and focused on her. "Why?"

"Well, for one thing, you've been laying in bed all morning. Come downstairs and have something to eat. Del is expecting a visitor this afternoon and you're to entertain him."

Neil groaned. "Who?"

Amy put her hands on her hips and tisked at him. "Get up and come downstairs. You can ask Crow."

Neil would rather stay put and starve but he figured if he didn't do as she wanted, it would only mean another taste of punishment from the collar.

He pulled on Malachai's hand-me-down jeans and shirt then made his way down to the kitchen. The other occupants of the house were already gathered around the table, bolting down toast and cereal. Crow was watching them from the window and there was no sign of Vargas.

"About fucking time," the whiskery creature muttered at the sight of him.

Neil glanced at him but didn't bother to respond. He sat down at the table and grabbed a piece of toast. The bread at least was decent wholemeal and there was plentiful butter and a bowl of scrambled eggs. He felt his stomach complain—his dinner had been interrupted the other night, after all. He ate three rounds of toast and as much of the eggs as he could grab.

Crow stood and beckoned him curtly into the next room when he'd finished.

Neil rose and dragged his feet as he followed. Crow pointed toward a couch. He could have made a show of refusing to sit, but what was the point? Once he flopped down, Crow opened a box that sat on the table in front of him and pulled out a sheaf of papers. "Delilah found your tricks last night adequate."

Neil snorted softly. "Watch out, don't want to give me an ego or anything."

Crow narrowed his already narrow eyes and went on as if he hadn't spoken, "Get the man that's coming over to sign these papers."

He set them down and Neil took a look at them without picking them up. Something about property lines and a deed. He read further.

"This is the deed to this house?"

Crow nodded. Before Neil could respond, Vargas joined them.

"I see Crow has set your next task before you."

Neil glanced from one to the other, both watching him expectantly. He looked down at the sheaf of papers again. Getting a name of a competitor was one thing, stealing a house from someone was another.

"I don't know if I can work that big of a compulsion...and who's to say if this guy will even be interested in me. If there's no lust, I can't make him do anything." That last part was true, but the first part was a lie. If there was enough lust to work with, he could get him to sign everything he owned over to him. People were almost always willing to part with money and things to get what they wanted — the nature of that sort of barter was something indelible in humans.

"Oh, he will be interested, little demon, don't you worry about that," Vargas laughed. It was not a pleasant sound. "Our arrangement with him has always included...entertainments."

Crow snickered at that last remark.

All the food he'd just eaten suddenly sat ill at ease in his belly. No wonder the strays Vargas collected were moving on to greener pastures as soon as they could. Maybe he should have thrown himself on Drasnil's mercy to escape Vargas after all. This had to end. He'd been fooling himself to think he could just do what Vargas wanted and pacify him until an opportunity to escape presented itself. If he did this, if they saw how easy it was for him to manipulate the man to hand over a house, they would watch him like hawks, maybe keep him under lock and key. What he could do was valuable but he'd made a mistake using it to bargain.

If he secured the house for Vargas, that would only be the beginning. He would use him to seduce, manipulate and steal until he was either caught or killed. He'd have to fail.

It was as if Vargas could see his thoughts because the evil smirk left his face.

"Be warned, chicken. If you let me down again today, I'm taking you straight to the police. We'll see how gentle they are with you, little demon."

Crow laughed like a hyena at that and even his master's disapproving glare didn't quite shut him up.

Neil glared at him indignantly. "What do you mean 'again'? I got you the name you wanted last night."

"Can't do anything with what you gave me, demon. Drasnil is out of bounds to me. The information is about as much use to me as a chocolate teapot." Vargas sighed. "Must do better."

"That's not my fault." Neil stood up to face Vargas and only after he was on his feet was he reminded of how much taller Vargas was and the fact that the fae's magic torture device was around his throat.

He felt the collar tighten, though Vargas said nothing nor did he move a muscle. Impassively, the dark fae observed as Neil's fingers flew to his throat, trying to keep the band of steel from crushing his larynx. Crow tittered eagerly, staring at him with glee in his ugly face.

The pressure didn't tighten any further but was just enough to keep him from getting any air. In desperation he reached out toward Vargas and grabbed his arm, his eyes wide and pleading. Vargas barely reacted, just a twitch of his arm that flicked Neil off like he was a fly. Black spots started to form in the center of Neil's vision and he sunk down to his knees. A moment or two later—moments that felt like an eternity—the pressure stopped and he gulped in air in big, heaving gasps, coughing and choking on the floor as he filled his lungs.

"Let that be a lesson, demon. Go and get changed into something easier to remove," Vargas told him, turning toward the door. "You have twenty minutes."

* * * *

Neil would have rather faced twenty Madrans than the man that was introduced to him as simply 'the landlord'. Not that Madran had any better intentions, but at least he had given the illusion of choice to Neil and had spent a few minutes talking to him, treating him like a human being, even if he technically wasn't.

This man closed the door of the bedroom Neil had been waiting in, gave him a cursory glance and told him, "Strip. Time to pay the rent."

Neil stood slowly. He almost asked, "Are you serious?" but stopped himself before he said the words.

"Hi, I'm Neil," he said, trying to stall.

The man looked up from unbuckling his belt. "Well, Neil. Get your kit off and get on your knees, I haven't got all day."

Neil licked his lips. "Don't you want to...talk some, first?"

The man snorted and looked at him fully for the first time since he'd entered the room. "What the fuck would we talk about, huh? I only want your mouth open for one thing, got it?"

Neil peeled the mesh shirt off under his half-hungry, half-angry gaze but hesitated with the filmy pants. A small coil of lust rose up like perfume from the landlord and Neil reeled it in like a sponge. There was a part of him buried deep inside that was always hungry, a part he liked to ignore and pretend didn't exist. It scented other men's lust like a hound on the trail of prey, blooming and racing to the surface. The experience was something like being taken over by another personality entirely, and that personality knew exactly how to move, how to take a small step and cant his hips forward. How to turn the corners of his mouth up into a sultry smile. How to hook one thumb in the edge of his pants and run it just under the band back and forth teasingly.

"What's the rush?" Neil asked. Even his voice changed, growing smoother, huskier, loaded with promise. "You want to take your time with me, don't you?"

The slap came out of nowhere. Neil stood with his cheek stinging, frozen, and before he could do more than register that he'd been hit, the man grabbed his arms, digging his fingers deep into the muscle before giving him a hard shake. "I'm not going to tell you again," he said through gritted teeth. He let go of Neil's arms and yanked at his pants. Neil heard the sound of threads snapping as they were pulled off his hips. The garment was loose enough it dropped to the floor, tangling around his feet as the man shoved him down as well.

All of it happened so fast Neil couldn't get his wits together quick enough to think how to stall, how to slow him down long enough to use his lust against him. And that was another problem. There was way more anger in the man than lust. He unfastened his jeans as Neil knelt, stupidly stunned. His face was so close to his crotch the faint, musky scent hit him when he unzipped and long-buried memories tried to surface from the murk in his mind.

"Just sit on his lap, Nielub. It will only be a few minutes and I'll come back for you."

Neil brought his hands up, maybe to fend him off, he wasn't sure, but when they weren't smacked away he rubbed them over his crotch, over the thickness behind his underwear. The back of his throat fluttered and he swallowed the nausea.

"That's better, take it out for me," the man said.

Neil lowered the front of the landlord's underwear and his cock was freed. Panic was gibbering at him but Neil kept a lid on it, seeking the scraps of lust the man was barely putting out. He looked up at him, making his eyes go wide and doe-like. "Slow down." He put a surge of power behind the words but it was like trying to push a cart through wet cement. There just wasn't enough lust to work with yet. The man took a handful of his hair and pulled his head back and took his cock in his other hand, guiding it to Neil's lips.

Tamping down the revulsion, Neil opened his mouth and closed his eyes. He tasted salty and musty at the same time but the man's cock grew thicker between Neil lips after only a moment or two. Fine threads of lust rose and Neil grasped for them, getting ready to try for a bigger burst of power. The landlord pushed deeper into his mouth, thrusting his hips until his cock butted the back of his throat and made him choke and gag. He pulled out again and Neil gasped, still gagging a bit, eyes watering. The glossy head of his cock smacked against his cheek and Neil drew on every ounce of lust he could reach. He looked up and caught his eyes, staring deeply, unblinking.

"Sit on the bed." The muscles in his legs went watery and his heart started to pound when the landlord didn't move, but he took a sudden step back and sat down on the narrow bed. Neil took a shaky breath and wiped his mouth on the back of his hand. He stood, stepping out of the pants hobbling his ankles, and let his nakedness fan more lust in the man. He pointed to the pen sitting on top the papers on the small bedside table. "Sign those papers before you touch me again."

The landlord's eyes narrowed and he looked at the papers. His lust wavered like smoke on a breeze and Neil turned instinctively, putting his backside into his view, practically under his nose. "Sign them. They're nothing important," Neil murmured, swaying his hips. A hard hand grabbed his arse and he jumped but resisted the urge to pull away. The lust steadied and Neil glanced over his shoulder. "Jerk off for me," he told him and immediately the man's hand went to his cock and started stroking while the other still fondled his ass. Finally a big surge of lust came rolling in like the tide. Neil sighed and let it flood into him, wrapping it up around metaphorical fists.

"Oh yeah, that's it," the landlord groaned.

"It certainly is," Neil said determinedly. He reached over and grabbed the pen. "Sign the paper." He put every ounce of seduction he could into the compulsion as he placed the pen in the hand that had been stroking his ass. "Sign it and I'll make you feel so good…" he whispered, pushing his power through the words.

The landlord's hand shook as he set pen to paper and scrawled his name on the line. Neil flipped the page and he signed again, and one more, all while he stroked his cock faster and harder. "One more, do it," Neil murmured in his ear and he signed the last page just before he spattered his cum onto the floor.

He reached for Neil but Neil danced out of his reach, snatching the papers up.

"Come back." The landlord slurred like he was drunk, and in a way, he was.

Neil ignored him and slipped out of the door, not caring he didn't have a stitch of clothes on. He'd rather run through the house naked than spend another second in the same room with the man. Crow was lurking not too far from the door and Neil slapped the papers against his chest with a snarl, not caring if it got him in trouble. Crow sneered at him but he grabbed the papers as Neil let them go, and he didn't try to stop him as he took off toward the stairs and ran up to the bathroom at the top.

He slammed the door and locked it with the flimsy, useless hook and sank down with his back to it. He had to put his head between his knees and take some deep breaths and still he didn't know if he was going to throw up or not for a long time.

When he finally got back up, he was calm. He splashed his face with the tepid water from the tap and went to the room he'd slept in last night. He was more than glad to find the room empty. He didn't think he could face Charlie and Eithne naked. How had he ever thought he could bluff his way through this, play along and do what they wanted until he could find a way to escape? He had been colossally stupid. He'd rather have prison, or the noose, than day after day of this.

If he looked deep enough, he had also held on to a small kernel of hope that Malachai might somehow get him out of this mess. He needed to let go of that stupidity too. Malachai either couldn't or wouldn't help him anymore. He was on his own.

Neil found the clothes Malachai had given him and put them on. He went to the window and pulled the torn curtain back. Unlike downstairs, this window still had its glass. Unfortunately it also had bars on the outside. There was no getting out this way. He left the bedroom and moved as silently as he could down the hall, away from the stairs. Two doors he tried were both locked. The third was a closet. The last door was unlocked, another bedroom with a single bed and a dresser. The window in this room was neither boarded over, nor did it have bars, but it wouldn't budge no matter how hard Neil tried to open it. He could break it, but he had been hoping he would have a least a few minutes head start before anyone discovered him missing. Oh well. There was nothing for it. He'd already made up his mind he wasn't staying here another minute, collar or not. He'd find a way to get it off.

There was a small box on the dresser, the only item he saw. It had some weight to it and Neil hefted it for a moment, getting ready to send it through the window.

"What the devil are you doing in here?" Crow asked, his voice harsh. Neil jumped and Crow saw what he had in his hand. "I knew it! Filthy demon scum. Thieving little bastard!"

"I wasn't stealing..."

Crow apparently didn't have the same control over the collar that Vargas did because he didn't bother trying to use it, he just lashed out with a fist that caught Neil on the chin and sent him reeling back. He dropped the box as he reached out to steady himself and ducked his head when Crow swung at him again, this time missing his head and clipping his shoulder.

Neil yelped and tried to dodge for the door but Crow grabbed him in a surprisingly strong grip. "I'll teach you how we deal with thieves that steal from the hand that feeds them!" Crow roared. He dragged Neil from the bedroom and down the stairs and by the time they reached the bottom, the whole house was roused at his cursing. Except Vargas, who was nowhere to be seen. Neil wasn't sure if he should be relieved or worried.

He twisted in Crow's hands but couldn't break his hold. Still, he was more angry than anything. Until Crow started heading toward the cellar stairs.

"Let go of me!" Neil yelled, planting his feet. "I wasn't going to take it!"

Crow ignored him and dragged him forward, stronger than he looked. In a last-ditch effort Neil threw himself to the ground and tried to hang on to the doorjamb, but Crow just took a hold of his legs and hauled, ripping his hands way. Neil hit his chin on a step about halfway down and saw stars for a second. It was pitch black at the bottom, the only light coming from the stairwell, but that didn't seem to hinder Crow. A rough rope was looped around Neil's wrists and tied tight before he was hauled to the center of the room and up onto his feet. Crow threw the rope over a beam in the ceiling and pulled on the end until Neil's arms were stretched over his head and he was lifted right up, his toes barely scraping the floor. As Crow tied the rope off, Neil could hear whispering on the stairs, Amy's more feminine pitch sounding worried.

A match flared and Crow lit an oil lamp on a table and picked something up. Neil's eyes were dazzled and he blinked, squinting until he made out what Crow had in his hand. It was a length of hose, longer than his arm. Neil frowned. It didn't seem like much of a weapon. He tried to keep Crow in sight but the evil little man moved behind him. He heard the whoosh before it struck his midsection and knocked the air right out of his lungs. The hose was filled with something heavy, sand maybe, or rocks. His body jerked, then went numb for a second before the pain came rushing at him. If he'd had any air, he would have screamed but all he could manage was a grunt then the hose struck him again. Crow laid it right across his kidneys and this time the sound he made was bigger.

"Filthy demon!" Crow spat, grabbing his hair and wrenching his head back. "I'm going to enjoy this."

Neil had no doubt he would.

The weighted hose struck again across the backs of his thighs, then again on his ribs before Crow moved around him and dealt a vicious swipe to stomach. Neil tried to tense his body for the next blow but Crow changed directions and whacked him across the thighs again. After a while the pain throbbed through him from what felt like every square inch of his body. Every time he tried to catch his breath, it was whipped out of him again and every time he tried to flinch away, it only made Crow more vicious. Neil had no idea how long it went on. It seemed like hours, days... It all started to blur and blend together and finally he hung limp, with the world wavering in and out of darkness.

Chapter Eleven

Malachai ached all over and he was so cold that his teeth chattered. It was the shivering that woke him from a dark dream where Vargas stood over him in a gown the color of blood and slit his back from his shoulders down to his ribs, twice, leaving long bloody scores in his flesh.

"Show me your wings. I will not give you peace until you show me."

He shook his head, but the movement hurt his neck — hurt all the way down his spine. He felt the tingle of pain right down to his knees. For a while he thought he would be sick.

"I can't! I promised..."

But the words corrupted on his tongue and what came out of his mouth was, *"Yes, Master. Whatever you wish."*

His eyelids fluttered and for a moment the real world flooded in, stuttering images that made no sense, until he tilted his head, ignoring the pain that screamed through every nerve. He was on the floor, in his own kitchen. Merc lay face down, just out of arm's reach, bleeding from a nasty cut on the back of his balding head.

Mal blinked harder but the image did not falter.

"Merc!" he said hoarsely.

The other man stirred when he heard his name and Malachai felt a wash of relief. He rolled awkwardly onto his stomach then levered himself to his hands and knees. His limbs were weak as a newborn colt's but he somehow managed to crawl to his friend's side and touched his fingers to the short, jagged split in the thin skin of his scalp. He could not feel broken bone beneath the skin and Merc grumbled at him, trying to reach up to swat him away, clumsy as a drunk.

"Fuck! That hurts, Malachai!"

"Shhh...let me stop the bleeding at least," he breathed. "What happened?"

Merc turned his head just a fraction, squinting up at him out of one bloodshot eye. "You don't remember?"

"Vargas was here," Mal said, gently pressing the edges of the wound together so that flesh met over the cut. He closed his eyes and put as much of himself as he could into the shift, transmuting the ragged skin, making it knit and come together, as whole as he could make it.

Because he'd thrown just about everything he had into altering the Smoke Dragon that Vargas hurled at him, in a life or death game akin to Rock, Paper, Scissors. Only more lethal.

Vargas' unseighlie roots meant he had darker magic to dip into, but like Mal, he could use that power in defense alone They had fenced around each other, both waiting for the other man to make the first move. His feint had forced Vargas' hand and when his opponent had unleashed the Smoke Dragon to smother him, Mal had cast a powerful transmuting spell to turn the smoke to spun glass. As it had tightened its coils around him, the glass had shattered and he still had glittering shards of it in his hair and clothing, as he did what he could to stop his friend bleeding out.

Why had Vargas been here?

Mal pushed at the clouds obscuring his memory. His gaze scanned the chaos in the kitchen. There had been a struggle. The table lay in countless pieces.

Damnit, that was a fine table.

Three plates, one still whole, the other two broken, were scattered around the room. Three tin mugs. The frying pan lay on the floor beside Mercurio.

Why three?

It came back to him then. A rush of memory so hot and angry that he almost burst from the rage inside. The boy. The incubus boy with the big, vulnerable eyes and that sweet, soft mouth.

"Where's Neil?"

"They took him, Malachai. Nothing I could do. That wretched shit Crow must have hit me with something. Last thing I remember was seeing one of Vargas' thugs dragging him out to the front. Then it all went black." Merc sat up and rubbed his head cautiously. He examined his hand but it came away unbloodied. "Thanks, Mal."

The strength went out of him then and Malachai sagged, his hands hitting the floor, fingers splayed, bracing himself against another undignified collapse. Mercurio must have moved because suddenly the man was beside him, hands on his shoulders, steadying him.

"Keep it together, Mal. No time for fainting fits, kiddo. We need to get rid of that fucking car."

"No." Mal lifted his head to stare at Merc. "Neil. We have to –"

"The kid's long gone. It was still light when they came over. It's full dark out there. If they've taken him to the cops, he'll have spilled everything that happened and they'll have him on a charge sheet longer than your arm. We don't need that car anywhere near this place. Do you hear me? We take a spotlight and the pickup and we ditch that bitch in the fucking river. It's a damned shame but if the cops and their enforcement enchanters turn up here and that car is still in the loading bay, we are eff-you-cee-kay-ee-dee." Merc glared at him and Malachai knew better than to argue.

"Okay," he said, dropping his defiant stare and focusing on not passing out.

He was still weak, still nauseous, but he could do this. Once the car had been vanished, though, he was going to go after Vargas. And the end results were not going to be pretty.

Mal grabbed a beaker from the cabinet over the range and knocked back half a liter of cold water from the bowser in the corner, which made him feel a bit more alive. He joined Merc in the garage bay where the older fellow already had the pickup revved up and ready. Merc was having a last look for the tracer spell and Mal couldn't blame him for that. If cops and Bone Men were teaming up to find the damned thing, they'd swoop on it like a hawk on a mouse the minute he and Merc broke cover.

Mercurio seemed to read his mind because he said, "If they have him in custody, they'll have stepped down the search for the car. And even if they haven't, they'll have to track it to Corvo's first, then figure out which way it went after that spellstorm you escaped through. We have time. I'd feel it if we were being watched."

Even so they waited until the first hints of daylight were lightening the city skies before winding open the two sliding doors that guarded their scrapyard from interlopers. Merc had the floodlights blazing and damn any neighbors that might have been trying to sleep. This wasn't a residential area so much, these days, but there were people dossing down in the buildings around and about and in the main part they were all pretty respectful of one another. The alleyway that ran down the side of the building and around the back of the yard was empty and quiet in the glare of the spotlights.

Merc got the pickup lights fired up and Mal gave the winch on the back one last check over to make sure the Maserati was securely fastened on, then hopped up into the passenger seat. He usually drove when they went out but he was faster on his feet, if there was anyone lurking, and he knew it. Also he was still a bit mazy from the shadow-fog Vargas threw at him. Okay, Mercurio possibly had concussion, so they were level on that count, but the old bastard still wanted the wheel.

They kept to the back roads because Merc figured that they would be less likely to be watched, even when Mal pointed out that they were also better for ambushing people in the dark. The pickup's engine rumbled softly as Mercurio kept it in as high a gear as he dared on these narrow, winding streets, minimizing the noise as much as possible. He wasn't one to spook at shadows but Mal was picking up on his unease and that in turn made his skin prickle with wariness. He kept a close watch on the wing mirrors, alert to anything moving in the shadows on either side of the street but there was no one around at this time of the morning. They reached the outskirts of the old Downtown area within half an hour and climbed up onto the old Westmacott Bridge that arched over the broad, fast-flowing Princeville river.

Merc slowed to a stop on the crest of the bridge but kept the engines running. He pulled on a pair of thin suede gloves and reached over into the well behind the seats for a set of bolt cutters then swung down from the cab. Mal followed and unhitched the Maserati before lowering the front wheels gently back to the tarmac while his partner removed a ten-foot section of the railings with the bolt cutters then dragged it around and heaved it in pieces into the back of the pickup.

Mal stared at him for a moment.

"Waste not, want not," Merc said with a shrug.

"You're about to dump a Gran Cabrio in the river and you're stealing railings from a public highway! Shut up!" Malachai huffed.

He got into the car, which turned over smoothly for him, and drove it around the pickup, taking his time, lining it up with the gap in the railings, nudging the front wheels up onto the curb before he jumped out again. His hands moved over the gleaming carmine flanks of the beautiful car and he sighed. "Sorry about this, old girl."

"Don't be soft," Merc told him. "It's a car and it's hot. And it's now got your fucking fingerprints all over it."

"River will see to that," Mal said. He bent to rest the heel of his hand against the edge of the windscreen. "Give me a hand then, mastermind!"

Merc put his back into the passenger side and together they pushed the car forward until it was right up on the curb and its nose was poking out over the river. Mal moved around behind it and his partner quickly followed suit as they gave it a last good push and the car went over the edge with a bang and a squeal of metal undercarriage. The weight of the engine carried it trunk over hood off the edge of the bridge and it flipped in the air, landing on its back in the water below with a splash that they probably heard in Richensboro.

Mal peered over the edge and watched as it resisted gravity for a few moments, spinning on the powerful tide, then succumbing to the currents as the water found its way into the chassis, dragging it down into the depths of the cold, gray river. Merc tapped his shoulder.

"Get in the truck."

When he looked up, it was to see what his partner had spotted. A local patrol car crawling up the far embankment toward the bridge had put its lights on and was heading their way. He swung himself behind the wheel without waiting for Merc to argue about it and his partner was in the cab beside him in double time. Mal rammed it into drive and floored the accelerator, spinning the pickup around in a full U-turn and heading back down into the sprawl of the Downtown area. They would lose the cops there before that cruiser had even pulled itself onto the bridge.

"What happens if they find it?" he asked, eyes on the road.

"We pray that it doesn't have a black box as well as a tracer spell," Merc said without humor. "They won't find it, Malachai. That river flows fast at this time of year. It'll be halfway out to Lac de Prince before we get home."

Less than thirty minutes later, Mal pulled up outside the shop but he kept the engine running. Merc turned his head with a frown. "What now?"

"I drop you here. I have something to do," Mal told him.

"If it involves that fucking kid, like hell you don't," Merc grumbled. "Forget about him, Malachai. He's trouble, I warned you he was, but you wouldn't listen."

"I'm going to talk to Vargas, find out which nick they took him to. Maybe I could — "

Merc caught him by the front of his shirt, pulling Mal forward in his seat roughly. "Listen to me, kid. There is nothing we can do. The brat is demon spawn. If his own kin don't come for him, then why the hell should we risk our necks?"

"Let go, Merc." Mal felt the tremor in his voice but hoped that his partner didn't hear it. In truth he could have just walked in the building and gone up to his bed and slept for the next two days. He was bone tired. But he could not get Neil's scared and unhappy face out of his head. The kid had no one. Nobody from his family was going to come for him. If they found him guilty of murdering his mother, he would die. And execution for anyone with demon blood, or found guilty of using dark magic to commit a Grade A Felony, was a slow and horrible end.

"Let go of me," he repeated, with more determination. "I understand that you care, but I'm a grown up, Mercurio. I can take care of myself."

Merc glared at him for a few seconds more then shoved him away with a snort of disgust. He got out of the truck and unlocked the shutter over the front doors of the store, let himself in and rolled it back down again, behind him, with a bang. Mal adjusted the front of his shirt and pulled the nearside door shut with a sigh. Then he put the truck in Drive and was about to pull away when he saw something that gave him pause. There was a smoke-gray metallic Lincoln MKZ Hybrid parked in the passageway opposite the shop, with two shadowy figures inside, watching him. Mal stared back at them, uncowed then — when they did not move — he turned off the engine and got out of the pickup, crossing the street to confront them. They were not cops, he knew that much. No cop would stake out the place in a car like that. It stuck out like a glass of champagne in a line of chipped beer mugs down here. If they were Bone Men, they would have come for him and Merc before he'd even spotted them.

Mal stopped in front of the Lincoln's shiny front fender and folded his arms as he recognized the passenger in the front seat.

"What the fuck are you doing down here, Drasnil? You're a long way from any of your usual haunts." He did not speak in a loud voice but he knew that the cluricaun would hear him perfectly.

The nearside door opened and the dark fae stepped out with a smirk. His hair curled around his tiny, nacreous horns like oiled pewter and his eyes gleamed like moonstones. The smile he bestowed on Mal was too wide, too bright, and had too many sharp little teeth.

"Lord Valentine, always a pleasure."

"Cut the crap, Drasnil. What do you want?" Mal tapped the finger of his left hand irritably on his right arm as he waited.

"I have a message, Your Sublime Rudeness," the immaculately clad fae mage declared, adding in a small bow for good measure.

"Spit it out." Mal chewed on his lips to stop them twitching. Drasnil was more fun than his half-brother, but Delilah Vargas would usually come straight to the point whereas Felipe Drasnil preferred to grandstand for a bit first. He outranked them both, even if he had never been forced to pull that rank with either. He hoped that it wouldn't be necessary today. Not when he had so much to do.

"Charming as ever," Drasnil demurred.

"I'll charm your designer arse if you don't stop queening and tell me," Mal prompted him.

One silvery eyebrow slid all the way up to Drasnil's hairline but if he was annoyed, he did not let it show.

"Very well, my lord. I like my derrière the way it is."

Mal draw a pair of circles with his index finger, to indicate that he was still waiting.

"Last night it was my very great pleasure to entertain a most charming young creature, sent to La Sala by my esteemed brother, to spy on me. Can you imagine such a thing?" Drasnil said, making his petrol-blue eyes very wide and imploring.

"Are you trying to enlist my aid to declare war on Del Vargas?" Malachai put a hand over his mouth, pretending to yawn.

"As if I would do such a thing. Though he vexes me without cease." Drasnil let those huge eyes roll, extending the drama.

"Then how may I help you, Felipe?" Mal inquired. "The short version, if you please? I have things to attend to."

"Then I will be brief. My brother has acquired an incubus. I know…" he added when Mal's eyes widened in astonishment that he could not quite contain. "I could not believe it, either, a child of demonic blood in my brother's house. Imagine how Three Crow Tree's wretched skin will creep right off his nasty back at the idea of it."

Malachai managed a chuckle at that. Since being hexed by a demonic mage, Crow had a mortal fear of dark magic.

"He is still there then? With Delilah?"

"As I understand it, yes." Drasnil let his lips frame a half-smile. "He was most eager for you to hear that, by the way."

Mal blinked. "Delilah was?"

"No, my lord. The boy. The incubus. He seems…quite taken with you. I see these things." The cluricaun executed another compact bow.

"Is this some mischief you are devising?" Mal narrowed his eyes with more than a hint of suspicion.

Drasnil clapped one hand to his chest, feigning outrage. "As if I would do such a thing. You wound me, my lord."

"I'll wound you if I find out you've been spinning me wild tales, Drasnil. What do I owe you for this mercy mission?" Mal rocked back on his heels, surveying the smaller fae critically.

"With respect, sir. I come out of the goodness of my heart." Drasnil batted his silver lashes.

"Your heart is made of granite, Felipe." Mal fought to suppress a smirk.

"Not true. You ask what I desire? I would make matters right between my court and that of my brother, but he will not speak with me." Drasnil wagged a finger his way.

"I am an alchemist, not a miracle worker, Felipe." Mal shook his head. "I will try. That is all I can promise you. Del has put up a wall of concrete around his own heart. Can't I tell that the two of you are related?"

"We are the children of our fathers, my Lord Valentine," Drasnil declared with another sweeping bow.

"Maybe some of us are," Mal muttered under his breath. He pressed a smile. "Thank you, Master Drasnil. I will do what I can. I must be off now."

"Indeed. He is a fine boy, it would be a pity to keep him waiting." Drasnil flashed a grin with lots of sharp teeth in it. "Please, also, send word to Charlie that Chesney is pining for him."

Mal half-turned on his way back to the pickup. "Will you not be sated until you have stolen them all from him?"

"I am the Master of all Mischief. It is what we cluricaun do." Drasnil winked at him.

Mal leveled his index finger at the fellow. "One day that will come back to bite you, Felipe. Take care. And thank you."

Drasnil saluted him with a cheeky smirk then slid back into the softly purring hybrid vehicle. As Mal hopped back behind the wheel of his pickup, the silvery car pulled out softly and melted away into the brightening morning. Once it had vanished, he set off in the opposite direction.

* * * *

The first slivers of gold were sliding up over the eastern horizon as Malachai turned onto Delancey Boulevard and that ragged thoroughfare was briefly gilded and faintly glamorous again. Long shadows hid the heaps of junk and the grille-covered doors, the broken windows and missing slates. He could almost imagine the place in its heyday, back when the city of Or d'Roit was in its prime, rich on the transatlantic traffic flowing in and out on the Princeville River, a hive of industry.

Then he pulled up outside Vargas' place and the dream faded as he locked the pickup and strode up the uneven path. Mal rang the doorbell twice then hammered on the piece of wood that had been nailed over the missing glass panels in the door.

"Open up! There must be someone in there!" he called. "I'm going to stay here and be a pain in your collective arses until you let me in."

To his surprise, he didn't have to wait long for a response. The door opened a crack and a slim young man glared through it at him. Charlie.

"What do you want?"

"I've come to speak with Del. He has something that I want." Mal leaned both hands on the door frame, looming over him.

"Go away. Delilah isn't home." He started to close the door but Mal put his hand out to stop it.

"Ah, c'mon, Charlie. You know that's bullshit. Tell him to stop hiding behind kids and face me, or I will burn this place down."

There was furtive scuffling on the other side of the door for a moment. "For Pete's sake, Charlie, let him in!" Amy pulled the door open and that was all the invitation that Mal needed but she still said,

"Malachai...Crow's gone crazy. He caught the new boy stealing and he's got him in the cellar."

"Thanks, Amy." Mal pushed by Charlie but patted his shoulder and added, "No hard feelings, mate."

Then he set off at a run for the kitchen and the door into the basement. He could hear the crack of rubber on skin even from up here and rage bubbled up in his chest like a wildfire, burning out the moment of hesitation he had at his own dark memories of being hauled into that cellar. The scars across his shoulder blades prickled but he forced the discomfort aside and practically kicked the paint-peeling door off its rusty hinges.

The sight that met his eyes would be emblazoned on his retinas for many moons. Neil hung limply by his wrists from the iron loop in the low ceiling, his head lolled from his shoulders and Crow stood with his arm drawn back to deliver another blow with a sand-filled length of hose Mal was intimately familiar with.

Oh, Neil, I'm sorry. I should have come sooner. The blasted car be damned.

"Three Crow Tree! Put that down. If you touch him once more, I swear by all the powers Underhill or Over, I will use it on you, and I will not stop until you draw your last breath."

He advanced down the stairs as he spoke. While he did not raise his voice, his command gave the smaller man pause.

"Lord Valentine, this is not your business," Crow hissed and it would have been convincing if he hadn't betrayed his nervous fear by asking, "Who let you in?"

"What? Tell you, so you can beat them too? I don't think so." Mal stalked him until he was close enough to reach out and jab at Crow with one finger. "Who gave you permission to treat him this way? What has he done that you would be so cruel?"

"I caught the demon whore stealing." Crow's dark eyes gleamed in the light of the oil lamp, greedy with a twisted desire, his pale face flushed with more than the effort of the beating. "He belongs to Vargas now." He emphasized this by grabbing the collar at Neil's throat.

The movement caused Neil's body to sway and his eyelids fluttered, a low, pain-filled moan on his lips.

"But apparently Delilah is not here." Mal looked around as if he were expecting the cluricaun to strut into the room at any moment then sighed with mock disappointment. "Nope. Not a sign of him. Such a shame. I was interested to hear from his own lips why Neil is still here instead of at the police station, when he was so adamant that his only reason for taking him was the reward money."

He strode around Neil's dangling body, running a gentle hand across his shoulders. Then he touched the fingers of his other hand to the jewel at his throat and his eyes gleamed like moonlight.

"Lord Valentine, you may not work your magic here. The C-Compact…" Crow stuttered.

"Was broken the moment your master entered my property and used magic and lies to steal what is mine, Three Crow Tree. The Compact is invalid."

If it was petty to feel gratified at the way Crow shrunk back from him and cringed, he didn't care. The odious troll was just lucky he was too worried about Neil to want to waste time giving him the same retribution he'd dealt out. Instead he funneled his anger into breaking the charm on the slave collar. It flared a dark, evil green as he pushed his transmuting magic into it, subtly altering the spell so that it became a harmless protection rather than a malevolent punishment, then he shifted his attention to the slender torque itself, altering the very substance of it so that it was brittle as chalk. A tug and it snapped in two and fell from Neil's neck. The pale skin underneath was rubbed raw but unbroken.

Malachai exhaled a sigh he hadn't realized he'd been holding inside. There was always a risk with nasty little charms like these that they would snap the trap as soon as someone tampered with them, forcing him to rush the second transmutation. But Neil was safe. He reached up easily to push cold fire through the ropes around his wrists, burning them harmlessly to ash. Neil dropped like a sack of coal but Malachai was ready to catch him and hefted the lad's limp body in his arms.

Crow backed away. He might be a cruel toady but he wasn't stupid. He knew a how a direct confrontation without Delilah's support would go for him. Cowardly creature that he was, he wasn't going to stand in Mal's way.

"We'll be off then," Malachai said, keeping his voice cool and steady as he carried Neil back to the stairs and up into the kitchen. "Give my regards to your master, please. Oh..." he added, setting eyes on Charlie's still-grouchy features as he reached the top. "I almost forgot. I spoke to Master Drasnil this morning before coming here. He asked me to tell you that your brother is pining for you, Charlie Cooper."

The expression on Charlie's face shifted, for just a moment. Hard to say what was in there — worry, certainly. It was gone just as quickly and the hard, angry mask he usually wore was back in place.

Amy followed Mal outside and opened the passenger side door on the truck for him so he could set Neil inside.

"Is his new hair color your work?" Mal asked her.

She nodded, a fleeting smile crossing her lips. She was probably the kindest soul in Del's house. "He's a pretty one. You'll take care of him, won't you, Mal? Del had him out all night and he sent the landlord in to him earlier. I think he was crying in the bathroom after."

Mal pressed his lips into a hard line, somewhere between grief and frustration, neither of which was fair to take out on Amy. She was a good girl, brave and tough.

"You should come with us," he said on an impulse.

"And who would keep an eye on that old Crow?" she said. "Go on, take him home. Before Del gets back."

He leaned out of the cab and kissed her hair, wishing that he was able to give her a useful gift like a protection charm or some such thing. "Take care, Amy. Thank you."

The internal debate over whether to hurry back to the shop and get Neil seen to or carefully navigate to avoid as many potholes and bumps so as not to jar him lasted only to the end of the street. The sun was well up in the sky and the roads were getting busier, and Neil started to come around as he shifted the old truck into second around the corner.

"Are you—?" Mal was interrupted by Neil's pained hiss.

"Fuuuuck!" The single word died away to a whimper.

"Shhhh...try not to move. I'm going as steady as I can but this heap of rust doesn't have the best suspension, I'm afraid." Mal kept glancing to him as he drove, worried for him after the beating he had taken. The tubing that Crow favored was supple enough not to break the skin in most cases but carried enough weight to do serious internal damage if it was landed in the wrong places. "Mercurio and I will do our best to fix you. I swear."

Neil slumped down on the bench seat and curled up. His eyes were shut again but the way his face was scrunched and the shudders that ran through him as he breathed told Mal he hadn't passed out again. It would probably be better if he had — this journey was going to be a small slice of hell for him.

After a moment or two, Neil said something that he didn't quite make out, cleared his throat and tried again. Mal tilted his head to hear him.

"You're okay. I was worried."

Mal blinked at that, surprised, and caught by the sensation of having something in his eye. He scrubbed the brief wetness away with his knuckles.

"You were worried? Why? I'd have thought you'd have enough to worry you without worrying about me, kid."

"You were hurt. Merc was hurt. I couldn't do anything." Neil's voice was still soft, strained. Mal glanced down when Neil lifted his hand to his throat. "It's gone."

"Yeah. It didn't suit you. I'll get you something new if you miss it." Mal cleared his throat awkwardly. "I...uh — I have a confession to make."

He could see the way Neil tensed then winced before he said, "What?"

"We had to lose the car. Um, your car. I'm sorry." He said it quickly.

Neil was silent for a second then made a small sound and another. He lifted his hand and put it over his eyes. Mal thought he was going to cry for a moment, but Neil heaved a sigh and let his hand fall. The silence as he just stared at the dash in front of him was almost worse than tears. Finally, he said, "What choice did you have?"

"Not much," Mal admitted. "We tried to find the trace spell but in the end we just had to get rid of her. I promise you that we'll do everything in our power to keep you safe from those bastard Bone Men, though. And if they're looking for the car still, they'll be looking in the wrong direction. So, uh, that's good."

"Why?"

"Why is that good?"

"No, why would you promise to keep me safe? The car is gone. There's no more reason for you to keep me around. Not that I'm not grateful you came and got me."

Mal glanced his way again with a frown, wondering if he'd read Neil wrong after all.

"Well…it means they won't look for you here. Which gives you time to get well," he said, choosing his words with care. "And, for what it's worth, I don't believe that you killed your mother. I don't really think that Merc believes it, either but he'll probably play hardball for a while."

Neil went quiet again and Mal let him rest. He groaned a bit when they hit unavoidable bumps but otherwise said nothing while Mal took them back to the shop. He half-expected Vargas to be waiting to cut him off, but he ran into no trouble. Merc must have been keeping an eye out for the truck because he pulled open the gate to let him in and locked up behind while Mal pulled it into the garage. He cut the engine but Neil didn't move to sit up.

"Let's get you inside," Mal said.

"I don't think I can," Neil said.

"Don't be silly. I can carry you. How do you think we got you into the pickup?" Mal offered him what he hoped was a reassuring smile.

He got out and went around to the passenger side, opening the door. Neil had managed to uncurl from his fetal position but his face had gone gray.

"Easy, go slow," Mal told him.

"I think I can walk," Neil said.

"You didn't think you could sit up a second ago. I can carry you, it's really no problem." Mal didn't see the need to let him put himself through an agonizing walk upstairs just to appease some latent shreds of machismo.

Neil turned on the seat and moved to put a leg down. "Let me just…"

Gravity got him out of the truck more than anything, but once he was standing, Neil's face went from gray to milk pale. He clutched the door of the truck with one hand and Mal's arm with the other as he swayed.

"What in the nine hells is going on?" Merc asked as he came in.

Mal had been resisting the urge to give his partner snark but the words were out of him before he could censor them. "Something that might not have had to happen if you'd let me go after him when I wanted to."

He swept aside the rest of Neil's attempts to tough it out and slipped one arm under the younger man's shoulder and across his back. He bent and, as gently as possible, hooked his other arm behind Neil's legs and lifted him up, carrying him into the house.

Whatever protests Neil might have made were buried under hisses and groans as he carried him upstairs. He set him down on his bed and heard Merc stop in the doorway. He ignored his partner because it would do no good to take his anger out on him.

"Let's get this shirt off and take a look," Mal said in as mild a tone as he could manage.

Neil hesitated and Mal wasn't sure if it was just pain or something else, but after a moment he reached for the hem of his shirt and pulled it off.

Neil's skin was light enough to show the exact shape Crow's makeshift whip had made on him in vivid blue-black and purple lines. A dozen or more on his front and his back was just as covered. It was no wonder Neil's eyes were just great big dark circles of pain. It might have started out a punishment but Crow's hatred had obviously gotten its teeth in him to administer such a beating. More grape-sized bruises dotted Neil's jaw where fingers had grabbed him and his chin had a big scrape on the bottom.

"This might sound odd, but it's important. Does any one place hurt more than another? Do you have any sharp pain, like around your middle?"

Neil shook his head.

"Where does it hurt the worst?" Mal asked.

Neil thought for a moment. "My knee."

"Your knee?"

"Yeah."

"Let's take a look."

Reluctance practically oozed from Neil but he unfastened the loose jeans and wriggled them down. More stripping marred his thighs and his left knee was swollen about twice the size of the other. Fresh rage poured into Mal at the sight. Crow must have been completely out of control to risk maiming him like this.

"Little sadist!" he hissed through clenched teeth.

Beside him, Merc straightened and whistled softly. "You're tougher than you look, kid. I'll get some ice. Get that swelling down then we can see what we're messing with."

Neil waited until they heard Merc's tread on the stairs before asking under his breath, "I know he hates me too. Why is he helping?"

Mal forced a chuckle but it came with some effort. He was still furious at the damage Crow had done to Neil and mad at himself for hesitating to go after him. "Mercurio Geiger likes folk to believe he's a hard man with no time for anyone, but he wouldn't turn his back on someone that's clearly hurting and needing his help. He's not a monster. I found that out myself, the hard way. You can trust him."

"What if Vargas comes back? What if he tells the police where I am?" Neil still looked despondent.

"If he tries it, which I doubt, we'll have to hide you. There is no way on this earth that I'm letting him take you away again." Mal hoped he looked as fierce as he felt. If Vargas came back here, he fully planned to kill the bastard, not just for lying to him but for letting Neil suffer. And for his own suffering too. Yes, he owed the cluricaun a great deal — without Vargas' intervention his own gifts would still be locked down and useless. He was not ready to forgive the rogue fae yet, though.

After another pause Neil said, "He was going to turn me in, for the reward. I convinced him I'd be more valuable if he kept me around. Now he understands what I can do...but I didn't have a choice."

Mal took the words in and tried not to look puzzled. He was only telling him what had happened, but the way he said it was...defensive. Like he had to explain himself for simply using his wits. "I don't see that you had much choice. You did what you had to, Neil."

His shoulders eased down a fraction and some of the guarded look in his eyes came down a notch or two. That was interesting. Neil didn't need his approval for anything, but maybe subconsciously he sought it anyway.

"I am not here to judge you, Neil," he said, sitting back to give his patient more space. "You're an adult. You make your own choices. But I'm getting the feeling that things haven't always been that way for you. And I'm sorry if that's been the case. I just want to help. Because when I was in your place, people helped me. Call it karma, if you like."

Merc came in with a bucket of ice and towels. He set them down and Mal started wrapping the ice into a pack and getting it situated on Neil's knee. He was beginning to get used to Neil's long pauses.

"Maybe the house will be enough for him," Neil murmured, shifting his leg a bit to settle the ice more comfortably.

"The house?"

"I got the house for him. For Vargas."

"What do you mean, got the house for him?" Merc asked.

"I made the landlord sign the deed over to Vargas. That should make him happy, right? That's worth more than the reward for turning me in."

Mercurio blinked at him. Mal opened his mouth then he closed it again without saying anything.

"Fucking hell!" Merc said at last. "If that doesn't put a smile on his sour face, nothing will."

Mal was less sure. "If they're so cock-a-hoop about it, why did Crow take the lamm to him?"

"Cos he's a nasty bastard that likes to hurt people," Merc replied with a huff of disdain.

"He thought I was stealing something," Neil said, glancing up at Merc, probably because it wouldn't be a stretch for them to assume he actually had been stealing something. "I wasn't. I was just looking for something to break the window."

"And he didn't even stop to ask what you were actually doing? That sounds like Crow." Mal barely kept the growl from his voice but for once he didn't care.

"That one doesn't know when he's well off," Merc agreed. "How's that knee feeling now, kid? Looks like the swelling's already coming down a bit."

"Cold." Neil paused then said, "I don't think he much cared if I took it or not. He wanted to hurt me from the moment he saw me."

That was probably true enough.

"How'd you get the landlord to sign over the deed?" Merc asked.

Neil shifted the ice pack again, keeping his eyes down. "The same way I got away from the pirates. I told him to sign it and he did."

"You just told him to sign it and he did," Merc repeated.

Neil sighed. "I'm an incubus, Mercurio. If enough lust is involved, I can make people do a lot of things."

"Vargas sent you in there to seduce him?" Mal didn't really need an answer to that question. He knew without details that Del would not have blanched at the idea if it got him exempt from paying rent for the rest of his unnatural days.

"The only thing I could do to prove I was worth more than the reward was to tell him what I could do. He gave me a test, to see if I could get a name of an enemy from someone named Madran. I got the name and that was it. He was already planning what else I could get for him. He wanted the house, said certain things were a part of the rent." Neil practically spat out those last words, then continued, "So all I had to do was pretend I was part of the rent...encourage his lust and use it make him sign the papers."

Mal muttered under his breath in the old tongue. Sometimes the English language was just inadequate when it came to the expression of opinions. Merc patted him on the shoulder in consolation.

"That one's a prize-winning cunt and we both know it. But the Crow is worse. That piece of shit's got a redwood-sized chip on his shoulder. He'll guard his position as Del's second-in-command with his miserable life."

"And he won't let old grudges go. You're best off staying clear of them both," Mal agreed.

That went without saying and Neil must have thought so too because he let the conversation drop. Mal examined him thoroughly, top to bottom, and the knee was indeed the worst of it. With any luck nothing had been torn. They would have to wait and see once the swelling was gone. The rest of Neil's injuries were superficial. Deep, painful bruises and some scrapes, but nothing was broken or burst that he could tell. Other than the blond hair, nothing seemed permanently changed, which was always a possibility when dealing with the fae.

Merc left them, saying he was going to see to food.

Once he was gone, Neil said, "I'm sorry."

"You've got nothing to be sorry for," Mal said.

"I cost you a customer."

"That was your fault, was it? You made Del's greed override common sense? You made him come and break the Compact to take you?"

"No…"

"No is right. You didn't. There's plenty of time to accumulate blame and guilt in this life, Neil, no need to take it on when it isn't rightfully yours."

Neil stared at him. Those big blue eyes still looked sorrowful, but not as much, and there was curiosity in them too.

"What's 'the Compact'?"

Mal sucked in a breath and heaved it out as a long sigh. "You know how I told you Vargas is fae, right?"

Neil nodded and Mal sat back, looking at him solemnly.

"Well, we both come from family lines that can trace their heritage back to the Tuatha de Danaan, a race that some folk say were gods and some say were space aliens, but just about everyone these days tries to pretend didn't exist."

"Did they?" Neil probed.

"Well, there's no one alive these days that recalls those times but enough lore remains to suggest that they did. They passed down a whole heap of earth magic through their bloodlines, though. And as human sorcerers and witches found out about that magic, they tried to steal it and use it. As the fae multiplied and bred into human bloodlines, there were some gifts that got weaker and some that got stronger. Which caused squabbles when one group of fae tried to poach magic users from another group. Squabbles bad enough to start a turf war."

"Did people get hurt?" Neil was sprawled on the mattress, propped up in the pillows, looking tired but determined to stay awake.

"Worse. Lots of folk died, on both sides." Mal heaved another sigh. "And as a result, the Compact was drawn up, forbidding the abduction and forced use of fae magical labor. Most clans abide by it, even the unseighlie, the dark brotherhood. But Del clearly got greedy and decided he could bend the rules with you, since technically you aren't fae."

A loud bang came from downstairs and they both jumped. Mal listened, heard Merc's muttered cursing and relaxed. He had lived with the old bastard long enough to tell a domestic grumble from something more serious. Beside him, Neil was still tensed, spring tight.

"Easy, he just dropped something."

Neil nodded slowly. "Can I have my clothes back?"

"Sure, if you feel up to getting dressed," Mal said, though he thought Neil would probably be better off trying to get some sleep. "Are you hungry? Merc is probably gonna cook stuff. He cooks when he's stressed. It'll be good, though. Scouts' Honor."

"Maybe in a while," Neil said. He picked up the shirt Mal handed to him and very gingerly slipped it back on.

"The shirt is long enough on you, why don't you leave the jeans off until the swelling goes down. Easier to keep ice on the knee," he advised.

Neil seemed to mull it over and he lay back with a sigh and a wince.

Mal tried again. "I haven't got much to deaden the pain…unless you want to try some whiskey."

"Okay," Neil said, eyes closed, and he got the impression that the lad would say 'okay' to anything so long as it made the pain go away.

Mal slid soundlessly across to the storeroom out front and rummaged in one of the crates in there until he located a decent bottle of Kinvarra single malt that he had cooked up in case they needed a bribe to hand. The local plod liked their whiskey and it was fascinating how quickly they lost interest in whatever he and Merc were scrapping when the amber nectar came into play.

"Just a drop," he said, pouring some into a water beaker he kept by the bed. "It's potent stuff."

Neil didn't even sniff it. He took the glass, lifted it to his lips and carefully tipped it back, swallowing in one. He held out the glass for more and Mal eyed him.

"A little painkiller is one thing, but go slow. You don't want to start puking in your condition, trust me."

Neil took a couple of cubes of ice from the bucket Merc had brought and dropped them into the glass. "Just one more. I won't get sick."

"You say that like you've been here before." Mal poured a slightly smaller shot this time.

Neil looked up at him, paused with the rim of the glass touching his lip before he took a more careful sip. "My dad sometimes would give me some before we went out."

Mal rubbed away the small frown that creased his forehead between his eyebrows. Something about Neil being plied with alcohol by his own father didn't sit easily with him.

"Was it that grim? Going anywhere with your dad?"

Neil looked back at him, like he was studying him. Then he drank the rest of the whiskey, the ice clinking gently in the glass before he set it on the bedside table. With a series of slow and careful movements, Neil lay back against the pillow, arranging himself so he was lying on one side, his damaged knee bent with the ice pack still in place.

Just when Mal figured he wasn't going to answer at all, Neil said, "I'd rather go back to Vargas... Hell, I'd rather have to stay with the pirates than let my dad find me."

"Do you really think he would have killed you, if you'd stayed?" Mal asked.

"Eventually, yes," Neil said, feeling a tightness in his throat. "He's a sorcerer. He's killed with magic many times. He's waited nearly twenty years to have my soul to keep him alive and able to keep killing. If he doesn't bond me as his familiar, I don't think he has much longer before the madness gets him, and from there death isn't far behind."

Mal said, "I still can't fathom how he could do that to his own son."

Neil went still. "Because I was never a son to him. I wasn't the result of passion, or even violence. I was a calculated plan. I was only ever meant to be a tool for him to use."

Malachai did not argue or try to find virtue where there was none. "I guess that's one more thing we have in common. We could raise a glass to shitty fathers and a long sojourn in hell to them both."

"Is your dad...gone?" Neil asked.

"Not yet," Mal said darkly. "Worse luck!"

"He's not trying to kill you too, is he?"

"That's questionable." Malachai sighed, drawing one hand across his forehead. "My father only has one love. Gold. He married my alchemist mother to that end and it's my belief that he worked her to death in the pursuit of more and more of the stuff. The gift did not breed true in my elder brother, Mordecai. He went into finance after university in an effort to appease our father, who turned his attentions to me. I joined the army to escape him, but while I was out in Afghanistan, I learned that my brother had died. I always suspected that the old man pushed him to suicide. But I can't prove that."

"I'm sorry," Neil said. "With a dad like that…I guess you can understand why I don't want mine to find me."

"In that case, we'd best make sure he doesn't," he said, pouring himself a small shot of whiskey and raising the tumbler briefly to Neil before consuming it. The burn was harsh on the back of his throat but its warmth was a comfort to his belly.

He got up. "I'm going to check on dinner. Do you need anything?"

Neil shook his head. Just as he reached the bedroom door, Neil said, "Thanks…for coming to get me."

Mal stopped in the doorway, one hand on the lintel. The hesitant note in Neil's voice made his gut clench and he was angry with himself again. If he'd put his foot down and got there sooner…

He turned and made sure a smile was on his face.

"It will be okay. Nobody is going anywhere with you again, not if you don't want to go."

Down in the kitchen, it appeared Merc had decided that every single vegetable in the house had needed chopping and dicing. A big pot was over a low flame, bubbling gently. Mal leaned one shoulder against the door frame, crossing his arms and watching, waiting. This was the part where normally he'd expect a lecture on running off half-cocked, or bringing home troublesome strays, or getting involved when there was no profit to be had. Merc was uncommonly silent on all fronts.

"Nothing to say?" He tried not to sound antagonistic but couldn't help the deliberate poke.

Merc looked sidelong at him but carried on stirring the pot.

"Is the kid okay?"

"He could be better," Mal said, watching his partner with a scowl.

At last Merc pulled out the big metal spoon and set it down more firmly than necessary. "It was better to be safe than sorry. How was I supposed to know that twisted fuck would bang up their new toy so fast?"

"You were nursing me for long enough after I got away from them," Mal growled, but he could not keep up the hostility in the face of Mercurio's hangdog expression. "I got there before the vicious cunt killed him. He seems fragile but I think he's tougher than he looks."

Merc grunted and went back to stirring his pot. "Chicken soup will fix him up."

He must have been feeling guilty if he had put their last chicken in the pot. Still, Mal needed to make sure things were clear. Because while the sniping and grousing were just part of Merc's nature, they worked better as friends and business partners when certain lines were clear, rather than left ambiguous.

"I've offered him shelter. I'm going to keep him safe for as long as he wants to stay."

Merc sighed but gave no argument this time, and no countermands. "I figured you would," he said simply then added, "Just...be careful, Malachai. You heard what he said, what he admitted he can do if he gets under your skin."

"I understand," Mal told him. "But I was there at the docks when he escaped from that ship. I saw the fear in him. He could probably have done worse to them but he didn't. He understands what he's capable of."

Merc snorted. "Just because you understand that your weight will crush a bug doesn't make the bug any less dead if you step on it in the dark."

"You wouldn't stand for him in the house if you thought he was a danger to us," Mal said with a wry smile.

"He's bloody dangerous, but I'm not gonna fight with you over this," Merc said. "I know what you're like when you get yourself on a mission. Don't screw this up, though."

"He's fragile, Mercurio. He needs our help. No one else is going to help him," Mal implored. "He's just a kid."

Merc set the spoon down again and turned to give him as incredulous a look as he could manage. "Fragile? Fragile? You watched him jump from a height that should have — at the very least — shattered his legs. We both watched him tear apart a car in about half the time it ought to have taken and haul it all out to the trailer, on his own. He took a beating that probably would have laid a normal man low for a week, if not killed him outright, and come away from it with some bruises and a swollen knee. You're already blinded by that new shiny blond hair and those wounded looks he throws around, if you think he's 'fragile'."

"That's not what I'm talking about. Stop changing the subject!" Mal pushed away from the door frame and began to get dishes and cutlery down from the cabinets because he needed to keep his hands busy or he couldn't say what he might do with them. "He's emotionally fragile. Something is bothering him, Merc. And I want to help him."

"Emotionally fragile." Merc huffed. "How emotionally fragile can he be if he can fuck a man into giving away a house?"

Malachai turned fast and took a step toward him and Merc went very still. The air between them seemed to thicken, almost crackling, but neither of them took any move to set a spark to the potential tinder. "You heard his words same as I, but you weren't listening if you can say that. Did he sound like he came up with the idea on his own? Did he sound like he wanted to be put in a room with a man 'to pay the rent'?"

"I'll grant that he didn't sound pleased with himself or the situation. He is part incubus, though."

"Just because he is something, or can do something, doesn't mean he likes what he is or what he does."

Merc managed a rueful half-smile. "That sounds like someone standing not a million miles away. A skinny, ginger Irish brat running away from his pot of gold."

"At least my inheritance isn't out to kill me," Mal said drily.

"All right, so the kid is staying. Fine. How exactly are we going to keep him hidden? Even if Vargas isn't likely to go squealing all the way to the cops, he's still wanted. That's a problem."

"Leave that to me," Mal said, busying himself setting out the plates and the knives and forks on the makeshift folding table that Merc had dragged down from the storeroom, getting the cutlery positioned so that each piece was perfectly symmetrical with its neighbors. "The car is out of the way. I can put a shield on the block that will keep prying eyes away."

He looked up through his hair when Merc didn't immediately argue about this, his hands falling still on the table. The gremlin was watching him with that odd tolerant expression he sometimes got when he knew Mal was doing something wrong in the garage but was waiting for him to figure it out for himself.

"What?" he said irritably, at last.

"Nothing... Gimme the heads up when you've got the table arranged to your liking, mi'lord, and I'll serve dinner."

"Fuck you. Spit it out or shut up." Mal pulled away from the table, annoyed with himself as much as his partner. He hadn't come down for a fight but Merc was right. He got defensive over Neil, but with good reason.

"You know I'm right," Merc told him with a shrug. "He's trouble. The only times you get all OCD on me are when you believe I'm right about something but you can't back down."

"I don't have OCD, which is a real medical condition by the way. I am meticulous and I'm also giving myself a reason not to come over there and kick your stubborn arse around this kitchen, and you know it." Mal glared at him.

"Come on then. I'm ready for you." Merc carried on inspecting the contents of the pot as if it held all the mysteries of life. "Whenever you are."

"Fuck right off." Mal's voice shook and he clamped down hard on his temper. It would not do to start a row with Mercurio tonight. The shop was Merc's and he would be well within his rights to throw them both out on the street if he thought they would bring trouble to his door.

"Then you run out of smart answers," Merc added, nodding. "How you gonna keep a shield up, day in day out, on the whole shop, when you're hurt and just about ready to drop?"

"Let me worry about that." Mal twitched one of the forks a fraction of an inch to the left and studied it critically so he didn't have to meet Merc's eye again.

Merc didn't reply this time but his canny silence was almost worse than his pointed arguing. As Mal was reaching to adjust the fork again, a small sound carried down from the stairway, nothing alarming, but enough to make Mal pause and listen. Another tiny noise filtered down. Definitely a whimper.

Mal moved faster than his companion could react, running for the stairs, his heart suddenly pounding hard. He should have stayed up there and made sure Neil didn't overstretch himself. He was too badly hurt to be left alone. What had he been thinking?

"What is it?" he called as he reached the foot of the stairs. "What's wrong?"

No answer. Everything was quiet.

He hit the stairs running, taking them two at a time in his rush to get to the top. His first thought was the bathroom. Maybe Neil had decided not to wait for help and taken a fall, but the small, tiled toilet cubicle was empty, as was the shower room. Which left his own room...

He pushed open the door ready to throw up a shield in case of attack, but Neil was alone, still writhing uncomfortably on the bed. Mal stopped in the doorway, perplexed.

"What is it? Can I help?"

Neil jerked then went still. He blinked a few times then focused.

"What's wrong?" He repeated Mal's words back to him.

"Are you okay?" Mal panted.

Neil looked at him, his eyes big and dark but mostly confused. "Not really. Sort of. I was sleeping… I think. Did something happen?"

"You shouted. I thought you'd…" *Been attacked. Been abducted again. Killed, maybe?* Mal bit down on the insides of his mouth for a second, trying to push that fleeting moment of panic away. "Hurt yourself," he finished lamely.

True to form, instead of being angry with Mal for waking him, Neil said, "I'm sorry." He paused. "I-I was…" He pressed his lips together for a moment. "Just a nightmare."

"Oh." Malachai caught his breath for a while longer. His pulse was slowing but the shock and concern still had his adrenaline running high. He forced a wan smile. "There's nothing to be sorry for. We all get bad dreams from time to time."

Neil slowly struggled to sit up, wincing all the way. "Need to use the bathroom," he said, looking like he was dreading the prospect.

"Okay…" Mal hesitated. "You need a hand…or should I just get out of the way?"

Neil looked uncertain. "I think I can…" He stopped mid-thought as he touched a foot down on the floor. Mal winced in sympathy. Neil had heroically refused his help to get down from the truck and back indoors but, since then, he had been pretty much immobile and now he was hobbling like a three-legged calf.

"Uuuhh..." He exhaled. "I might need help getting there."

That much he could do. Gallantly he crouched to let Neil reach up to his shoulder. "Put your arm around my neck and lean on me. Let me walk you over," he said, practicality coming to the fore.

Neil put his arm around him, moving gingerly. Inch by inch, Mal shuffled him over to the bathroom but when he got him to the toilet and let go, Neil swayed and grabbed for the wall. He took a couple deep breaths and swallowed. "Okay, I can..."

"You might wanna sit," Mal said with a crooked smile. "I won't think badly of you, if you do."

"Not sure I'll be able to get back up." Neil's pale cheeks were a bit pink when he said, "This is so embarrassing. Can you hold me up for a minute, please?"

This time Mal hung back for a few moments longer. Which gave Neil's blush time to deepen to a soft, rosy hue. That made up his mind for him. If this was manipulation as Merc always seemed to think, it was damned subtle stuff.

"C'mere," he said gruffly, sliding one arm back under Neil's with difficulty, since the toilet cubicle was barely large enough for them both to stand abreast. "Is that...? Um, can you manage with one hand?"

From downstairs he heard Merc's yell, compounding the awkwardness of the situation. "Hey! What's going on up there? You want me to crank up the radio and put out a nine-one-one?"

Which was a joke because they both knew, even if Merc could get a signal, no one would send a paramedic unit Downtown with darkness falling.

"It's fine. I'll be down in a minute," Mal yelled back while Neil was fiddling with his zipper.

After a moment there was the sound of his stream hitting the water in the bowl and, ever so slightly, Mal could feel Neil relax against him. Neil finished up and got himself zipped. Mal took a step back, his arm still around him, and Neil took a stumbling step as well. Figuring it would be easier and less painful, Mal just bent and scooped him up and carried him back to bed. Neil's face was a lovely shade of red by the time he got him there.

Merc came in as Mal was setting Neil down, two steaming bowls in his hands. He set them down on the bedside table without a word and left just as silently.

Mal looked from Neil to the door and back again with a tiny twitch of his lips.

"Oooookay, so maybe someone's nose is a bit out of joint."

Neil must have been in too much pain to worry because he didn't apologize.

"Are you hungry?" Mal asked. "It's good stuff."

Taking his time, Neil reached for one of the bowls, picked it up and tried a spoonful. Mal smiled encouragement and took the other bowl before sitting down beside him. They ate in companionable quiet and Neil got most of the soup eaten then set the bowl aside and lay back. Mal finished his own soup and stood.

"I dreamed my dad found me," Neil said. "He sent the shadow fire after you to get to me."

"Meh, I can handle shadow fire." Mal was disturbed by the dream but he made sure not to let that show. And he hoped that he wouldn't have to prove that to Neil any time in the immediate future because the last two days had him exhausted.

Neil stared at him then looked away. Disappointed not to have garnered more of a response, Mal shoved himself to his feet and had started to go when Neil said, "Could you stay a while?"

He didn't try to check the brighter smile that put on his face but turned back to Neil, tucking his thumbs into the pockets of his jeans and leaning against the wall, just watching him. Neil was thin and starved and wary, like a stray cat come in from the street, but all of that could be fixed, given enough time. He was evidence enough of that.

"Sure," he said, moving the dishes and coming to sit by the low bed again. "If you want me to."

Neil tucked a hand under his cheek and bent his knees, curling up on his side, facing Mal. "Tell me something," Neil said.

"What?" Mal tilted his head back to look at him.

"I don't know. Anything. Tell me something that makes you happy."

He had to think about that. It was not that he was unhappy here, but since coming to the States, he had been forced to redefine his criteria for happiness. Thinking back to his life before this was akin to remembering some old movie that he'd watched on the screens back at his family home in Ireland as a boy. He was detached from all that and it felt weird to think that once such transient things had been so important to him that he couldn't imagine life without them.

"This makes me happy," he said with a smile. "Having a place that I can be safe in, somewhere that I feel at home. I think I spent my whole life looking for such a place. And it took me a long time to realize that it's not always true, the nonsense they tell you in stories and school, about family being your home. You can make family out of anything. It took me a long time to understand that I didn't have to accept the way things had been mapped out for me." He paused because Neil's eyes had glazed. "Sorry. I'm rambling. I'm not used to talking about myself, I guess. Out of practice."

A tiny smile flicked across Neil's lips. "No, I was just thinking, that sounds nice. How did you meet Mercurio?"

Mal laughed at that. "It's kind of embarrassing. He...ah, he bought me out of a contract. Mercurio collects shit like me, stuff that's broken. And he — he fixes it. Then, usually he sells it on, but I guess no one wanted a second-hand alchemist, so he's stuck with me."

The fledgling smile vanished from Neil's face. "Oh."

Mal sat up quickly, shaking his head at the expression his words had conjured. "It really isn't as bad as all that. I must be useful and that's a good thing. Apart from when I was in the paras, I'd never been much use to anyone before, not in a practical way. I mean, when I was driving, I was a commodity and I made a name for myself but none of it was really worth anything. What I do here helps people out. It's a good thing."

"I didn't realize he...owned you," Neil said, so quiet it was almost a whisper.

"He doesn't, but I work for him. I kind of owe him. Not in a bad way." Mal pressed a grin on his face again. "He's a grumpy old bear, but he's a good boss. The best I've had. I know where I stand with him. And I'd trust him with my life. He's my family now. And that's what makes me happy. Since...well...since I was a kid really, I never had that."

"But you said he bought you," Neil said.

"No. He bought me out," Mal corrected. "I was working for Vargas and he owed Merc money for a job. He couldn't pay up and so Mercurio said he would take me on as collateral. Del told him that I was worth more than he owed Merc. So they worked out a deal. Part of that is the fuel consignment that I make for them."

A small line appeared between Neil's brows. "You worked for Vargas?"

Mal nodded. "Uh-huh. When I first came here, I was looking for a community that would accept me for who I am. There's plenty of prejudice against those of us with fae blood in this city. The cops don't like us. The sorcerers don't like us. Underhill is the New Black, if you'll forgive the analogy. Vargas might be a dick but he's one of us."

"At least you're not demon bred," Neil said.

"There are worse things to be," Mal replied, opting for diplomacy. "At least demons are natural creatures. Being demonic doesn't make you any more prone to evil than any other man is. Those that actively choose a dark path..." He broke off and shuddered.

"Like my dad," Neil said.

And they were back around to that, and Neil's nightmare. Surprisingly Neil didn't dwell on it and moved onto something unexpected.

"Do you trust Drasnil?"

Mal uttered a short laugh and turned it into a cough because, from the look on Neil's face, that wasn't the response he was expecting.

"About as much as I'd trust any of the cluricaun," he elaborated. "Drasnil isn't malicious like some of them. He's been sober for about thirty years. That's pretty much unheard of amongst his kind. When his brother's had a skinful, he can be a vicious bitch, but Felipe... Yeah, I guess I trust him. Why?"

"He wanted me to trust him and I told him I might, if he told you where I was."

"You did, huh? Well, he did as you asked. I guess you have your answer right there. He didn't have to come looking for me." Mal leaned back against the wall again. "Though I have no doubt he will also figure out a way that this will cost me." He waved away the look of concern in Neil's eyes. "Don't worry. I'll sort it."

"Why should it cost you anything? I'm the one that asked him."

Mal laughed at his question. "Because that's the way we roll, baby. If one of us does you a favor, there's generally a fee involved. And Felipe has already worked out that he's done me a favor too. It will be okay. He's not going to get me to build him a palace of gold and move it Underhill in a night. He moves with the times. Shame we don't still have the Maserati. He'd have taken that as payment, no hesitation."

Neil blanched. "How could you possibly owe him that big of a favor just for telling you where I was?"

"Take it easy, I said not to worry, didn't I? You could say it's a fae thing. A repayment of significant value is always a good idea."

"But...that's not fair."

"Neil. Relax."

Mal didn't think he would, but Neil surprised him again by subsiding, some of the tension leaving his body.

"Maybe you should try and get some sleep," Mal suggested.

Neil nodded then went still. "I'm afraid I'll have nightmares again."

"Doesn't anything make them better?" Mal asked, more tenderly. When he had been small, his mother would sing to him to keep bad dreams at bay. He still slept better when he had music to listen to. The small wind-up radio that had been part of a vast salvage lot Merc had picked up for about twenty-five bucks on Cheapside lived under his pillows permanently. "Would it help if you had something to listen to, to take your mind off things?"

Neil started to shrug one shoulder but stopped with a wince. Mal thought he might get the radio anyway. He waited, sensing Neil was on the verge of saying something but was hesitant about it. At last, Neil said, "Would you stay and talk to me? Until I fell asleep?"

"I'm that exciting, huh?" Mal winked at him when Neil looked as if he might take that remark seriously. "It's fine. What else d'you want to hear about?"

"Can you tell me about where you grew up? What it's like there?"

Mal had to cast his mind back hard to remember what was real and what just felt that way. His childhood had been a sequence of trips, back and forth from England to Ireland, passed from his parents to his grandparents and back again then, when he was old enough for school, another stop on the merry go round. So he talked about his maternal grandfather's house in Berkshire and his memories of the seemingly endless polished corridors with their familiar treasures — the huge vase at the top of the split staircase that for most of his childhood was taller than he was — and the enormous stuffed bear in the hall that had always scared him when he was a tot. He briefly closed his eyes and once more he was in the expansive gardens with his grandmother, watching her trimming the roses and listening to her talk about the past, when there had been huge parties held at the house with all the great and the good, up from London for the weekends.

As Malachai continued to talk about how he imagined some of those parties to be, he turned his head and watched Neil's eyes start to close, then flutter open, then softly close again. He seemed to be fighting it but before long his breathing evened out into sleep. Mal leaned his head back against the wall and closed his own eyes again, for a moment.

He woke up to darkness and a small whimpering cry. Neil had rolled over at some point and had his back to him, all scrunched up against the wall. His shoulders shook, whether with cold, or fear, or something else, Mal wasn't sure, but the next sound he made was more of a sob.

"Hey!" Mal kept his voice soft, but he could not bear to hear it. That small, strangled noise ripped at all the defenses he kept wrapped so tight around his own heart, threatening to drag him down into Neil's solitary sorrow. When the lad did not respond, he struggled awkwardly to his knees, biting down on his lips to keep from growling in pain as his muscles and joints protested after the long period of stillness. He held back for a moment then reached out and touched Neil's shoulder, kneading there with his fingertips. "Hey…shhh… It's just a dream. It'll be okay. I'm here. I won't let anything hurt you."

Neil's shoulders shook, but he didn't startle or struggle away when Mal touched him. In the dark Mal could make out that Neil had his hands covering his face and he was taking ragged breaths as he tried hard not to cry, and failed.

"I don't know what to do anymore," Neil murmured in a broken voice.

"What do you mean?" Mal asked, keeping his words as gentle as possible. "What do you think you need to do?"

He levered himself up to sit on the edge of the bed so that he could still stroke Neil's arm without crippling his knees.

"I mean, what comes next...? My mom's gone and I just ran away and left her..." He wouldn't uncurl from the wall, or lower his hands, and if anything he only shook harder as he fought back the tears.

Mal was torn. He could empathize because he had been far younger than Neil when his own mother was taken from him. Neil was no longer a child, though. How to comfort him was a conundrum. He lowered himself onto the mattress and put his arms around Neil, careful of his injuries. He did not pull Neil back, just let him steer things, but he rested his cheek against Neil's shoulder gently.

The crying didn't stop, but Neil didn't draw away from him, either. Whatever else Neil might be feeling — grief, pain, whatever — he was too hurt to play hard and resist the offer of comfort. Neil let Mal hold him until he cried himself out and slipped back into sleep.

Mal lay there for a long time after Neil's little, hiccupping sobs died out and his muscles went slack. He remained sprawled on the bed with Neil against his chest and listened to the sounds of the old building that had become as familiar to him as his own breathing. He heard Merc's slow, steady tread up the stairs and steeled himself for the rebuke as the old man passed by his door, but it never came. Merc went into his own room and shut the door solidly. After a while the light under his door went out and the bedsprings creaked as he settled down for the night.

Mal closed his eyes again. This time he let the world slip away for a while and dreams claimed him.

Chapter Twelve

Neil woke to stiffness and pain, also to the strange sensation of warmth all along his back and the weight of an arm around him. He stayed as still as he could so he wouldn't wake Mal. The crying had been even more embarrassing than needing help to pee. A part of him had wanted to tell Mal to leave him be so he wouldn't see the tears, but it had felt too good to hear his soft murmurs and be held.

Comforting, yes, but dangerous. He wished he could turn over and burrow into the strong arms wrapped around him, snuggle into his warmth…maybe kiss him good morning. And the warming coil of fantasy died there. He could never do that, not to Malachai. It would be too easy to ask for things…ask him to stay in the knowledge that there was no chance he would refuse. It would be an awful thing to repay all his kindness by twisting it into something Mal didn't want.

Malachai shifted, rolling to his back and taking his warmth with him. Neil carefully rolled over too. The bed was narrow enough that there wasn't a way for them not to touch while he did it. When he could see Mal's face, he filled his eyes for a moment, saving how he looked in his head for later when all he'd be able to do was steal glances. Then Mal opened his eyes. If he'd torn his gaze away, he might have been able to play it off like he'd looked for only a moment, but once those silvery-gray eyes settled on him, he couldn't look at anything else. Before he could talk himself out of it, he leaned in and pressed his lips to Mal's.

To his surprise, Malachai did not throw him off the bed and stalk out. He lay on his back a while longer, just watching Neil, and his mouth moved under the kiss as if he was trying to speak but unable to make words. Mal stroked one gentle hand up and down his back and when Neil finally broke the kiss, he offered a perplexed smile.

"What was that for?"

"Because...I wanted to. Because every time I've thought I should go one way, lately, it's turned out I should have gone another. I didn't want to talk myself out of kissing you."

Mal reached up to stroke a wisp of Neil's hair away from his face. His gaze shone like moonlight through the darkest clouds and his words were still very mild and bemused when he said, "I had no idea that you were even thinking of me that way. What with everything that's been going on with you. I'd have kinda thought that kissing was the last thing on your mind."

"Should I not have done it?" he asked, wondering if he'd gotten things wrong again.

"Don't get me wrong, it was a very pleasant wake up call," Mal assured him. "But I wasn't expecting it. That's not why I stayed with you last night."

Neil studied his expression, tried to fit it with the words, see if there was something he was missing. It didn't feel like there was any hidden meaning behind them, just concern. Making sure he wasn't misunderstanding anything.

"I know that," Neil said softly. "I didn't kiss you to repay you. I really did just want to."

"Well...that's fine then. Thank you." Mal gave him another of those lopsided smiles. Neil was starting to recognize that he did this when he was a bit unsure of himself. Mal didn't often give himself away — he kept what he was feeling pretty tight — but that smile was a brief window into his mind and the glimpse that Neil was getting through that window was of a person that didn't open up easily. "I wouldn't let Merc see you do that, though. Not that I'm embarrassed about it. But he'll put two and two together and make six, you see."

Neil had been just about to ask if he could kiss him again but that stopped him cold. He couldn't argue it. He'd thought it himself, that it was too easy to get caught up and make Mal feel things he didn't really feel. "I can't blame him for thinking I might do something to you, use you, that way." He pulled back some. "It was just a kiss, though, I wouldn't try to...do anything bad to you."

Mal smiled and drew his face down closer so that he could return the kiss, but just briefly to the tip of his nose. "That's good. I'm relieved to hear it."

Even though he'd just said he couldn't blame Merc for being wary of what he might do, it hurt him more than he cared to admit, knowing Mal was relieved that he wasn't using his abilities on him. He pulled back, telling himself he was being stupid. He didn't even trust himself. Why should he expect Malachai to?

That gentle hand stroked his hair again, though. Mal said, "It was nice to wake up with someone this morning. I've been on my own for a long time. Thank you for not wriggling out and running away."

A shivery tingle ran all the way from Neil's nape to the bottom of his spine at the touch of Malachai's fingers brushing his hair. He had been trying to put two words together in response, but every last one scattered when Mal smiled at him. Then it hit him. He'd been so worried about using Mal's lust against him that he'd failed to notice there wasn't any. Oh, how stupid could he be? If ever he'd wanted the ground to just open up and swallow him it was now.

"Oh my… Mal, I'm so sorry. You don't have to be nice to me. I won't kiss you again, okay."

An odd expression flitted across Mal's features but was gone just as quickly, stored behind that mild, interested expression again. Was he annoyed? Disappointed?

"You're right," he said at last and Neil's spirits sank. "I don't have to be nice, but it's the decent thing. And I genuinely have no problems with treating you nicely, Neil. I just want to get you back on your feet again."

"I didn't mean nice like that. I mean you don't have to tell me things you think I want to hear. I can tell you didn't feel anything when I kissed you. You could have just said you didn't like it."

Mal blinked. His features gave nothing away but he said, "I could. That wouldn't have been true, though. And you just said you didn't want me to lie."

"I... What?" Neil stopped mid-thought. "But...are you sure?"

Mal glanced around the room as if he was expecting something to happen then grinned at him. "I'd like to think I know my own mind. It was nice, Neil. Yes. I enjoyed it."

Neil frowned. He had to be just placating him. There was nothing, not a whiff of lust on him. But it didn't feel like a lie. And why would he lie anyway? So what was he supposed to believe, his senses or the words? Maybe he'd just been more asleep than awake and somehow missed it. Without thinking he asked, "Can I kiss you again?"

Was he imagining it, or was that the tiniest hint of a blush under Malachai's dark-golden skin and the redder shadow of his stubble? Interesting.

"I — um — er...yeah. I suppose so. If you want to." Mal settled back down among the pillows again and looked up at him with a curious twinkle in those silvery eyes.

Conscious that this was not exactly an enthusiastic invitation, Neil searched deep into his eyes. It was oh so tempting to try to pull him under, but not only was the idea repellant, it would also defeat the purpose. He lifted his hand to Mal's cheek, spreading his fingers so they fanned over his jaw. His fingertips tingled at the touch of his skin. He leaned closer, until there was only a breath between their lips, and savored how warm he was. Then he nudged that extra bit closer to touch his mouth to Malachai's.

This time Mal's long copper lashes brushed like delicate feathers on his skin as he closed his silver eyes. Mal's jaws parted and his lips moved in effortless synchronicity with Neil's, kissing him back.

Disturbingly, he still didn't get the familiar buzz of lust, but if he pushed his senses deeper, he was enveloped in a warm fuzz of protectiveness that made him quiver all over.

There should have been at least a trace of lust, but Neil's seeking found none. There was something — something that felt warm, and Neil dove after it. He slid his hand into Mal's hair, cupped his fingers around the back of his neck. He flicked his tongue teasingly between his lips, then deeper, tasting his mouth.

There was more of that elusive heat and Neil chased the spark, pressing not just his mouth but his body up to Mal's side. Something changed, that sweet warmth spread over him, raced down with a rush of blood. Hot now, and not just coming from within Mal, but like Neil was the source as well.

He couldn't remember the last time he'd kissed someone because he wanted to, but he recognized the desire when it hit him. His cock stiffened and he rolled his hips then gasped as his injuries protested.

Mal rested gentle hands on his arms and nudged Neil's nose with his own. The heat still blossomed but spread its flickering flames through him gently, instead of rising to an inferno. Mal's lips came back to his but caught them lightly, sucking and nibbling on the lower then the upper one, like he was teasing him back into orbit.

"Shhh…" he whispered and the softness of his breath caressed Neil's wet skin like balm. "There's no rush, take your time. You're hurting and I'll still be here later."

Still be here for what? Neil almost asked him. Instead he gave in to the pain and settled back in a more comfortable position. Mal slipped out of bed and left the room, and Neil closed his eyes. He could still feel the softness of Mal's lips on his own, taste him on his tongue. The pleasant warmth lingered on his skin and deeper inside. He hugged that feeling to his middle, wanting to hold on to it as long as possible. It wasn't lust, but he craved more of it, was hungry for another long taste already. It didn't feel at all like the usual hunger he kept chained. This was actually…really good.

* * * *

By the end of the week, Neil's bruises were faded. He healed faster than someone with purely human blood and, while he still was tender, he was at least up and moving around under his own power. Mal kept trying to get him to sit, to rest, but the stillness was starting to drive Neil crazy.

On top of that, he couldn't stop thinking of the kiss he'd shared with Mal and that wonderful feeling of warmth that had come with it. There hadn't been a repeat and Mal hadn't slept in the same bed with him again. If anything, Mal seemed to be taking pains to make sure he gave Neil plenty of space. It didn't stop Neil craving him.

The last two days Neil had sat in the garage, watching while Merc and Malachai worked on various projects. He'd tried to help but Mal wouldn't let him lift anything and kept shooing him back to his stool. Neil tried not to be obvious but he watched Mal—just from the corner of his eye, if Mal was facing his way, but when he turned his back, Neil filled his eyes with the way Mal moved, the breadth of his shoulders, the lean lines of his back and especially the curve of his ass in those tight, ripped jeans.

Mercurio had been weirdly cordial since Mal had brought him back from Vargas' house. He had said nothing gruff or accusatory at all and pretty much ignored Neil while he sat watching them work.

Mal had just bent over the engine compartment of a beat-up Buick and Neil's eyes were instantly drawn to his backside, imagining how he had looked when he'd walked in on him that one morning in the bathroom, fresh from a shower.

Mal straightened and Neil glanced away again quickly, before Malachai saw the smoldering look — and noticed Merc looking right at him. *Caught.* He tried to stop it but his damn cheeks felt like they were about to burst into flame and he knew he was in all probability glowing red. He shifted on the stool and pretended to be very interested in something on the floor.

"This is screwed," Mal said, extracting the ragged fan belt and tossing it over one shoulder.

"I have a spare up in the storeroom that should fit this bitch," Mercurio told him. "In the box with the distributor parts we took off that old Chevvy. We might as well give it a try."

"I'll get it," Neil said, glad for an excuse to flee, but Merc stopped him before he even reached the doorway.

"Let Malachai get it, he'll be quicker. He knows what he's looking for," Merc said in his practical way.

Mal peered over the engine compartment at him quizzically for that but his partner just tipped his head in the direction of the stairs and, with a frown, Mal straightened and wiped his oily hands on a strip of rag before heading up the stairs. Once he was safely a floor above them, Merc came over and confronted Neil.

"Malachai Valentine is a good man, for a fairy," he said in a low, warning tone. "A good friend. If I catch you putting the moves on him, in any way, I will make sure that you are out of here. Do you understand me?"

Neil laughed and the brittle bitterness of the sound surprised him. "I don't think you have anything to worry about. Even if I was trying to 'put the moves on him', which I'm not…not in the way you're thinking, he doesn't have any interest in me at all. He couldn't be any safer from me."

"I've seen the way you look at him and I call bullshit," Merc grumbled, shaking his head. "Clearly you've been looking for an opportunity to get your hooks in. He's way out of your league, kid. And in ways you can't even start to imagine."

That struck far too close to the mark for comfort. He looked up at Merc, ignoring the sour churning in his stomach that was part anxiety but mostly anger. "You think I don't already understand that? I told you, he's not interested in me. If there was any bit of lust in him when he looked at me, I'd know it. There isn't. Not that I would ever use that against him if there was. I like him, that's all." *A lot! So much it hurts.*

Merc fired an odd look his way at that, as if it were a concept too far out there for him to grasp that someone like Neil was capable of basic human emotions like friendship.

"Well, I like him too," he said at last. "So long as I can see he ain't coming to any harm, you and me will be fine. I trust his judgment, young man. But sometimes he lets stuff blind him and he ain't so careful. That's all."

Merc looked as if he might have said more but Mal called down from the landing, "Damn it, Mercurio. I can't find that fucking belt. Are you sure it's up here?"

"Look in the tool case!" Merc bellowed back up at him. Then raised an eyebrow and added, more quietly, "You see? He can't spot what's right under his nose. He's not worked out how to be around ordinary people, yet. How's he meant to cope with a thrice-damned incubus?"

Neil clenched his jaw so tight it made a muscle in his cheek twitch. He wanted to stare Merc down, make him take back those words, but how could he when he agreed with him?

"I may be demon-bred but I'm human too. I would never hurt him. Just the opposite. I tried to protect him, when Vargas attacked him. Didn't you see the shadow fire? Do you have any idea what it cost me to do that?"

Merc's lips tightened too, but he just said, "It was in all of our best interests not to let that bastard take you."

Neil huffed and gave up. Merc was determined to think the worst of him and Neil had no ammunition to defend himself. He was after all an incubus and there was good reason not to trust him.

Mal came back down so quietly that he made them both jump. That had to be some kind of fairy trick because Neil had pretty sharp senses, but the red-haired man just seemed to appear out of the shadows at the entrance to the stairwell.

"What's up?" he asked, casually tossing Merc the replacement belt, which must have been in the tool case all along. "You both look like someone ate your last donut or something."

Mercurio shrugged and turned back toward the car he'd been working on. Neil had no idea how he could tell Mal about the conversation without sounding like he was tattling, or bitching, so he just said, "Nothing," with his eyes fixed on Merc's retreating back.

Mal followed his gaze and frowned briefly but he didn't push the issue. He did make a point of chatting with Neil about the stuff he was doing on the car from then on, presumably to keep him in the loop, but it could have just been because he was kind like that.

* * * *

Despite Merc's warning Neil couldn't keep his eyes off Mal. As one day rolled into the next, and the next, he watched him more and more. While Merc occasionally shot him a glare, he didn't try to warn him off again. Nor did Mal seem to notice. The one night spent in Mal's arms and the kiss in the morning began to feel like it was a dream.

Eventually Mal let him start helping in the garage, and even while he was working on his alchemy, which was really interesting. Neil couldn't quite put together how he took one thing and made it shift into another thing but he felt the energy of it clear enough and got a big charge out of it. By the time the beating Crow gave him was nothing more than a memory and could no longer be traced on his skin, he knew intuitively what items Mal was going to reach for when he was brewing something up, and handed them to him before he'd done more than extend a hand in the direction of his workbench.

Mal was working on an order for a potion that would cure a certain virulent form of tree rot and stretched his hand out. Neil thought he needed the wolfsbane but second-guessed himself. "Wolfsbane or henbane?"

Mal lifted his head and peered through his forelock, briefly deliberating this before he agreed, "The Hyoscyamus niger, I think. Henbane. It may just do the trick. Don't get it on yourself, it's a bit lethal if you want to stay awake. I don't recommend the hangover that comes with it." He flashed a smile as Neil handed the vial over carefully. "How'd you learn about herbs?"

"The greenhouses where I worked grew all sorts of plants, not just vegetables. I had to learn what they all were because some of them were meant to be used for medicine as well as food."

Mal glanced sidelong at him, not taking his attention off the vials he was working on for more than a second. "That's useful to know. How does a sorcerer's son come to be working in a glasshouse in the first place, anyway?"

Neil ran his fingers lightly along the labeled jars of herbs, gathering his thoughts on how to answer that question. Or rather, how much to answer, how truthful to be. A lifetime of conditioning to avoid questions, hide what he was, lie if he had to, warred with the desire to put his trust in someone. No, not someone. In Malachai.

"My dad took good care of my mom." He paused, testing to see how truthful that statement was. It was not untrue, but he didn't really know how to express the complexities of his homelife without sounding like he was spilling his guts to a counselor. "In a way. I mean, financially, he took care of everything. The house, the car, anything she could want, he made sure she had. But all those things, they came at a price. Once I was old enough to figure that out, I wanted to make sure I wasn't completely dependent on him that way. So, I got a job. I liked it, working with the plants.

Helping things grow. My mom liked plants too. She knew which herbs were good for healing, she even worked them into the amulet I used to get away from the Bone Men."

Mal's expression sobered but he murmured, "She sounds like a smart lady."

"She was smart and she taught me some of what she knew. I think she would have taught me more if...if I wasn't going to be my father's familiar."

He saw the look of disgust flit across Mal's face then retreat behind his customary placid mask, but all Mal said was, "Sometimes life gets away from us. All we can do is try to be smart like your mother and take all the precautions we can. What did she use in the amulet she made for you?" Mal asked as he applied a few drops of henbane carefully to his concoction then corked the vial securely again, wiped it down with a clean cloth and passed it back over to Neil.

"Cayenne, rue, black pepper...um, monkshood, belladonna...black cohosh. I think that was all," Neil answered as he tucked the henbane back on the shelf.

"Sounds to me like she knew her stuff," Mal told him with a knowing smile. "Living with a sorcerer clearly rubbed off on her. Unless she learned her herb lore before she married him. Sometimes, mages make power bonds when they marry. It's a shame she didn't—" He closed his mouth on the sentence as if he'd changed his mind about uttering it. "We can put together something similar for you, if you'd like it. A protection charm."

"I don't have the same sort of magic she did. I can put the herbs together, but they would still just be herbs," Neil said.

"That's okay. I can do the mixing. The alchemy I use isn't all that different to charm building. I worked with a charm maker once." He finished off what he was working on and rose, fetching down some more jars from his shelves and adding small amounts of each into his retort. Neil noted a few of the herbs that he put in there but Mal asked him, "What else would you use, if you were making this?"

Neil gave it a moment's thought before saying, "Agrimony. Because it's good for reversing things. And cinquefoil."

"Why cinquefoil?"

"Because it's so common no one thinks to use it. But it strangles out other plants when it spreads." Neil shrugged. "I just think it's good at surviving."

Mal laughed. "Interesting. Okay, pass me that blue jar up there on the shelf end."

When Neil handed it down, he added a little to his mixture, but not very much. A few other ingredients were added until the formula was bubbling away with some vigor in the glass bulb and some small objects like dark beads were beginning to form inside the retort.

Neil bent to get a closer look.

"Not too close. Breathing those fumes wouldn't be healthy," Mal warned and Neil straightened.

"What are we going to put the charm on? I don't have the amulet I used on the Bone Men anymore."

"Hang on," Mal said and got up to rummage in one of the drawers of a long, metal unit that took up most of one wall in his little workshop. He came back holding a piece of silver chain with small silver keys and stars hanging off it at regular intervals. "Thought I remembered picking this up with a salvage lot recently," he said. "It's not got a catch, but I can fix that if it will do the trick."

Neil took the bracelet Mal handed him, looking at it thoughtfully.

"If you don't like it, I can find something else," Mal said.

"No, I like it. It's just, I was thinking of how the other charm worked. It was meant to be thrown on the ground to break the glass and that's what made the barrier. But, if those same Bone Men found me, or even if my dad found me, they wouldn't fall for that. I might not get a chance to take it off and throw it."

"What if the charm was in the catch?" Mal asked. "If the catch was forcibly broken, it would trigger the charm. Would that work?"

Neil looked from the bracelet to Mal. "Like, if someone grabbed it off my wrist?"

Mal nodded. "Exactly. Although we'd have to put a delay into it. Don't want it blowing your hand off or anything like that."

Neil wasn't sure if he was serious. "Um…yeah. I'd like to keep my hand. What are you cooking up in those herbs?"

Mal grinned at him. "A little something to put the stops on anyone that gets in the way of it. It should only be temporary, but if you trigger it, make sure that you back away and don't walk through the effect field. If someone is coming toward you, it should be enough to tie up their minds in confusion for long enough that you can escape."

Neil smiled back at him. "That's a pretty complex charm. You can really do that?"

"It's simple enough." Mal grinned at him. "I'm used to fixing stuff so it works properly. It's part of my job."

"I thought your job was working on cars?"

"That's part of it," Mal agreed, watching the combination of ingredients in his glass alembic until they emitted a bluish smoke. He removed it from the heat and capped it at both ends deftly.

"It seems like two very different things...making potions and things, and fixing cars. Did you always figure you'd do one or the other?"

Mal turned to him and heaved a weighty sigh as he set the smoke-filled globe on the worktop between them.

"Do you think I planned to spend my days hunkered down in a filthy garage cooking up cures for people that can't usually afford them? It wasn't on my itinerary when I was your age, I promise," he said.

Neil saw his lips twitch but Mal didn't quite manage a smile this time.

"So, what did you want to do?"

Mal shrugged. "I wanted to win every long-distance motor race on the international calendar, basically. Cars have been pretty much my life. I couldn't see beyond that future once I'd left school. I upset my mother by not taking my alchemical heritage seriously enough. I upset my father by... Where do I start? I wasn't ever enough for him. My father is an important figure in our society — one of the most important. He wanted me to go to university and study business finance, like he did. When my brother died, he planned to groom me to inherit his title and estates. I went into the military instead and bided my time there for a couple of years 'til I was twenty-one. All I really wanted was to claim my grandparents' trust fund, blow it all on fast cars and just get the fuck off that green rock on the edge of the Atlantic as fast as possible. My father's response was to disinherit me. He has remarried. Thus far, to the best of my knowledge, his only children with his new wife are daughters, which I'm sure will infuriate him."

Mal rarely sounded bitter about anything but there was no disguising the loathing in his voice when he spoke about his family.

"You raced cars?" Neil asked, changing the subject. "Like, combustion engine cars?"

"Exactly like those, yes." Mal managed a rather less forced grin. "Had I paid attention to my political and socioeconomic history classes I would have been more aware that the petrol engine was living on borrowed time, but—" He brought his hands together and heaved a sigh. "I didn't, so I lived in very blissful ignorance for about three and a half years, until I had a bad smash that basically wound up my career before the petroleum axe could."

"Is that what happened to your back? From the crash?" Neil asked.

Mal blinked again and Neil saw his face do that rapid recalculation where he was trying to think what to say instead of being completely frank.

"My back? Um...no. Well, I suppose the accident didn't do it much good, but it was my legs that were the most injured. I couldn't walk for about seven months. I came out here to see a specialist and it cost me just about everything I had. I wound up having to start again from scratch, with nothing."

"You couldn't walk? For seven months? That must have been really scary." On impulse, Neil leaned over and hugged him.

Mal managed a humorless laugh but he didn't wriggle away. "It was frustrating more than anything else," he said. "I was pretty much dependent on nurses and stuff. For everything. It was kind of embarrassing."

"That must be why you took such good care of me. You knew what it was like."

"I guess so." Mal shrugged. "I didn't really think I was doing that great a job. Not used to looking after other people. But I suppose I just...um... I dunno. I'm glad I did okay for you. And you seem a lot... *Better* feels like the wrong word but you seem like you're getting stronger."

Neil nodded and let him go, settling back to watch him finish up with the potion. He chewed on the fact that Mal had noticed he was well on his way to being completely healed and wondered if that was his way of leading up to saying it was time for him to go. He hadn't suggested it yet, but Neil figured it was only a matter of time. He thought there would have been more anxiety over that, where he would go and what he would do, since wherever he ended up, it wouldn't be with the money from the sale of the car. Instead, all he could think of was how he could talk Mal into letting him stay.

Chapter Thirteen

It had been a day over two weeks since Mal had walked into Del's cellar and taken Neil back home with him. In that time, the incubus had quickly become a fixture at the auto store and even Mercurio seemed less prickly around him. Mal felt okay to leave the pair of them together while he ran deliveries or picked up salvage. Most of the time, they managed not to wind up sulking at each other in his absence.

Neil had not tried to kiss him again and Malachai tried not to think too much about the reasons behind that. Maybe Neil had just been giving him what he thought Mal wanted from him in exchange for a roof over his head. Whatever his reasoning, Mal didn't feel comfortable pushing him for more, if that wasn't what Neil was happy with.

So they knuckled down and got on with their work and slowly Neil got stronger and less wary around them. He had an aptitude for the salvage side of things that Mercurio appreciated and the two of them had wasted no time, stripping down nineteen vehicles in that short period. The money and other goods—including, to his delight, a rather splendid Regency-period dining table—flowed in exchange for spare parts and scrap metal and all three of them ate well.

Mal came back from one of his drop-offs with a folding box bed in the back of their pickup. His back was not being helped by sleeping curled up on the sofa in the store front, which was way too short to be used as a permanent place to sleep. Neil had not extended an invitation to spend the night curled up with him again, so he figured it made more sense to get a proper mattress and try to actually get a decent night's sleep for once.

Neil came down from the workshop with a broken alternator unit from a Dodge van as he was trying to wrestle the box base down from the flatbed.

"Need a hand?" Neil asked.

"Sure," Mal said. It wasn't that it was heavy, but it was unwieldy. Neil hopped up into the truck and grabbed an end and that made the going much easier. It wasn't until they got it down that Neil seemed to notice what it was they were moving.

"Is this...for me?" he asked.

Mal flashed a grin at him as they got it down and he went back up for the folding mattress. "If you like. I was thinking I could sleep on it. I reckon it's a bit longer than the sofa. But you can try it out if you like." He wrestled the mattress down and dumped it on top of the box unit. "No idea where I'm gonna put it yet."

"Oh. Um, you don't have to do that. I mean, it is your bed and I'm really grateful you let me use it." They pushed and carried the new bed through the workshop and up the stairs while Neil talked, even though Mal still wasn't sure where to go with it. Neil stopped in the kitchen, as if he too were trying to figure it out. "We could just put it in your room?"

Mal laughed. "It's a bit of a tight squeeze with two in there, don't you think? And don't you... I mean, we have the room... I just need to rearrange stuff. It's your call."

Neil didn't answer him. He just grabbed the bed again and started tugging it toward the stairs. Mal helped to shove it from below and together they pushed, pulled and wedged it up the narrow staircase. At the top, Neil steered them into his room. He wriggled the bedside table out of the way, then moved the new bed up next to Mal's and unfolded it.

"It fits here," Neil said.

"Cozy." Mal laughed, but he went back down for the mattress and dragged it up, positioning it on top of the box. Once in place, it wasn't a bad height match for his old single, and he went in search of some sheets to complete the arrangement.

Neil was sitting on the bed when he returned and Mal dropped the bedclothes in his lap. "Comfortable enough for you?" he asked.

"It's okay actually," Neil told him.

"You do realize I am going to have to climb over you to get out?" Mal observed.

Neil stood with the sheets in his hands, one of his rare smiles flitting across his lips. "Help me get these on."

Mal took an end and they each went to a corner, tugging and adjusting to make the bed up. Once they got that done, Neil reached across to the oversize quilt on Mal's bed and tugged it over both mattresses so it looked like one double bed instead of two.

"Happy?" Mal raised an eyebrow but couldn't quite keep his grin at Neil's determination in check.

Neil turned toward him and the hint of a smile that had been there before had bloomed, softening his features from the serious expression he usually wore.

"Yes," he said simply. He took a step. Just one, and Mal had no idea how he could put such sultry suggestion into a single step. Neil slid a hand up his chest. "When I kissed you before, you said there was time, you'd be here later. Is it later yet?"

"Ah, I see where this is heading." Mal laid one of his hands over the cool fingers on his sternum and moved to sit down on the edge of the new bed. "I'd say it's probably a good bit later," he conceded, patting the duvet beside him.

Instead of sitting next to him, Neil moved between his knees and cupped his cheeks in his hands. The look he gave him was focused, but the scrunching between his brows suggested he was also quite confused. It didn't stop Neil from laying a kiss on him.

Mal returned it, curling his fingers around Neil's lean hips to pull him in closer. It had been long ago, in another life, when he had last felt anything like the urge to kiss and touch another person the way he wanted to with Neil. As their lips parted and he drew a breath, he already knew that today would probably bring that dry spell to a close.

Damn it, Merc was going to be mad at him, but he could not be a monk for the rest of his life. Mal could count on the fingers of half a hand how many times he had even felt desire for someone since coming here. None of those urges had been acted upon.

He stroked one hand up the nape of Neil's neck and lay back, gently pulling Neil down with him. Screw what Mercurio thought! He needed this and his needs were no one's business but his own.

And Neil's, of course.

"Are you okay like this?" he whispered against Neil's cheek.

"Yes." Neil murmured agreement, trailing more kisses along Mal's temple and into his hair. Neil shifted, moving one leg over the top of Mal's and reaching over the end of the newly combined beds to nudge the door so it swung shut. The movement pressed Neil's thigh between Mal's legs, then Neil's lips were back on his, hungry kisses that pulled at him and delved in at the same time.

After a few moments, Neil pushed up on his arms and looked down at him, and that puzzled look was back. "Do you want me to stop, Malachai?"

Mal knew that his eyes must have widened because Neil kind of mirrored him and he shook his head right away.

"Good grief, no. Why would I want you to stop?"

"You tell me," Neil ventured and Mal reached up to stroke his loose, dark golden curls tenderly.

"I don't want you to stop," Mal confirmed and he had never been surer of anything in his life. "This feels amazing. I love it."

"Are you sure?" Neil asked.

Mal just lifted his eyebrows a bit and Neil's expression turned sheepish.

"I mean...it's just... I can't feel the, um... I don't feel any lust coming off of you."

Mal blinked then laughed. He couldn't help it. The laughter bubbled up from his throat.

"We're only just kissing, Neil. Steady on!" he exclaimed. "Did you never hear the phrase, 'don't run before you can walk'?"

"I can tell if someone wants me without them touching me, sometimes from a just a glance. I can't tell anything with you."

Mal brushed the backs of his fingers along Neil's cheek and the curve of his jaw. He was so beautiful. Even more so when he was perplexed like this. He could almost taste Neil's frustration.

"Did you ever try to seduce someone that was half-fae before?"

"Madran. I don't know if he was half, though. But, I wasn't trying to seduce you, honest."

"Oh really?" Mal grinned and Neil blushed.

"Well, not using the incubus power. It doesn't matter, I'm glad you don't want me to stop. It's just a strange feeling, not being sure if you, um…like what I'm doing."

Mal snaked his arms around Neil and pulled him up close again then applied his mouth to those soft lips, letting his tongue wriggle between them to taste Neil's mouth. There was nothing remotely unpleasant about that experience, so he enjoyed it for a longer while then stroked his way down to Neil's backside, squeezing him gently there and pushing up more intimately with him until their bodies were joined from chest to knees.

"Mm-uhh…" Neil moaned as Mal kneaded his ass. Neil bucked his hips, one hand tangling in Mal's hair as the kiss grew more passionate. He was riding his leg and squirming against him. The top of Neil's thigh brushed his balls and the underside of his cock and Neil went still for a moment, like he skipped a beat, then relaxed, almost melting into Malachai's arms. The hungry edge to his kisses came back with a vengeance, like he wanted to devour him, or maybe dive into him.

Mal locked his arms around him and rolled, bringing Neil under him, and Neil reached up, his hands gripping the back of Mal's shirt, a short gasp on his lips before he bucked his hips up, rubbing on him more firmly. Having satisfied himself that Neil was not uncomfortable beneath him, Malachai settled back down on him, letting his body roll in smooth waves against Neil's. It felt so good that he even questioned why he'd held off for so long after his split from Emeline. But he did not want to think about her now. Not here with Neil beneath him, hungry for him, as he was for Neil.

He broke the kiss for a moment, touching his lips to Neil's soft cheek, just above the line of his razor, then to his ear.

"This feels good. You maybe wanna do more?" he whispered as he squeezed Neil tight in his arms. They were so close that he could feel the ridge of Neil's lean hip digging into his side and the outline of Neil's cock nudging up against his jeans, pressing against Mal's swelling erection.

Neil nodded and tugged at Mal's shirt impatiently. "I want to touch you, everywhere."

He reached for the fly of Mal's jeans. Malachai caught his breath and knelt up, astride him, to unbutton his shirt. He kept it on his shoulders for the time being. It still felt weird to uncover his back and though he trusted Neil well enough, he reached down instead to pull up the borrowed T-shirt Neil was wearing, exposing the long, pale stretch of his midriff and admiring the tone he was already beginning to get on his abs from good, regular meals and all the hard work he'd done on the cars. Mal stroked his palm down Neil's belly and hooked his fingers in the waist of his jeans, just tugging on them lightly as he watched Neil wrestle with his unfamiliar belt and fly. He found himself wondering, was this the first time Neil had tried to get another man undressed, or was it just eagerness making his fingers temporarily clumsy?

A few more fumbles and Neil got Mal's jeans unzipped for him then yanked harder at his belt loops, working the coarse denim down his hips. He fanned his hand over the bulge at the front of Mal's briefs, stroking the outline of his cock with the gentlest of touches. Some of the confusion smoothed from Neil's brow as he mapped the hardness of his cock. Mal could see Neil's pupils slowly dilating as he caressed him.

"You are truly stunning, you know," he murmured as he watched Neil's face, the way his curious expression softened as he touched him. He deftly unbuckled Neil's belt and popped the buttons at the waistband of his pants. "I need to see some more of you."

Neil lifted his hips helpfully as Mal tugged at his jeans. The boxers beneath slid down his hips as well, while Neil pulled off his own shirt and dropped it over the side of the bed. He was lithe and sleek, like a creamy mink, under his clothes and Mal eased up off him for a moment to wriggle out of his own jeans, then get free of his shorts. It suddenly felt as if he was wearing far too much. Before getting back onto the bed, he went over to the door and made sure it was firmly closed. There was no need for a lock. If the door was shut, Merc would knock first. They both respected each other's space that way.

His cock bobbed as he settled back on the bed, straddling Neil's slim thighs, running his fingers over his smooth, bare chest. He teased the side of Neil's left nipple with his fingertip and watched the smile that coaxed to his lips and the way his cock twitched in immediate response.

Bending over him, he touched his mouth to Neil's lips again, kissing him with long, light presses of his mouth and tongue. He explored Neil's torso with one hand then moved the left one lower to stroke his hip and run a finger down his dark blond trail.

Neil's chest and belly rose and fell under Mal's hands as his breathing deepened, hitching as his hand moved down his quivering abs. The way Neil kissed him back told him that quiver was only anticipation. When Mal looked down at him again, Neil opened his eyes and the pupils were blown so wide there was only a slim line of blue ringing them. His lips were wet and parted. Mal slid his hand lower, his fingers fanning around the base of his thickening cock and Neil exhaled a soft moan, still looking up at him.

"I want to suck you," Neil murmured.

Mal's dick jumped at the idea and he crawled forward to straddle Neil's midriff, whispering, "I want you to suck me too."

Neil ran his hands up Mal's thighs and over his hips, drawing them inward to frame his cock and balls. He lifted his head and licked a wet line up from his base to just under the head, teasing back and forth over the tip a few times.

"I still can't feel any lust from you," he said. "But there's this warm, thick feeling instead, and it's amazing." He breathed the last word over the head of his dick, dragging his bottom lip just under the flange, then opened wider and took the whole crown into the heat of his mouth.

Mal shuddered and tipped his head back so that strands of his hair caught in the collar of his open shirt worked their way down between his shoulder blades, tickling his back. His wings fluttered once or twice in response and he issued a silent caution to them.

Stop that!

He reached over Neil, gripping the pillows behind his head and focusing on the ceiling because he thought that if he looked at the lad, he was going to come so hard he'd see stars for a week. How the hell Neil wasn't feeling lust was beyond him, because as far as Mal was concerned, he was hornier than he'd been in years.

His shoulders itched, the scarred skin pulled tight across them. Muscle and sinew, tucked against his shoulder blades, were flexing like they wanted to unravel and spill away from his body. It was the weirdest feeling, but not one that was alien to him.

"Not now," he whispered, cautioning his body almost inaudibly. "Not today. Please."

He'd forgotten how sharp Neil's hearing was. Neil lifted his head and looked up at him. "You want me to stop?"

"No, no...don't stop!" Mal choked out through the tightness in his throat.

Neil blinked at him with curiosity in those bright eyes but didn't press, thank the stars. He wrapped his fingers around Mal's cock and stroked him slowly before lowering his lips again, pushing the crown of his cockhead against their plush fullness, then between. His lips formed a tight seal around his shaft, just above his fingers, and he inched up and down as he continued to stroke him.

"Oh yeah…" Mal crooned, the words gone hoarse in his throat the moment they were uttered. "I love that. Feels so good. Don't stop."

He brought one hand down to run his fingers through Neil's loose curls, stroking through his hair then gripping it tighter when Neil's lips almost brushed the very root of his cock and the head nudged up against the back of his mouth. This time the ripple ran right down his back and he struggled to keep it in check, to keep his mouth shut, determined not to have this rare moment of enjoyment ruined. Absolutely nothing was going to get in the way of his climax. Not even…

His shoulders pulled tight and he almost screamed. The old scars didn't hurt anymore but the muscle beneath them was striated and rapid movement could be painful. His back undulated again and he squeezed his fingers tightly in Neil's soft hair, focusing on that.

"That's good. Make me come," he begged, his voice little more than a husky whisper.

Neil moaned, the vibration lifting from his chest into his throat and carrying right down Mal's cock to his balls, where Neil had shifted his hand to caress and knead them gently in his palm. His finger tickled just behind his sac and he went faster, drawing on him in long, hard sucks with each lift of his head, and laving with his tongue along the underside as he plunged down again and again. Someone had definitely taught him how to give great head. He was a hundred percent focused and knew just the right pressure and speed, and exactly when to shift gears for more.

Mal let go of his hair and slammed his hands hard against the wall above Neil's head. The energy that clever mouth stirred up in him built up like a lightning ball inside him and he just needed to let go of it. The concerned human part of his brain wanted to slow things down, to reassure Neil, to warn him that he was almost there, to give him choices.

But the other, darker, fairy part of him didn't care about any of that shit. It just wanted pleasure. It wanted release.

He brought his palms down hard again and again, and with the third slap of flesh against plaster, his senses unraveled and he let go. As his cock began to spurt, he felt the ripple run down his back again, harder and more urgent this time. His wings wanted out and he didn't have the strength to fight them, just hoped that they would not do more damage, straining against the adhesions and the old magic that kept them locked down tight.

Neil took him down to the root again, groaning sweetly as he swallowed his spend, one hand still caressing his balls and the other gliding over his own cock. His eyes were closed, a look of bliss on his face as he slowed down to draw out the last few shuddering spurts from him.

Mal kept his eyes on Neil's face, kept watching him, because that helped to calm him down. The aftershocks continued to roll through him like lightning through a thunderhead for a while. He managed to get his breathing back under control and leaned his forehead against the wall, just looking down at Neil, watching the incredibly peaceful, happy aura that radiated out from him. If he had known that coming in a person's mouth could make them that happy, he thought disjointedly, he might have done it more often.

One shoulder twitched and he resisted the urge to growl at it.

Cut that out, damn it!

What he actually said, as Neil opened his eyes and looked up at him, letting Mal's cock slip wetly from his lips, was, "My turn. I want to taste you."

"You do?" Neil asked, voice sleepy and bemused. "That would be..." He pulled his bottom lip between his teeth for a moment, giving Mal such a smoldering look it was a wonder he didn't set the bed on fire. "Mmm, that would be awesome."

"It definitely would," Mal agreed and shuffled carefully back down the bed on his knees until he was perched astride Neil's lower left leg. He slid his hands between Neil's thighs, opening him up wider so that he could bend and kiss his way up the insides of Neil's slim, white legs, taking his time, letting the pinking sensation in his balls subside enough that he could concentrate on the task in hand. Neil's body was so soft. It felt like warm plush against his lips and he sucked gently on the skin, leaving temporary hickeys there as he moved higher.

He cupped Neil's balls, rolling them in his palm as he leaned over to kiss Neil's belly, which rose and fell more rapidly as he got closer to his target.

"You are really stunning," he whispered, tilting his head back to look up at the gorgeous half-demon in his bed.

"I know," Neil said simply. "I can't help it. It's the demon side." From anyone else the words would have sounded conceited, but Neil was so matter-of-fact he was almost apologetic.

"You mean your whole paternal line is seriously hot?" Mal knelt up for a moment, leaning on one hand while continuing his gentle manipulation of Neil's ball sac with the other. "Wow."

Neil uttered a shivery whimper and exhaled a breathless, "Y-y-yesss…" It was hard to tell if that was in answer to his question or in response to what he was doing.

Whatever his motivation, the response was so sweet that Mal just kept watching him for a while until he decided that this was wholly too voyeuristic of him. Instead, he lay down and wrapped his fingers around Neil's cock, sucking it gently into his mouth and closing his eyes.

It had been a long time since he'd been with a man in this way. He had been barely out of high school the last time he'd sucked a guy off. Or at least, the last time it had been his idea.

Mal didn't want to dwell on his time with Vargas, not here with Neil under him. This was something way different to the work he had done for Del Vargas.

For a start, it didn't feel like work or an obligation of any kind. Neil was cool and smooth and…beautiful. Malachai had never thought of another man as beautiful before, but it fit Neil to perfection. He was beyond sexy. Sexy didn't fit him nearly so well, although Mal was undeniably attracted to him.

Neil had said something about not feeling lust in Mal and he supposed that was right. Mal recognized lust. He knew it for what it was. There had been plenty of one-night stands when he'd been on the racing circuit and he'd felt plenty of lust then—the blind, disconnected impulse to spread someone, to drive into them, to fuck them until he was exhausted, then to sleep until they crept out of bed in the pale morning and wriggled into their clothes to leave before they thought he was awake. He had never felt hurt by that, oddly. It seemed like part of the game for him. Mal hadn't wanted them to stay any more than they had wanted to sit around and make aimless small talk over breakfast.

Ems had been the only one who was different. Or he had thought she was, at least, but he had been wrong about that.

Malachai took Neil deeper into his mouth and nodded faster, pushing those thoughts away too. He did not want her in his head when he was trying his best to satisfy Neil at least half as well as the semi-incubus lad had done for him. He figured he had his work cut out, though. Neil had sex in his blood. How did a mere leprechaun compete with that?

Still, he tried. He worked Neil steadily with his hands and his mouth, stroking his tongue up and down the curving length of his gorgeous cock to flick at the sculpted curves around his tapering head and lick deeper into the salty slit, running the very tip back and forth there until Neil wriggled and gasped aloud.

Neil combed the fingers of one hand into Mal's hair, his fingertips gently caressing along his scalp. It was yet another layer of contrast, because Mal had certainly had other hands in his hair before, but couldn't remember any of them being able to convey so much longing in a simple touch.

He blew on Neil's wet skin, loving the sinuous way his body moved in response. He was like a living, breathing work of art and Mal wanted to see him in a state of ecstasy. Once more, he took Neil's delicious cock in his mouth and dipped down on him, smiling around the hot, hard muscle as Neil began to buck and thrust against him, wanting more.

"Uhh-yes, ohh, Mal…" Neil tipped his head back, sliding his other hand into Mal's hair too. He didn't pull him down, or guide him, just let his hands ride there, his touch sensual but undemanding. "Mal...Mal, ohh, I'm gonna come..." he whispered, fingers tightening in his hair.

Mal sped up, not much but just enough to tip Neil over. Neil's hips kicked as he lifted them in short thrusts and his heels dug into the mattress, his knees spread wide. For someone so serious and composed most of the time, he didn't hold back when it came to passion — he embraced the pleasure with abandon.

Mal was glad of that because he wanted to experience it again and again. He wanted to hover over Neil and watch him as he came. He wanted to come with him, sharing the pleasure, and collapse into his arms afterward.

That was a new emotion. For most of his adult life, sex had been about his own pleasure, almost exclusively. Was that where he'd been going wrong?

Neil made a pleased sound, almost a purr, and Mal kissed his quivering belly then kissed higher until he reached his mouth. Neil opened his eyes after their lips parted, looking perfectly content and happy.

"Well..." Mal exhaled, managing a smile that was probably as shaky as he felt. "That was interesting."

Neil nodded. "I never really thought about it, but if I had, I would have thought not sensing someone's lust would have been like feeling nothing. It wasn't like that at all, though. More finally learning what it's like to want someone without a coat of something dirty all over it." Neil touched Mal's face, tracing his finger lightly over his cheekbone.

Mal nodded thoughtfully. "Yeah, it was kind of like that. I can't imagine what it must be like to be bombarded with other people's lustful feelings all the damned time, but even I could feel that this was different...different to how it's always been for me before. It was more than just sex, if that makes sense. Which is just weird because...well, I mean...we hardly know one another. Right?"

"Right, so...we'll have to do it again, to see if it was just a fluke," Neil said, totally deadpan, but his eyes glinted with mischief.

Mal blinked at him for a moment, then the humor filtered through and he cracked a slow smile.

"You," he said, pointing directly at Neil's too-pretty face, "are a very bad boy. Which I like. A lot."

Neil kissed the tip of Mal's finger then gave it a nip and laughed and Mal realized, with a pang of sadness, that it was the first time he'd heard the sound from him.

"I like you too, Malachai. A lot."

Mal might have said more but at that point he was interrupted by the creak of boards outside the room and the rattle of Mercurio's knuckles on the door. His partner's gruff voice was muffled by the heavy wood. "How long does it take to get some furniture shifted, fairy boy? Get your ass downstairs if you still want lunch, or I'm taking it all to a homeless shelter."

Neil went still in his arms but Mal just called out, "We'll be down in a minute."

After a moment he heard Merc move off.

"I thought you wouldn't want him to find out," Neil whispered.

"Too late for that, sprout." Mal laughed bitterly. "Merc may be an old guy but he's not completely green. He knows."

The pink flush crept up Neil's cheeks and chased any misgivings Mal had about having to deal with Mercurio away.

"C'mon, let's get dressed," he suggested.

Chapter Fourteen

Neil waited for Merc to corner him about Malachai, to warn him off again—or worse—but it never came. The day after he and Mal had brought the bed upstairs, Mal and Merc went out together and when they came back, something had shifted. Merc no longer glared at him or watched him warily from the corner of his eye. The lectures and dire predictions of how much trouble Neil would bring them stopped and as far as Neil could tell, Merc was choosing to ignore what went on when Malachai closed the bedroom door.

As one day rolled into the next, Neil began to relax. With the car gone, maybe he had slipped away without a trace. At least, no assassins or police had come looking for him. It was a very weird feeling to have his fear slowly replaced by happiness. He had never been happier than when he and Malachai were together. He still stole looks at Mal while they were working, but more often than not, when he did, he caught Mal looking back at him with eyes that pinned him and stripped him where he stood. Those looks Mal gave him scattered all his thoughts and made him throb with need.

They were sitting around the kitchen table one evening, about a week or so after he and Malachai had begun to share a bed, when someone knocked at the door out front and they all exchanged wary glances immediately. It was dark outside, the late autumn skies already leached of sunlight—which meant that whoever was out there was not the bringer of good news.

Merc rose and went over to the cabinet by the refrigerator, the one he kept locked. He had the padlock off it in seconds and turned back from the closet with an armored rifle in both hands.

"Is that necessary?" Mal raised an eyebrow.

"No cause to take chances, is there?" the gremlin replied gruffly.

"Do you have any more of those?" Neil asked, on Merc's side for once. He remembered what had happened the last time someone had come knocking all too well.

"Nope. You know how to use a gun?" Mercurio headed for the doorway into the front of the shop and Mal grabbed the biggest of their utility knives and a wrench that was sitting on one of the counters where he'd left it when he came up from the garage earlier.

"Yes. Handguns mostly, but I'm not picky," Neil told him.

He could see Merc file that away somewhere for future reference before he headed back to the doorway, grunting, "Try not to get yourselves brained or abducted this time."

"Nice that he cares," Mal said under his breath but the look he flashed at Neil was one of solidarity.

Whoever it was outside hammered on the shutter again, just as Merc reached the door. He opened the inner door a crack and bellowed, "Whaddaya want?"

There was silence, then a small, female voice wailed, "I need to speak to Mal. Please! Something bad has happened. Really bad!"

"Amy!" Mal dropped the knife on the counter right away and ran to the door, wrestling with the padlock on the shutter. Merc grabbed his collar.

"What the fuck do you think you're doing?"

"It's Amy, from Vargas' place. She's a friend." Mal stared at him in disbelief.

"And if she was sent here to get those bastards in again?" Merc said. "Are you deranged?"

Mal's lips tightened. He turned back to the door. "Amy, are you alone?"

"Please!" she called back, banging on the metal roller again. "It's dark. Please help me. Everyone is dead. Or gone. We all just ran...I don't know where. I don't know what to do. You're the only other people I know here."

Mal turned his head to glare at Merc. His partner barked, "Were you followed, Amy? Be very sure before you say yes or no."

"I don't think so! It's dark out here! I'm scared," she whimpered.

"Open it, Mal," Neil said calmly. "You can't leave her out there, even if she was followed."

"You two are made for each other. You're both dumb as fuck!" Merc grumbled. He grabbed the keys from the wall hook and tossed them at Malachai.

"Step well back from the shutter, girl. If anything follows you in here, I will shoot you all. Get it?" Merc called, raising the shotgun to his shoulder as Malachai bent to open the lock and bring up the steel shutter.

Amy had smartly taken a step back while the door was opened but as soon as the shutter was halfway up, she darted inside, running right to Malachai and latching on to him. Neil crouched and scanned the dark quickly but didn't see anything moving out there. He got the shutter down and locked, then shut and bolted the door while Amy sobbed and babbled incoherently in Malachai's arms.

"Who brought you here?" Merc demanded. "Stop hollering and talk sense, kid. It's dark out there, so who brought you?"

"I drove myself. In the van," Amy said, trying to pull herself together.

"What happened?" Neil asked her.

"Bone Men," Amy said and his blood ran cold. "They walked right through our wards. Del and Crow...they fought them, but they used shadow fire. It got Crow. I heard Del screaming and hid... They kept asking Del where Nielub was, then...then they killed him."

Neil watched as Mal's silver eyes flared wide. They had all witnessed Vargas fend off shadow fire and that was no small ability. Though he knew Mal probably had no great affection for the cluricaun, this was a neighbor and a business associate, and his death ripped into their lives. If Bone Men had come to the house on Delancey, of course they had come for him.

Mal looked at him with shock written all over his face. Mercurio shook his head. "They will follow her here. We have to leave. Now."

Mal said, "They tracked him to Vargas, but not here, or they would have got here first. Let's not panic. Amy, did you hear all that Del told them? Did he say anything to them about Neil?"

"He told them Neil ran away."

"You're sure? He didn't tell them anything about where Neil might have gone?" Merc countered. When Amy just looked scared and shook her head, he muttered, "I still think we should leave. She came through the dark. Alone. Anything could have tailed her."

"And if we go out there...?" Mal drew himself up to his full height, glaring defiantly at his friend. He put one arm around Amy's shoulders as she tried to make herself smaller.

"If they followed her, we're not going to outrun them in the truck," Neil said, thinking fast. "They'll find us. If we have to fight, would you rather do it here or on the road?"

"At night our chances are better here," Mal said quietly, before Merc could open his mouth to argue. "We have defenses up around the whole building and we know the layout."

"And if they breach our wards?" Merc grumbled. "Vargas might have been a piece of shit but he knew how to ward a building, Malachai."

They were all silent for a second. Neil said, "If you leave and I stay, they might not come after you once they've found me."

"If he stays, I stay," Mal added quickly. "I won't let him face this on his own."

"Well, hell! This is my unit. Why don't you all piss off and leave me in peace? They ain't gonna bother me if you ain't here," Merc said, without any real animosity in his voice.

"They bothered Vargas," Neil couldn't resist pointing out.

"We stick together," Mal said defiantly. "Whether we stay or go."

"Mal," Neil said. He put his hand on Malachai's arm to make the half-fae look at him. "I got away with a trick before. That's not going to work again. They'll kill us. There's no reason you have to die. Take Amy and Merc and get out while you can. If they were asking about me, it stands to reason they'll stop going after anyone else once they have me."

"You hope." Mal clenched his teeth and gave a single shake of his head. "But even if you're right, that's still not a good excuse to just leave you to it. We've stood by you this far. If they wanna take you, then they have to come through us."

Neil looked at him and for the first time, he thought it would have been handy if he could use his power to make him get in the damn truck and drive away. Instead, Malachai locked eyes with him and something else entirely passed between them. His belly went fluttery and he caught his breath.

"Aw, fer... Cut that out." Merc told them. "We have fuck knows what coming at us and you two are making moon eyes at each other."

"I think it's sweet," Amy said.

"Shush," Mal told her, firing a last, helpless smile at Neil before checking the door was secured. He hustled them all through to the back of the shop where no light would show out on the street and it would hopefully be safer.

* * * *

No one slept well that night. They took it in turns to get a couple of hours, except for Amy who was practically passed out on her feet from fear and exhaustion. At first light, over breakfast, Mal announced that he was going to take her over to the River District and ask Drasnil to take her in.

"Ches is there, you won't be on your own," he told her, gently when she looked anxious about this. "Felipe isn't a complete bastard. He doesn't drink any more, for a start."

"I could go with you," Neil offered.

"No. Stay here. If they haven't come yet, it means they've lost the trail, or they would have struck while it was dark and they had the advantage. When I get back, we'll think what to do next."

"Okay." Neil wasn't happy about letting Malachai go on his own, but it did make sense. Mal was probably safer away from him.

They had a problem over what to do with the truck Amy had driven down from Delancey. In the end, Malachai took Merc's pickup to drop her at Drasnil's place down in the River District, and Merc stowed the armored truck she'd liberated from her late employer in the garage out back, muttering about how they would probably find it useful before too long. When he and Merc had shut the gate and retreated into the kitchen, the shop felt a lot quieter.

Neil paced for a few minutes and Merc finally said, "They don't have no reason to look for you here, boy. Settle down."

"How did they track me to Vargas?" Neil said, still pacing.

"Malachai said Vargas took you to La Sala. I imagine it wouldn't have been too hard for at least a dozen people to tell a resourceful snoop they'd seen you there, and who you were with."

Neil froze. "Vargas took me there, but I was with Madran and Drasnil too."

"Kid, anyone that messes with Drasnil's people has picked the wrong fight. I don't care what kinda superpowers they got." Merc chuckled. "If they were chasing those sources last night, they'll have been and gone. Drasnil will have told them you weren't there. And even if they searched, they're not gonna find you. There's no reason for them to go back there."

"Maybe we should —"

"No, we should not." Merc cut him off before he even finished his idea. "What we need to do is wait for Mal to get back. Sit down."

Neil sat.

Merc had just put the kettle on the stove and was beginning to debate whether they ought to scrap the armored car or try to sell it when they heard the shutter rattle out front again. It wasn't a deliberate knock, like Amy's — more a sound as if someone was trying it out to see how resilient it was. Merc took the kettle off the hob and went to the doorway between the kitchen and the shopfront. He peered around the door frame warily.

"Someone out there. Twenty bucks says it's just some schmuck cruising for gas," he said, and his voice was steady.

"Merc, take the shotgun with you," Neil warned.

Before Merc could make a move, one way or another, the sound of screeching metal jarred their ears and the shutter came up in a twisted mess. A tall, imposing man with dark hair and piercing blue eyes stepped inside.

"No." The word barely made it past Neil's lips in a whisper.

"Nielub," the man said, no surprise or pleasure in the tone.

"No," Neil said it again, more firmly.

The man smiled. "Don't be foolish. You're lucky I found you before the Bone Men did. Come, Nielub." He held out his hand and said the words like he was calling a dog to heel.

"He's not going anywhere. He's made it clear what you want with him," Merc said, his gruff voice low and serious. "Go on and burn your own black soul with sorcery if that's what you want, but you're not using his to pay the cost."

Neil sucked in a breath. Malachai must have told Merc why he didn't want to be found by his father. A lot of people were prejudiced against those with demon blood, but sorcerers were universally reviled for their use of familiars to fuel their magic.

"Watch how you tread, old man. It wouldn't take much to stop your heart."

Neil watched the black creep over his father's eyes as he spoke. "No, please don't hurt him. Please."

"You plead for his life, but did you plead for your mother's? Of course not, you were too eager to run away," his father sneered.

The words struck Neil as surely as a fist. "I had no time to plead for her, they killed her the moment they saw me," he growled low. "And it's your fault! What did you do to make them come after us?"

"What did I do?" His father smiled condescendingly. "I spawned a demon brat."

Neil stared blankly and his father uttered a humorless laugh.

"You thought the Bone Men had come for me? Oh no, my son. They were after you. Until you're bonded as my familiar, you're a juicy plum, ripe for the picking to any sorcerer that takes you. Your unfortunate mother was simply in their way. Your existence is the reason she's dead."

No. That couldn't be true.

Even as he fought to deny it, he knew his father spoke the truth. Bile burned the back of his throat and his stomach churned as, in his head, he saw the blood gushing from her neck and her eyes starting to glaze.

"The reason this lad's mum is dead is because some cowardly piece of shite murdered her, and no other reason," Merc snarled. "You're not taking the boy and that's that. You need to leave."

"Who's going to stop me taking him? You?" He spread his arms and gave Mercurio a mocking smile. "Go on and take your best shot, gremlin." His eyes bled completely black as he said it and there was a crackle in the air like static that spoke of dangerous power.

"No! Dad, please. Leave him alone. I'll...go with you," Neil protested.

"Neil!" Merc erupted.

"No, it's all right, Merc. I'll go. Enough people have been hurt or killed," Neil said. He walked to his father then stopped, heart pounding. He looked over at Merc and reached for the charm bracelet around his wrist. "Can you give this back to Mal for me?" he asked.

His dad grabbed his wrist.

"Don't you dare!" he growled and pulled the charm bracelet off.

Neil yanked his arm away, jumping back. A flare of emerald green dazzled his eyes but he was already turning to run.

"Go! Run, Merc!"

His father cursed as ghostly green tentacles grabbed and wrapped around him. Neil didn't wait to see how long they would hold. A few seconds, or a few minutes, it didn't matter — it was all the time they were going to get so they had better make the best of it. Merc retrieved the shotgun from the kitchen cabinet, on the way out, as they both ran for the back door.

"Get Amy's van running. Keys are in it!" Merc instructed, following him halfway down the stairs into the garage then stopping and loading the gun.

"Where are you going?" Neil asked, panic edging his voice.

"Never you mind. Just get the van and bring it round the front."

Neil didn't have any time to argue. He ran into the garage for the van while Merc ran through the scrap yard, opening the shutters and gates, and disappeared around the side of the building. For one gut-wrenching moment, the door on the van wouldn't give and he thought it was locked, but a harder yank on the handle pulled it open. Neil jumped in and turned the key. He threw it in reverse and put his foot down, the tires screeching a protest as he careened backward down the ramp before hitting dirt and throwing up a cloud as he spun it around to face the gates. No mean feat, as the van was reinforced with heavy steel plating and drove top heavy like a tank, threatening to tip over when he turned too sharp. It kept its wheels under it, though. Neil jammed it in gear and tore up the side alley toward the road.

He spotted Merc at the front of the shop, slamming down the hood of an expensive black sedan that he recognized. He had barely rolled to a stop when Merc ran over on surprisingly light feet and jumped in the passenger side.

Merc pointed left. "Let's go, kid."

Neil pulled out in the direction he indicated and hit the gas. "Where?"

"Drasnil's place. We'll catch up with Malachai there."

Chapter Fifteen

Felipe Drasnil held court in an old cinema up in the Malasañas district, between Silver and Vine Streets. The building had once been the Trocadero movie theater but for the past seventeen years, it had belonged to Drasnil and his cohorts. A number of young half-fae and humans swarmed out, carrying discreet weaponry when Mal pulled up outside and jumped down with Amy close behind him.

"Lord Valentine." One of the half-born nodded to him, in reluctant acknowledgment of his birthright. "What brings you to our court?"

"I owe your master thanks for some information he brought to me," Mal said in a calm voice, while Amy's sharp gaze passed over the assembled ranks of Drasnil's court. "I also seek another favor."

"Who is the girl?" one of them asked, staring at Amy who glared back at him.

"She is a friend to Chesney, who is one of your own." Mal put a steadying hand on the small of Amy's back. "She needs a place of safety."

"Will she not be safe with you, Lord Valentine?" the half-fae snickered.

"My home is known to our enemies. She has only Mercurio and myself to protect her there," Mal said, shaking his head at the fellow. "Will you be so kind as to convey my request to your master?"

They consulted among themselves and finally one of them went back inside. He was gone for a few minutes and when he returned, he beckoned to them imperiously.

"Master Drasnil will see you."

"About time," Mal murmured for Amy's ears alone.

"Stupid assholes," she whispered back.

"They take their work very seriously." He grinned at her. "They're good people, on the whole. And Ches is happy here."

They were shown to a vast auditorium that had once housed rows of seating and a stage with a screen. All of that was gone, in favor of more comfortable armchairs grouped in clusters. The stage had been reduced to a raised dais where Felipe sprawled sideways across a plush chair as if it were a throne. Malachai suppressed a chuckle at the affected posing, which told him more than anything else that Felipe was not feeling nearly so casual about this meeting as he pretended.

"Lord Valentine," Felipe said, his voice carried clearly to their ears by some weird trick of the acoustics. "Isn't this an un-surprise. And you come bearing gifts?"

"You love each and every one of your children, Felipe. I thought you might like another. Amy is very resourceful. Plus she brings information regarding the foul creatures who killed your brother." Mal bowed his head respectfully.

For a moment, Drasnil stared at him. His expression was hard to read.

"Am I to believe it is coincidence that Bone Men hunting for your charge found their way to Delilah's home so quickly?" he asked in rigid tones.

"Delilah took him to La Sala," Mal said, just as stonily. "You know as well as I how word travels when a pretty new face is brought in. Your brother made no effort to hide him, in fact flaunted him. I'm sure it was no great task for an assassin to make an inquiry or two and trace him back to Del."

Drasnil bared his teeth but he did not call bullshit on that line of defense. La Sala was a meat market and gossip was stock in trade there.

"Now you bring another of my brother's waifs to me. Charming," he said, his pale eyes falling on Amy and studying her until she shivered. "How am I to afford another mouth to feed?"

"I'm no waif," Amy said, lifting her head and straightening her shoulders. "I'm perfectly capable. I've lost my home, not my abilities. I'll offer you the same cut I gave Del for room, board and protection. Half your hooligans come to me for their charms anyway."

Felipe lifted his silver eyebrows and Mal hid a smile behind a deliberate cough.

"Is that so? Interesting." The little half-fae rolled smoothly from a lounge to a sitting position, leaning forward with his elbows on his knees, hands laced between them.

At his shoulder, the goblin who was his bodyguard grunted, "I can vouch for her charms, sir. They work very well."

"If I didn't know you better, Klosky, I'd imagine you were being salacious," Drasnil said, tilting his head to look at the stocky youth.

"I ain't sure what that means, sir," Klosky said, shuffling his feet. "Sorry."

"Of course not." Drasnil uttered a short, sharp bark of laughter. "Don't worry, Klosky. It doesn't matter. She's kept you alive, that's what's important here, correct?"

"Yes, sir," the goblin said, sounding relieved to be asked a question that he understood. "She makes good safety charms."

"And they are not inexpensive," Drasnil acknowledged, returning his gaze to Amy. "Very well. You may stay, young lady."

Amy performed a half-bow in his direction but didn't say thank you, as per the old ways. Drasnil offered her a small smirk and a nod.

"Since our business is concluded, would you join me for tea, Lord Valentine?" Drasnil asked.

Malachai measured that offer. He wanted to get back to Neil and Merc, to make sure they were safe, but at the same time, he was being offered a courtesy and it would be rude to decline. For a mortal, acceptance might constitute a binding contract, but he was not mortal and considered that he was already more than lightly indebted to the self-styled King of the Trocadero Court. "Tea would be most acceptable, Felipe," he replied, inclining his head once more.

Felipe rose and escorted Malachai from his 'audience chamber' into the hall and through what could only be described as a crack in the wall, which led to something quite amazing. An inner courtyard that was awash with growing things and blooms, even a few saplings. The old theater wasn't a gateway to Underhill, by any stretch—it might not have even qualified as a shallowing—but the place certainly held some magic.

Felipe slowed to a stroll among the neat beds of edibles and flowers, leading Malachai along a narrow winding path and obviously enjoying his reaction.

"My brother was quite enraged when you stole the boy back out from under his nose. Charlie tells me Crow was near apocalyptic. It was a good thing your little demon had already rewarded them so handsomely, they were loath to risk their good fortune."

Mal's lips quirked a tight smile. "I had rather hoped that Charlie would find his way to you."

"Where else would he go?" Drasnil asked with a smirk, shaking his head and making his pewter curls bounce. "His brother has been in my service for a long time. They pined for one another." His expression grew more solemn. "It is hard for twins to be apart."

Mal sobered. "I truly am sorry for your loss," he said. "I'm aware you and Del did not always see eye to eye but even I don't believe you would wish him dead."

"No, I wouldn't. But perhaps I lost him long ago. This benighted land made him greedy and incautious, and that caught up to him. There's a lesson in there for you, leprechaun." Drasnil chuckled humorlessly. He led Malachai to a small table set between comfortable wingback chairs, beneath an arbor of verdant foliage and fragrant blossom, where they sat, making small talk until a younger half-fae girl with enormous lavender eyes and sharply pointed fangs brought them tea in a delicate porcelain pot and fine, near-translucent cups.

Mal was conscious of each minute that ticked by but told himself Neil was safe behind the wards, and it was full daylight still. The Bone Men had no reason to know where he was.

Even so, after two polite cups, he was just about ready to tell Felipe he needed to get back home, when a goblin that could have been Klosky's younger brother came trotting up to them, out of breath.

"Beg pardon, Master Drasnil, there's a problem."

Mal started to his feet at once and Drasnil laid a hand on his arm, wordlessly calling for caution. Mal's family line might have precedence over his but Drasnil was the elder here and these were his people. Mal held his tongue, though he had to bite it hard.

"What's happened, Kalden?" Drasnil inquired, rising with him.

Kalden looked from Drasnil to Malachai and back. "Mercurio Geiger is here. He drove up in an armored van and is demanding to be let inside."

"Where is Neil? Something is wrong. I need to go to him," Mal said at once.

Drasnil nodded, a brief frown between his silver eyebrows. "I will accompany you, Lord Valentine. Permit the gremlin to enter the delivery bay. Secure the doors and keep him there," he told his goblin attendant.

The goblin nodded and flew off at once. Mal ran after him, protocol be buggered.

Malachai arrived at the rear of the building, prepared for injury or chaos, and found neither. Through the small window he could see Neil, standing in the yard, talking to one of Drasnil's guards. The way he stood was relaxed, the tilt of his head as he looked up at the half-fae appeared more flirtatious than alarmed, and even from a distance, Mal recognized the sultry slant of his mouth and suggestion in his eyes. Eyes that were fixed on the man in front of him.

Before the order was given, the guard, who was supposed to let no one pass, calmly opened the door for Neil, his head swiveling to watch his arse as he walked inside.

"Open the gate for Mercurio," Neil told him over his shoulder, making serious eye contact, his voice husky, honeyed with power. The fae let go of the door, eyes glazed over as he turned to get the gate open.

Neil took a deep breath and shook himself, taking a determined step, then stopped as he saw him with Drasnil.

"Mal!" Neil rushed over to him, the air of seduction shed like water off a duck, a warmer look and obvious relief taking its place.

Drasnil's silver eyes narrowed on the security detail who had the good grace to look embarrassed as he realized just how he had been worked over. By then the heavily armored vehicle was in the secure yard behind the theater and the gates were closing, shutting them off from any possible pursuit.

"What happened? What are you doing here?" Malachai wanted to know, once he had assured himself that Neil was unhurt.

Neil let his eyes cut to Drasnil, obviously debating how much he could say in front of him then reaching some sort of decision as he looked back at Malachai.

"My father found me," he said quietly. He touched his bare wrist. "I'm not sure how long the charm will hold him, but Merc did something to his car too, before we left."

Mercurio bounced down from the cab of the truck with the shotgun slung casually across his shoulder and, right away, he was placed in the line of fire of about eleven smaller fae pointing tasers and bolt guns in his direction.

Mal moved between his friend and their hosts immediately, holding up his hands. "Calm down. He means you no harm. On my word. He will not hurt you," he called out.

Drasnil waved a hand toward his clan. They lowered their weapons fractionally but kept them leveled in Merc's general direction.

"Am I to assume that the Bone Men already looking for you are in the employ of your father, since you seem to be hiding from both?" Drasnil asked.

"No…or at least, I don't think so," Neil said.

"Sonofabitch ripped the front grille out and walked right through the wards," Merc said to Malachai in a low tone.

"Shit!" Mal said. "If warding isn't going to keep him out, then we will need to go on the offensive against him."

Drasnil had moved closer and was eavesdropping most indiscreetly on their conversation.

"You will bring him here," the cluricaun said, but he looked more thoughtful than angry. "He is searching for this one."

Drasnil pointed to Neil and the tasers slowly moved in the incubus' direction.

"Shooting him is not going to help you," Mal told them blandly. "If his father thinks he is here, he will break in first and ask questions later. And if you kill the boy, he will still take his due in blood. Either way you will have to fight him."

"Or, we could stake him out like a goat in the street," Drasnil said. "And be done with the matter."

"We shall not." Mal turned and met his silver gaze head on, steel in his own glare. "Not unless we wish to discover how that feels."

"Threatening me, in my own court?" Drasnil asked, his tone still mild.

"If you leave Neil out there as a lure, I will have no need to threaten you. His father or the Bone Men will do that for me," Mal told him without flinching. "Do you actually wish to bring them to your door? Are you so hungry for a bloodbath?"

"My, you are besotted, aren't you?" Drasnil said, and while his tone was still light, it held an edge of bitterness too. "I don't owe him — or you — protection, Lord Valentine. I was thinking more of an offering than a lure."

"Neil is under my protection. If you hand him out like sweets to any random passing strangers, you will have me to contend with, Felipe." Mal pulled himself up to his full height. "You may consider that a warning."

Silvery eyes flashed at him, but after a tense few moments, Drasnil turned his gaze back to Neil, affecting a more relaxed pose. "Well. I suppose if we're going to be the shelter in the storm, we should be aware of exactly what may be coming down from the clouds. What kind of demon are we facing here?"

Neil licked his lips and cast his eyes around at the group of onlookers uneasily. "He's an incubus," he muttered.

"Hmm, that explains Madran and Tomalin's reactions to you. Not so hard to deal with then…"

"If he were just an incubus, you might be right. He's also a sorcerer," Neil told him. His arms hung at his sides and he looked at the ground as he spoke in a monotone. "When he comes here, he'll send in a wave of dread and nightmares. Whoever doesn't run away, he'll exploit their weaknesses. Stopping their hearts, rupturing their liver, causing an aneurysm. Whoever survives that, he will attack with shadow fire."

"What a lovely fellow," Drasnil said with a sarcastic snicker. "I have to say, Lord Valentine, I do not envy you your father-in-law."

Mal raised one golden eyebrow in response but he did not counter that jab. Instead he slid a comforting arm around Neil's shoulders.

"We should be ready to fight him, in that case. Does he have any weaknesses?"

Neil shook his head. "No. Except...he doesn't have a familiar." The word *yet* hung between them. "He can't just attack indefinitely."

"Then we have to spread out," Merc said, leaning against the wheel arch of the truck nonchalantly, the gun still propped against his shoulder. "Give him a bigger target. Keep him on his toes."

"Use magic against him that will tie up his own spells in firefighting," Mal added, considering his partner's advice.

"He won't face you directly if he doesn't have to, not when he's outnumbered," Neil said. "So don't count on being able to wear him down. He'll pick us off one at a time, if he can, and save his power."

"He's going to have to spend a lot of time hanging around waiting. That gives us more opportunity to pick him off in turn," Drasnil suggested, having listened with interest to this exchange.

"I don't think you understand," Neil said, his voice soft. "He's very good at killing people. He'll have his defenses high, you won't get close to him, most likely won't even realize where he is. The spells will come one after another. He doesn't have infinite power, but it won't matter. By the time you recover from one thing, he'll have another ready to go. He can keep that pace up for days…weeks. I've seen it. Multiple targets, large spread-out areas, closed areas with tight defenses. He has ways of defeating almost any scenario he comes across."

"You are not making me feel optimistic about keeping you within my walls," Drasnil said with a thin-lipped smile.

"I don't want anyone to die," Neil responded, running a hand through his hair and sighing. "If there was a way to get him to expend a lot of power, all at once, then you might get inside his defenses."

"But if we throw ourselves at him en masse, he will take us out one by one. Is that what you are saying?" Drasnil sighed. "Boy. My opinion of you is decreasing by the minute."

"Hang on, there may still be a way that we can get him to spend his energy without throwing everyone under the train first," Mal said thoughtfully, tapping his front teeth with one fingernail. "We don't have a sorcerer. We can only use defensive spells against him. He isn't going to be geared up for a full-on assault. Can we get him into a part of the building where we could come at him from all directions?"

Drasnil nodded. "There are corridors in this building with access vents in the ceiling and no let-out for an intruder on the ground."

"If we could bombard him with defensive spells from above, he'd be tied up trying to combat those and maybe less aware of what he was heading into. It would give us the space to set up a trap spell for him." Mal was pacing again.

"It would take you some serious energy to create a cage out of magic that could contain a half-demon sorcerer," Merc pointed out.

"What if he had help?" Neil asked.

"What you got in mind, kid?" Merc asked. Drasnil was also looking thoughtfully at him by this time.

Neil swallowed and Mal heard the click in his throat. He said, "If you used me to —"

"No." Mal cut him off.

Neil stopped talking.

"Drawing power through him, especially for an entrapment spell like this, it's close to his natural ability anyway. That's not a bad idea," Drasnil said.

"I said no," Mal stated more firmly.

"Don't be so prudish, Lord Valentine. It's not like you'd be bonding him to you. It's only the first step for a familiar."

"And it leaves him vulnerable to his father, which we're trying to avoid, unless you'd failed to notice." Mal glared at him.

"Only if it doesn't work," Drasnil said. "If it does work, he'll have nothing more to worry about from Daddy."

"Until he regains his strength."

"He won't do that if he's dead," Neil said softly.

"I like this boy." Drasnil patted Neil on the shoulder. "He thinks like one of us."

Mal narrowed his eyes and stalked the length of the armored truck, then back, while his temper cooled. Merc caught his attention.

"He has a point," the gremlin said when Mal stopped pacing beside him. "We've seen what he can do. And between you, you cooked up that bracelet, which stopped the bastard in his tracks. Nice work, that."

Mal grunted but wasn't going to be so easily cajoled out of his mood or into a rash decision. This was serious. Pulling power through Neil would be…almost a violation. It was practically what his father was after. Even if Neil did volunteer. No one should be used like that. Granted it wasn't exactly the same as what his own father wanted to do to him — Mal's defensive magic wouldn't eat his soul, for one thing. Still, it was a level of trust he wasn't entirely comfortable with. If he pulled too much power too quickly, he could kill Neil. Or damage him permanently.

"Mal, can we talk for a minute?" Neil asked him, glancing meaningfully toward a spot that was away from everyone else.

He exchanged a quick look with Merc, who merely shooed him away, so Mal ambled over while Drasnil was busy ordering his security detail around and making sure that his wards were all in place and strengthened to the max.

"I'm only trying to look out for you," Mal said when Neil was in earshot.

Neil sighed and leaned up against a side of the building. "Mal, my father kills people for a living. It's what he does. When someone wants the best, when they have the money to pay to make sure their target is eliminated, my father's name is one of those that are whispered. You know what will happen if he gets me back. He won't wait any longer. He'll bind me to him and I'll be no more than a battery pack, until I'm drained and dead. It could take years and every time he uses sorcery to kill, I'll feel it, a piece of me will be lost." Neil looked up into his eyes. "I trust you."

Mal thought he might struggle to breathe for a moment. He'd looked out for plenty of lost souls since coming here but none of them had made the impact on him that Neil did in such a short space of time. He understood why Merc had initially distrusted the boy but Mal lived by his instincts and those sharp senses were telling him that he wasn't being played. Neil was like no lover he'd ever taken. Okay, he was part-demon for a start, but that wasn't the whole of it. Mal wanted to be around him and he was pretty sure that wasn't enchantment. He was half-fae. He'd feel it, if he was being hexed, he was fairly certain.

It worried him because he wanted to be equally sure that he could live up to the faith that Neil was putting in him. He was a two-bit alchemist, not a sorcerer. All right, maybe a bit better than that, but even so…

"I wish I was the sort of guy that could promise you'll be safe," he said at last, quietly. "I'm not a hero, Neil. I'm not even a mage. But what I can promise is that I will not give up on you, not while there is breath in my body."

Neil smiled crookedly. "I have mass-murdering Bone Men after me, my father, who wants to use me to pay the cost of his dark magic, after me, and am in the shelter of a fairy that hasn't decided if he'd rather throw me to the wolves or kill me out of revenge for his brother's murder, and I'm still safer here with you than anywhere else, Malachai."

"That doesn't say a whole lot for your chances," Mal told him.

"We have time. He couldn't follow us and Merc destroyed his car. It'll be a while before he finds me again. This time we can be ready."

"I still don't want to use you like that," Mal said.

Neil gave him some heavy eye contact then took pity on him. "Good thing for you, you're immune to me."

"You're so sure about that?" Mal managed a smile at last. Even Merc was coming around to the idea that he was safe with Neil. Otherwise he wouldn't have brought the young incubus here.

"One hundred percent. I can't twist you around. If you lust after anything at all, I haven't seen it yet."

"But I still want you," Mal mused, enjoying how that confession put a hit of color in Neil's cheeks. "Nearly all the time. I don't think I've ever felt like this about anyone."

"Whatever you're feeling, it's not just lust," Neil said.

"What is it then?" Mal leaned closer, putting a shoulder against the wall beside Neil and grinning at him.

A small line appeared between Neil's brows and Mal had to resist the urge to pull him into his arms and kiss him. He was too damn cute when he was perplexed.

"Well... I don't, um... I'm not an empath... I mean, the desire is there." Neil's eyes flicked to somewhere south of Mal's beltline and traveled slowly upward, and Mal knew full well how it would feel to have his hands following that same path. "I mean, you couldn't...um, if you didn't feel any desire you wouldn't be able to...you know."

"There's no doubt the desire is there," Mal agreed, murmuring the words into Neil's ear and positively delighting in the way it made Neil's breath catch in his throat and his cheeks flush.

"For some reason my incubus side can't feel it, but the rest of me can," Neil said, finally bringing his eyes back up to Mal's. "Why do you think that is?"

"I have no idea," Mal replied, his voice gone husky as he leaned close enough to feel Neil's warm breath on his face. "Maybe once we've sorted this business out, we ought to experiment with it a bit more."

Neil might be confused about why he couldn't sense his lust, but Mal had no trouble picking up on the spike of heat that put a glazed look in Neil's eyes and made him lick his lips. Separated as they were from the group milling around, they were by no means alone, but Neil still looked ready to pounce on him. Mal dropped an arm around his shoulders and pulled him close, touching his lips in a soft kiss.

A throat was cleared next to them and Mal looked up.

"Beggin' yer pardon, yer lordship. Master Drasnil says if yer done staking yer claim, he wants to see you in the big hall to make plans."

Chapter Sixteen

Once the initial planning for how they would deal with a sustained attacked from a sorcerer was laid, the alert remained high for a few days, but by day five some of the tension was starting to ebb, if not the vigilance.

Malachai and Felipe consulted often and both were of the opinion that Neil must have given his father the slip. It was a continued possibility that he was out there somewhere, biding his time and waiting to strike, but the probability was higher that he was still looking. This meant that Neil needed to stay inside as much as possible and certainly not venture beyond the boundaries of the compound. That was fine, for now, but Neil wondered exactly how long Felipe's patience would hold and how long before the self-imposed confinement drove him crazy.

He was safe at the moment but felt more like a prisoner every day. On top of that, the safety was only an illusion and he knew that, but it was hard not to be lulled by it.

"So how often do you have to feed?"

Neil jumped at the question. He'd been so wrapped up in his thoughts he hadn't even heard Eithne until he spoke, practically in his ear. The subtly androgynous young man had found his way to the Trocadero Court with Charlie after the house on Delancey was attacked and his room was just down the hallway from the one he and Mal were using.

"What?"

"You know. Like, how often do you have to…" Eithne made his forefingers into hooks and put them up to his eyeteeth.

"I'm not a vampire," Neil told him.

"Not an undead one, no. But an incubus still needs to feed, don't they?"

"A full-blooded one, yes."

"Oh…so you don't suck Malachai off?"

Neil stared at him and Eithne laughed. "I'm just joking, Neil. Relax. I was only asking because vamps can't keep feeding off the same person all the time."

"I'm not a vampire," Neil repeated.

"I know, hunny." Eithne leaned in closer, putting his hand on Neil's arm with a sultry smile. "But it doesn't hurt to offer."

Oh. Neil almost smacked his forehead. The fae here seemed to exist in varying degrees of perpetual lust all the time and Neil had been doing everything he could to ignore it and tune it out so he could live in such close quarters with all of them. So much so that he apparently couldn't even tell when someone was flirting with him anymore.

"Um, thanks. But I don't need to feed like that."

"Oh." Eithne looked surprised but not offended.

He had shown up at the old cinema the day after Mal, Merc and Neil, looking very much the worse for wear. Given what he must have seen or heard when the Bone Men attacked their home, plus a couple of nights sleeping rough and evading the creatures that moved through the nighttime city, it was hardly surprising. Neil wondered, and not for the first time, what Eithne was, because he certainly wasn't human. No human could have crept up on him like that.

"Crow said that you had to fuck to stay alive."

Neil suppressed the urge to bristle at him. It was maybe a bit tactless to bring it up, but he thought Eithne was just blunt, rather than snide. Unlike Crow himself.

"If I wasn't mixed, that would be true."

"Ah," Eithne said, still studying him with keen interest. "Right. You can still fuck me if you want to."

Neil had been put in any number of situations where he'd been pawed at, groped, propositioned and worse, but he'd never had someone just flat out offer like that. As far as he could tell, Eithne was only mildly turned on. His lust was just a hint, like a faint perfume that was put on hours ago, but you knew would be stronger if you put your nose against his skin and inhaled.

"Um, you realize I share a room with Malachai, right?"

"Everyone knows you share a room with the very delicious and oh-so-unobtainable Lord Valentine." Eithne pressed even closer and Neil moved back.

"Well, then..."

"You can ask him to join us. I don't mind doing you both."

"No. Um, no, thanks. But no."

Eithne blinked at him, looking perplexed. "Are you scared of me? I mean... I kind of thought... You must have done it before? Right."

Actually, Neil hadn't. Not, like, all the way anyway. But that wasn't any of Eithne's business. "I'm not afraid of you," Neil said. "But you should be afraid of me. Wait...I didn't mean that to sound like a threat." He put up a placating hand, although Eithne's expression hadn't changed from mildly perplexed. "What I mean is, I'm with Malachai and no one else. Okay?"

"Wow." Eithne blinked. "Seriously? Like...*with him* with him? Wow. I didn't think he was...well...was interested in any of that."

Neil wished this conversation would stop. No, he wished it had never started. Would explaining that he had no idea what Eithne meant by 'with him with him' help or only make it worse? And what if Eithne went running his mouth? What if it got back to Malachai? How would he explain that?

"I don't know what he's interested in," Neil said because Eithne was still staring at him and he felt like he was supposed to say something. "I only know what I'm interested in."

"So...you haven't actually done it with him yet then?" Eithne had a glint in his eye that said he'd probably imagined as many times as Neil what it might be like to go further. "Interesting."

Could this conversation get any more embarrassing?

"I don't see why that's interesting," Neil said.

"Just franks a few theories about lovely Lord Valentine, that's all." Eithne winked at him.

Neil opened his mouth to ask what he meant by that but someone beat him to the punch.

"What sort of theories would those be then?" Mal asked from the doorway, making them both almost jump out of their skin.

How the hell does he do that? Sneak up like that? Neil thought wildly.

Eithne was biting his lips. "Um...just stuff that Del used to say. When he was drunk, mostly."

Mal laughed but the sound didn't hold much humor. "I wouldn't give much credence to that then."

Eithne smiled like he didn't quite buy it, but apparently his blunt questioning didn't extend to Malachai because he kept his mouth shut. Neil meanwhile felt pretty certain Mal could probably hear his heart pounding from where he stood. How would it sound to blurt out that he wasn't talking about him behind his back? *Probably bad.*

"Well, I guess I should just leave you two lovebirds alone then," Eithne sighed. He canted his hips in a way that suggested he'd like to test out some of those theories for himself and put so much swing into his walk as he crossed the room toward Mal that Neil thought he might dislocate something. The eely way he passed Mal in the doorway ensured that he made plenty of contact too. Neil watched every move he made, but the stab of heat he felt, watching him glide a hand over Mal as he left, had nothing to do with lust. He had a vivid, fully fledged image of snatching that hand and making Eithne eat it. He had to look away before he went after him.

Eithne's footsteps faded along the corridor and Mal closed the door with a bemused smile.

"Well, that one's growing up way too fast for his own good," he said. "You okay? You look like you want to burn things with your face."

"I'm fine," Neil said, making himself look up and forcing a little smile of his own. "Eithne was just being nosy. And blunt. I hope you don't think I was talking about you behind your back."

"Of course you were. I don't mind, though." Mal shrugged. "It really doesn't matter. It doesn't change how I feel."

Neil should probably just let it drop. Mal wasn't given to saying things he didn't mean. He still felt guilty about it, though.

"He thought I was feeding off you and said I could feed off him too. I told him I didn't need to do that and he said he still wanted to sleep with me, with us, anyway. Who does that? Just says things like that?"

"We all have our own needs, Neil. Just because you don't crave intimacy from everyone doesn't mean that there aren't others out there still struggling to get a handle on their own yearnings. Don't think badly of him. I think, for what it's worth, he does actually like you." Mal sat down on the edge of the bed and leaned back with his hands splayed on the duvet behind him. "My weakness is shiny things. His is the buzz of ecstasy. What's yours?" He winked playfully.

Neil scowled at him. "You. Or chocolate. I do like chocolate."

Mal grinned and said, "C'mere." He lifted one hand, beckoning Neil with a crook of his index finger.

Neil resisted the urge to glide over to him to prove he could move just as silkily as Eithne. That would be petty and it would feel too much like it did when he let his demon side out. He did let his eyes roam up and down Mal's body and, instead of stopping in front of him, he leaned in, putting a knee on the bed between

Mal's thighs and lowering until he was arched over him. "Yes?"

"I don't have any chocolate," Mal said with an easy smirk. "But I'll remember that for future reference. In the meantime, I guess you're just going to have to make do with me."

The hand he had used to call Neil over came to rest in the small of Neil's back and Mal walked his fingers up Neil's spine.

Neil bent his head the scant inch it took to touch his lips to Mal's. Kissing Mal wasn't like kissing anyone else. He had a taste to him. It wasn't minty toothpaste or what he'd had for breakfast. It was sort of spicy, like cinnamon maybe. The way he moved his lips and tongue sent shivers down his back to where Mal's fingers were touching him. Neil still hadn't figured out how his lips could be so soft and coaxing and at the same time turn so hard and demanding when he got really turned on. He just knew he liked the contrast.

"I think you taste better than chocolate anyway," Neil breathed when their lips parted.

"Mmm...you too." Mal touched noses with him.

Neil bumped him back gently, nudging his lips again for another kiss, a deeper taste. He slipped a hand between them and caressed down Mal's chest and abs over his shirt, and the conversation with Eithne popped back into his head, unwanted. Ever since the day Mal had brought home that bed they'd pushed next to his old one, they hadn't slept alone, but sometimes that was all they did. Sleep. And sometimes they kissed and stroked each other off and a few times they'd used their mouths on each other. Neil was perfectly happy with all of that, but Eithne made it sound like it was odd. Mal would tell him if he wanted something more, though, wouldn't he? Neil moved his hand lower as they kissed, tracing his fingers over the outline of the bulge behind Mal's zipper.

Mal lifted his hips under his touch, pushing the swell of his cock into the palm of his hand. It felt comfortable there and he framed the fullness of it with his fingers and thumb, gently stroking back and forth and enjoying the way that it stretched and thickened for the attention, as if preening. Malachai stroked his fingers up into Neil's hair and caressed the nape of his neck and the back of his skull while they were joined at the mouth. His kisses grew hungrier as Neil caressed his cock. His tongue darted between Neil's lips rapidly, flickering against his teeth and tongue as his breathing quickened.

Mal's warm touch moved down to his hip and he lay back, drawing Neil onto the bed with him as he slid both hands under Neil's T-shirt, pushing it up to his shoulders and stroking over his lean, warm body, up and down his back, then his sides, making him shiver at the ticklish sensation above his hips. He caressed Neil's bared torso and flicked at his hardening nipples with his thumbnails, causing Neil to gasp and laugh into his mouth.

"Let me take this off," Mal whispered, pulling the shirt right up over Neil's head then looking down at himself.

"You're wearing too much," Neil agreed, quickly tugging buttons out of their buttonholes in his hunger to see Mal exposed.

They had slept in at least T-shirts and underwear since arriving here. This was not their home and Drasnil had so many people housed at the old theater that they were in constant expectation of someone barging in on them unannounced but right now, someone walking in was the furthest thing from Neil's mind.

When he got Mal's shirt open, he skimmed his hands over his chest, loving the way his skin felt, so hot and silky, with just a dusting of dark-golden hair around his nipples. He flicked his thumb over Mal's nipple, like he had done to him, his lips twitching at the way it stiffened. He moved his other hand down and unbuttoned and unzipped him one handed.

Mal grinned at him, a sexy, feral smirk that never failed to get Neil hot. He was hard just from the kissing and touching. Whatever Eithne thought, there was nothing wrong with his reactions. He was perfectly equipped and clearly enthusiastic when it came to getting off.

"I've missed this," he said, as if confirming Neil's thoughts. "Me and you, and a bit of privacy."

"Do you miss other things?" Neil couldn't resist asking. He knew he was letting Eithne get way too far under his skin with that question, but he couldn't stop thinking about it.

"Like, what kind of things?" Mal asked.

"Like…like sex things. Um, more than a blow job, I mean?"

Mal's silvery eyes widened and darkened briefly, shimmering like pools of oil. He curled his fingers around Neil's hips above the loose waistband of his jeans, running them lightly under the denim, teasing the sensitive upper curves of his ass cheeks.

"I can't miss something I've never had, can I?" he said at last, gnawing on his lower lip.

Neil stared at him, waiting for him to chuckle or something. When he didn't, Neil finally said, "You've never done it with anyone?"

"I've never done it with you," Mal said cryptically. Then, when Neil just stared at him, "I've fucked women. And I've been had by…well, let's not call them men, shall we."

His gaze flickered toward the ceiling for a while and the admission most definitely dampened his ardor.

Neil brought a hand to his cheek, brushing his thumb over the high cheekbone and waiting for Mal to look at him again. He kissed him, light and tender. "I'm sorry."

"So am I." Mal looked down at the hand on his face then back up into Neil's eyes. There was a kind of weary resignation in his expression. "Don't be sorry. It isn't…wasn't your fault. But I guess I lost interest in sex for a while, because of that. You've brought me back to life, Neil. You can be proud of that."

Neil kissed him again, a long, slow kiss that was still sweetly tender but full of longing. When they broke the kiss, Mal asked him, "What about you?"

"What about me?"

"Do you want more than what we've done so far?"

"I like everything we've done," Neil said. "I don't know if I want more."

"We don't have to do anything you don't want to do, Neil. I hope you understand that."

"I do. Understand. I just… I've never done it, so I don't know what it's like. And don't say we don't have to again, I get that we don't. But maybe I do want to."

Mal drew him down so they were practically face to face and Neil could feel the length of his warm body pressed up close against his, from his lips down to his feet.

"What do you want to?" he whispered and a ghost of his old mischief returned. "Tell me."

Warmth trickled down all the way from the top of Neil's head to somewhere just behind his balls. It was so sweet and good and churning with all kinds of emotions that Neil shivered. "You're going to make me say it?" he whispered back.

"Yes."

Neil licked his lips, then trailed the tip of his tongue over Mal's bottom lip. "I want to find out what it feels like...to have you inside me."

Mal's tongue flickered out like a serpent's, sparring with his for a second then retreating. "I'd love to know what it feels like to be inside you too. Some guys say it's amazing. Tighter. Than being with a woman, I mean." A slight flush rose to Mal's cheeks just for a moment, then it was gone. "I'd be happy to...if you really want me to."

Neil slid his fingers back into Mal's hair. He kissed him again, undulating on top of him so they pressed together tighter. Mal still had his hands resting on the top of his ass and when Neil curled his hips, he squeezed, making him buck faster and groan into his mouth. Mal's hands slid even deeper into the confines of his jeans, getting a good handful of both cheeks before he squeezed again, harder. Neil gasped.

"Yes, I really want you," he said breathlessly.

Mal covered his mouth with his own, kissing him more fiercely and tugging Neil down against him so that he could feel just how into that idea Mal was. His lovely, long cock was firm and hard, leaking against Neil's bare belly as they rubbed together. Neil's own hard dick pressed uncomfortably against the fly of his jeans and he wriggled a hand down there to unfasten them. It freed his erection and served the dual purpose of giving Mal's hands more room to squeeze and fondle his ass cheeks.

"We're gonna need something for lube," Mal said when he came up for air. "I don't wanna hurt you and dry fucking is bloody painful."

He spoke with the tones of bitter experience. He was already pressing against Neil's channel with his fingers, massaging skillfully around the flexing nub of his hole. Neil itched to feel them inside him but he made himself focus.

"There's rose oil in the bathroom cabinet, the bottle Drasnil gave you for your...your scars. Would that...would it do?" he panted.

"Clever lad." Mal chuckled. "Go get it then. And lose your pants!" he called because Neil was already scuttling off the bed and into the compact bathroom that adjoined their room. When he came back, shutting the door behind him and making sure it was locked this time, there was a very naughty grin on Malachai's face. He lay naked on the bed, having shucked his own pants, stroking his cock slowly. Neil shivered with need as he dropped his jeans and boxer briefs to his ankles, kicking them away, then wrestling his boots off, and his socks.

Finally, gloriously nude, he clambered onto the bed and wrapped one hand around Mal's hard, curved, beautiful penis. He was not so thick that Neil couldn't wrap his fingers around it but a shade longer than his outstretched hand. The plump glans was still wrapped in a fine shroud of foreskin. Most of the men Neil's father had encouraged him to raise spell energy with were cut and Neil loved to stroke Malachai's silken cowl back and forth over the head of his cock, watching the glossy dome play peek-a-boo for a while before he swallowed and sucked on it.

"Mmmmmhhhh...take it easy down there," Mal sighed. "It feels amazing but you want me to save something for your ass, right?"

Neil flushed at the reminder and Mal grinned at him.

"C'mon. Shuffle around this way so I can eat that sexy hole. I wanna get you nice and slippery while you're sucking me."

Neil still found it strange how Mal could say the most deliciously frank and dirty things, while Neil had his cock in his mouth, and the only surge of lust he felt was his own. No, that wasn't exactly true. His demon side couldn't sense it, but Neil was learning to feel it with his human half. He wiggled around on the bed until they lay facing opposite directions. He was about to straddle his head but Mal gripped Neil's thighs and rolled a quarter turn, so they were both on their sides facing each other. He bent one of Neil's knees up so it was pointed at the ceiling.

The position was comfortable in clothes. Naked it felt hyper-exposed and, weirdly, that seemed to be turning Neil on as much as the way Mal touched him.

"You have such a beautiful body," Mal mused, before diving in and doing things with his mouth between Neil's legs that he'd have once blushed to think about. He took time to kiss the insides of Neil's lean thighs, running his hands up and down them as he explored with his lips and tongue. That felt as fantastic as the compliment, even more so.

He shivered and sucked in a breath, as Mal's tongue skated over the sensitive stretch of skin behind his balls. Every nerve ending down there prickled and tingled with anticipation as Mal slowly laved him with his tongue, back and forth. When that tongue touched his ring, those prickles turned electric and he had to come up from Mal's cock with a gasp. To his relief, that didn't stop Mal from circling around with the tip and even pressing inside a bit. Neil's lungs were working overtime and he closed his eyes with a groan. The feeling was so intense he was quivering.

"You okay?" Mal whispered and his breath was like the touch of an angel's wingtip over his wet skin.

Neil exhaled in a rush and licked over Mal's cockhead.

"Don't stop, that feels so good," he murmured.

"Just checking." Mal nuzzled deep between his cheeks and kissed him there, sucking gently on the loose skin behind his balls until Neil was almost jolting up off the mattress with every touch. The forefinger of one of his hands traced up and down the cleft of his ass, tickling his ring while the other hand reached down and stroked through Neil's hair, offering gentle encouragement to take him deeper.

He sighed between kisses as Neil nodded lower on him. "Oh…oh yes…that's sweet."

Neil hummed his agreement of how sweet it was and quickened the strokes of his mouth, drawing back slow before plunging down again and finding a rhythm. If he focused on that, it was easier not to get so caught up in what Mal was doing to him that he couldn't breathe. Until Mal slid an oiled digit inside him, then every thought he had scattered. That was ten times the intensity of what his tongue had done.

He pushed his lips down the length of Mal's cock, sucking him hard as a sound of pleasure rose in his throat. He didn't know what he would do if Mal stopped.

Mal seemed to have no intention of stopping. His finger moved steadily, alternating a gentle, rhythmic sawing motion in and out of Neil's body with a slow circling of his fingertip over that ultra-sweet spot just inside him. Neil was not sure if he wanted to scream or cry, it felt so good. To make matters more complicated, his lover's warm mouth moved back to his balls, absorbing them one at a time, tugging gently on them, letting them go, swallowing the other.

That was so hot and so amazing, it was tipping Neil forward too much. He came up off Mal's cock again.

"Malachai... Mal... Oh, you're gonna make me come."

Mal sat up and grinned at him lazily. "Isn't that the point?"

Neil sat up too and reached for him, pulling him in for a kiss. "Yes, most definitely yes. But not yet." He lay back and pulled Mal down with him this time, still kissing him, until they were situated with Malachai between his legs.

"So this is more what you had in mind, then?" Mal punctuated his words with slow, hungry kisses, undulating so that their bodies were in constant, restless contact, his cock stroking up against Neil's and stirring his need again.

Neil nodded then added, "Actually, I'm not certain what I had in mind, but this feels right."

He stroked his hands over Mal's arms and shoulders and bent his knees up, because that felt good too, even if it also felt vulnerable.

"It's fantastic," Mal agreed. "I want you so much, Neil. I can't remember ever feeling this way about a guy before. But I love it."

Neil smoothed a hand down Mal's chest to where their stiff cocks rubbed together and took hold of them, giving a good few strokes. He almost changed his mind. The feel of them both in his hand was amazing, urging him up toward the edge again, but he made himself slow down before he got there. He was so hot and wanted to come so badly, but he also wanted to discover what it would be like to have Mal inside him. His finger had certainly felt good in there.

He started to move Mal's cock down but Mal stopped him. "Put some of the oil on me first," he advised.

Neil fumbled with the bottle but got some in his hand and slicked it over Mal's cock, taking the opportunity to jerk him a bit more before Mal wrapped his fingers around his dick as well and moved back between his legs, pressing the head against him.

It felt big there, snuggled up between his cheeks and pushing on his hole. Like, really big. He wanted it, though. He was so turned on, so ready, and when Mal finally did ease inside, Neil tipped his head back, eyes closing. A long, low moan worked its way up from what must have been the very bottoms of his lungs.

"Neil…"

"Yes…more…ugh, yeah! Don't stop, please don't stop."

"Just unwind a bit, will ya? You're crushing me, here!" Mal's chuckle was a deep, dark, sultry sound and it vibrated through Neil's body like the aftershock of a quake.

Everything Neil had heard whispered by snickering friends at school, every snide joke, everything he'd surreptitiously read in anatomy and sex ed books at the back of the library while keeping one eye peeled for nosy librarians, none of that was anything like reality.

From all he'd gathered, he'd been expecting it to hurt — or at least be uncomfortable. He'd been prepared that he might not even like it. Wrong. So wrong. He wasn't sure he was going to make it until Mal got it in all the way. Not before he came.

He tried to relax like Mal said and maybe he managed it because Mal's features softened, but he couldn't stay still. He gripped Mal's arms and rocked his hips, and the feelings that shot through him like fireworks made him gasp and moan again.

At last Mal knelt back and pushed his sweat damp hair out of his face to look down on Neil with a bemused smile.

"Let's try something a bit different, okay?" he suggested, climbing over Neil's thigh to drop down beside him on the mattress, huffing for a moment, though he was still hard and eager. He stroked some more of the oil over his cock, taking his time and ignoring the look of anguish on Neil's face.

Neil was trying not to hyperventilate. He managed to stay where he was a moment or two longer, then swung his leg over Mal's thighs and sat up astride him, his hands on Mal's chest.

"Neil?" Mal said the word almost tentatively.

"What?"

"Are you okay?"

"Yes. Better than okay. Why?"

A strange look crossed Mal's features for a moment then was gone. "Nothing."

Neil smiled. "Is this okay?" he asked, sliding his hips back and forth so they rubbed cocks again.

Mal reached down and slowly wrapped his hand around both of their cocks, stroking slowly until Neil was calmer. He stretched up then, hooking one hand around the back of his neck and drawing him in for a kiss.

"That's great," Mal whispered as their lips parted. "How about you try sitting down on it, see if it goes in easier that way?" He leaned back in the pillows again, looking up at Neil with a twinkle in his eyes. "You can control how fast we go like that. If it works, I can roll you over again. How's that sound?"

To demonstrate how that sounded, Neil took hold of Mal's cock and lifted up, guiding him back. He still felt thick and very big, like it wasn't going to fit, even though he knew it would, but it was only for a moment or two. Only until he got the head past his ring. He stopped there for a few seconds, adjusting, then sank down lower and pushed back up before easing even farther down. Neil bit his lips but not from any pain, just to keep the noises of sheer pleasure from getting out. Mal had a hold of his hips but he was only resting his hands there. He glanced up and caught Mal's eyes.

"Better?"

"That feels good, hot stuff. Still nice and tight, but it's doing it for me," Mal said, just a bit breathless. "You like that?"

"Yeah…oh yeah…a lot." Neil crooned. An actual croon, and nothing he'd planned, it just came out like that. He brought both hands back to Mal's chest and balanced there, rocking his hips again nice and slow, finding a glide that felt amazing. "That is so fucking good." He sank all the way down until his cheeks met Mal's pelvis and ground there for a second before resuming the slow up-and-down motion.

Mal let him find his rhythm for a few minutes, just holding on to his thighs and watching Neil move astride him. Then he rolled his pelvis upward in time with Neil's downward motion, thrusting slow at first then latching on to his hips and bucking faster into him. The steady slap, slap, slap of their bodies coming together was another level of heat on top of the vigorous stimulation of Neil's asshole and the rising tension in his balls.

"Gods above and below, you're fucking beautiful," Mal growled.

Neil made an incomprehensible, strangled sound and leaned down over him. He only realized he'd been digging his fingers into Mal's chest when he let go. He grabbed the sheets on either side of Mal's head instead, bunching them in his fists as he kissed him hard, delving his tongue inside to dance over Mal's.

Mal's body curled upward between his thighs as he leaned forward, keeping that deep penetration going as his mouth pressed harder on Neil's lips. His strong hands gripped Neil's ass cheeks almost roughly, tugging him down on his cock as he surged harder, no clever words, just vigorous rutting and the hoarse sound of his ragged breathing. Sweat jeweled his torso and the ripples of his belly as he fucked Neil like his life depended on it.

Neil's breath huffed out with each thrust. His cock was so hard, the head brushing Mal's belly where it pressed between them.

"Uuhh, Mal…uhh, I'm gonna come," he whimpered.

This time, Mal did not make a joke or try to stop him. He leaned back into the softness of the bed and his body arced up to meet Neil's, pounding him with short, fast, urgent thrusts that tore fractured sounds from his throat and rolled his eyes back in his head for a moment as he tried to match Neil, stroke for stroke.

Neil's gasps and cries joined Mal's as he went hurtling over the peak. Not only was it more intense than he'd ever felt before but the orgasm seemed to last and last, one big shuddering spurt after another until he saw spots behind his eyelids and collapsed on Mal's chest in a sweating, panting, heap.

"Mal, oh fuck... Uh, so, good." *Good* didn't really cover it but his mind was just a swirling mass and he was afraid if he didn't say something he might do something ridiculous like start crying.

Mal was grunting from the sheer exertion of powering up into him and he kept going for about a minute longer before Neil felt the thickness in his ass swell even more and Mal went still under him. A sharp cry, like the bark of a kicked animal, burst out of him and his long, lean body trembled briefly. Then he flopped back down and stroked shaking hands up and down Neil's naked back, huffing hard.

"Uhh...thank you. Thank you." The words were no more than a whisper against his skin.

Neil murmured words back to him that didn't make any sense and he didn't care. It felt like every bit of tension he'd been carrying around for weeks had been drained from him. He'd never done drugs, but he imagined that this must be what it felt like when people talked about being high. After a long while — after they had cooled down and Mal had softened and slipped from him and their breathing had slowed — Neil shifted to Mal's side and curled up with his head on his shoulder.

"That was nothing like what I thought. It was way, way better," he murmured.

"It was amazing," Mal exhaled in a sleepy whisper. "So good. Haven't shot like that in ages." He wrapped his arms around Neil, pulling him closer.

Neil snuggled in and while he meant to just close his eyes for a moment and enjoy the lovely, honey-warm feeling he was getting from Malachai, the lure of sleep proved too much and he drifted off.

Chapter Seventeen

Malachai had a little bounce to his stride for most of the following day. It was weird really, he'd never put much store in sex as a therapeutic aid. He enjoyed the actual, physical act but beyond the moment and the pleasure, he didn't usually think about it much. He'd woke up wrapped around Neil, the morning after they'd...well, he wasn't really sure what to call it. Fucking didn't seem adequate, even if it was undeniably what they'd done. Making love seemed too flowery. It had been more like a binding, a piece of energy magic. Maybe that was down to Neil and what he was, but it had seemed more balanced than that. Like they'd somehow worked magic together.

This morning he felt like he could take on the world. And it did not go unnoticed. People grinned at him as he passed by, all the way down to the first floor. Mercurio raised an eyebrow but just patted him on the back, without saying a word, miraculously. Drasnil greeted him in the main auditorium of the theater, which was his makeshift war-room, with a knowing smirk.

"Well, someone got his oats last night!"

"Hush, you." Mal leveled a finger at his face. "Don't ask questions, I'm not going to answer them. What have you got for me?"

"One of my runners heard a rumor down by the docks that a tall, redheaded witch stole a cabin boy out from under the nose of Captain Kenneally. That news is a few weeks old, though, so I'd say that's how the boy's father found you."

"Damn it. I should have figured that dockside gossip would get back to him. I guess I was thinking that the Carraroe Canary would have been long since sailed and the fuss died down by the time he came hunting." Mal drummed his fingers on the edge of his host's elaborate desk. The piece could have been discreetly removed from any of the fine houses that once stood up on King's Mile. "Does anyone have any idea where he is currently? The sorcerer, I mean."

"If I had that piece of information, Lord Valentine, I wouldn't have waited for you to roll out of bed at your leisure." Drasnil smirked again. "My scouts are making inquiries. They have to take care, though. The rumor mill works both ways and the last thing we want is for the bastard to hear we're searching for him. Which brings me to my other piece of news. Madran reports that someone was asking questions last night at the club. Seems now that the trail has gone cold with my dearly departed brother, the Bone Men are backtracking."

Mal cursed under his breath.

"Look at it this way, at least we know they are still on our trail. It's when they stop that we need to worry," Drasnil said in a conciliatory tone.

"If they come here, at least we can kill them," Mal said, lacing his fingers and cracking his knuckles.

"We can certainly try," Drasnil agreed, looking no less supportive of this measure. "We have the firepower, both magical and less…ethereal. And the warriors to wield it."

"We are fighting demons and sorcerers. And a sorcerer who is at least half-demon himself," Mal reminded him.

"Once, our people and demonkind walked side by side on the face of the world," Drasnil told him with a knowing smirk. "Some of us do not forget."

"Did you learn how to kill them?" Malachai asked him seriously. In his opinion, the half-fae exuded more levity than the situation required.

Drasnil's eyes flashed, silver and feral. "They are not immortal, much as they would like you to believe otherwise. They bleed just like anyone. It's the ones that have a bonded familiar that are truly dangerous. Without one, they are more vulnerable. Easier to wear down."

Before Mal could respond, they were interrupted by a surly voice.

"Easier would be to just give him up before more people have to die for him." Charlie was staring at them bitterly when they both looked round. He looked smaller and more wan than Mal remembered from his visits to the house but given what he had probably witnessed there, he was hardly surprised.

"Easy is not always right," Mal reminded him, turning to lean back against the desk so he could survey the youngster. "If your master had handed Neil over to the authorities as he intended, or even left well alone and not meddled in my business, Death might have passed him by." He felt Drasnil go very still beside him and nodded to the cluricaun. "My apologies, Felipe, but it is true."

"Del never could resist a pretty whore. You should know that, Malachai," Charlie sneered. "This one turned out to be the death of him. You're right, he should have handed the thieving bitch over when he had the chance. I don't get why everyone is being so stupid about it."

"I don't understand why you're being so vindictive, either. What did he ever do to you, Charlie Cooper?" Mal asked sadly. "If the Bone Men came looking for you, we would have your back, the same as for any other fellow here. Why do you hate him so much?"

"He's demon scum!" Charlie spat out. "No better than the Crow."

"Better a whore, a thief and demon scum than one willing to sit by and watch someone being tortured and do nothing," Neil said from the shadows at the edge of the room. "I'll take what I am any day, over being a coward."

"Says the demon that ran away while his mother was being killed!" Charlie glared at him, practically shaking with rage.

"Enough!" Mal barked at him, making him jump. "That's enough. I understand that you're upset. I comprehend your loss but sniping at one another is not going to bring your mother back, Charlie. It won't bring Del and Crow back, and it is not going to defeat Neil's father if he returns with an army of Bone Men at his heels."

Neil went silent. He had gone pale and his lips were pressed together. Charlie was red-faced and looked ready to fight.

Neil spoke first, quietly. "I did what I had to do to survive, just like you would have. I didn't ask Vargas to take me. What happened to him isn't my fault. I don't know why you hated me from minute one, but I'm willing to put it behind us if you are."

Charlie took a step toward him, curled his lip and spat at his feet, then turned and stalked out.

"That would be a 'no' then." Drasnil sighed and smoothed his silver hair around the small, curved, nacreous horns self-consciously. "I have no idea what we are to do with that one. If his brother was not such a sweetheart, I would feed the little sod to the Bone Men, personally. Master Markovic, please come in properly and take a seat. It is a joy to see you looking so...vibrant."

Mal glanced from Drasnil to Neil and he realized what the cluricaun meant. Neil's aura practically shimmered with energy, even if he looked so despondent that, were he fae instead of demon kin, his ears would practically be drooping. Was that what Felipe saw around him?

A bit of heat climbed to Mal's cheeks and he lowered his head.

Neil came closer and when he got near enough that they were within touching distance, Mal swore he felt the same sensation as when two magnets pulled close. If Neil sensed it, he gave no sign, other than perhaps a slight sway of his body before he took the seat Drasnil offered.

Drasnil sat too, across the corner of the table from him, and waved Mal toward the empty seat on Neil's other side. As he sat down, the cluricaun appraised Neil of the continued search for him and asked, "Does your father possess any weakness that you are aware of, anything that could perhaps be used to our advantage?"

Neil was quiet for a few long moments. Instead of answering the question, which he had already answered at least a dozen times for Drasnil before, he said, "Maybe Charlie's right. Maybe I should leave here before he finds me."

"There's a fool idea," Mercurio spoke up from where he'd been propping up the wall. He snorted. "C'mon, kid. I thought you were made of sterner stuff. You're not going to let a little shit like Charlie Cooper get under your skin, are you?"

"No," Neil said. "It's not that."

Merc snorted again. "Are you lying to us, or to yourself?"

Neil bristled. "I'm not lying. It's just…"

"It's just…you don't want anyone getting hurt on your behalf," Merc supplied for him and when Neil nodded, he continued, "Boy, these fairy folk might make a big fuss about it, but when it comes down to it, they practically wet their panties over a chance to fight demons. You won't find a one of them here that isn't itching to shed some demonic blood on their turf."

"Is that supposed to make me feel better?" Neil asked, although he was almost smiling.

"Present comp'ny excluded." Merc winked.

"I'm glad to hear it." Malachai exhaled then moved over to let Merc come and sit at the table, since he was already eavesdropping. He did not miss the long, appraising look that Drasnil ran over Mercurio's well-muscled frame. Interesting, that—he hadn't believed that Felipe formed attachments, at least not physical ones. But then Mal hadn't thought *he* was capable of it anymore either, until last night.

His face grew hotter again and he steered his thoughts away from that.

"Mister Geiger is not incorrect," Drasnil said, dragging his eyes away, but not before they darkened considerably. "We never shy away from a good fight. Not if we believe we can win. And we usually do."

"Believe or win?" Merc asked him and those intense, gray eyes shifted back to his face.

"Both," Drasnil told him, without a shred of modesty.

They talked some more about various plans and contingencies, and Mal was relieved that Neil didn't bring up the idea of leaving again. He was under no illusion that they were safe, but they stood a better chance here than on their own, unless they could simply outrun the man. The idea of running didn't sit well with Mal and even if they went far away, he'd always be looking over his shoulder and trying to keep Neil hidden as much as possible. That sort of life was not one he wanted, for Neil or for himself.

Breakfast was brought in while they were still deep in discussions and they all ate well. As the plates were being cleared away, the goblin Klosky came rushing in and accorded Drasnil a sketchy bow. "Beg pardon. We have an issue, Master Drasnil."

"Don't keep us waiting, what is it?"

"This morning when Rita and Baathy went to relieve Tonton and Zefe of the guard, they found the post abandoned. Baathy reported it of course but we didn't think much on it, except to be irked. Zefe was new and Tonton likes his drink so we figured they'd gone off on a bender. Baathy says he and Rita weren't on post an hour before he started feeling twitchy and Rita began mumbling, like 'what are we doing here', and 'it's madness to stay', and just as he was about to come down and see if anyone could take his shift as he's feeling out of sorts, Blanor and Gaelyn come scrambling in like they was being chased by the night creatures and spouting how 'it's hopeless and we're all gonna die'."

Mal saw from the corner of his eye how Neil had gone stiff in the chair and gripped the arms so tight his knuckles were white.

"Heart's Fear hex," Neil murmured.

"So it would seem." Drasnil looked at Neil, eyes narrowed thoughtfully. "We'll need to counter, and fast, before panic spreads. How are your singing voices, gentlemen?"

* * * *

Within minutes, everyone able to carry a note was in the walled yard. Many of those with goblin blood brought drums or pipes. By the time they had all gathered, a palatable aura of dread had permeated Drasnil's people. Mal felt the edges of it tugging at him, a darkness that wanted to chip away at his heart, but his defenses were better than most and while he was aware of it, it didn't affect him.

Neil, he noted, was grim and focused but showed none of the nervous tension many of the others did. He didn't fidget, or dart his eyes around looking for danger, or start yammering doom and gloom, as was happening all around them.

"It's getting bad," Neil observed. "You'd better hurry," he said quietly to Drasnil, who gave him a 'no kidding' look in return.

"Since you're so eager, lead them off. I'll start the weaving."

Mal half-expected Neil to beg off, but instead he nodded and licked his lips. If Mal was surprised at that, he was just about floored when Neil started to sing.

"Sweet, o sweet, is the sun shining high
And light with love is my heart
Dance, o dance, til your feet they do fly
And know we shall ne'er part."

It was a very old song, one that Mal had probably heard sung three dozen different ways, although it had been years since he'd heard it last, in another country and another life. More surprising than the song was the way Neil sang. Sweet as the sun shining high, was right. His voice was clear and strong, lilting over the words. Mal glanced at Felipe, who lifted both eyebrows and grinned as he started to weave the song into spell form. Other voices joined in slowly, and the instruments. Mal had heard the song most often in melancholy tones, but the way Neil led the chorus infused the words with an undercurrent of joy and hope. Mal spotted Amy, who smiled at him and grabbed the hand of the young man next to her, pulling him into the loose circle and laughing as they twirled into a fast, bouncing jig.

When the last verse was sung, Neil kept right on, starting over from the top without pause. More people joined in the middle, singing while they danced.

With each pass the song grew in strength and vibrancy as the power of the counterspell coursed through their band. He thought that he even saw Charlie smile but it could have been an illusion because their dancing circles were all spinning madly by the time the song came around for the fifth or sixth time.

Drasnil, like a deranged conductor on the stairs above them, steered and channeled the counter-hex and Malachai felt the euphoria spilling beyond their corporeal bodies and out into the wards that fizzed and crackled around the compound. Most would have seen nothing at all but he had watched his father ward their properties Overhill and knew what he was looking at. Energy danced in time with the rhythm of their song. It coasted like a wave of pure ultraviolet light, around the walls and into every nook and cranny of their physical defenses. The magic made his blood course with fierce effervescence.

He kept control of his senses but some were already giving way to the tide of euphoria.

Mal experienced a wash of mild anxiety. They could not lose control. It would be almost worse than letting them yield to the Heart's Fear. This was how Wild Hunts were unleashed...

He looked up at Drasnil but the cluricaun had already seen it and he was drawing the energy back, reining it in. As if they were one being, Neil softened the vibrancy of the song, turning it from exuberant to a gentle confidence. The moment of madness was averted but their assembly looked at one another with new eyes as the music slowed and came to a stop.

A whoop and cheer went up and the everyone seemed to start chatting at once and eventually moving away in pairs and clusters to get on with their day, or in some cases probably to sneak off to a private corner. There was no circle cast to worry about—fae magic on the whole tended to be less formal than all that. The wildness of it was powerful but came with the cost of being more difficult to control. Felipe was indeed a skilled mage and the spell seemed to have worked perfectly. Everyone was full of smiles and laughter, not a trace of the dread and despair that had dogged them earlier.

Neil looked like his head might be floating about three feet above his shoulders, high as a kite and soaring aimlessly.

"Neil...?"

Neil closed his eyes and swayed on his feet, a smile curling his hips.

"Time. It's bought us time," he said dreamily as Mal reached him. "He won't have the energy for another big working for a few days."

Mal slid his arms around him and bent his head to touch his forehead and nose to Neil's.

"Come back down. Focus, little falcon," he said, letting some of the tenderness he was feeling flow out into Neil's vibrant aura. "That was...beautiful."

Neil slid closer, fitting himself against Mal like a puzzle piece clicking into place. He tipped his head back and kissed him, maybe only meaning to brush his lips reassuringly, but instead the kiss sizzled between them. Mal broke off the kiss before it grew more heated and Neil opened his eyes. They were bled black, just like when they'd been tangled in the sheets together and Neil had crawled so eagerly on top of him. He hadn't told him then what he'd seen because he hadn't wanted to scare him or spoil the mood. He seemed wholly unaware of it then, just as now.

"Earth some of that energy," Mal said more firmly.

Neil smiled and Mal swore it held a rebellious edge for just a moment, but Neil took a deep breath and let it out. The crackling energy in Neil's aura came down to a more normal level and the blue came back to his irises.

"Better?"

"Better," Neil confirmed.

"You are amazing," Mal told him, drawing Neil to him harder and burying his face in his dark blond curls. "I can't wait to find out what effect you have on transitional magic. But you unfasten hexes better than anyone I know. And I've met some damned fine charm-smiths."

"I just sang a song. Felipe did the heavy lifting." Neil beamed at him.

"I've watched Felipe Drasnil work a charm before and trust me, he didn't do that all on his own," Mal said but couldn't help a smile at the innocent look on Neil's face.

Okay...maybe not innocent. But he certainly looked bemused. Did he really have no idea how strong his own powers were?

At that moment, said charm-smith came trotting over to them, all agrin.

"That was a thing of beauty." Drasnil echoed Mal's sentiment. "If this one doesn't lay claim to you when all is said and done, Master Markovic, you are more than welcome to a place in my court. I would love to have you at my side," he said shamelessly.

Mal was surprised by the sudden spike of emotion that casual offer roused in him. A spear of possessive heat surged through him from his heart to his loins and he had to sit down very hard on a growl.

The thing was, he could see how such a match would work out well for Neil. The boy was already beautiful. With Felipe on his arm, with the sartorially immaculate cluricaun for a partner, he would become incandescent. And the magic they would work together could easily become a thing of modern legend.

It would do Neil no harm and plenty of good.

"I don't think that will be necessary," he managed to say. It came out smooth enough, he thought. Not snarly at all.

Felipe still raised one of those immaculate silver eyebrows and the look the cluricaun gave him was pure fairy mischief. But all he said, in his driest, most elegant way, was, "Of course not, Lord Valentine. However, if you did not—"

"Thank you, but I'm with Mal," Neil said. The words, and the way he said them, were simple. No declarations or explanations. And yet they had the power to smother Mal's sudden flare of possessive jealousy in a soothing blanket.

He stifled the grin that wanted to plaster itself across his face but could not resist nodding agreement and pointing in Neil's direction. "What he said."

Chapter Eighteen

When Neil was younger, he had made friends easily. It was only when he'd gotten older and become aware of the life his father was grooming him for that he'd started to withdraw and cut ties. It had seemed pointless to socialize, knowing that one day his soul would be eaten as fuel for killing magic. Maybe it was even dangerous to let anyone get too close. When he'd felt lonely during those years, he'd filled the void with worry and fear and kept to himself even more.

He hadn't set out to befriend Malachai, much less actually care about him, but he couldn't deny that Mal filled the place inside where all that fear and loneliness lived so completely he couldn't even look at him without smiling.

"You're too cute," Amy said, low enough so only he would hear. He was sitting on a bench under a tree in the courtyard, pretending to read while stealing glances over toward where Mal was working with Merc on an old radio.

"I've no clue what you're talking about," Neil said, hiding a smile.

"That. Right there. The smile you think you're hiding when you look at him," she teased.

Neil's face warmed but he didn't try to deny it. He hadn't realized he was so obvious.

"Oh, you got it bad." She chuckled. "Have you said the *L* word yet?"

"No."

"You should tell him. He's totally gaga over you, you know. And, he's hot."

Neil couldn't disagree there. Malachai stood out, even when he was just quietly tinkering with something. The flame-red hair got your attention, then you saw the fine cheekbones and defined jaw. He had a movie star face and a tall, willowy frame a lot of people would kill to have. And Neil got to see him naked, which was even better. He had run his fingers and tongue over the firm muscles beneath his light-copper skin and watched that perfectly tensioned body dance and flutter for every touch.

"How do you even start to tell someone like him that you feel…" Neil looked away, watching Mal again. He was quibbling with Mercurio over some technical issue and the expression on the older man's face was fond and tolerant, like they'd had variations on this argument many times and he knew exactly how it would go.

He understood that Merc too loved Malachai, in his way. But Mal did not sleep with Mercurio, did not writhe in ecstasy under him. That was not how their relationship worked. Neil could not even figure out whether that was something Merc regretted. He was as much a closed book as Mal in that respect.

Malachai lifted his head and ran his fingers through that tangled, fiery mane. His silvery gaze met Neil's for a second, through his forelock, like he knew he would find Neil watching. A frustrated grin tugged at his lips, then he returned to the debate, tapping one finger on a component of the radio for emphasis.

"Silly." She laughed at him. "He knows how you feel."

Did he? How could he, when Neil had barely figured it out for himself? Amy tousled his hair with one hand as she rose and mumbled something about checking to see what was on the menu for dinner and Neil sank back on the padded bench to let his thoughts tumble around. He had Bone Men looking for him and it was only a matter of time before his father sent another attack. He should be wholly focused on that, but instead all he could think about was how it felt when Malachai peeled him out of his clothes, how it gave him shivers when he pinched his nipples and nipped at his neck, how it nearly turned him inside out when he kissed and stroked him.

He squirmed and tried to sink deeper into the cushions. The words on the page in front of him were a jumble of black squiggly lines that blurred and made no sense, no matter how much he tried to pull his thoughts away from a private fantasy of walking over to Mal and whispering in his ear to meet him upstairs.

A crackling sound got his attention then mutated into a guitar-driven ballad from a few years back. Mal jumped to his feet with a bark of delighted laughter and came over holding out his hand with an impish grin.

"Wanna dance?"

Neil dropped the book beside him and slid his hand into Mal's, letting him pull him up to his feet. He felt kind of silly but any excuse to touch Mal and have his arms around him was a good enough excuse for Neil. He grinned back when Mal pulled him close and spun him around a few times. It wasn't the most graceful of waltzes but it gave Neil the opportunity to press up against Mal for a few moments.

He was vaguely aware of a few whistles and catcalls from watchers on the sidelines but he only had eyes for the man before him, who was wriggling those lean hips of his in time to the music as the song switched to something with a faster, salsa-inspired beat.

When Madran had tried to dance with him at the club, it had felt awkward and Neil had looked for the first excuse to stop, but dancing with Mal felt totally natural. He put his arms up and moved with Malachai to the beat and Mal dropped his hands to his hips, steering him a bit, but mostly just riding there. They danced all around the courtyard, together, apart, together again, and every time Mal touched him, pulled him close, Neil had to fight the urge to kiss him and yank his clothes off.

"You're good at this," Mal whispered, moving in so that he could touch his lips to Neil's ear then shimmying back again, making him follow. "If I didn't worry that we might be jumped any moment by your dad or a squad of Bone Men, I might just drag you upstairs for an hour."

Neil tilted his head to one side and widened his eyes, feigning an innocent look.

"What would we do upstairs?" he asked, trying to keep his lips from twitching.

Mal wriggled his hips, sliding away from him then moving back in close, never quite relinquishing the touch of his fingers on Neil's hips. His grin was positively feral.

"We could figure out how to incapacitate your father," he suggested, as if he knew just how much that would frustrate Neil.

Neil stuck out his tongue at him. "We could do that right here."

"If you'd rather?" Malachai teased him. "I just thought we could maybe do it naked, if we went upstairs. But if you'd prefer to stay here..."

"Stay here and get naked?" Neil teased him. "Pretty shameless."

"We're amongst fae. They don't care if we strip to our skin, on the whole," Mal said, winking at him. "Merc might get a bit shirty with you, though."

Neil laughed then wondered how he could feel so happy when the future was so uncertain, but of course he knew the answer. He was looking right at the answer. The music slowed down again and Neil slid his arms around Mal's neck, stretching up for a kiss. Not quite as hot as the one he'd been fantasizing about, but sweet. Did he love him? Yes, he was pretty sure of that. Should he tell him? Maybe he should.

As their lips parted, he took a breath and said, "Mal... I—"

His words were drowned out by a booming sound like thunder, so loud it rattled the windows and made everyone startle and freeze. In the frozen half-second afterward, Mercurio snapped the radio off and stood. Another deafening boom rocked the courtyard, followed by the tortured shriek of rent metal.

"The wards," Neil whispered. Mal must have already come to that conclusion because he let him go and sprinted for the door. Every instinct Neil had told him to run the other way, away from the sound of that terrible crash, but he forced his feet to move, following Mal. Not that he would be able to do much good against whatever had just smashed through a ward as strong as the ones Drasnil had protecting his people, but he wasn't about to let Mal face whatever it was alone.

Behind the old theater was a walled courtyard that at one time had served as a parking lot and now contained greenhouses and tiered garden beds as well as some vehicles and equipment. There was a gaping, ragged hole in the back wall with bricks strewn around, like a giant fist had punched through. The physical damage was bad but that wasn't the worst. The wards for the entire back wall had been shattered, leaving them open and vulnerable to the night creatures.

Mal skidded to a halt so fast Neil almost ran into the back of him. He spit out a few words in a tongue Neil didn't understand, but he couldn't mistake them for anything but cursing.

Others were rushing out around them and there was more cursing that Neil could understand. Drasnil was suddenly there, shouting orders.

"Get the bus moved over! Block that breech! Where are Sabine and Rilk? We need to get new wards set. Move, people!" he barked.

All around them, people were hopping to it, but before they got that far, another sound split the night around them. This one unmistakable. A shrill, undulating cry echoed eerily from just beyond the gap. It was an animal sound but strangely like human speech. Like it should be possible to pick out words, but he couldn't quite grasp them before they slipped away. A night creature's hunting call.

"By the Dark Goddess..." Drasnil swore vehemently under his breath then shouted, "Get the bus! *Move!* Get up on the walls! Get the crossbows ready, shoot anything that comes through that hole!"

Malachai ran forward with Drasnil, peering down into the chaos and Neil stuck to him. As they reached the ledge overlooking the yard, he was able to see countless figures swarming around the crumbling hole in the wall while others tried to maneuver a long vehicle into the gap. Mal turned and shook his head at him.

"Get back inside. It's not safe out here."

Before Neil had a chance to argue that inside wasn't any safer than outside, the first of the creatures slithered through the hole. It was dark, oily black, with hairless skin stretched over a burly frame. Its muscular body was built stocky, like a bulldog, but far bigger. Maybe the mass of a lion. And there any resemblance to human world animals ended. This creature had six legs for one thing and the legs ended in long, scaled feet like a dragon's, tipped with dagger claws. Its skull was flattened at the front, and rather than two eyes it had a yellow-orange band that went all the way around its head. Its snout bristled with dark teeth.

Shadow Beast, his mind whispered. He'd never seen one like this before, though his whole life he had lived under curfew because of these creatures. They were born of the same plane of existence that his own bloodline came from, but in this world they only thrived at night. It was large, and powerful. Dark magic was woven into the very fabric of its being. His father had once told him that they were stunted runts with a fraction of their real power here in this world. He couldn't imagine what kind of horror they would be in their natural environment.

Someone on the opposite wall loosed a crossbow bolt. It sailed right on target to take it in the chest, but just before it hit, the beast blurred and moved and the bolt struck the fender of the bus. The creature lifted one of its front paws and raked its claws over the metal, curling four gouges out of their makeshift barrier. This was why the shadow beasts were not hunted to extinction. This was why it was safer to stay behind the wards after dark rather than risk trying to take back the night. It was damn near impossible to kill something that was mostly made of magic.

Malachai swore in that curious, musical language that Neil was coming to think of as belonging to him.

Another crossbow bolt sang through the air and again the beast blurred for a moment and the bolt stuck in the ground beneath it.

Neil was watching closer this time and saw that the creature didn't just disappear, or move out of the way, it actually changed.

"Smoke," he murmured under his breath. That's what it looked like to him, anyway.

The creature raked the bus again, this time its claws catching the door and tearing it off its hinges. The fae who had driven it there scrambled to the back and out of the emergency door. The pit of Neil's stomach turned to ice as the beast leaped forward after the fleeing man.

As it moved, so did Mal, jumping onto the low parapet around the ledge and focusing his attention on the creature. The hairs on the backs of Neil's arms rose in response to the energy that flowed from him. He had watched Malachai work his magic before, in less pressing circumstances, and had been aware of the way he channeled and applied that power. But it had never made his skin want to shiver off his body like this before.

Instead of blasting the shadow monster with the magic he controlled, Mal wrapped it around the beast, reeling it back in a ways, trapping the monster in a kind of alchemical net. Then he pushed again.

All the while, determined fae defenders launched their arrows and bolts at the thing, dodging around as it flailed and clawed at them. Their missiles flew through it and clattered on the concrete under the monster, then, without warning, they *didn't*. When the first bolt hit home and stuck in its hide, a cheer went up and the defenders redoubled their attack. And as they fired on it, Malachai held it in place, held it in a physical form they could attack.

And Neil felt how much that pulled on him. Though his features were impassive, he could sense just how much it cost Mal to keep that transformative spell in place, anchoring the creature where they could attack it.

Enraged now, the creature bellowed, rearing up on its hind most legs and thrashing. It ripped one of the arrows free and black blood gushed from the wound. Just as it was slowing down another creature, twin to the injured one, jumped through the wall, landing on the hood of the bus and screaming in fury.

Drasnil turned and grabbed Neil by the shoulders. "We have warded nets in the storage area. They might work on them. Can you go get them?"

Neil nodded. Reluctant as he was to leave Mal out here, at least he could do something to help. He took off at a run.

Chapter Nineteen

Mal heaved a small sigh of relief as Neil followed Drasnil's bidding and retreated to the store. He was able to focus all his attention on the attackers, though a niggle of worry stabbed at the back of his mind all the time that Neil was out of his sight. At least if one of those creatures escaped his control and swarmed up here, Neil would be safe from it. For the time being.

He siphoned off some of the energy he was using to wrap the first shadow creature and pushed it toward the enraged beast on the hood of the bus. The second creature had already sent a couple of fae archers flying with a swipe of its claws and was dodging the arrows of their defenders as its companion had, by melting into smoke until the missile ceased to be a thorn in its side. Mal caught it by the tail and wrapped it in his spell energy as he had the other. This time, however, he did not merely hold it in physical form, he squeezed the magical net tight and pushed a second spell into the weave, seeking to discover how it had come to be here.

Someone, or something, had killed a pair of beings governed by the Night Compact, then sent them here. That much he learned plainly from the last traces of sentience in the second beast. He felt its rage and incredulity, that a mere mortal should have thwarted it and it's sibling so easily.

Mal drew the net in tightly and pushed fire into the weave of alchemical energy.

The fae down below fell back automatically as the creature they were fighting began to glow, turning scarlet then gold, then bursting into pure white flames. He felt its last quiver of rage as it was consumed then collapsed into ashes over the chassis of the bus.

The first one panicked as it saw its sibling fall and he had to fight to hold it long enough to work the same transformation. When it too crumbled to white hot ash, Mal dropped to his knees and buried his face in his hands.

Drasnil moved to his side at once. "Are you ailing, Lord Valentine?"

He shook his head, but for a few moments, he was beyond movement. He had never used his alchemical gift to destroy something before and it was not a sensation he wanted to get used to.

"That was a nice bit of work there. Quick thinking." Drasnil patted his shoulder. "Just catch your breath, my young friend."

Although the words were meant to be reassuring, Mal could hear the undercurrent of worry in them. Worry for him, maybe, but more likely a deeper concern that there was more fighting to be done yet, and Drasnil needed him on his feet. He put a hand to the floor and pushed up, and under his palm a vibration ran through the concrete. Moments later they heard another boom, muffled by the bulk of the building behind them.

Drasnil spun on his heel and Mal was running into the old theater even before the little fae shouted to his archers below, alerting them to the new danger. Mal didn't care what it was. Neil was down there somewhere, inside. Alone. If another of those things had broken in at the front...

He did not want to think too closely about it.

"Neil!" he bellowed as he careened down the long passageway back into the area behind the original cinema screen then clattered down the turning staircase that led toward the ground floor where the stores were. "Neil! Find some cover!"

Mal stopped, looking left and right. If another creature had come through the front, it could still be out there. If he went that way, he might stop it before it got any farther. If there was a creature, and if it hadn't already moved on. He looked the other way, the direction Neil was most likely to be, back toward the stores, somewhere in the maze. He hesitated only a moment more. If he made the wrong choice, it could cost lives, but he had to be sure that Neil was safe. He headed to the right, into the storage area.

He was right to have trusted his instinct. It took him only a minute or two to find Neil, but it was no slavering night beast he was facing down. Neil stood with his back to a wall as an imposing figure stalked toward him, dressed in a dark suit, perfectly tailored, not a hair out of place. The man had fine features, so perfect they probably made hearts melt wherever he went and so familiar it was almost a jolt to his senses.

"You've put me to a lot of cost and trouble, Nielub. Enough of this. You will submit and come with me, or I will kill every one of those that have harbored you."

Mal risked a quick glance at Neil then wished he hadn't. The stricken look was enough to stab him in the heart.

In a last-ditch effort to save himself, Neil threw the net he was holding at his father.

Malachai tensed and as the handsome man facing Neil — like a strange mirror image of another, older Neil, in a different plane — lifted a hand to fend off the glamoured mesh, he moved. In the outside world, Mal was bound to human conventions. He moved and acted like a human. He blended in, as part of the arrangement he had made with his own sire when he'd left home to try to make his way in the world.

But here, in places like this, he was free to be what he had been born to be. He could do things that were forbidden to him in the human world, under the Daylight Compact.

Mal moved faster than blinking, sliding from shadow to shadow like a flash of lightning, touching here and there, at different points of the room, coming to a brief halt before the man who could only be Neil's father.

The sorcerer. The one who had herded them to this place. The one who had never seen Neil as anything more than a weapon — an energy crop to be harvested.

Before he could divest himself of the net, Malachai threw up both hands and pushed his own magic into the delicate looking mesh, turning it to tempered steel, hard as nails and sharp as a thousand, interlaced blades. A cage made of razor edges.

The sorcerer lifted his own arms to shield himself and let out a shout of rage and pain when it cut into his arms and hands.

"Mal!" Neil cried out behind him, but Malachai held out a warning hand for him to stay back, out of range.

The razor mesh settled around the sorcerer, but only for a moment. Power surged and a moment later he flung the net down. Blue eyes a few shades darker than Neil's glared at him. "Get out of the way or die."

"Original." Mal smirked at him, moving more slowly, making the sorcerer track him as he shifted away from Neil. "I don't think so."

The sorcerer narrowed his eyes. "He's of no use to you. Whatever he's promised you for your protection is a lie."

"You see, that's where you're very wrong. You think that just because you see him as a possession, something to be used up and thrown aside, that everyone else must see the same thing. I don't want anything from him. But if you want to take him, you will have to come through me." His lips quirked again. "See… I can be original too."

The man made an impatient sound. "He's seduced you. You do realize that? What he is, I mean?"

Mal clutched at his ribs and gasped. "No! Really? I'm ruined!" He dropped the act just as quickly and pointed one long finger at Neil's father. "You'll have to try harder than that, Mr. Markovic. Yes, I know what he is. I also understand that whatever he does to most humans, it doesn't work in here."

He tapped his chest again, twice, with the same finger. Neil was still in the room and he wanted to turn and tell the boy to get the hell out, but he didn't dare take his eyes off the man in front of him.

The sorcerer glanced at Neil. "You've made him think he loves you. Very impressive, Nielub. I didn't think you had it in you. Of course, now I have to kill him."

He wasted no more time on trying to talk Mal into giving up. Shadow fire leaped up all around the sorcerer's feet, racing up the walls and across the floor in front of him. This was no controlled burst like Neil had used on Vargas, not even the conflagration the Bone Men had sent after them in the garage. This was an inferno of dancing shadow flames that sprang up all around them, instantly.

"No!" Neil screamed somewhere behind Mal. "No!"

Malachai had to admit that it was impressive. He didn't waste his breath on compliments, though. If that black flame touched him, he was a dead fae walking. Instead he ducked and grabbed two of the nets, throwing one of them out like a shield, or an umbrella, while he spun the other on his fingertip until it was whirling in front of him like a Catherine wheel.

"Get out, Neil!" he yelled. "Run. Keep running!"

"No!" Neil yelled again and suddenly he was in front of Mal. Neil flung his hand out and black flame arced toward the sorcerer. It was nowhere near the level of power his father was expending but it made the man take a step back, a snarl on his lips. Another wave of power surged and knocked Neil down, flinging him back from the flames that were just as much a danger to him, demon blood or not.

"Oh, for fuck's sake!" Mal growled and he pulled with his magic instead of pushing at the shadow fire, extending his net and drawing back hard so that the black flames licked at the magic-infused mesh that spun like a tiny tornado on the tip of his finger. He began to spin the second net so that he was drawing the black flames down on himself, but channeling them into the nets. There was a serious amount of power in those flames and he cocked an appreciative eyebrow at that before putting himself back between Neil's sprawled form and his father's upright one. "You know something, Neil. You really shouldn't have made me think I loved you. A bloke who thinks he's in love might do all kinds of unpredictable things. Especially when someone hands him a shitload of volatile demon magic. Bloody hell. Just imagine what he might do with that, eh?"

He focused his attention on the flames again, still pulling them in toward him, and feeding his alchemy through the mesh to meet them there, in the twin funnels he had created with the spinning nets. It was almost a thing of beauty as the flames hit the mesh and threw up silver sparks, then turned into the same white fire he had used to melt the shadow creatures in the yard. The heat filled him but did not consume him. Malachai contained it as he had contained the creatures. It was a worry that he had no idea how much more of it he could keep in check without spontaneously combusting.

Peripherally he was aware of Neil, saw the movement from the corner of his eye as he pushed himself up and shakily got to his feet. He couldn't see enough of him to see his expression but considering what was in front of them, it was a pretty safe bet there was a good bit of fear. He couldn't think about that. He had to keep all his focus on the nets and funneling the power bearing down on him.

He was worried Neil was going to try something else, something that would make him have to stop, and he wasn't even sure at this point he could without being killed. Instead he felt Neil move behind him.

"Malachai... Mal, you need more power."

No kidding. Only, he was using just about everything he had. There wasn't any more power.

"Take it from me," Neil whispered. "Please... Mal, before it's too late."

Malachai Valentine had always thought it was a romantic turn of phrase when people said their lives flashed in front of them at times of great peril, but right then he understood that they weren't being metaphorical at all. Only what he saw was primarily his life with Neil in it and that was a pretty short movie, all things considered.

He saw Merc giving him grief for shacking up with an Incubus. He saw Delilah's disbelief and Crow's crafty sneer. He saw this man, Neil's father, congratulating his son on...what? *Enslaving him? Capturing him?*

If that wasn't bullshit and he opened himself to the power that was within Neil, he was probably fairy toast. And wouldn't Mercurio laugh like a drain about that?

Mal kept his eyes on the man trying to melt his resolve, and probably melt the rest of him, given the chance. Sweat trickled down his face, running down his body beneath his shirt. His damned wings itched. Their urgent twitching under his skin was a distraction he could do without. He could say no and pretty soon his useless wings would be the least of his worries.

He could say yes and take the risk that the end would be faster for all that. Would Neil be merciful, in light of what they'd shared? He hoped so.

Don't let me down! he prayed silently.

Then he dropped his personal barriers and reached out to Neil.

There was no thunder clap, no huge surge of egomaniac-inducing power, no bright flashes of light or whirlwinds. What came instead was incredibly subtle. The first noticeable thing was the strain of holding the spell in place vanished. Not just became a little easier, it vanished entirely. He felt like he could siphon those infernal flames all day with only half a thought on it. The fatigue of using so much magic in so short a period was gone as well — he was suddenly as fresh and sharp as if he'd just gotten out of bed after an excellent night's sleep. On the heels of those realizations came another, deeper feeling.

Power was an inadequate description but there wasn't another good word for it. Not just his own, but Neil's. Bright and warm, and seemingly endless. A small tug on that source and Mal felt invincible. Neil stood beside him, and behind, completely open and unresisting. He would be hard-pressed to ever think of another time in his life when he'd felt such utter trust and support.

"Take more. Strengthen the spell. You're not even scratching the surface," Neil murmured in his ear.

Damn it, but under any other circumstances that invitation would have sounded almost sensual and he could not afford distraction. He didn't even dare to blink. Neil's touch was almost cool compared to the heat he was channeling and the funnel spells were doing their job. With that additional power coming from Neil, he was able to absorb so much more of the transformed shadow fire. At this rate, the first time he touched something electrical he was going to blow every fuse in the building. And it was working — he could see the frustration on the face of Neil's father as he realized he was losing control of his magic.

Mal reached deeper and leaned back into Neil's hands, and they soothed the frantic fluttering of his trapped wings, encouraging them to be still for a moment as he let a stronger flood of energy into himself, something that filled him with incredible euphoria. He wanted to soar to the lofty ceilings and he had not flown since he was a teenager.

His grip on the nets strengthened too and he pulled harder, faster, sensing that the prey was in his trap.

The sorcerer let lose a snarl, blasting more energy into the shadow fire until the whole room was dark with it—only then did he start to sense his mistake and it was too late. He flung himself back, coming perilously close to his own flames. He wrenched his body first one way then the other in attempt to cut off the power he was feeding into the fire. The moment he truly figured out what Mal had done—what he was still doing to him—flashed across his face in sudden shock, followed immediately by terror.

He twisted and turned frantically but the flames did not die, they only grew, racing toward Mal's trap to be devoured, and all the sorcerous energy it took to create them was drawn with it. When Mal had first set eyes on the man, he'd looked more like Neil's older brother than his father. Now, he could be his grandfather, maybe.

"Stop this!" the sorcerer shouted, panic edging the once confident arrogance of his voice as the twin vortex slowly sucked the life force out of him with his magic. "Stop!" He began to struggle in earnest and he went from grandfather to ancestor to shriveled shell. His mouth opened for another scream, but no sound emerged. The shadow fire drew back from the walls, narrower and narrower until it was just a thin thread running from the desiccated man to Malachai's trap and when it disappeared altogether, he collapsed. Nothing but a dried husk on the floor.

Mal let the funnels slow and, as the last threads of power vanished into him, he let the nets fall from his shaking hands to the ground. For a few moments, there was silence all around him and he finally let his eyes fall closed. It was like the aftermath of a drunken binge. He felt half-crazy and more than a bit nauseous. And he was scared of even touching anything.

Neil's hands were still resting against his shoulders. Mal wanted to turn around and hold him but after the weirdness of the last few minutes he barely dared to look at him, afraid of what he might see in Neil's eyes.

I just desiccated your father.

We just desiccated your father!

Bloody hell!

"Is he…?"

Neil's voice trailed off and Mal finished the thought for him. "Dead? Yes."

"Are you sure?" Neil asked.

"Very sure," Mal said, his stomach doing a slow rolling churn.

Neil exhaled a shaky breath that shivered along the back of his neck, then Mal felt him press his forehead into his shoulder blade. One wing twitched in response to the pressure there. Funny how the lack of them didn't bother him for ages, then something set them off and he could not stop feeling for them, like a phantom limb.

"We should…" Neil didn't seem able to finish anything he started to say so Mal leaned back into his warmth for a moment. Since he wasn't channeling incessant shadow fire, his body temperature was normalizing and Neil's touch no longer felt cool.

"Get rid of the body, yes."

"I was going to say, we should tell the others it's over." Neil's arms eased around him. Mal wanted to be relieved but he could feel how his companion was shaking and folded his hands over Neil's, squeezing them reassuringly.

"We could do that. Yes. Although, with the ringmaster dead, I suppose his reanimated circus will have gone back to wherever it came from too." Mal turned his head so that he could feel Neil's rapid breaths against his cheek. "That was…" He wanted to say 'amazing' but that seemed inappropriate after they had just immolated Neil's only known relative. "You were incredible. I've never felt magic like that."

"I guess most people don't mix demon and fae magic together." Neil pulled him closer and Malachai reached up to touch his face. His fingers came away wet and he turned abruptly, folding his arms around Neil.

"Are you going to be okay?"

Neil looked up at him and for once all his guards were down. Malachai felt like he could fall right down inside those deep wells and drown in his soul. Slowly, Neil nodded.

"You know all he said to you was a lie, right? Not the wanting to kill you part, but everything he said about me…a-about making you want me. I never used power against you."

Mal drew him in and kissed his forehead. He had wavered, but Neil did not need to hear that. The important thing was that it felt so very good to hear Neil say those words.

"It doesn't matter," he said, opting for diplomacy. "I don't care what he thinks, Neil Markovic, I only care about you. And..." he added, to lighten the mood, "he underestimated me if he figured I'm so easily influenced! What a fool!"

Neil looked like he might be about to say something more but the sound of running feet drew their attention.

Several of the fighters from outside came bursting in, along with Merc toting his shotgun. Mal pulled away from Neil as they all more or less came to a halt, most peering around as if confused as to where the danger lay.

"What's happening outside? Where's Drasnil?" Mal asked.

"We drove out the last of the creatures. They're working on getting wards up." Merc shouldered his weapon, but the fae warriors who had accompanied him glanced uneasily from Mal to the body lying on the floor.

"Dead sorcerer. You're welcome," Mal said, gesturing toward the husk of their late opponent. "Not sure what your local recycling services are like on bodies, so I kind of left him there, sorry."

Merc grunted and slung his shotgun up on one shoulder. The others still looked uncertain until one of them finally stepped up and took charge. "Get a sheet, wrap the body and take it out to the wagon. We'll find a watery home for it come first light."

Orders given, everyone was suddenly busy because no one wanted to be the last left to actually have to carry them out.

"You're wanted upstairs, Lord Valentine."

"Upstairs?"

"Amy sent for you. Drasnil was injured in the fight."

"He got his hands dirty? Bloody hell!" Mal managed a grim chuckle and turned to pat Neil on the shoulder. "I'd better get a move on then. You wanna come with me?"

Neil nodded and Mal could imagine that he probably didn't want to stick around to watch the body of his father being wrapped up and taken away like so much trash.

He started to head toward the stairs but Merc called to him and he stopped.

"That's a neat trick, taking on a sorcerer on your own. How'd you manage it? You don't even look winded. Not that I'm not glad to see you still standing and him growing cold."

"I have hidden depths." Mal winked at him.

"Cocky little bastard!" Merc fired him a look that said he knew better. Malachai was pretty sure that look wasn't overconfidence.

"I'll tell you later," he said, more quietly, with a small tilt of his head in Neil's direction. He didn't want to give the surrounding fae any ideas by explaining in detail. "Let's just say, I had some help."

Merc didn't look happy, but he didn't push the issue. Mal continued up the stairs and Neil followed.

Chapter Twenty

Felipe had a suite of rooms on one of the upper floors of the theater. Neil had time to imagine severed limbs, broken bones and all sorts of possible maiming before they finally made it to the door and were shown through by Felipe's bodyguards. The tightness of Neil's muscles uncoiled when they saw their ebullient host was merely walking wounded, or sitting wounded in this case, as two of his people were attempting to keep him in a chair, away from the windows, while dabbing wet cloths on the cuts to his face and arms.

"What happened to you, Master Drasnil?" Mal asked as he perched on the arm of a plump, upholstered seat by Felipe's side. Neil chose to stand next to Mal, afraid if he sat he wouldn't be able to get back up, and how embarrassing would it be to fall asleep in a wounded man's room? "You look like you've been scrapping with a weretiger."

Drasnil laughed, but it clearly took some effort. There was blood all over his fine jacket and the costly cloth was torn in several places.

"A handful of smaller versions of that beast that ruined my lovely wall managed to wriggle up the side of the building and we had to exercise extreme prejudice in order to prevent them moving in." He sighed and batted away one of the young fae with the washcloths. "That will do, I'm quite clean, thank you."

Mal leaned in and examined the rent marks in his coat. "I'm not sure what I can do about this, Felipe," he said, tugging at the tattered cloth. "But I can probably put a few patches on your flesh wounds until they can heal on their own."

"Thank you, Lord Valentine. I would not have bothered you, but my people do like to fuss."

That might be, Neil thought, but Drasnil still looked pleased with the attention. The cluricaun tucked a strand of blood-streaked silver hair behind one of his horns as Mal gently pinched together the edges of one of the wounds. The torn skin began to meld and knit back together. Neil felt a fierce tug inside on his own magic and quickly stifled a reflexive twitch. The feeling was hard to describe. Sort of like finding your own hand was writing a note without you having thought about what you wanted to write.

All these years since finding out the destiny his father had bred him for he had dreaded, with cold terror, becoming his familiar. Dreaded what it would feel like to have his magic drained away and the shadows eat him from the inside out. And here he let Mal link to him and take all that he wanted.

Not that it compared. Mal's magic wouldn't eat his soul, for one thing. Allowing him to draw on his power, on his energy, was not the same as being bound to him for the rest of his life, either. Either of them could close the link any time they chose, until it was sealed in blood. Of course, he would no longer have to worry about becoming his father's familiar. It was over. Well, over in the sense that he didn't have to fear the man any more. There was still the matter of being wanted by the police...and if his father hadn't been lying, then someone had sent the Bone Men after him specifically. He didn't see why father would lie about that. Which meant he still had plenty to fear.

He was too exhausted to think on that too closely so he focused on Mal and Felipe. The largest of the wounds was nearly sealed, a dark red line where the tissue met. He'd seen the work of healers before, ones that used magic. What they did was something like coaxing the body to fix itself, but more rapidly than it usually took. Mal's alchemy couldn't do that. He needed something to transform. Whether that was muddy water into fine whiskey, or a net into a magic siphon, or blood into whole flesh.

When he finished with the jagged wound, he sat back and Felipe took a look. "Nice work, Lord Valentine. Maybe I should convince you to give up tinkering with scrap metal and sign on as a healer?"

"Blood freaks me out, Felipe. If you don't mind, I'll pass on that," Mal said in such mild tones that Neil wasn't sure whether it was a joke or not.

He applied himself to fixing the worst of their host's scrapes nonetheless, and each time, Neil lent him more power until, by the last of them, he had a sense of just how bone weary Malachai was as he withdrew from the fix. He offered his arm in silence and Mal leaned on him gratefully.

"Thank you, that is much better," Felipe said. "I suggest you also both find a place to lay down before you fall over."

Only as they made a move to leave did Neil realize he hadn't said a word. He turned back but any words died in his throat. Felipe stared at them with such sharp interest it made Neil think he really hadn't been very hurt at all.

A silvery brow lifted in question and Neil started to stammer his thanks but Mal interrupted him. "Let's leave Felipe to recover. You can talk to him tomorrow."

And before he knew it, Mal had steered him out and all the way to their room before Neil could say, "I was just going to thank him."

"I know. That's why I stopped you."

"Why? I don't want to be rude."

Mal sighed and sunk down on the bed. "You aren't being rude by not thanking him. It's a fae thing. An expression of gratitude implies an obligation. If you thank him, since we're in his domain, it's saying he fought the battle for you."

"Oh." Neil thought for a moment. "But he thanked you for fixing him up."

"He's our host, it's different."

Neil wasn't sure he understood how but he didn't want to get entangled in a lengthy discussion of fae etiquette. He sat down next to Mal and put a hand on the back of his neck, kneading into the taut muscles.

"Are you okay?"

"Exhausted. I'll live." Mal leaned against his shoulder and rested the side of his head against Neil's.

Neil put his arm around him and kissed him tenderly. "It's okay for me to tell you thank you, isn't it? You saved my life. How did you know to do that with the nets?"

Mal shrugged. "It's a variation on a spell I've used to siphon diesel out of old trucks. Saves time and manual suction and stops it going all over the floor. I wasn't sure it would work." He returned the kiss with a weary grin. "And you're welcome. I won't count it as an obligation, since I'd have been chopped liver if you hadn't helped me out back there."

"You should sleep, you're barely keeping your eyes open," Neil said, kissing him softly again.

"That would be nice," Mal agreed. He leaned back into Neil's embrace with a sigh. "It's rare to feel this comfortable with someone. Thank you."

Neil got up and helped pull Mal's boots off. Mal chuckled and said he could do it himself but Neil helped him anyway because he wasn't so sure he could stand back up. They both wiggled out of their jeans and crawled under the blanket. Usually Neil curled up and Mal fit himself around him but tonight Mal sprawled out on his back for a few moments before rolling over and Neil spooned up behind him. It was not long at all before Malachai's breath deepened and evened out in sleep, but as tired as he was, Neil found sleep elusive. He kept replaying the moment when he'd turned, with the nets in hand, and saw his father standing there. He'd had a moment of crystal clarity when he'd realized the breach in the wall was an engineered distraction, and while everyone was outside fighting the night creatures, their foe had come in the front as easy as you please. He had thought he would be terrified when father finally came to take him, and he was, but not for the reasons he'd imagined. He had been afraid he wouldn't get to ever see Mal again, then he had been afraid he would and he'd have to watch him cut down by shadow fire.

He tightened his arms around Mal, who murmured in his sleep, so he loosened his hold again. So close. He'd come so close to losing him. He still wasn't safe, not for so long as he was unaware who had sent the Bone Men after him. And if he wasn't safe, neither was Malachai. He'd been running and hiding for weeks. With his father dead, he needed to stop cowering and start planning. The Bone Men weren't the only ones that could ask questions and trace steps.

With that thought, he finally closed his eyes and sleep found him.

Mal slept fitfully, disturbed by dreams in which Bone Men invaded the sanctuary of his home and he was forced to watch as they tore apart everything he cared about, then worse nightmares where he watched Neil fade, as his father had, sucked dry by the magic that Mal himself was wielding. No matter how hard he tried to stop, he failed and in every dream, Neil crumbled to dust in his arms.

Those nightmares were worse than the ones when he dreamed he could spread his wings again and woke screaming in pain from the fire under his skin.

When he woke, shouting and shaking, it was to find Neil's cool hands on his face and to hear Neil's gentle voice, repeating his name, over and over, telling him to calm down until his pulse stopped hammering in his throat and he was able to pull his lover close, without shaking. He ached inside, though, and dreaded to imagine how Neil was feeling this morning. For all his quiet bravado, Neil had watched his father die last night. Mal knew it was a fate that had to be, but even so, he was not proud of himself.

"I'm sorry. I'm so sorry." He murmured the words over again like a mantra, holding Neil tightly in his arms.

Neil slid his arms around him and made soothing sounds, shushing him gently until he finally pulled back to look him in the eyes. "You've nothing to be sorry for, Malachai. Nothing."

"I feel as if I've left you with nothing," he said and his voice sounded hoarse and pathetic in his own ears. "I orphaned you and I never even asked if that was something you wanted. I don't want to do that to you too, Neil."

"Mal, you didn't kill him. You did what you had to do to protect yourself and keep him from making me into a slave. If he hadn't used sorcery, he'd still be alive. His fault. Not yours."

"But I used your power to do it. Does that make me any better than him?" Mal closed his eyes but the images from his nightmare assailed him and he quickly opened them again, focusing on Neil, whole and alive. That was a much better vision, even if Neil did look quite exasperated with him.

"Malachai, there is no comparison. You borrowed power I willingly gave you. Your magic is so different it cost me almost nothing, a bit of energy. It's not like you paid to use dark magic with pieces of my soul."

"I just... I never want to hurt you, Neil. You're too important for that." He snuggled up to Neil again, wondering how these feelings had crept up on him so suddenly. If he lost Neil, he would be bereft.

Neil snorted softly but Mal could feel how the tension in his muscles relaxed under his hands and Neil laid his cheek on his chest.

"I'm hardly important," he murmured. "I've been a burden to everyone that's set eyes on me and the one thing I can do, I hate using."

"You're not a burden to me." Mal sat up for a moment, looking down at him. It made him unaccountably sad to learn that Neil felt that way. "You would never be a burden to me. Just so you understand that. Right?"

Neil shifted around, pushing himself up on one arm. "I'm glad you don't feel I have been. Still, you can't say I've done much but bring you trouble. You didn't even get anything out of the car. Not that I'm not grateful for all you've done. So please don't feel guilty about anything. What happened to my father…you only did what I couldn't do myself."

Mal stroked the backs of his fingers down the side of Neil's face, exploring the sharp lines of his lovely features tenderly before leaning in to kiss him. He had not been with so many men that it came naturally to him, but somehow, with Neil, it felt right. The kiss was light, just a soft brush of his lips against Neil's really, but it warmed him inside.

Neil leaned in for another kiss when Mal pulled back and more warmth threaded through him. Neil's voice was low and husky when he said, "Mal… I wanted to tell you —"

The knock on the door was soft, but Mal still jumped and Neil froze.

Mal sighed and swung out of bed, his stiff muscles protesting every movement. He opened the door a crack. Merc stood in the hall, his customary scowl in place.

"I'm going to see what's left of the garage," Merc said. "Do you want a lift or…?"

"Damnit, Mercurio, your timing stinks. We'll be down in a few minutes." Mal narrowed his eyes at his partner but kept the dry smile on his face.

Merc sketched him a salute but his expression was far from repentant. He closed the door and turned back to the bed but Neil was already shimmying into his clothes.

"Sorry about that. He can be an arsehole sometimes." Mal scowled.

"I hadn't noticed," Neil deadpanned.

Mal had to chuckle. "What was it that you wanted to tell me?"

"It'll keep." Neil pulled on a clean-ish shirt. "I hope Merc will cool it long enough for us to get breakfast."

"He'd better," Mal grumbled, shaking his head as he pulled on his jeans. "I'm friggin' starved. What with all the hassle last night, I haven't eaten since breakfast yesterday."

He mellowed then and smiled at Neil through his tangled, copper-colored hair.

* * * *

The denizens of Felipe's court were up early, or maybe had never slept. Spirits were high and the food hot as they celebrated successfully defending their home. Neil was quiet while they ate but Mal couldn't tell if it was from his natural reticence or if he were just tired. Maybe it felt too disloyal to celebrate his father's death, even if he had hated the man.

"Mercurio tells me you will be leaving this morning," Felipe said, sauntering into the long art deco refectory as they shoveled down food, conscious of time ticking by.

The cluricaun was immaculately turned out, in a mauve silk shirt and silver embroidered waistcoat that matched his ridiculously tight pants and artfully curled hair. His little horns coiled through his mane, shimmering as if they had been polished with stardust.

"Merc wants to get back to the store and make sure we've not been cleaned out. I kind of get his point," Mal said, once he had swallowed his last mouthful.

"Perfectly understandable." Felipe nodded. "And what about you, Neil?"

Neil looked startled and before he could respond, Felipe said, "Now that the danger is over, what will you do?"

"I'm going back to the garage with Mal," Neil said, though he sounded less than entirely confident.

"I see. And after that?"

Neil toyed with his toast and didn't answer.

"Well, my offer stands. You are welcome to join my court, if you change your mind about a tinker's life."

Mal looked up from his plate when Neil held his tongue. For a second or two, his heart felt like it might stop. He peered through his tangled hair, hardly daring to meet Neil's eyes in case he saw pity, or worse still, dismissal there. After all they had come through to be here together, it would be the final kick in the nuts to lose him to what was, undeniably, a better offer.

Felipe would look after Neil well. He recognized an asset when he saw it, but he was not unkind to his crew. They were a strong, unified team. Neil could flourish and grow here.

The 'tinker' jibe rattled him, but in all honesty he could not refute it. This was what he had fallen to. Without going back, cap in hand, to his father, there was no other lifestyle open to him. This was what Drasnil acknowledged in his mocking fashion when he addressed Mal by his former title. He was Lord Valentine truly in name alone.

Neil would be better off here.

As he lifted his head, he spotted Merc in the doorway, nodding toward the exit pointedly. That made up his mind for him and he pushed himself up from the table, sweeping his hair out of his eyes with one hand and extending the other to Drasnil.

"Felipe, it has been an honor and a privilege to hang out with you guys. You'll forgive me if I don't say we must do it again some time," he chattered as he shook the cluricaun vigorously by the hand to cover the awkwardness inside. "But my lieutenant is ready to be off and I think it's time we got out of your hair." He took a quick breath and licked his lips before risking a glance at Neil. "That is…if you…want?"

For a young man with such lovely, delicate features Neil looked very serious when he scowled like that. Mal's heart did a stutter against his ribs and he braced himself.

Neil's chair scraped on the floor as he pushed back from the table and stood. He also extended his hand to shake with Felipe and Mal couldn't help the tiny kernel of satisfaction to note he pulled away rather quickly when Felipe held on a bit too long.

"It's nice of you to offer me a place here," Neil said and Mal hid a smile of pride at the careful way he didn't say 'thank you'. "But I'm not going with Malachai just to be a tinker, not that there's anything wrong with that.

I'm going with him because I want to be wherever he is."

Felipe's eyes sparkled. "Ah, it's like that, is it? Well. I suppose you'd better have this then." He reached into his coat pocket, withdrew a small box and handed it to Neil. "This was found before we disposed of the sorcerer's...remains."

Neil thrust it back. "I don't want it."

"Then you can throw it in the river or give it to the first person you see. But I'll not take it back. It's a key, by the way, so you might want to think on it before you do either of those things."

"Here." Mal held out his hand. "Give it to me."

He saw Felipe hesitate for a moment, then, when Neil did not object, the cluricaun handed it over. Mal tucked the box in a pocket of his coat and looked at Neil.

"Are we good to go?"

Neil nodded. "Ready when you are."

Mal grinned at him then, his spirits lifted by those four small words. "C'mon then. Let's go home."

* * * *

The shop was untouched. Other than the metal shutter on the front of the building that needed repair, everything else was just as it should be. Even the car that Merc had jinxed while he and Neil were making their escape was still sitting where it had been left. The three of them made quick work towing it into the garage out of sight.

"We'll call the spares from that baby part-payment for all the hassle the bastard put us through," Merc grumbled once they'd got it out of sight.

"What's the other part?" Mal asked. "He's dead and gone."

He glanced apologetically at Neil but the lad just shrugged.

"Whatever that key opens," Merc said.

"No," Neil said. "I'll figure out a way to pay for the shutter. Throw the key in the river. It can't lead to anything good."

Mercurio narrowed his eyes. "If you know what that fucker is for, spit it out right now, kiddo. I don't like nasty surprises creeping up on me."

Mal slid his fingers into his pocket and curled them around the key. It felt cool still, in spite of its long proximity to his body. He thought he felt it vibrate in response to his touch, but perhaps he was imagining that. Steadily, he withdrew it and held it out in his open palm.

Just an ordinary-looking iron key from a mortice lock. Maybe quite old, the shaft and bit were blackened, save around the edges of the wards, and the only signs of recent use were the silvery rub marks on the bow and shoulder where someone must have held it or turned it.

From the corner of his eye, Mal saw Neil's shoulders twitch in a shiver. "I don't need to know what it opens to guess that I don't want any part of it."

"You've never seen it before?" he asked in a gentler tone.

Neil shook his head and Mal watched him more closely, saw the gradual way his eyes dilated wider, the black swallowing up the blue, and how his face drained of color when he moved the hand holding the key closer to him, how he flinched from it. Mal couldn't feel anything malicious in the piece of metal—it wasn't cursed—so he didn't understand Neil's visceral reaction to it if he'd never seen it before.

"You're sure?" He tipped his hand so it rolled from his palm to his fingertips and held it up for Neil to examine. He'd meant only for Neil to take a closer look but Neil recoiled, his upper lip curled in a snarl.

"No! I've never seen it! Throw it away!"

Mal closed his fingers around the key. He watched how Neil eased down off the edge of panic once it was out of sight. He was almost certain Neil had seen the key before, although he didn't think he was lying about having not seen it, either. Maybe the key locked more than just a door.

"Is it possible you just don't remember having seen it before?"

Neil started to shake his head then stopped, his throat working as he swallowed. "I've never seen it," he insisted.

Merc made a disgusted sound in the back of his throat. "Throw the fucking thing in the river, Valentine. It's been in the house for all of ten minutes and already it's more trouble than it's fucking worth."

Mal shoved the key back into his jeans pocket with a shake of his head.

The rest of the morning they spent taking stock and cleaning up. Mal kept an eye on Neil but he seemed his normal self.

"I'm going to hit the shower. You wanna share?" Mal asked Neil at last, once the garage and downstairs areas had been tidied up and Merc had some pigeons and a bowl of chopped veg stewing merrily on the reinvigorated stove in the huge kitchen.

A lovely shade of pink rose up Neil's neck but he didn't hesitate to follow Mal from the kitchen and up the stairs.

They crossed the threshold of the bathroom and Neil said, "Mal...?"

He turned. "Hmm?"

Neil slid his arms around his neck and kissed him, nipping lightly at his bottom lip and slipping his tongue between like he'd been waiting all day to do this. Mal somehow managed to smile and kiss him back at the same time. There was something so demanding about the way Neil kissed him, like it was imperative that he respond in kind. And so he did.

When their lips parted, he murmured, "So...was that the whole sum of your question? Or did you want to ask me something else?"

"Did I have a question? I don't remember it," Neil said, pressing closer and kissing him again. Neil's fingers crept under the edge of his shirt and tickled over Mal's belly. He lifted his arms and Neil released his lips long enough to pull his shirt off before diving in for another kiss. When they broke apart again, Neil looked up at him, the serious frown making his eyebrows scrunch.

"I was afraid this morning that you were going to try and talk me into staying with Drasnil," Neil said quietly.

Mal unbuttoned his shirt and slid it down off his shoulders, then peeled off the T-shirt he'd worn under it, dropping it to the floor. He pushed his fingers through his hair, shoving it out of his eyes.

"Is that so? Funny, that... I was kind of scared that when he offered you a place, you might decide you were safer with him."

"I thought of staying there," Neil said and Mal stilled his hands, looking into Neil's eyes. "I wouldn't be any safer, but you would have been, without me to bring danger to you." He paused, licking his lips before saying, "I was too selfish to stay, though. I-I wanted to go with you. I want to be wherever you are."

"Neil…"

Neil went on in a rush before Mal could say more, "Because I've been trying to tell you, I love you."

He blinked because suddenly his heart was racing too fast and his mouth felt too dry. He'd hardly dared to talk about the way his precious incubus left him feeling, mostly because he worried that Neil would just laugh and tell him that was how people normally felt around incubi.

"That… That's good," he said in careful, measured tones. *Yes. Good. Very good.*

Neil's eyes tracked back and forth minutely, searching his face, and Mal forced himself not to drop his gaze under that scrutiny. Finally Neil pulled back, just a fraction, but it was enough for Mal to catch the trace of hurt before Neil quickly hid it. "You think I'm being stupid."

"No!" Mal caught his arms before he could withdraw completely. "No. Neil. I don't think that at all. You're so smart. Too smart for a country boy like me. At least that's how it feels sometimes. But none of that matters. You're here, with me, and that makes me happier than I've been in a long time. When I thought you might stay with Felipe… I didn't know how I was going to cope with not having you around."

Neil was still looking at him in vague bewilderment, so Mal pulled him close and held him tight, relishing the warmth of his lean body so close to him. "I want you here. I don't ever want to lose you, Neil," Mal murmured into his hair.

Mal exhaled a long, shaky breath when he felt the tension in Neil's body flow out of him. He'd half-expected Neil to try to wriggle away but instead he put his arms around Mal. Although he knew he'd not said exactly the right words, he was grateful that Neil seemed to accept them. Too afraid of making a wrong move, Mal simply held him until he felt Neil's hands kneading gently on his back and his soft lips pressing to the side of his throat and along his jaw, then they were kissing again like their lives depended on it.

It felt good. Better than good. Way, way better. Mal had been in so-called relationships. He'd even thought vaguely that he might be in love, once or twice. But none of his experiences matched up to this. The rush of heat he felt from his loins to his throat every time he held and kissed Neil like this...it was nothing like his previous trysts.

If this was love, he wanted more.

One of Neil's hands tangled in Mal's hair and the other moved to the fly of his jeans. His palm brushed over his cock then caught him in a gentle grip, slowly pumping up and down.

"Oh, baby... That's so good," Mal gasped, rolling his hips to push into the touch of Neil's hand. This was crazy. They weren't even naked and already he was on fire for the guy.

Incubus. His conscience sounded an awful lot like Merc and he flipped it the mental equivalent of the bird.

Neil smiled, his lips teasing, only brushing his own with the lightest of touches. Mal caught his breath as Neil traced the outline of the head of his cock with one finger, swishing it back and forth over the tip. He groaned as a spot of dampness spread there. Neil flicked his button open and unzipped him with far more deftness than he had the first time they'd gotten naked together, his slim fingers sneaking inside to lift him out and take him more firmly in hand. He stroked him once, twice, before he bent his knees and dropped down. Mal reached one hand behind to the sink to steady himself as Neil licked the underside of his shaft and closed his lips around the head.

A breathless Gaelic epithet escaped Mal's lips as he watched Neil swallow him and gripped the basin at his back tighter. It was a battle to remain still and not thrust furiously as his cock swelled to full hardness in Neil's mouth.

"How could I not love you when you do this to me?" he exhaled in a jumbled rush.

The glide of Neil's lips and tongue stopped and Neil looked up. Mal touched his free hand to his cheek, cupping his beautiful face, and Neil closed his eyes, his whimper shivering up his shaft before he sunk down on him again. Neil gripped his hips tighter, taking him down deep and sucking hard on the up stroke.

Mal echoed that fragile whimper of sound as his knees threatened to give out on him. He grasped at the basin behind him like it was a lifeline, his jeans cascading down off his lean hips as he gave in to the compulsion to thrust into Neil's mouth.

"Oh, baby... I want to fuck you," he panted.

Neil made a low, needy sound that shivered up Mal's cock. He nodded a couple more times up and down before pulling off him with a gasp. He lips were full and wet when he looked up at him. "I want you too..." Neil's breath caressed along the wet length of his cock.

Mal reached down and tugged on the buckle of Neil's belt, quickly popping the buttons of his jeans so that he could touch his lover all the way down between his thighs, caressing the silken softness of his skin there, cupping his firm balls and stroking his hand up and down the curve of his hard cock.

"You feel so good. I've missed being inside you," Mal whispered in his ear. "It's so sweet to be home again."

"Mmm…" Neil hummed his agreement, swaying on his feet into Mal's touch. A shift of his hips and his jeans joined Mal's on the floor and they stood naked, pressed up against one another. Neil tipped his head back and Mal kissed just below the swell of his Adam's apple while he stroked him.

Neil laughed at him. "We aren't getting much showering done. Did you want to go to the bedroom?"

"Unless you want me to fuck you in the shower. Kill two birds with one stone." Mal grinned at him, loving the way that Neil's smile set off fireworks inside him. "The bed might be more comfortable, though."

Still smiling, Neil took his hand and they left their piles of clothing on the floor. As if he hadn't a care in the world, Neil brazenly pulled him naked across the hall to the bedroom. The two pushed-together beds were waiting just as they'd left them, with the wide comforter covering both.

Mal closed the door and Neil sprawled across the bed, lifting one knee and smiling up at him in a wordless invitation.

"There's no place like home," Mal declared as he crossed the room in three strides and leaped onto the bed, reaching down the side for the bottle of oil that he had stashed there. Neil arched and crooned as his fingers got to work, slicking him and pressing gently into him, preparing the way for his eager cock. He leaned over Neil, kissing his mouth with ravenous hunger again.

Neil's lips moved with his own and their tongues met and traded back and forth in a flexible dance. He felt Neil's hand on his chest then lower, grasping and stroking his cock. Mal pressed his finger up against the gland inside and Neil bucked his hips, whining in eagerness into his mouth. They were both breathless when their lips parted.

"Ooh… Mal…want you…" Neil gasped, stroking him faster.

"You got me," Mal agreed, kneeling up so that he could watch the expression of bliss on Neil's face as he touched him. "Oil me up, babe. I am so ready for you."

A drizzle of sweet-smelling oil in the palm of Neil's hand was all it took. He stroked him deftly from crown to base, the slick glide almost enough to undo him.

"That feels amazing," Mal told him, dipping down to kiss him again. "Let me get inside you."

He knew he wasn't a sweet talker. Plenty of girlfriends in the past had accused him of being anything from crude to insensitive. But he knew how to get a job done. Not that making out with Neil was a job, but…he knew what needed doing.

Neil seemed to have no objections as Mal wriggled down between his thighs and positioned himself so that he could press his cock into him with a few smooth, firm strokes then buck himself deeper. It felt delicious. Neil was hot and sleek inside and it felt so right to push into him hard like this.

"You okay?" he whispered as he settled into a rhythmic thrusting motion, pushed up on his elbows so that he could watch Neil's face as they fucked. His eyes were scrunched closed and his teeth were sunk into his bottom lip. "Neil…?" He started to pull back when he didn't answer, and he couldn't tell if that expression was pleasure or pain, but Neil dug his fingers into his shoulders and slung a leg around to keep him from backing out.

"Nnooo, don't stop…" Neil gasped.

Mal lowered his head and brushed his lips along Neil's neck. Such a simple thing, compared to how their bodies were enmeshed, but Neil arched and tipped his head back, baring his throat and bucking his hips. There was no denying he was hardwired for sensuality and pleasure. How much was from his incubus heritage and how much was just Neil was hard to say, and Mal didn't think it much mattered. Certainly not at the moment.

He nibbled along the curve of Neil's slim neck to the lobe of his ear and licked him there. He tasted salty — after the last strenuous couple of days, Mal wasn't really all that surprised. Bringing his mouth to Neil's lips again, he sank his tongue into a deep, enthusiastic kiss as he bucked harder between his lover's thighs.

Neil's fingers dug into his shoulders and he hooked his legs around Mal's hips, clinging to him like a limpet as they moved together. Neil's hungry growls and whimpers told him when he had things just right. He pushed his hands into Neil's hair at his nape and tugged his head back. Neil gasped, lifting his hips to meet his thrusts.

"Yess…ohh…" Neil exhaled. "Ooh, I'mgonnacome…" he got out in a rush.

Mal slowed his strokes, not quite ready for him, still enjoying the heated sounds he was conjuring from the half-demon's throat as he tugged and pounded him.

Before Neil had come along, he'd almost forgotten how much fun sex could be. And Neil was pushing all his buttons at once, for sure.

The way his sexy ass clenched and squeezed around his cock was doing almost as much for Mal as the friction of fucking him.

"Ahhh, you're so beautiful," he rumbled low in his throat as he kissed Neil again, quickening his thrusts once more.

Neil stroked his feet down the backs of his thighs, planted them square with Mal's knees on the mattress and curled his hips, changing the depth and angle for Mal to something wholly irresistible. Mal leaned up over him, his hands flat to the bed, on either side of Neil's heaving chest, and Neil opened his eyes. Drowning in black, just the thinnest edge of blue around the pupil. It would have been scary if his face weren't so suffused with longing.

Mal hovered over him, the tip of his nose almost brushing Neil's. His long hair caressed Neil's face as he drove in deep, again, and again, fast and hard, taking him up to the edge, if those sexy huffs and squeaks of need were anything to go by. He hoped so because he was dangerously close to losing control. And he wanted to lose control more than anything.

"You there, baby?" he huffed out.

"Uh-nnagh…" Neil groaned. The muscles of his stomach tightened and so did everything else. His flushed red cock painted opalescent ropes on his belly, spurt after spurt while he panted and moaned.

Mal abandoned all efforts at holding back. The sight of his gorgeous lover coming hard under him tightened his abs and his pelvic muscles like a magic spell. His eyes screwed shut and the way Neil's body tightened and gripped around him milked his thrusting dick until at last he burst, and for a short while, he saw stars erupt behind his eyelids. Mal subsided onto Neil's sweat — and cum — slick body and clung to him, shuddering in ecstasy. His climax was just about the best he'd ever achieved and he hung on to every last delicious moment of it. When his arms and legs couldn't hold him up a moment longer, he flopped over, almost boneless, onto his back, pulling out of Neil with a quiver of shock at how cold the air felt brushing over the incandescent heat of his softening cock. He lay there catching his breath for a moment.

"That was…out of this world."

Neil rolled, sticky and languid, and plastered himself to Mal's side, resting his head on his shoulder. He sighed, sending a cool breath over his heated flesh. "I was wrong."

"Hmm?" Mal murmured, drawing slow circles on Neil's back.

"I was just using the wrong part of me to feel your lust." He could feel the grin on Neil's lips where they touched his chest.

"Since you've found the right part, should I be worried?" Mal asked. Interestingly, he didn't feel too worried. In fact he wasn't worried at all. It was a good emotion. He drew Neil in closer to his chest.

Neil laughed. "I'm not sure if you should be. Maybe my ass should be worried."

"Maybe it should." He stroked one hand up into Neil's sweat-damp hair and pulled his mouth onto his own for another of those long, slow, delicious kisses. As their lips parted, Mal turned his head to look at him with a wicked glint in his eyes. "It's going to be very busy in the immediate future, I predict."

"Mm, I see you're branching into fortune telling. So, what does the future hold for us? Are we going to take a long journey where we'll meet a tall, dark and handsome stranger?"

"I'll have to consult the tea leaves and let you know," Mal said. "In the meantime, I think we've earned a break from running around. What if we just kick back and enjoy that we're together and we're both still alive? No sorcerers trying to kill us. No meddling fae getting in the way."

Neil grinned. "Sounds like a perfect plan to me."

Want to see more from these authors? Here's a taster for you to enjoy!

Elemental Evidence

Breathing Betrayal

Bellora Quinn & Sadie Rose Bermingham

Excerpt

Rain *pink-pink-pinked* against the window pane and *drip-drip-dripped* into the pot that Jake had placed under the leak in the hallway. Murky gray morning light greeted him when he opened his eyes. Another drizzly day. He had thought that was just some persistent stereotype, a comic exaggeration—about how rainy it was in London—but so far, this month, it was turning out to be true.

Jake was steadily getting used to the weather. It really wasn't all that different from his native Michigan. He had been told by his colleagues this was an unusually wet November and that when winter finally kicked off, it wouldn't be as severe as he was accustomed to. That was something to be glad about, at least.

The weather was not the only thing he'd had to get used to after moving a little over three and a half thousand miles away from the only place he'd known. London was worlds away from Detroit. It was still alive for one thing, not a dying husk. It was cleaner too, even with more than ten times the population. London had its crime and its dangerous places just like any large city, but even the urban degeneration here had a certain vibrancy to it that was unlike the desperation and decay of Detroit.

Enough of that.

Thinking about home was a guaranteed way to put him in a bad mood. At least he didn't hate his new abode.

The apartment was small and leaky but it was clean and bug free and he didn't have a lot of stuff anyway. Four rooms — kitchen, bathroom, small living room and a closet-sized bedroom that was barely big enough to hold a double bed and the armoire. The kitchen was equally tiny. A small fridge, sink and an ancient two-burner stove. There was just enough counter space to plug in his coffeepot. He was not complaining. The small space made it easy to keep warm and clean and discouraged clutter. It was also paid for, which was another big plus.

He hadn't liked that idea at first. He thought the university should just pay him outright and let him figure out how to deal with the rent and utilities, but he had to admit that having them take care of the bills took some of the worry off his mind. Unfortunately he still had plenty of other things to worry about.

No, he told himself firmly. He was not going to start off the day thinking about home and everything he'd deliberately left behind when he got on the plane. That was over.

Jake dragged himself out of bed and across the living room to the bathroom. After a quick slash, he washed his face, finger-combed his hair with wet hands then threw on some sweats and he was ready for his morning run. There would be time for a shower and food later. Back in Detroit, he would have started his day by driving to the track or the gym to work out before heading to the station house. Here he could walk or use public transportation to get just about anywhere he needed to go. At first the idea of not having a car, of not being able to just hop in and drive wherever he had to go, any time he wanted, had given him more of a panicky, trapped feeling than being an ocean away from everyone he knew and everything familiar. A car was the very first thing he'd asked about, after moving his meager belongings into the apartment. The research assistant who'd been assigned to ensuring he got settled in and had what he needed had told him to give it a week or two and, if he still wanted to purchase a car, the university would arrange it. At the time, Jake had thought there was no possible way he could survive for so long without a vehicle at his disposal, but by the end of his first week he had explored the Tube, the cabs and the buses, got himself an Oyster card and found he could get around remarkably well without having to fight through traffic behind the wheel. He hadn't brought up the need for a car again.

There was a small park only one street over from where he lived, and several right around the university, but they were little more than decorative green space — compact garden squares hemmed in by the tall, dark façades of houses and office buildings — nice for a picnic maybe, but not big enough for a run. Fortunately Regent's Park was fairly close to where he lived and the paths and trails there were perfect. The park was never truly empty but this early in the morning, especially on such a wet, gray day, only the dedicated were out. They all had little earbuds or headphones on and their eyes were fixed forward, everyone in their own private bubbles. No one stopped to say good morning. No one drew him to one side to ask if he could touch their grandmother's wedding ring and tell them if she'd hidden cash somewhere in the attic. It was great. It was almost perfect, except for one thing.

There was one other person from the university that liked to run the same route he did and while Jake didn't see him every morning, it happened often enough that he'd started looking for the guy while he ran. That annoyed him. Running was his time to clear his head. It was meditative. He could tune out and think of nothing. Or at least he could until he started paying more attention to the people he passed than he did the simple rhythm of putting one foot down in front of the other. Now during his morning runs, he was distracted by looking around to see if he'd catch sight of a particular slender figure whose long legs ate up the distance like the wind.

Jake told himself that he was only looking so that he could avoid him, and thereby avoid having to make polite conversation. It definitely wasn't because of the way the ridiculously tight Lycra leggings he wore outlined every muscle in his lean thighs or the way his perfect ass looked so tasty in them. No, not at all.

Jake never had been very good at lying to himself. Even so, admiring that sexy little derrière from a distance was all he would do. He had learned his lesson about getting involved with coworkers. Anyway, it was unlikely he'd see him today, given the dismal weather. He could stop looking around and just concentrate on pushing himself.

* * * *

The park was usually Mari's first call of a morning, though he sometimes gave his running a break when the weather was this grim. Today the rain was that fine, persistent drizzle that evaded umbrellas and invaded just about all items of clothing that weren't a wetsuit. He was used to it, having spent almost the last three of his twenty-seven years here, at UCL, but after the sunshine of his previous job in Barcelona, it was still kind of a comedown to walk out of his front door on a morning like this.

Fortunately the park was just around one corner, and the university campus just around the other, one of the perks of living in town. Papi had wanted to pay for a place out in the countryside, arguing that it would be more peaceful, but his Mama would hear none of it. The London house had been her grandmother's then her father's. He had been renting it out for years while the family lived abroad but now it was finally useful, even if the reason behind its new purpose was a less than happy one. Plus, Mama argued successfully — because no one, not even Papi, would dare to fight with her right now — it was also a short cab ride to the hospital, not an ungodly trek through the suburbs every time she had treatment or saw her oncologist.

He pushed those thoughts away, determined not to dwell on what might be, knowing she would not thank him for it. She had not wanted him to come to London at all, but on that point he had dared to defy her and anyway, he'd already been offered and had accepted the post at University College London. It was a decent job, even if London was not Barcelona.

There was no one quite like Tomas here, but maybe that was a good thing too.

Mari put his head down and pushed on into the clinging miasma of the chill London rain. Tomas

Arregui was something else he would rather not think about right now. With the clarity of hindsight, perhaps it had been for the best that the job had come up with UCL when it did. Given longer to chew over the frustration of his on-again, off-again lover, he might well have been driven to do something he would most certainly regret.

Damn it, though! The memory of Tomas was like a persistent tic that wouldn't let go of his hide once its nasty little fangs had sunk in.

He was glad of the distraction presented in the form of another early-morning loper and his spirits perked up even more when he was able to make out the familiar form and easy gait of the new guy who was working with the Web Security Team. Mari had spotted him striding through the park before, though they had never spoken. Lester in the print room said he was American, though Mari thought there was a slightly Hispanic look to his rough-cut, thick black hair and darkly handsome features. Maybe Romani, even? He couldn't be sure.

He was well built without looking chunky, except when he was bundled up in several layers of damp running gear, and almost as tall as Mari's six-foot-two-inch frame, which was a plus. It got embarrassing trying to flirt with men who were forced to look up at him all the time.

Not that he had any idea if Mr. Tall, Dark and Handsome was even that way inclined. But that never stopped him testing the waters. Alicia in his department said that one day some guy was going to punch his lights out for flirting the way he did, as if every man in the world was automatically gay and, by definition, hot for him.

He'd made her laugh with his mock-horrified response. "You mean they *aren't*?"

About the Authors

Bellora Quinn

Originally hailing from Detroit Michigan, Bellora now resides on the sunny Gulf Coast of Florida where a herd of Dachshunds keeps her entertained. She got her start in writing at the dawn of the internet when she discovered PbEMs (Play by email) and found a passion for collaborative writing and steamy hot erotica. Soap Opera like blogs soon followed and eventually full novels.

The majority of her stories are in the M/M genre with urban fantasy or paranormal settings and many with a strong BDSM flavour.

Sadie Rose Bermingham

A storyteller since before she started school, Sadie also enjoys reading, photography, live music and long walks on the beach.

Sadie has worked as a bookseller, a pedigree editor for the racing industry and a local and family history researcher. Originally from the north of England, she has been working her way across the UK ever since. She currently resides on the south east coast with her long term partner, where she hopes to buy a mobile home and establish a whippet farm.

Bellora and Sadie love to hear from readers. You can find their contact information, website details and author profile page at http://www.pride-publishing.com.

www.ingramcontent.com/pod-product-compliance
Lightning Source LLC
Chambersburg PA
CBHW031306280626
47169CB00017B/293